HEAR THIS WOMAN!

HEAR THIS WOMAN!

By *Ben and Ann Pinchot*

NEW YORK

FARRAR, STRAUS AND COMPANY

FOR SUSAN

Chapter One

1. The United Air Lines plane landed at the St. Croix airport at noon. Charlie Turner pulled his old hat over his forehead, walked down the ramp, and hailed a cab.

"What's the best hotel in town, bud?"

"Lake Shore."

Charlie raised the collar of his rumpled gray jacket against the damp wind blowing in from Lake Michigan. "Okay. Let's go."

At thirty miles an hour, the battered yellow taxi creaked and groaned like the shutters of a haunted house. Charlie stared out of the window with professional curiosity. The sprawling factories which lined the lake front bore names he recognized from national advertising. Lane-Crandall Farm Implements. Trout Celluloid Company. Wolverine Motors. That's my baby, he thought. Mark Holmes—Wolverine Motors.

"Quite a burg," he said. "About eighty thousand population?"

"Just about. Place still crawlin' with war workers."

Charlie split the cellophane on a pack of Luckies and handed it to the man. "Doesn't Faith Holmes come from here? The dame who's been stirring up a political rumpus?"

"Yeh," the gray-haired driver said bitterly. "An' every damn fool female is all for her. Including my missus."

"She got any relatives in St. Croix?"

"I wouldn't know, mister. I ain't been here long myself."

After Charlie registered in the lobby of the old hotel, he went out for a quick look at the town. Main Street, he thought, is suffering from an over-active pituitary. War prosperity. Old sandstone buildings dwarfed, like poor relations, by modern concrete structures. He counted a half-dozen seafood, chop suey and steak houses; two movies, the Palace featuring Humphrey Bogart, the Odeon an old Western picture with Roy Rogers; Woolworth's, the conservative Bon Ton Department Store and the elegant Fashion Shop; and at the end of the block, Willie's Cocktail Bar, all chromium and gleaming black glass. The narrow faded brick building across the street housed the local paper, *The Observer*. He caught a glimpse of the headlines chalked on the bulletin board.

HENRY WALLACE RESIGNS

STOCK MARKET NOSEDIVES

NO MEAT IN SIGHT!

He took the worn flat steps two at a time, entered the cool dark hall, and asked the lethargic boy at the desk for Steve Pringle.

"Down the hall, sir. Then to your right."

"Thanks."

In the noisy main room, he found the editor working at a scarred oak desk beside a dusty open window. He was a thickset, middle-aged man, whose regular features were too small and feminine for his bloated, heavy-jowled face. He was chewing on a fresh, unlighted Panatella.

"Mr. Pringle, my name's Turner. I'm from Homer Sweet's office in New York."

"Homer Sweet's?" A genial expression larded Pringle's face. Every newspaperman in the country was familiar with the name. Pringle frequently used releases coming from his office. "Glad to know you. What's on your mind?"

"One of St. Croix' fair daughters. Faith Holmes."

"Since when does she need a public-relations counsel? I've always been under the impression she does right well blowing her own horn."

"We're not working for her. Mr. Sweet wants this information for himself."

"Yeh?" suddenly wary. "What's the idea?"

Charlie shrugged. "Magazine article, I suppose. Maybe a Profile for *The New Yorker*. Mr. Pringle, do you know Mrs. Holmes?"

"I know her."

"She apparently boasts that she worked for Vrest Macklin, the old editor of *The Observer*. Is that true?"

"It's true."

Pringle was suspicious. You never can tell, Charlie reflected, when a guy may turn out to be an old pal of Faith Holmes's.

He said disarmingly, "You've a right to be cagey, Mr. Pringle." And handed over the letter Homer Sweet had wangled from the New York head of the Rentschler Allied Newspapers, the syndicate which now owned *The Observer*.

"This puts a different light on it," Steve Pringle said. "What do you want to know?"

They talked for a half hour, then Pringle suggested Charlie visit the principal of the Holmes High School.

"I'm pretty sure he can dig up a yearbook for the class of 1924," he said.

And he was right. Charlie leafed through the volume the old man found for him until he came to a postage-stamp picture of a girl in a shingle bob, with friendly eyes and an ingratiating smile. Faith Andrews, her name was then.

> *The Outstanding All-Around Student.*
> *Destined for Future Fame: Faith Andrews.*

The judgment of her classmates had proved correct. Faith had certainly gone places!

The principal sent him to Miss Lovejoy, Faith's first teacher. She was a small withered woman, retired now and still living in the past.

"Yes," she said tartly. "I remember Faith Andrews well. Very well! I taught both her and Mark Holmes, you know, when they were children. She was a common little thing—ordinary background—but clever, and bold. And right from the beginning, she attached herself to Mark Holmes."

"What about her family, Miss Lovejoy?"

"Her mother was a highly neurotic woman—though we didn't use that term in those days. Very emotional and possessive."

"What do you know about Mark Holmes?"

"He's head of Wolverine Motors now."

"So I heard."

"The schools in our town are named for his grandfather, Eben Holmes," she rambled on. "He was a great man."

Miss Lovejoy sent him to Winona Kraus. "Her father, Mr. Kraus, runs the big supermarket on the Heights. She was Faith's best friend in high school."

Mrs. Kraus refused to let him see Winona. "My daughter is sick," she said bluntly. But Charlie was thoroughly trained in Homer Sweet methods. He could be most friendly and persuasive.

Winona turned out to be a straw-colored, weary woman of forty. Charlie's imagination couldn't stretch far enough to visualize her as a schoolgirl, class of '24. She wasn't interested in talking to him until he suggested lunch at the Lake Shore. One thing he'd learned about these frustrated women: fortified by a brace of martinis, they'd get right chummy. He ordered steaks, which weren't on the menu, French fries and coffee. Winona drank her lunch. She kept mum about Faith until Charlie mentioned Mark Holmes. Then she admitted Mark's family had sent him abroad to forget about Faith.

"It didn't work," she added, looking at Charlie with pale, disillusioned eyes. "You couldn't put anything over on Faith Andrews. She always knew what she wanted. When Mark came back from Paris, she got hold of him—but fast! Of course, everybody wondered why they got married so suddenly. There was talk . . ."

Once started, there was no stopping her. She told him of Faith's affair with Phillip Latham and her wretched behavior to Mark. And all the while she discussed her old friend's actions, envy corroded her voice. Funny about women, Charlie reflected. It's not the lady they admire, but the adventuress.

Two weeks later, he sat on a chair in his fourth-floor room at the Lake Shore, portable typewriter on the table beside him, and looked over a stack of notes. He was pleased with himself. Pringle had been generous with his information, and although he didn't exactly confess to it, there was something in his manner which led Charlie to believe he'd been very friendly with Faith Holmes once upon a time. Now that he'd lined up the information on her youth, he was going back to New York to dig up the rest of the story. Not from the morgue. No one had pinned any scandal on Faith Holmes; she was too clever. But he meant to interrogate the people who knew her well. Harvey Jessup, for example, and Christine Ostbergh, and Eric the Great. . . .

Another week's work and he'd be finished, ready to place the dossier on Homer Sweet's desk. He had an astute suspicion of how desperately Mr. Sweet needed this dope on Mrs. Holmes. There should be a fat bonus in it for one Charlie Turner.

Whistling cheerfully, he closed his bag, locked it, and rang for the bellboy.

2. In his private office on the thirtieth floor of a Rockefeller Center skyscraper, Homer Sweet fidgeted behind his Chippendale desk. His pale prominent eyes scanned the note at the top of a large memo pad:
2:30. Re: Faith Holmes
They lingered on the words briefly, then wandered across the polished surface of the desk, cluttered with telephones, a dictaphone, a pipe rack and the newest books on public relations, including his own

best-seller, *Publicity, the Shortest Road to Success,* to the pile of clippings assembled beside the manila folder, which he considered Exhibit A.

"Faith Holmes," he muttered, glaring at a picture of a slim, handsome woman in a dark tailored suit, standing before a microphone. "She's made the front page again!"

The *New York Times* announced: FAITH HOLMES ADVOCATES GOVERNMENT BE TAKEN OUT OF HANDS OF PARTY POLITICIANS.

The *Herald Tribune:* MORE THAN LEADERS, COUNTRY NEEDS INTELLIGENT CONSTITUENCY, SAYS FAITH HOLMES.

The *Daily News* was flippant: FAITH HOLMES ACCUSES MEN OF MAKING WOMEN THE SAPPY SEX.

It was foolhardy, Homer thought, to dismiss her lightly. That had been their initial mistake. For in the beginning people said, What can one woman do? Nobody will take her seriously—probably another publicity stunt, anyway. A columnist dubbed her the "Messiah in Mink." That had been a mistake, too. For in the end, a million women succumbed to her silver-tongued wiles. The Messiah in Mink, indeed! She was a demagogue—and infinitely more dangerous than any male.

The soundproof room was deadly quiet. In a corner, Harvey Jessup was hunched in a green leather club chair, a highball in his hand, a scowl on his handsome self indulgent face.

Homer Sweet glanced surreptitiously at him. Jessup was sulky and ill at ease, lacking his customary affability. Homer hadn't seen much of him recently. Today, Faith Holmes was instrumental in bringing them together. How did Jessup feel, Homer wondered, now that they were finally in a position to silence her for good? Was his vehement cry for retaliation sincere—or was he still in love with her? Even Homer admitted wryly it was not easy to forget Faith Holmes.

Then, abruptly, Jessup finished his drink and struggled to his feet. His well-fleshed, ruddy face reflected his tenseness. He's afraid, Homer realized maliciously. Afraid of meeting Ostbergh, who, seven years ago, dismissed him brutally. He's riddled with fears.

Miss Kelly, Homer's secretary, looked in reverently. After serving him for a decade, she was still in awe of him. He was, to her, a great man, practically a genius.

"Mr. and Mrs. Ostbergh are here," she said.

"Show them in, please."

Eric Ostbergh's name was familiar in financial and industrial circles as the head of the International Petroleum Company, but few people knew the man himself. He was over six feet tall, massively built, with the muscles of a wrestler. Yet as he strode into the room, wearing a conservative blue suit, a white Oxford shirt, a knitted black tie, he looked as harmless as a deacon. On closer inspection, however, he was more formidable. The square skull, the pale blank eyes, the blunt flat nose accentuated by a heavy jaw, gave him the cast of a death's head. When *Time* wrote up the fabulous Ostbergh Enterprises, the editors referred to him as *The Man Who Never Smiles*. Even his wife, Christine, now a personality in her own right, was never entirely relaxed in his presence.

Homer jumped up to greet him.

"It's good of you to take the time, Mr. Ostbergh," he said. Not once in all the years he had handled public relations for International Petroleum had he dared address this man by his Christian name.

Ostbergh nodded brusquely, then ignored him. And Homer was free to turn to Christine.

"You're looking very handsome, my dear," he said in an undertone, as if this were a secret between them.

Christine smiled demurely, her official smile, which her admirers had been privileged to see in hundreds of photographs during the time she served as a Congresswoman from New York. She slipped the Russian sable stole from her narrow shoulders and searched through her petit-point bag for a cigarette. The expensive black frock might have enhanced the beauty of another woman; on Christine's thin figure it resembled the unobtrusive black she had once worn as Eric Ostbergh's very efficient private secretary.

"When is Faith supposed to be here?" she asked.

"Any moment." Homer noticed that while Christine sent Harvey Jessup a pleasant glance, Eric Ostbergh ignored him completely.

Homer marched back to his desk and stationed himself by it, a director ready to give the cues. He was small, plump and as colorless as lard. His round body was bundled into a custom-made, brown chalk-stripe suit, boasting a white carnation in the lapel. Although his blue silk tie flaunted the head of a painted horse, he was not addicted to sports. Actually, he loathed any form of exercise, since it reminded him of his bucolic youth. He was wise enough to keep his origins shrouded in secrecy, and the elegant soundproof offices were home to him.

The telephone rang. He answered and then turned deferentially to Ostbergh.

"For you, sir."

Ostbergh lumbered across the deep pile of the sand-colored rug. Why hadn't the woman arrived? He had postponed several urgent appointments to come here—a senator from the Midwest; a representative from the Saudi-Arabian government; engineers about to depart for his South American refineries. As he waited for his confidential secretary to decode the cablegram which had just arrived, his mind kept reverting to Faith Holmes. She was the only one who had possessed enough courage to oppose him. She had laughed at possible retaliation, secure in the knowledge that during the war years, when she was "Our Faith" to the G.I.'s, his hands were tied. Even the smear campaign Homer had tried to put over had backfired miserably.

Now, however, the time was auspicious. The war was over. And, he reflected sardonically, already the gullible public had forgotten his ties with alien powers. Homer Sweet was showing the ingenuity for which Ostbergh paid him a munificent yearly retainer.

"I'll be back within the hour," he told his secretary, and hung up.

Jessup stirred restlessly. "Shall I fix you a drink, Christine?"

"A whisky sour, please."

After handing her the glass, Jessup debated with himself whether to offer some Irish whisky to Ostbergh, who was at the window, impervious as granite. Seven years ago, Ostbergh had withdrawn the International Petroleum account from Jessup's agency, damn near ruining the business as well as Jessup's morale.

"Drink?" he asked hesitantly.

But Ostbergh remained immobile, looking down at the golden Prometheus on the sunken terrace, where the crowds loitered in the ripe October sunlight.

Homer Sweet watched the interplay with veiled satisfaction. Jessup was a weakling at heart. No guts. Not enough of a man to accept a share of the guilt. He had let Faith Holmes take the punishment alone.

Eric Ostbergh swung around abruptly. "Homer, what are your terms to her?"

"Terms?" Homer savored the word. "Mr. Ostbergh, we have no intention of bargaining with her. Either she resigns as the head of this new National Women's Committee, or we release the story of her private life to every newspaper in the country."

Mr. Ostbergh appreciated the value of blackmail.

"Faith knows the power of publicity—good or bad. I am confident we'll have no further trouble with her."

"She's as slippery as an eel," Jessup warned him quickly.

"I'm sure you know whereof you speak," Christine said sweetly.

Hank Jessup scowled. He was thinking sullenly that these people regarded him as the culprit. For Faith Holmes was still his wife.

"You needn't fear," Homer said. "She won't squirm out of this trap."

The idea had first taken root in his mind a month ago, as he pored over her speeches, seeking the inadvertent admission that might be used to incriminate her. But she was too smart to lay herself open to such an error. She made use of every weapon Homer himself had given her, and she used them exceedingly well. Yet he was convinced they could find a way to stop her. They must! She was a public menace. As her power increased, women flocked to her standard like children to the Pied Piper. She was growing bolder. Now she lashed out violently against men like Eric Ostbergh, denouncing them as the greatest obstacle to world peace.

"There's only one way to deflate her and to crush this movement," he had told Ostbergh three weeks ago. "Find the skeleton in the closet —that is our problem. There's a scandal somewhere in her life. There must be! No woman as personable as Faith can stay out of mischief forever."

While she was working for him, Homer had never found out much about her past. She had refused to discuss it. Just as she had refused to fill out the questionnaire when she first applied for a job. Had she been hiding something even then?

I should have been wary, he thought morosely. Then we'd be saved all this trouble today.

He did know, however, that she had worked for Vrest Macklin, the great liberal editor of the Midwest, and that her first husband was a member of a wealthy Michigan lumber family. Hank Jessup could add little more to this information.

"She never liked to talk about what had happened," he admitted. "She said only the future was important to her."

So Homer Sweet dug for dirt and struck gold.

Miss Kelly entered. "Mrs. Holmes is here," she said breathlessly.

Deliberately, Homer Sweet took a straight-backed chair from its place at the wall and stood it in the center of the room, in the spotlight of the afternoon sun. Then he turned to his secretary.

"Show her in."

The door opened slowly. Faith Holmes hesitated, as her dark luminous eyes measured them coolly.

"Good afternoon, Homer."

"Come in, Faith," he said. "We've been waiting for you."

She smiled courteously, as if this were a casual meeting, utterly without significance. Her tall figure in a tailored blue greatcoat was still slim and willowy. She was a beautiful and distinguished woman and, consequently, all the more dangerous.

"I'll stand, if you don't mind," she said in a voice that matched his for softness. She remained at the chair, composed and unruffled as she appraised each of them in turn. Her level glance met Christine's indifferently, turned into a challenge as it rested on Ostbergh's grim features, ignored Hank Jessup entirely.

This wouldn't do, Homer decided testily. It wouldn't do, at all! To reassure himself, he looked at the manila folder containing the detailed report which had involved such effort and expense, not to mention the services of his best man, Charlie Turner.

"Faith Holmes," he began pontifically, "you are the head of an organization that is deliberately misleading thousands of gullible women. You've made ugly accusations you cannot substantiate. You've sullied the reputations of innocent people who have done you no harm. You've turned traitor to your old friends—"

Again he glanced down at his desk, conscious of the potential value of the evidence in the folder, and a triumphant smile broadened his pale, fleshy lips.

HOMER SWEET'S REPORT ON FAITH HOLMES

Birth. May, 1906.

Place of Birth. St. Croix, Michigan.

Parentage. FATHER: Tod Andrews, drunken, shiftless printer. Never wanted to settle down. Mechanic at Wolverine Motors, later foreman. Tied up with a Mrs. Hussar, disreputable woman who ran the local pawnshop.
(*Source.* Present owner, Willie's Tavern and Bar.)

MOTHER: Maiden name unknown. Something odd here. Possible parents weren't legally married. Charlotte Andrews moody, hysterical, superstitious woman. Perhaps obsessed with shame daughter was illegitimate? Died in insane asylum. Daughter missing from bedside.

SPECIAL NOTE: Use this illegitimate angle and mother's insanity in campaign against Faith Holmes.

Early Youth. Only child. Precocious. Tricky. Adept at getting own way. Parents ill-mated, quarreled bitterly. Girl played one against the other. But dominated by neurotic mother.
(*Source.* Miss Lovejoy. First-grade teacher.)

Even in youth, Faith Andrews snobbish of environment. Snubbed neighborhood children. Set her sights on richest boy in town, Mark Holmes, grandson of pioneer founder of St. Croix. Attached herself to boy. Repulsed anyone else he was interested in.
(*Source.* Miss Lovejoy, who had occasion to watch Faith Andrews through formative years. And still has same picture of stubborn, aggressive, ambitious girl.)

High School. Outsider, socially. But repaid snubs by monopolizing young Mark Holmes. Joined glee club and debating team because he was interested in them. Bound him to her with oldest female trick in the world.
(*Source.* Winona Kraus, Faith Andrews' best friend.)

At this time, first signs of her glib tongue. Her devilish talent for persuading listeners she is right. Love of limelight, pugnacity and insubordination—as shown in glee club incident. Made fool of old instructor.
(*Source.* Miss Lovejoy.)

Her hold on Mark Holmes source of worry to his family, who took him to Paris to forget her.
(*Source.* Winona Kraus.)

During his absence, she ingratiated self with his grandfather, Eben Holmes. Persuaded old man to arrange job for her with Vrest Macklin, editor of local paper. Used bit of blackmail here. Old Holmes devoted to grandson and heir.
(*Source.* Winona Kraus.)

Made herself deliberately attractive to elderly bachelor, Vrest Macklin. Rode roughshod over staff. Used wits to get opportunity to cover event at local country club in order to charm local big shot, Lewis Trout. Was rebuffed.
(*Source.* Lewis Trout and Steve Pringle.)

SPECIAL NOTE: This may be reason she gunned for Trout last year. Vindictive woman.

On young Holmes's return, she persuaded him to elope. Moved into mansion of Eben Holmes. Rejected her parents. At this point, mother committed to institution.

(*Source.* Steve Pringle and *The Observer.*)

Early Years of Marriage. Faith's character already hard, calloused. Mother's tragedy had no effect on her. Used her charms on Eben Holmes. Wangled priceless string of pearls from him. Made herself First Young Matron in St. Croix. Got the Lewis Trouts to sponsor her.

(*Important note.* Lewis Trout, today St. Croix leading industrialist, most co-operative in giving trenchant picture of her early married life. Dropped old school friends. Tried to implicate Trout in clandestine flirtation.)

No children. Why? Obviously healthy young couple. Resented entanglements? No impediment in her climb upward?

Chapter Two

1. Godawmighty! Charlotte was still whining. Ever since they had stepped on the greasy deck of the *Lady Marquette*, the overnight ferry to St. Croix, she hadn't stopped complaining. Her thin face had a greenish cast, her thickened body was slack as a half-empty sack of meal, but her tongue went on and on with the unflagging drive of a dynamo. She sat hunched against the stained pillows, her dark lustrous eyes burning, her narrow lips curved down with the taste of bile. The smell in this filthy cabin. She was going to be sick again.

"Tod, open the window!"

"Porthole's been open all night."

"I can't breathe. I feel *awful.*"

He was helpless against this introverted hysteria. Only way to shut her up was to outshout her, and he couldn't do that. Trouble was, he was too patient, too easygoing. He couldn't be rough with a woman, especially one in the family way. Nope, he'd just keep his trap shut. Patience was his armor. Had been for six months now. Ever since that old goat, the Justice of the Peace, in Rockland, Wisconsin, had mumbled the words which made them man and wife, all the while staring lecherously at the bride's thickened waistline.

Soon the boat would dock at the slip in the tranquil St. Croix harbor, the trip over, the prospect of getting a job as a printer at *The Observer* bright as the May morning. Tod didn't mind the ill-smelling cabin, the greasy food, the bawdy revelers. He never fussed about lack of comfort. After all, an itinerant printer couldn't travel like Teddy Roosevelt. Besides, Tod Andrews always kept his eyes open and found amusement in the sights. The *Lady Marquette* had been used shabbily. Her rank odor reminded him of the Halsey Street ghetto; Olivera Street in Los Angeles; Chinatown in San Francisco—they were all mixed up in his senses, bologna and brine, enchiladas and tortillas, joss and spices. Now, suffering Charlotte's fretful voice, his sensitive nostrils discovered the fragrance of Pinaud's lotion, mustache wax, Bull Durham tobacco. He pictured the swaggering drummers in their stylish suits, straw lids cocked at an angle, setting out from Chicago for the exile of a hundred commonplace little towns, their battered sample trunks bulging with Easywear Shirtwaists, Rib-Iron Union Suits, Northern Spy Mackinaws. He could see the prostitutes, unobtrusive and flamboyant at the same time, reeking of musk and cheap whisky. And the stolid fair-skinned Dutch farmers, their clothes impregnated with the acrid odor of humus; the blond Swedish fishermen and the dark lumberjacks, coming down from Canada to hew timber for Eben Holmes—a shaggy, brutal, virile crowd.

"Lotte, think of all those folks—going to new places—starting fresh. Just like us! All different . . ."

Her dark, fanatic eyes regarded him with contempt. "Sure, they're different. Not much good, either. Ain't a decent woman on this boat!"

Tod sighed. Nothing ever pleased her. "You'd better get your clothes on," he said. "We're docking soon."

Awkwardly she fastened her blouse and pulled a worn black jacket over her shoulders.

"I only hope we'll find us a place to live. An' I'm tellin' you now, Tod. No more traipsin' around. This time we stay put—start savin' for the future!"

The martyred lines in her sallow face spoke of poverty and worry. Why can't we make roots like other folk? It's all your fault, Tod Andrews, you led me into this. . . .

It seemed unbelievable to Tod that only a short time ago he had been smitten with her dark beauty. He had been stuck in a one-horse town, Rockland, Wisconsin. He was bored and restless and the summer sun warmed his blood, and Lotte was there, innocent and ardent. She was an orphan, raised in a dreary institution, conditioned to poverty, plain food, ugly clothes. In her lonely, thwarted life, headaches and hysterical dreams compensated for reality. To her simple mind, a black cat crossing her path, a violent thunderstorm, a broken glass, conjured up dire and portentous omens.

She had been farmed out at sixteen to a Rockland lawyer and his wife. When Tod met her six years later, she was docile, inarticulate and pathetically eager for affection. A good girl was a novelty in Tod's life. And in his affair with Charlotte, he unwittingly garnered a whirlwind. Her moods of gaiety and depression baffled him, and her sudden fits of crying unnerved him. Yet, one evening when she told him she was pregnant, he made no fuss. What the hell. He was twenty-five, he'd knocked around plenty. Maybe it'd do him good to settle down.

Then, too, Lotte acted as if she loved him. And being loved meant a lot to Tod Andrews.

However, immediately after the ceremony, her attitude underwent an abrupt and terrible change. Shame took the place of wanton passion. She was chained to a man who'd been forced to marry her. She had conceived a child in sin. Now she lived in perpetual fear that the baby would be marked, spiritually and physically. She feared retribution, and made a nervous wreck of herself and Tod.

"What're you fretting about?" he asked again and again. "We're married. We're gonna be happy. And our kid'll be a helluva nice kid, you wait and see. What more do you want?"

"Tod . . ."

"Yeh?"

"How much money we got left?"

He was jarred out of his reverie, pulled back rudely to the hot, smelly cabin where his wife crouched on the berth, her bloated abdomen giving her a hunched, monstrous appearance.

"You got it all in your pocketbook, Lotte."

She counted glumly. "Seven dollars. I figured we had more. Tod, what about the cash you had?"

"It's gone."

"What'd you do with it?"

"Lotte, for heaven's sake! We ate last night—that was a buck apiece." They'd had dinner in the salon. Chicken and the fixings. He figured they should eat decently for a change.

"People like us don't deserve chicken," she said.

"Why not? It's a free country!"

"For them with money."

"Oh, forget it!"

But immediately, he regretted his brusqueness and smiled to soften the effect of his words. He was a tall, exceedingly thin fellow, with high square shoulders and a narrow frame. His angular face was carved in raffish lines that lent themselves to caricature. His hair grew in a stiff bushy pompadour a shade redder than his skin. He looked like a clown out of costume: the long, foolish nose, the jug ears, the mild, dreaming blue eyes that revealed the ineffable goodness of his character. An itinerant printer, he had roamed the land, always planning, one day, to settle down in a small town with a printing shop of his own. And now he was optimistic, looking forward to the great day—and Lotte was giving him the dickens for having bought a decent meal last night!

"A quarter for the waitress," she grumbled. "I can fix us a whole supper for a quarter."

She sat there, a travesty of the slim willowy girl he had possessed. He thought bitterly, a man must love his wife dearly to put up with her in such a state. But he didn't love Lotte; at times, he wasn't even sorry for her. Nevertheless, he forced himself to sit down beside her.

"Lotte, I've been on my own for years—ever since I was a kid. I've never starved yet. And I won't let you starve, either."

"You sure you'll get this job?"

"Vrest Macklin promised it to me last year when I was working for him."

"It's six months since you wrote him."

"Stop fussing, Lotte. It's gonna be all right."

Ever since their marriage, they had been on the go. One small town after another. And each time, he'd grown restless and wanted to push on. Secretly, he knew the reason for it, and because he felt guilty, he tried more than ever to placate her.

The *Lady Marquette* collided with the pier; winches creaked; heavy footsteps thundered overhead. Tod reached down for his battered carpet bag and Charlotte's yellow straw suitcase.

"Come on, Lotte."

Up on the deck, he took a deep greedy breath of air, as he watched the sun make a majestic entrance over the horizon. The fishing boats were setting out for the day's catch, bouncing on the swell. He rehearsed his greeting to the editor of *The Observer*. "Better late than never, Mr. Macklin. I'm ready to start work."

Charlotte shivered in the chill air. "Doesn't look like much of a place," she said disparagingly. Her ankles were swollen and her back hurt again. They had seven dollars between them, and no real prospect of a job. She, for one, didn't believe Tod's confident words. I deserve it, she thought grimly, and because of me, my child will suffer, too.

She closed her eyes.

"How about some breakfast, Lotte?"

"I couldn't eat a mouthful."

"Hot coffee? It'll warm you up, make you feel better."

She followed him past the pier to the cobblestone street. In the narrow cafeteria, jammed with stevedores, he ordered coffee for both and a Western sandwich for himself. After he had eaten, he wiped his greasy lips with the back of his hand, pulled out a tin of Prince Albert and rolled himself a cigarette. He smiled reassuringly at her, but she turned her head away.

How weak is the flesh, she thought with bitter self-reproach.

"Ready?" Tod asked. "I guess we'll try Mrs. Hussar's. She takes in boarders. Last year I stayed with her."

She picked her way clumsily over the cobblestones, damp and slippery in the morning mist. He helped her into the trolley and as they rolled down Main Street, he acted as her guide.

"That's the Lake Shore Hotel," he said excitedly, pointing to the four-story red stone building. "And across the street—there's *The Observer!* That's the desk Mr. Macklin uses, right beside the window. And here's the Bon Ton Department Store. Jack Wertheimer runs it— fine fella. After the kid's born, you get yourself some pretty things."

"What'll we use for money?" sarcastically.

"Quit crabbing, Lotte." His enthusiasm boiled over again. "There's the pawnshop—Mrs. Hussar owns it. Wonder if she's still got the gold watch I hocked. Got the ticket somewhere."

The trolley swung drunkenly around the curve, and they caught a glimpse of Lake Michigan, reflecting the silver-blue of the sky. Now a column of black smoke corrupted the pure air.

Tod stretched to the end of the wide seat and nudged the conductor. "What's up?"

"New factory," the conductor said.

"Factory? What's it gonna make?"

"Auto-mobiles. Guess it'll mess up the town some."

Tod raised his sandy brows. His face looked guileless, as he stared at the charcoal whorls and the huge, new sign below the formidable smokestacks.

WOLVERINE MOTORS.

It was May, 1906.

Tod and Charlotte Andrews had arrived in St. Croix on a red-letter day; the day which marked its end as a sleepy village, dependent on fishing, fur-trading and Eben Holmes's timber camps, and its inception as a great industrial city.

2. Mrs. Hussar was a huge, hearty woman of Dutch extraction. Her hulk was unmarked by breast or rump, a mammoth block straight up and down, like the trunk of a redwood. Her small round head sat uncertainly on her shoulders, and her tiny feet strove valiantly to support the mass of solid flesh.

Years ago she had married a supercharged little Hungarian pawn-broker, who had been foolish enough to outsmart a Canadian trapper, and had his head blown off for his efforts. Mrs. Hussar took over the pawnshop, and became thereafter the loneliest woman in St. Croix. A gregarious soul, she was snubbed by the wives of the professional people and ignored by the wives of the Dutch farmers. And unfortunately, she found the language a barrier between herself and the Polacks and Slovenes who were migrating into town these days. Out of sheer loneli-ness, she took in a few boarders. She was content when the yellow bungalow rang with the shouts of lusty male voices, reeked with the good smell of tobacco and sweat, beer and wiener schnitzel. The clack of poker chips on the fumed-oak table was music to her ears.

When Tod naïvely assured Charlotte she'd be crazy about Mrs. Hussar, she made up her mind instantly to dislike the older woman. A tortoise-shell cat sidled around the Hussar porch and tried to seduce Tod, who squatted obligingly, murmuring gibberish to the animal. Charlotte watched in disdain. He was such a fool!

The front door flew open. Mrs. Hussar was blocked in the door-way, a mountain of spotless pink calico, her rosy face beaming.

"Tod Andrews! You sonofagun! Am I glad to see you!"

Tod grinned. His arm around her massive shoulder, he tried to answer Mrs. Hussar and introduce his wife at the same time. Charlotte held out her small, work-roughened hand, and saw it disappear in the maw of Mrs. Hussar's welcoming grasp. This grotesque creature was about to overwhelm her. She felt herself growing weaker and more help-less. Her head was spinning. She was filled with loathing for Tod, for this woman, for the town. She wanted to turn and run, to disappear forever from their clutches.

But her desperate need for roots, for an anchorage, was already stronger than her fear and revolt.

She knew she would stay.

How greedily they ate! Slabs of cold roast pork, steins of foaming beer, mounds of greasy home-fried potatoes, chunks of apple pie and cheese. They sat at the round oak table in the dining room, gorging themselves, laughing and drinking, totally oblivious of Charlotte.

The sight of them sickened her. This tidy little room, with its blue morning-glory wallpaper, its fumed oak, its cut glass and bright china was a prison for her. The cold pork looked dead on the plate.

"I think I'll get some air," she said nervously.

"There's a rocker on the porch," Mrs. Hussar boomed. "Make yourself at home, dearie."

Tod rolled a cigarette. "Guess I'll take a walk down to *The Observer*. I'll be back with a job," he added optimistically. "Then we'll find ourselves a place to live."

Charlotte sat on the porch rocker; her weight kept it immobile. She looked at the fragrant white lilacs and the crab-apple tree in the first blush of spring. Schatz, the tortoise-shell cat, nuzzled against her swollen ankles, but she pushed her away. A fly buzzed persistently at the screen door, and a noisy bee attacked the peony bushes. The air was luminous. Charlotte raised her pallid face to the sun, avid for its comfort and warmth; hoping it would banish somehow the consuming knowledge of her guilt. She coudn't bear to be alone. Yet she dreaded the voluble presence of Mrs. Hussar, who was coming out to join her.

She got up with clumsy haste. "I'm going out for a little while."

"Sure thing. But don't get lost. Main Street's to your left. Look in the Bon Ton windows. They've got some cute baby things. When are you expectin', Miz Andrews?"

"About a month."

"Well, don't tire yourself. If you get lost, just ask for Miz Hussar's place. Everybody knows me."

She didn't feel like walking, really. She was weary, her dark woolen garments weighed down her frail shoulders, and the midday heat exhausted her. She passed Willie's Bar and the Odeon, whose posters advertised a moving picture with Mary Pickford; the Bake Shop and a second-hand clothing store. At Terrace Street, she turned left, hugging the shade of the leafy elms and maples. Tod should be back now, she thought impatiently. With good news! She pictured a small place of their own, a few pieces of furniture—a home for her child. Since her marriage, it was the dream that gave her comfort when she was cold and wretched, the hope that kept her going. Home, roots, stability, all she had never known before, she would have one day. For this reward she could even tolerate Tod.

Returning to Mrs. Hussar's, she spied him on the cool porch, straddling a rocker, the purring tortoise-shell cat on his lap. He seemed even more genial than usual so she suspected something was wrong.

"Tod. The job?"

"No luck, Lotte. Macklin didn't have a place for me."

"But he *promised* . . ."

"It just didn't work out."

"You kept saying he'd hold the job for you. You were so sure."

"He *did* wait. Then finally he got somebody else."

"I told you we shoulda come straight here. I told you!"

"There you go again. Lotte, listen. I was thinking we'd take the Interurban to Great Falls. They got *two* papers in Great Falls. I'll find something."

She realized that their roots would never dig deep or permanently in any soil. Not unless she took the burden on herself.

"I won't go."

"Now, Lotte . . ."

"I can't keep traipsin' around. It's dangerous in my condition."

"Lotte, you aren't the only woman who's been pregnant. You aren't the only one who's been poor either. You haven't starved yet—and you won't."

"Sounds good. But how far do you think we'll go without a job? We'll starve all right!"

He glared at her, provoked beyond endurance. "I wish to God I'd never seen Rockland! I wish I'd never met you."

"That goes for me, too!" she cried hysterically. "I wish I were dead!"

3. Faith Andrews was born on Decoration Day in 1906.

Tod and Charlotte were living in a dingy brown bungalow down the street from Mrs. Hussar's. A shabby place with a leaky, overhanging roof that threw the small rooms into perpetual twilight.

Charlotte suffered the first severe labor pains late in the afternoon, as she was peeling potatoes for supper. When Tod found her she was huddled in the rocker, her swollen face contorted with pain. She was moaning piteously. He coaxed her to take a spoonful of whisky. Then he rushed to Mrs. Hussar, begging her to stay with Lotte while he went for Doc Williams.

As the night dragged on, shattered by Lotte's hideous screams, Doc Williams grew worried. But he tried to hide it. "Nothing to get upset about," he kept saying. "Everything's gonna be fine."

Charlotte pulled through, but she was ill for a long time after-wards, and she never allowed Tod to forget how much she had suffered because of him. He heard the litany each morning, before he left for his job at Wolverine Motors, and each night when he returned home. It was part of the daily routine, like the baby's howls and the smell of coffee brewing. Tod was a good husband. Every Saturday night, he handed Lotte his pay envelope. He tidied up after himself. He took

care of the child, rocking her in his big clumsy arms when she whim-
pered with colic. Only on Sunday, when Mrs. Hussar came to substitute
—she adored the baby—was he free for the day.

St. Croix had got under Tod's skin. Ambling down Ontario Place
in the pale wash of dawn, with the morning mist laying a smoke screen
across the lake, he'd think, This is home! He loitered a bit, studying the
pattern of the poplar and sycamore leaves. He listened to the saucy
nagging of a catbird. I've gotta remember that for Faith, he thought.
What curiosity the kid already showed!

On weekdays, he continued up Main Street until the low sprawling
buildings of Wolverine Motors came into sight. One last hungry look
at the burnished sunrise, the iridescent glitter of the lake, then the gates
of prison shut behind him.

A twelve-hour stretch day in and day out, six times a week.
Hunched over a lathe, eyes glued to the task, muscles aching with strain.
Half hour for lunch; squatting near a wall in the dusty yard, face to the
warm beneficent sun. Then back to the grind.

On Saturday night, the pay envelope. Two bills, a ten and a five.
You're supposed to support a family on that!

Night was a reprieve.

After washing up, he played with the kid. Cute little rascal, bright
as a new penny, and worth it all, he figured; the prison days and Lotte's
interminable nagging. But after she was put to bed, he left the house.
Walking up Main Street, he'd square his shoulders; his big, foolish nose
would sniff the air eagerly, like a hound's. And he'd remind himself
he wasn't thirty yet, and there was still life in the ole boy. Yessiree!

In those days, Main Street was about a mile long, boasting a hotel,
a couple of restaurants, the post office, a nickelodeon, stores and a saloon
or two. Same street repeated a thousand times in a thousand small towns.

Still, the sight of it never failed to give him a kick. Having adopted
St. Croix, he felt the pride of a foster parent. Up the west sidewalk,
stopping at Willie's Bar for a beer, talking politics with Willie, who
was a Socialist one week, a Single Taxer the next, and a good Republican at election time. Then Mrs. Hussar's pawnshop; the three gold
globes like an umbrella over the entrance, the windows cluttered with
guitars, coins, suitcases and jewelry, protected by a high iron grille. The
general store, displaying hardware in one window and children's skates
in the other. Burnside's Drugstore, the popcorn stand with its enticing
buttery aroma. The cigar store, the wooden Indian with a raised toma-

hawk, in front. The Bake Shop, featuring yellowish cream puffs. The Bon Ton Department Store. And *The Observer* office, its dusty window acting as a translucent screen for Vrest Macklin's desk.

Sometimes, Tod loitered before *The Observer,* like a kid in front of a candy store. He longed to enter, smell the ink, listen to the rumble of the presses, gab with Vrest Macklin, who was the most outspoken and courageous man he'd ever met. But he hesitated, shy, a little ashamed of what Macklin might think of him, working as a mechanic at Wolverine Motors.

Occasionally he stopped at the dock, while the car-ferries unloaded. Once in a while, he entered the ornate lobby of the Lake Shore Hotel, hung with tear-drop chandeliers and cluttered with red plush sofas and artificial palms. He'd get into a conversation with one of the drummers from Chicago or Kansas City. Those fellows invariably grumbled about the puritanical town. Said they pulled the sidewalks in at ten.

Tod defended St. Croix passionately. You oughta see it Saturday nights, when the lumberjacks pour in from the Holmes camps. Willie's Bar and Shaughnessy's do a landslide business. Below Grant Avenue, the red-light district is high, wide and open. The Salvation Army band plays its trumpets to drown out the rowdy laughter, the clink of broken glass, the first dangerous rumble of a knife fight. . . .

Of course, Sunday the town goes sober and pious again. The lumberjacks and fishermen disappear, carrying the livid marks of the wild night with them. Respectable folks go to church, St. Benedict's or the Dutch Reform or the Episcopal church, stuff themselves with enormous dinners, take afternoon naps, and in the summer drop by Holmes Park to hear the band concert.

Whenever Tod Andrews boasted about St. Croix, he usually added he wouldn't be working at Wolverine much longer. Soon as he paid Doc Williams, got a little head start, well, then, he'd scout around for a store and open a printing shop. . . .

He didn't expect to make a fortune. Hell, all a guy wanted was a little freedom and a chance to do as he pleased. He wasn't asking for the moon.

According to Charlotte, that was the trouble with him. He was content with too little.

4. Faith Andrews was truly the child of her parents, the result of their physical fusion, of their individual characters, environments and

backgrounds. But her childhood was conditioned mostly by their incompatibility. Her mother's perpetual brooding, the gloomy foreboding with which she met the new day, contributed as much to the molding of the child's personality as the genes which gave her Tod's tawny coloring, his long body, his gregariousness and his incurable optimism.

To the child, her mother seemed old beyond years—older than Mrs. Hussar or the mothers of other children. But her father was always young and full of fun. Although she was attached to her mother by habit and necessity, it was Tod who received her spontaneous affection. To her impressionable mind, the pattern of her parents' life was woven of arguments and tears. Marriage was worry over money, not having enough to pay Mr. Schultz the grocer, or Mr. Kraus the butcher, or Doc Williams. Marriage was the fearful tragedy of the unexpected sickness, like the time papa wrenched his back and there was no money in the house, no firewood to keep warm, nothing to eat. Marriage was mama's tears and complaints, papa's anger. Marriage, to the highly emotional, highly imaginative child, was like the gates of Hell mama always talked about. Sometimes Faith, lying in her small bed with the door open to the kitchen, listening to them quarrel, thought miserably, How awful to have to grow up and marry. Her small, flushed face buried in the pillow, she longed to comfort mama. She was awfully sorry for mama, but she pitied papa, too. It caused her considerable unhappiness and bewilderment, and at such moments, she longed fiercely to be a baby again, cuddled safely in her mother's arms, never having to fret about growing up. . . .

5. September. The first day of school. When Tod came into her room, clad in his heavy blue workclothes, Faith was already wide awake.

He sat down cautiously on the narrow bed.

"Big day, pumpkin."

She bounced up, tawny pigtails flying, eyes glowing like amber in the sunlight, smelling of soap and sleep, her Denton suit all rumpled, giggling with excitement.

"I want you to remember one thing, honey," he said. "Those teachers are as scared of you as you are of them!"

"I'm not scared." Full strong tone coming out of that pink child's mouth. Tod chuckled. Pretty little face and foghorn voice.

"That's fine, pumpkin. I like to hear you talk like that. Always remember you live in a free country. You don't hafta take any gaff." He placed his large hand tenderly on her well-shaped head. Her hair, gradually darkening at the roots to chestnut, had great life and vitality, springing back from the temples and curling over her low broad forehead.

"You be a good girl. Learn everything you can. Promise?"

"Promise." She lifted her small hand solemnly. "An' if I'm good, do I get another kitty?"

Last week Tod had brought from Mrs. Hussar's a tortoise-shell kitten. But Mama wouldn't let her keep it. Mama hated cats; they smelled up the house.

"When you grow up," Tod consoled her, "you'll have all the pets you want. 'Cause you'll be your own boss."

After he left the house, Charlotte came to the door. "Time to get up," she said. Charlotte never called her *honey* or *pumpkin,* for she avoided verbal endearments. Faith was the center of her life, yet she seldom fondled the child. It was as if she dreaded any reminder of physical emotion.

"Come on, Faith. Hurry."

Faith had learned to dress herself, all except the laces on her brand-new, white-topped shoes and the bow to her plaid jumper. She couldn't stand still. Why did papa ask if she were scared? Gosh, she couldn't wait to meet all the kids! She had no friends because mama didn't like the people living on Ontario Place. Cheap foreigners, mama called them.

"If you eat all your breakfast, I'll give you a present."

"A doll? A new doll, mama?"

"Something nicer than a doll."

"Skates? Mary Navotny's got brand-new roller skates!"

"I won't have you running around the streets, like those foreigners."

"Papa said I could have skates."

"Never mind what he said." Charlotte spooned cereal into a dish, took a cinnamon bun from a greasy paper bag. "Now be a good girl."

Faith measured her mother shrewdly. "I'll eat if you give me the s'prise first."

With a stab of jealousy, Charlotte realized the child never bargained with Tod.

"You're making my head ache again." There was a martyred air about Charlotte as she took a small box from her apron pocket and handed it to Faith. The girl opened it with clumsy haste. A tiny heart-shaped locket on a fragile gold chain fell to the table. Faith let out a wail of disappointment.

"You said it was somethin' to play with."

"I said nothing of the kind, Faith Andrews."

"I don't like it! I want a doll—or skates."

Charlotte caught the small arm. "Listen to me," she said fiercely. "This locket is worth more than all the dolls in the world! It's the only thing I have from my own mother—the only treasure in all this world! When you wear it, you'll be safe. Remember that, Faith. Nothing can hurt you!"

She placed the delicate tarnished chain around the child's neck reverently, as if it were an amulet, adding a prayer to keep her from harm. There were too many temptations facing an innocent girl. I won't let her be seduced as I was, Charlotte vowed silently. I'll watch over her. . . .

The strange consecrated expression on her mother's gaunt face moved Faith to sudden childish pity. She kissed Charlotte shyly.

"I'll eat," she promised. Then to cover her embarrassment, she grew boisterous. "I'll eat my whole darned breakfast—every bit of it!"

6. Years later, the first touch of autumn invariably brought up in Faith's memory a nostalgic image of her first day at school. She was back in St. Croix, the year was 1912, and she was walking with her mother. She remembered the pure, faultless blue of the sky, the first tinge of color in the dogwood and maples, the burning scarlet sumac by the pond and the lavender web of wild asters in the meadows.

They were taking the long way to avoid Mrs. Hussar's house. On this, of all mornings, Charlotte had no intention of sharing Faith with that dreadful old woman.

"Manistee Drive is a nicer walk," she said adroitly.

Faith didn't care which path they took, as long as it led to school.

The well-to-do families of St. Croix lived on Manistee Drive in large Victorian houses set back from the street, protected from curious eyes by evergreen hedges and iron grille fences. The massive gray stone house opposite the library was the Holmes place. Charlotte, who usually took little interest in the town's elite, had heard yesterday that Eben Holmes's grandson had just arrived from London to attend school here. The school his grandfather had endowed.

They cut through the park to the playground. At the Girl's Entrance, Charlotte knelt and straightened Faith's collar, then touched the gold locket with nervous fingers.

"It'll be a long day without you," she said.

The wistfulness in her mother's voice escaped the little girl. She kissed Charlotte obediently, and turned to the door. She meant to keep her pace controlled and reluctant, knowing it would please mama, but it was awfully hard. She loved mama, but she was eager to make friends. The world, the beautiful exciting outside world, beckoned.

7. Two hundred years ago, the French Jesuits stumbled on the cove that is now St. Croix harbor, and instantly recognized its possibilities. Indians had cleared a plateau overlooking the lake and the Jesuits built their mission, directly above the rolling white sand dunes. The mission languished until a full hundred years later, when the first Dutch farmers and Swedish fishermen settled in the wake of civilization.

St. Croix was still infant in the year of 1875 when young Eben Holmes drifted in from Rhode Island. He chanced on the virgin timber with the bewildered excitement of a poor man unearthing a hidden treasure. Great dark pine forests; mixed hardwoods; swamp cedars; spruce and balsam and white pine; beech and elm and sycamore; black and white oak.

It's mine, young Eben Holmes thought, awed. It's mine for the taking!

And here, in the timeless and impenetrable forest, the Holmes lumber camps mushroomed. Eben Holmes cut timber, erected sawmills, shipped lumber. He had tremendous energy, vision, and foresight. And the times were with him. He became fabulously rich and he contributed generously to the growth and expansion of St. Croix. He endowed the schools, the library and the hospital.

He built a vast gray stone house on Manistee Drive, where he lived in simple elegance with his wife, and his only son, Dick. He remained a man of no pretensions, blunt and outspoken but possessed of a great respect for the dignity of his fellow beings.

Since he did not epitomize the Victorian concept of a wealthy man, the town often misunderstood him. Even his employees considered his beneficence rather extreme, while his fellow lumbermen regarded him as a credulous eccentric. His views on labor and reforestation were too progressive for his time.

"Replace what you take out," Eben Holmes always said. And he carried out his own ideas years before the Federal Government got around to enacting them.

Chapter Three

1. When he received the cable from his son Dick, announcing that his grandson had been born in a Paris nursing home, Eben Holmes decided grimly Dick and Elinor weren't going to make a juvenile expatriate of the boy. By heritage and inheritance he was an American. His grandfather resolved that he would be brought up as one.

This decision involved a trip abroad which Eben Holmes did not particularly relish. He had never before left American soil; he harbored a provincial prejudice against Europeans. But he was determined at all costs to see the child.

Once reconciled to the voyage, he managed to enjoy it. Each morning, he stretched out on the deck chair for a period of reflection, and his aloof boldly sculptured face, touched with white at the brow and beard, grew tender as he thought of his grandson.

Other first-class passengers pointed him out as the fabulously rich and eccentric lumberman from St. Croix, Michigan, who had inaugurated extremely liberal policies for his workers. Free medical and hospital care, old-age pensions. Such socialistic notions would ruin the country!

During this trip, however, Eben was not concerned with economic problems. His son Dick was on his mind. Why was Dick such a failure? He was a good-looking young man who wore the right clothes and cultivated only the Right People. My son, Eben Holmes thought in candid disgust, has the soul of an oyster. Unquestionably, his mother had helped ruin the boy. Eben Holmes had been devoted to his wife, he mourned her death sorrowfully. But she had been a weak and doting mother, rather proud of her son's snobbishness.

What a pity, he mused, that we're so anxious to give our children what we've never had ourselves. It's nothing but an egotistic and misguided sense of love. Too much material security corrupts the moral fibre. He reflected ironically that the public, which accused the pioneer industrialists of growing rich at the expense of the country's resources, would be avenged ultimately when the younger generation took over the reins.

Three years ago, Dick had married a girl eminently suited to him.

Elinor was a Virginia girl, conditioned to the precept that a Southern lady born of an impoverished family must inevitably sacrifice herself on the altar of Yankee riches. Fortunately, her emotional needs were no more robust than Dick's, and easily placated by furs, jewels, dinner dances and hunt balls. Dick took her abroad for a honeymoon which turned into a protracted stay, for Elinor knew well if she returned to America, it must be to that dreadful little town called St. Croix. As for her stubborn, outspoken father-in-law, she preferred to know him only as the signature on a generous monthly check.

"What's keeping them?" Eben Holmes fumed to his wife. "It's time Dick decided what he's going to do. He can't loaf all his life!"

"Let him enjoy the money now," Mrs. Holmes had retorted, "rather than wait until he inherits it."

Long ago, Dick had warned his father the lumber business was not his idea of a suitable career.

"Have you something better in mind?" Eben had demanded sharply.

"Not exactly."

"You'd better give it thought. There's no room on this earth for a man who won't earn his keep!"

"The trouble with you, father," Dick was contemptuous, "is that you've been so intent on making money, you've never had any fun out of it." His lifted brow added, "Thank God, I don't take after you."

Dick hasn't taken after me, Eben reflected now, as the spray broke over the rail. But his boy will. I'll see to it. . . .

By the time he arrived in Paris, Elinor was home from the hospital, very pale and thin. Reclining on the Recamier sofa in the drawing room, she looked precisely like the Boldini portrait of herself above the Italian marble mantel.

"What do you think of your grandson?" she asked flirtatiously.

Eben, looking at the red-faced baby in the nurse's arm, was conscious of renewed hope.

"He's a fine lad," he said proudly.

During his three-month stay with Elinor and Dick in their spacious apartment on the Avenue Victor Hugo, Eben acquired a vivid and repellent picture of their social life. He was both astounded and revolted at the extent of the young couple's hectic and everlasting chase for pleasure. They hated being alone for a moment. They were wound up like mechanical toys which keep whirling madly until their sudden, inevitable collapse. It was a tireless round of luncheons, musicales, dinners, balls, the races and the opera; now London, then Cannes, and finally Paris again. Elinor's expeditions to Worth and Poiret were major events, consuming an appalling amount of time, patience and money.

They use up as much energy running away from themselves, Eben thought wryly, as I did building up a fortune.

He refused brusquely to be included in their gaiety. He spent much of his time in the nursery, partially relieved that they were too busy to attend the baby. He got along well with the nurse, a stern and anonymous Englishwoman with the face of a sorrowful middle-aged setter and an exquisite, cultured voice.

Often he accompanied her to the Bois, wheeling the pram, a tall erect old man in a blue serge suit and a high starched collar, his head with its magnificent shock of white hair bare to the sun. And while the baby slept, he made wonderful plans for the future. When Mark was old enough, he could surely come to St. Croix. . . .

The day he was to sail for home, he held a spirited conference with Elinor and Dick. Elinor was gay and ebullient, having been pacified by a diamond brooch from Cartier's.

"It was sweet of you to take the long trip," she said. "I know how you abhor crossing the ocean."

"Elinor," he began bluntly, determined to lay down the law, "I've been saving this for the last because you won't like it. I want a hand in Mark's upbringing. He's an American, and should be raised as one."

Elinor looked stricken at first; then she grew sarcastic. She was the continental who saw in the country she'd left behind only stupidity and crass materialism. When Eben reminded her icily that crass American dollars were giving her the questionable privilege of living abroad, she wept hysterically, and Dick railed at his father. But in the end, they compromised. It was expedient, since Eben assured them Mark was to be his sole heir.

Mark would remain with his parents until his sixth year. Then he would join his grandfather and attend school in St. Croix until he was sixteen. The choice of a college, either English or American, would be left to him.

Elated with his victory, Eben returned home. That year, as he studied the plans for the manual-training school he was giving St. Croix, he reflected. One day Mark will work in this machine shop. Every boy should learn to use his hands.

But in the end Elinor reneged. Mark's sixth birthday came and went, and still there was no sign of the lad. Finally, in reply to his urgent cable, Dick wrote that the boy was ill with bronchitis and they considered it unwise to subject him to a long voyage.

Again Eben waited. At last, after two years had passed, he decided on drastic measures. He ordered his bankers to withhold Dick's monthly draft.

Mark stepped off the train at Union Station at eight o'clock on the evening of September 2, 1912.

"Welcome home, son," Eben said, shaking hands gravely with the boy. He had been waiting for hours.

2. Since the death of his wife, Eben Holmes seldom used the rococo dining room with its somber paneling, heavy mahogany furniture and thick Oriental rugs. He took all his meals at the small table set in the sunny bay of the sitting room.

At breakfast this morning, his grandson was facing him. Eben could not believe it yet. He turned his eyes from the boy's bright, alert face to the garden, where the banks of purple asters and yellow chrysanthemums shimmered in the morning light. Had an old man the right to be so happy, he wondered.

He was such a nice lad! Eben smiled at the boy who was in his own image, lean, dark-haired, gray-eyed. But even more than the physical similarity, he sensed the spiritual kinship between them. You're the son I should have had, he thought fiercely. And it's not too late.

"Your first day of school in America. Excited, Mark?"

The boy finished his cocoa and wiped his trembling lips on a heavy damask napkin. "Rather, sir."

"You'll like school, once you get used to it."

"Yes, sir."

"Time to leave now."

They went through the great hall, hung with landscapes in heavy gilt frames. Mark put on his gray flannel jacket and Eton cap.

"You needn't wear the cap," Eben said hastily. "You'll go to school alone, Mark. It's just down the block. Through the Boys' Entrance, then ask for the principal's office. You can look after yourself, can't you?"

"I'll try, sir."

"Good."

From the window, he watched Mark cross the street and turn left to the granite building. His steps lagged. He stopped to watch a horse and wagon rumble by. Then he bestirred himself and quickened his pace, a thin leggy boy with a crop of thick brown hair. When he was finally out of sight, Eben Holmes stomped into the kitchen, where he found Mrs. Hanrahan, his housekeeper.

"Well, what do you think of him?"

"He's a nice little fellow."

"I hope the others don't make fun of his foreign ways."

"He'll get along—if you don't spoil him."

"Hard to spoil that lad!"

"You've made a good start," Mrs. Hanrahan snapped.

3. By four o'clock in the afternoon, Miss Lovejoy, first-grade teacher at the Holmes Public School, was ready to call it a day. The beginning of the term was always difficult, the children shy, nervous and clumsy. And what a grab bag this year, Dutch, Swedish, Hungarian, Polish; strange inarticulate children, with broad bland faces, heavy guttural speech, rough and rowdy manners. Miss Lovejoy, who came from Scotch pioneer stock, sometimes wondered what the country was coming to!

"I hope I never have to go through another such session," she confided to Miss Finney, the second-grade instructor. "Those dreadful little beasts ganged up on Mark Holmes! The Kolcheck boy started pulling his tie—then Joe Smolinsky joined in. Mark had a hard time defending himself. But before I could get to him, a girl took his part. You should've heard her scolding the boys!" Miss Lovejoy paused dramatically. "Afterwards, she kept telling Mark not to be scared, she'd help him. Can you imagine!"

"Who was the girl?" Miss Finney asked curiously.

"A bold little thing. Her name's Andrews. Faith Andrews."

4. The glorious September day ended at sundown in a violent thunderstorm. Mark Holmes was alone in the library of his grandfather's house. He tried valiantly to concentrate on *The Last of the Mohicans*, but his eyes kept wandering from the page. The room was shadowy, and the bookcases and paintings receded in the murky light. Rain beat sorrowfully against the window panes.

He was very much alone.

His mother wouldn't like it if he cried. She'd be ashamed of him. She was three thousand miles away, yet the very thought of her made his eyelids sting. His body ached, as if he'd had a whipping. His grandfather had been detained at the Lumberman's Bank, so there was no-body. . . .

At the sound of the door opening, he jumped. It was Mrs. Hanra-han.

"My, it's dark in here. Why don't you turn on a light?" She added gently, "Don't mope, son. It's natural to be lonesome in a new place."

"Yes'm."

"Your grandfather won't be home till late, so you better have your supper now. How'd you like to eat in the kitchen?"

His intense young face lightened. "I should like it very much, Mrs. Hanrahan."

The cheery sounds in the big warm kitchen drowned out the weep-ing of the rain. His back to the huge black coal-stove, Mark sat at a table covered with a red-checkered cloth and tried very hard to swallow morsels of roast lamb.

"Drink your milk, Mark."

"Yes'm."

He must remember to eat slowly and think of something quite gay. Then, before he knew it, he'd be ready for dessert. It was a game his mother had taught him when his nurse was away, and he treasured it, as he treasured each kiss, each visit, each trivial gift his mother had occa-sionally bestowed on him. There were moments when he felt that being sent away from her was more than he could bear. . . .

Strangely enough, his father had approved of his going. "Make a man of him," his father had said, as if it pleased him to ship Mark off to the other end of the world.

"Gingerbread and hot applesauce, Mark. That's a favorite Amer-ican dessert."

He managed to finish it and keep it down. Mrs. Hanrahan offered to help him with his bath, but he said politely he could manage, thank you. And his childish dignity almost wrecked her own self-control.

He stayed in the tub a long time, his lean young body slumped, his face empty and remote. He dried himself dreamily, stopping to inspect the scabs on his bony knees. Then a flake of soap got into his eyes, they smarted badly. He wasn't crying. It was the soap.

On the maple night table, he found a plate of butter cookies, a shiny McIntosh apple, and a book, *The Adventures of Tom Sawyer*. He slid between the cool sheets, wriggling his toes experimentally. He bit into the apple, and it crunched noisily against his uneven white teeth.

Beyond the pale-gold arc of lamplight, the room was blue-shadowed and mysterious. When he'd lived with his parents in the large apartment on the Avenue Victor Hugo or in the small London flat or even in the pink villa at Antibes, he'd never minded the dark. Indeed, he made friends with it, for it was a secret and special world, peopled with the characters of his beloved books.

And always, nearby, there was his governess, Miss Spencer, or Henry, his father's valet, or Yvette, his mother's maid. They were all fond of him, and he still remembered overhearing Yvette say to Henry once, "They don't deserve a son like Mark."

But tonight he was wary of the alien darkness beyond the lamplight. Shutting his eyes, he wished desperately it weren't so hard to grow up, to be a little man. He thought of his grandfather and Mrs. Hanrahan and that girl at school—Faith Andrews. How brave she was! Yet he wasn't at all sure he liked the idea of her jumping to his defense. His father would have laughed at him.

The door opened and his grandfather came in quietly.

"Good evening, Mark." He stopped by the window and raised the ivory shade. "It's stopped raining. The moon is out."

The boy was silent.

"How did it go today?"

"Quite well, sir."

Eben lowered himself in the chintz chair. The fresh damp air flowed in through the open window. The clouds parted obsequiously and the moon sailed through the black sky. In the elm a bird stirred in its sleep. Somewhere down the street, a quartet of boyish voices rang out in harmony. *Oh, you great big beau-ti-ful doll ...*

"Mark, have you ever gone fishing?"

"No, sir. But I'd like to try it."

"Good! Next Saturday, we'll go up to my camp in the north woods." He smiled. "Do you ride a horse?"

"Yes, sir."

"There's a piebald in the stable. And a cart. We'll have to get you a dog, too. What kind of dog would you like, Mark?"

A dachshund! Why, the kids would rag the hell out of him. He must convince the boy a terrier or a setter would be more suitable. He started talking, easy and relaxed, telling Mark about his own boyhood; of his youth on a New England farm; of his travels west to Ohio, and then up to Michigan. And under the running commentary of his experiences there was an undercurrent of compassion. He said gravely, as if he were thinking aloud, "After a while you'll get used to us, Mark. Then you won't be lonely any more."

His voice died to a whisper.

The boy was asleep.

Eben leaned down and kissed his cheek tenderly.

5. Faith Andrews hated the weekends, because she had to stay home, under her mother's thumb. By contrast, schooldays were a release, an actual holiday. She couldn't wait to leave the house each morning, starched blue gingham skirt swinging with her agile step; highlights on her healthy red cheeks; a grin on her full baby mouth. She looked like a glossy, radiant little animal, all warm physical senses. But the sudden, far-off expression in the bright eyes, the faint twitch of the full lips were already indications of her mother's influence.

Usually Tod went off by himself on the day of rest. And no matter how much mama nagged, he refused to stay home. Then, one Sunday, he said, "Pumpkin, how'd you like to go fishing?"

"Oh, swell!" Faith answered quickly. Anything to get away from mama who was in a blue mood.

They had fun, laughing and joking, and they caught some perch, too. And she said, "Papa, why don't you take me with you all the time?"

But mama put a stop to the excursions.

"Since Faith can't swim," mama said, "you've no right to take her out in a rowboat."

"If you keep on scaring her," papa said, "she'll never learn to do anything."

They didn't go fishing again. But they took walks through the woods or on the beach. In the spring, Faith liked to pull off her long, white, ribbed stockings, and race barefoot along the shore where the glassy waves rolled in leisurely.

"Papa, I got my dress wet!"

"Take it off, pumpkin. Sun's plenty warm."

"Help me."

As he unfastened the buttons on her brown serge dress, she stepped out of it hesitantly.

"Mama would be awful mad if she saw me."

"Why, pumpkin?"

"Well—because I'm almost nekkid."

The knowledge that Charlotte was corrupting her healthy young mind infuriated him. "Don't ever be ashamed of your body," he said. "Nature didn't mean you to hide it under heavy clothes. Babies aren't born with diapers!"

Faith giggled. Gosh, what fun papa was! She loved being with him.

After supper that evening, mama took her for a walk up Main Street. Faith loved the bright windows of the Bon Ton. Mama bought her a nickel bag of popcorn at Burnside's. If it weren't for women, mama said as they passed Willie's saloon, the world would be lost beyond redemption. But there were many pitfalls for innocent girls. . . .

Faith must realize, mama added, that the only friend she had on this earth was her mother.

"Don't ever forget that, child."

"I won't, mama. I promise."

"Your mother knows what's best for you."

"Yes, mama."

The following Sunday was clear and sunny. Tod said, "Pumpkin, how about a picnic on the beach?"

Faith's eyes sparkled. But then she remembered, and she said quietly, "I guess not, papa."

She sat on the porch swing and read the Katzenjammer Kids.

She felt terrible because she had hurt papa. But she had obeyed her mother.

6. Faith Andrews was precocious, self-possessed and aggressive. Mark Holmes was shy, reticent and painfully sensitive. Nevertheless, something more than Faith's impulsive defense of him the first day of school brought them together and made them fast friends. Each found in the other a quality lacking in himself. Compared to children coming from normal, well-adjusted households, they were both outcasts—Faith suffering from the quarrelsome, inharmonious atmosphere, dominated by her fretful neurotic mother; Mark rejected by his pleasure-mad parents. They were different from others. This humiliating knowledge bound them together; and was to influence their entire futures.

To Miss Lovejoy's intense annoyance, they were soon inseparable. They studied together, played together, did their chores together. Other children, excluded from their fiercely guarded unity, left them alone.

Privately, Miss Lovejoy questioned the wisdom of Eben Holmes in allowing his grandson to grow so deeply attached to a common child. Of course, he was known as a very democratic man, but wasn't this carrying democracy a bit too far?

As for Charlotte Andrews, she resented Faith's constant, enthusiastic prattle about Mark even more than Miss Lovejoy did. The Holmeses

were rich and well born, and therefore completely out of the Andrews'
sphere. Since no good could come of such a friendship, she was determined to thwart it. She begged Faith to play with the little Shannon
girls on Front Street. But it was too late. Faith wanted only Mark.

On pleasant afternoons that autumn, they played dodgeball on the
playground, just the two of them. One day, after a hard game, they
flopped on the damp grass, and soon were engrossed in their favorite
topic: their families.

"Mark, do you really like your grandpa better'n your pa?"

"Yes, sir!"

"But not better'n your mama?"

Instantly he was on the defensive. "Nope. Absolutely not."

With a grimy hand, she pushed back the chestnut curls from her
forehead. "I love my mother better'n anybody in the whole world," she
said smugly. "She loves me best, too. Does your mother love you best?"

Mark put his head down on the grass. To change the subject, he
said quickly, "Can you come over to play?"

He had invited her many times, but she had yet to enter the massive
iron gates of the Holmes place. Each day, her mother waited for her at
the school and walked her home. It embarrassed Faith to be treated like
a baby; she wanted more freedom. But when she asked if she could visit
Mark, Charlotte ordered curtly, "You stay where you belong—an' let him
stay where he belongs. Then we'll have no trouble."

Whenever they were together, they found plenty to talk about.
Faith listened avidly to stories of Mark's home life; the dinners which
he and his grandfather enjoyed before the crackling fire in the sitting
room, toasting apples and marshmallows afterwards; their trips to the
lumber camps in the new red cutter; the organ in the great hall, where,
once a week, Mr. Parks the organist from the Episcopalian church came
to play Bach and Scarlatti; the attics jammed with old trunks and fasci-
nating relics; and finally, the new dachshund, Putzi, given him by his
grandfather the week before Christmas.

"A puppy!" Faith cried ecstatically. She had to see him, she couldn't
resist, even if it meant fibbing to her mother. So she told Charlotte glibly
she had to stay after school—and went home with Mark.

At four-thirty, Charlotte appeared in the classroom. Miss Lovejoy
assured her Faith left at the regular hour. She and Mark went out together, as usual.

Nervously, Charlotte retraced her steps. The murky dusk was deep-
ening to black night. The air was chill and bleak. At the corner, she

hesitated, shivering. Where was Faith? What had happened to her? Then she remembered Miss Lovejoy's words. She moved clumsily up snow-covered Manistee Drive, sobbing to herself. If anything happened to her child, she couldn't bear it. She passed through the open gate and hurried up the low broad steps of the Holmes house and rang the bell.

After a moment, a middle-aged woman opened the door. Charlotte looked at her numbly.

"Yes?" Mrs. Hanrahan said. "Whom do you want to see?"

Charlotte caught a glimpse of a brightly lighted hall. Then she saw Mark Holmes rushing in from another room, and close on his heels, her daughter. Faith's rosy face was glowing as she cradled in her arms a small black-and-tan dachshund.

"Mama, just look at Putzi! Isn't she cunning—just like a baby!"

Faith was safe. No harm had come to her. Charlotte was conscious of a deep and blessed sense of relief. And immediately afterwards, a rush of uncontrollable fury.

"So you were here all the time!"

"Mama," Faith pleaded for understanding, "I just *had* to see Putzi!"

"You didn't stay after school. You lied about it."

The children were appalled by her white face; they retreated before her harsh accusing voice. Mark made a gesture to protect Faith.

"Get your things!"

Faith clutched the puppy, who howled in reproach.

"Did you hear me? Get your things!"

Before Faith could obey, Eben Holmes came into the hall. He put his hand on the girl's shoulder. "I'm happy to meet you, Mrs. Andrews. Won't you come in and have a glass of sherry with us?"

Brusquely, Charlotte refused. "My daughter has upset me. I've been looking for her." She snatched Faith's hand. "Come along," she ordered roughly.

In spite of the snow, her pace was so swift that Faith could scarcely keep up with her. For the first time, she was bitterly ashamed of her mother. How could she have branded Faith a liar before Mr. Holmes and Mark? Why did she act so peculiar? Other mothers left their kids to themselves, instead of fussing. Don't do this; you'll get hurt; something's going to happen. . . .

She was counting on her father to take her part, but Tod was out, probably at Willie's saloon. Stoically she undressed and got into her nightgown and when she was in bed, mama came in for the final rebuke.

"You don't realize how much you hurt me," mama said sorrowfully. "I want you to promise never to go near the Holmes place again."

Something exploded in the childish mind.

"I won't promise!" she rebelled.

"Faith!"

The round face was set in stubborn, antagonistic lines. "I'll go any time they ask me! I like it there better'n home! I wish I lived there. . . ."

Charlotte's sallow face turned livid. "How can you say such things to your mother? How can you hurt me so? After all I've done for you! You should be ashamed of yourself!"

"I'm not ashamed," Faith screamed. "And if you try to make me stop playing with Mark, I'll hate you!"

Afterwards, alone in her room, Faith lay in bed, holding her mouth against the pillow to stifle her sobbing. She was racked with humiliation, self-pity, and childish scorn. But not even for her mother would she stay away from Mark.

Not ever, she vowed, drifting off to sleep.

7. The assassination of a minor royal head in a far-off Balkan country had few repercussions in St. Croix, Michigan, U.S.A. However *The Observer* did carry a news item to the effect that Mr. and Mrs. Richard Holmes were trapped in Paris. Eben did his best to comfort Mark. The boy listened gravely, was lulled, and suffered nightmares in which the horrible Hun slaughtered his mother. Wolverine Motors developed a new combustion engine, and the owner, Zeb Whiting, made his first million. Long before the *Lusitania* was sunk and President Wilson declared a state of war, Eben Holmes was catapulted out of semi-retirement and caught in the exigencies of wartime production schedules. There were Wheatless Days and Sugarless Days; there were shortages of food and fuel. Mary Pickford and Douglas Fairbanks hawked Liberty Bonds. Women knitted for soldiers and Belgian orphans. The slogan of the day was *Make the World Safe for Democracy.*

Tod worked overtime, then loafed in Willie's Bar or on Grant Avenue with his cronies. He had learned to shut his ears to Charlotte's continual fault-finding. Were it not for the kid, he'd have walked out long ago. He was crazy about Faith, and protective, too, knowing that if he weren't the buffer, Charlotte would have made a little introvert of the girl.

Faith's friendship with Mark Holmes gave Tod genuine pleasure. He wasn't impressed by the boy's position as much as the soundness of

his character. Mark was level-headed and unassuming, and a good influence on Faith, who was apt to fly off the handle.

Although they were no longer in the same class (during the fourth
year Mark had skipped a grade) they still saw each other daily. They
sang in the glee club, all the songs popular during the war years, "Roses
of Picardy," "Keep the Home Fires Burning," "There's a Long, Long
Trail A-Winding." In the summer, they volleyed on the tennis court in
back of the Holmes place, or played in the park nearby, darting like
swallows among the granite statues. In winter, Mark taught her to skate
and ski; and after their exercise, windburnt and exhausted, they tramped
into the big warm kitchen, where Mrs. Hanrahan served them sandwiches and cocoa. Often they curled up in the huge red leather chairs in
Mr. Holmes's library and lost themselves in favorite books. Mark taught
Faith to read with imagination. Sunday afternoons, they joined Eben
Holmes in the great hall, where Mr. Parks played for them.

Faith had difficulty getting out of the house Sunday. Her mother
always objected violently. She resented Mark Holmes more than ever,
for he was the cause of all arguments between mother and daughter.
The older woman wept, begged, threatened, but the girl remained adamant. Tod marveled at Faith's resolute self-assurance. She was devoted
to her mother; in many ways she was deeply influenced by her, but
when it came to Mark, she refused to be swayed.

"You have no business getting friendly with the Holmeses," Lotte
wailed. "They're not your kind. You stay on your side of the fence,
Faith. Else you'll end up in tragedy. Your folks may be poor, but they're
respectable—and you're going to stay decent!"

"Fine way to talk to a young girl!" Tod interrupted. "I don't see
any harm in her friendship with Mark. You couldn't pick a nicer fellow!"

"A girl of twelve should be playing with other girls," Charlotte
snapped. "Not with boys. It's putting temptation in her path."

"You're not acting right with Faith," Tod reproved her bitterly.
Charlotte had a way of blighting innocence, of making everything ugly
and sordid. She was so suspicious. Maybe it dated back to their own
hasty marriage. But you'd think she'd be over it by now.

"I'm not upset about Faith," he added reassuringly. "She can take
care of herself."

To Faith those Sunday afternoons were the high spot of the week.
She and Mark sat on stiff gilt-and-brocade French chairs at either side of
Eben Holmes and listened, enchanted, to the music of Palestrina, Scar-
latti and Bach.

Eben Holmes said, "You don't have to be grown to understand Bach. He speaks to the good and simple in heart."

Listening to the strains of the Toccata and Fugue in D Minor, Faith was enthralled. Her spirit took wings, soaring above the dreary, commonplace pattern of her life. She saw herself as Elaine, the fair and romantic; as Joan, the fervent and impassioned. She dreamed of great deeds, of exalted sacrifices. . . .

Mrs. Hanrahan wheeled in the mahogany cart.

"Tea?" Mr. Holmes asked.

And Faith, jarred out of her trance, settled down comfortably to sandwiches, frosted cakes and cambric tea.

When Mark took her home Sunday night, she found the shabby bungalow on Ontario Place more depressing than ever. The overhanging roof threw the rooms in a perpetual gloom which was matched by her mother's dour moods. Why is our home always so sad, she wondered. Why can't we be happy like other families? Why was mother always warning her about "men," making her so wretched and embarrassed? Mother was a strange woman; born unhappy, dad said. The only way to get along with her was to give in constantly. Which was a lot easier for dad than for Faith. Dad had no problems.

Chapter Four

1. Faith was fifteen now, a big girl, five foot seven and well proportioned. Her eyes were the same luminous brown as her mother's, but
level and forthright where Charlotte's were feverish and fanatic. Her
mouth was large and sensuous; in repose, willful and undisciplined. Her
thick chestnut braids were pinned in a coronet around her large head, a
style she thoroughly detested. She longed for a shingle bob, the kind
her classmates Winona Kraus and Leah Parker wore. She envied their
flat, boyish bodies. Resolutely she gave up sweets, tortured her curved
young body into a tight girdle and a beige jersey tubular dress, knee-
length and belted at the hips. She looked simply awful.

When Winona got her first fuzzy permanent, Faith pleaded with
her mother for permission to cut her hair.

"I should say not!" Charlotte answered tartly.

"But I look so funny! Old-fashioned! Why do I always have to be
different?"

"The way girls dress today is a disgrace!"

"Mother, for Pete's sake!"

Charlotte folded her thin lips together. She was thirty-five, now,
and the spinsterish lines of her gaunt frame were obvious and there was
a morbid gleam in her magnificent dark eyes. The contrast between her
and Faith was so marked no stranger would ever have believed them
kin.

"Faith, I've done my best to bring you up decently. If you behave
like the Kraus girl, it will break my heart!" There was anguish in her
voice, as if she were re-living her own terrible humility. "I hope you'll
be smart enough to realize men want a girl only for what they can get
out of her."

Whenever her mother started a harangue like this, Faith escaped
as quickly as possible.

The following day at glee club rehearsal, Winona said, "Gosh,
Faith, you'd sure look wonderful in a shingle. Just like Clara Bow. Why

don't you have it done?" She giggled. "What can your mother do after-wards?"

Faith hesitated. Then she itemized all the hurts her mother had in-flicted on her. Mother wouldn't let her have a kitten, wouldn't let her be friends with Mrs. Hussar, wouldn't let her use lipstick, wouldn't . . .

I'll do it.

Winona accompanied her to the beauty parlor giving her courage. And she did look pretty in the bob; even the operator said so. When she got home, she braced herself for the scene. Mother wept, mother said she was headed for perdition. Mother finally went to bed with a sick headache, and a beautiful quiet descended. Faith prepared supper for dad. And while she set the table, she thought with a sudden and oddly mature fear, Are mother's actions going to dog me all my life?

2. She was one person with her folks, quite another with Mark and Eben Holmes. Meekly she accepted criticism and advice from Eben which she would have rejected bitterly from her family. Her friendship with Mark was the star on which she fixed her course. It afforded her the sense of security she found lacking at home, and it gave her also a special niche with her classmates.

At the Holmes High School, she presented still another facet of her character. Here, her already dynamic personality made itself evident. She had a capacity for hard work, which, combined with her energy and enthusiasm, helped make her an outstanding student. In her sopho-more year she was picked for the debating team of which Mark was captain. And the glee club. The girls admired her warily; the young men were frankly overwhelmed, though she was not aware of their adu-lation.

Among the fast set at school, Leah Parker and Winona Kraus were the ringleaders. They drove out to the casino on the lake in flivvers; they danced all night in the blind tigers on the State Highway; they drank bathtub gin, and boasted of their escapades. There were even rumors for a time that Winona Kraus was in trouble; but nothing came of it.

Winona was slight and exceedingly pretty, with long pale-blond hair, gullible blue eyes, and a porcelain skin. She was impressionable, easily led, and a constant source of anxiety to her old-fashioned German parents, who ran the meat market and delicatessen on Main Street. She had a small, pleasant soprano voice, a memory for all the popular songs and she did the Charleston better than any girl in town. She envied Faith for the many qualities she herself lacked—poise, maturity, self-sufficiency. She tried to make friends with Faith, who would see her, grudgingly, in the summer months, while Mark was away on a trip with Eben Holmes.

The rest of the year Faith was absorbed in her work and in Mark. She had time for nothing else.

3. It was a chilly Saturday afternoon. They had finished an excellent lunch, and Eben Holmes sat before the fire, a copy of *The Observer* on his lap. He looked at Mark, whose dark head was bent over a book; he noted proudly the wiry strength of the boy's lean body, the good shoulders, the narrow wrists and sensitive hands. Mark was eighteen and, Eben hoped, well adjusted. It had not been easy going. He missed his mother acutely, he had worried about her and his father when they were stranded in Paris. He was worrying even more now. Last autumn, Dick had written that Elinor was desperately ill with pneumonia, the result, no doubt, of the considerable hardships she had suffered. She had been sent to convalesce at a sanatorium near Basel, where the doctors discovered a lesion on her left lung. She had been there for six months now, and Mark received frequent letters from her, as well as snapshots of her and his father, stretched out on deck chairs in the sun. As soon as she regained her strength, they planned a trip to the United States. Mark looked forward eagerly to their expected visit.

Eben felt differently about it.

"In June you'll be finished with high school, Mark. Have you given any thought to college?"

"I'd like to wait until dad and mother get here before I decide."

He meant of course that he would heed Elinor's wishes. Eben realized her hold on the boy was still powerful. What a pity, for he needed guidance, understanding.

In many ways, Eben dreaded their homecoming.

4. In November, the high-school glee club was scheduled to give its annual concert. Faith Andrews and Winona Kraus were chosen soloists; Mark was in the male chorus. Two days before the concert, the music teacher called for another rehearsal. They took their places on the stage of the auditorium, amid laughter, shuffling of feet and slamming of seats. Winona complained, "Old Crandall's an awful crab. He takes all the fun out of the glee club!"

Winona was always having run-ins with Mr. Crandall, who flaunted such a rigid devotion to his duties that he aroused even in the most faithful students an aversion to music. To him, the basis of music lay in structure and technique; he was totally indifferent to the spiritual magic of melody. Winnie was his pet scapegoat. Her careless, impudent airs irritated him. It it weren't for her sweet voice, he would have made an example of her long ago.

Clearing his throat nervously, he took a thick gold watch from his vest pocket and tapped peremptorily for order. He was a tall man, given to salt-and-pepper worsted suits, stiff collars, funereal ties; he was so emaciated that he seemed in constant dyspeptic turmoil. His streaked gray hair was brushed back from a pale domineering forehead, and his small, alert eyes, shifting behind rimless glasses, were ready to pounce on any hidden move, any delinquent gesture.

Again he tapped for order. "If you need more time to quiet down . . ." he began sarcastically.

Fifty young faces watched him guardedly.

The young rowdies, he thought bitterly. Troublemakers, every one of them.

"Now, then—this is our last practice period before dress rehearsals. I want it letter perfect. We'll begin with the Brahms lullaby."

The Brahms lullaby, over and over again, until they were good and sick of it; the music from *Cavalleria Rusticana;* the Toreador Song from *Carmen.* Their young voices wove a pleasing pattern of sound, but still he was not satisfied. Mr. Crandall prided himself on being a perfectionist, and it did not matter to him at whose expense it might be. The afternoon dragged on. The air in the auditorium grew hot and stuffy. In the male section, the boys were listening enviously to sounds of football practice in the field across the way. Faith felt her eyelids beginning to droop, and she thought frantically, I mustn't get sleepy, Mr. Crandall will be furious.

She pictured the new dress Mrs. Hussar had made for her, white linen trimmed with Irish lace. I hope Mark likes it, she thought, sending him a winsome smile.

"Next," Mr. Crandall said, "we'll try Schubert's *Ave Maria.*"

The pianist struck the first chord, the girls' voices rose dutifully. But suddenly a new sound intruded, one which sounded very much like a squeal. A giggle ran through the chorus like a nervous shudder.

"Who is responsible for that idiotic noise?" Mr. Crandall demanded.

Silence, tense and uneasy silence.

"If you're ready, we'll try again."

Once more the sopranos lifted their voices. And once more the absurd squeal.

No one was laughing now. Mr. Crandall's face reddened; his light-struck eyes grew vicious. "No evasions. Who made that noise?"

Silence again, an insolent silence; they were no longer afraid of him; they were laughing at him, he could read it in their faces. The situation was untenable. He tried frantically to figure out a move to punish them without making himself ridiculous. And then Winona Kraus, unable to control herself any longer, giggled out loud.

He pounced triumphantly. Of course, she was the culprit, he should have suspected her before this.

"Miss Kraus, stand up, and tell us why you squeal like a mouse." She made no move.

"Stand up," he repeated softly. "*Stand up*, Miss Kraus."

Slowly, Winona dragged herself to her feet. Her classmates were watching her curiously. She clutched the top of the chair in front of her, and looked around in frantic appeal until her glance lit on Faith. Help me, she cried silently. Please help me, Faith.

There was a moment's uncertainty. Then Faith said slowly, "Mr. Crandall, Winona isn't responsible."

"Indeed?" So the Andrews girl wanted to make a laughingstock of him. "Then suppose you tell me who is?"

"I don't know. But Winona is here near us—and the sound came from the back."

"Obviously, Miss Andrews, you know more of the situation than you're telling me."

"Oh, no! I know nothing—except that I'm positive Winona's innocent, Mr. Crandall. I'd have heard . . ."

Winona was sobbing quietly. The others were watching him with contempt. Mr. Crandall was uncomfortably aware of the importance of this moment.

"Miss Andrews, unless you tell me instantly what is going on here—and unless you apologize properly—I will report you to the office for insubordination. And relieve you of your part in the concert!"

Faith hesitated only a moment. Then, without a word, she picked up her books and made her way down the aisle.

"Mr. Crandall . . ." Mark objected.

Crandall turned on him hysterically. "If you feel inclined to follow Miss Andrews, go right ahead!"

Mark and Faith left the auditorium together.

"The bully," Mark muttered. But Faith was thinking of her mother's reaction to this incident. "For heaven's sake," mother would say tartly, "why don't you keep your nose out of things that don't concern you?"

5. That spring, Faith developed into the star debater for the high-school team. She already had acquired a stage presence so persuasive that she didn't depend on facts or logic to impress her audience.

Mark, who was also on the team, helped write her speeches, clarifying her ideas with his own reasoning. The towns of Genesee, Montgomery, Ventura, Great Falls and Shawamie all bowed to them on their home grounds. The final debate of the season was scheduled to take place in Pine Bluffs.

"I'm not sure I can go," Faith said. "Mother'll never let me stay away from home overnight."

But Mr. Sears, the principal, promised that Faith would be strictly chaperoned by Miss Lovejoy and finally Charlotte grudgingly consented.

Faith was enormously excited over the prospect of her first trip away from home. She packed the cotton underwear, her good beige jersey dress, the string of amber beads Eben Holmes had given her for her birthday, the lipstick Charlotte knew nothing about. Tod, beaming, slipped her a five-dollar bill secretly.

"Have a good time, pumpkin."

When she arrived at Union Station, Mark, Miss Lovejoy and Paul Truit, the third member of the team, were already there. She was conscious of an exhilarating sense of adventure, and even her familiar companions took on a strange air.

"Hi, Faith!"

"Hi, Mark."

He looked different, too; taller, more manly in his gray suit, blue sport sweater and polka-dot tie. She watched him proudly as he carried her bag into the train.

The trip lasted six hours; through miles of fertile green flatlands bordered by leafing woods and sparkling lakes touched with the bright sheen of spring. They bought sandwiches and milk from the candy butcher; then, while Miss Lovejoy helped Paul with his speech, Mark and Faith talked quietly. This was the first time they had gone on a trip together. St. Croix was already fifty miles behind them when Faith realized abruptly she was experiencing nothing of the excitement she had anticipated. Away from home, she and Mark seemed to be losing their old camaraderie without finding a substitute for it.

What was the matter with her she wondered. What put such absurd ideas in her head? Why was she strained and ill at ease with him?

The constraint hung on the rest of the evening, through the time they registered at the Fulton Hotel, dressed and made their way to the Hayes Auditorium.

"Scared?" Mark whispered.

"Scared stiff."

"You needn't be. It's a darned good speech." He pressed her hand encouragingly. She moved away, agitated. I've got stage fright, she thought. I never felt like this before.

Then it was time to go on. She heard her name called, she stepped forward and, miraculously, her lips were forming the proper words. She had the odd feeling her real self was standing in the wings, looking on critically. . . .

St. Croix won the State Championship.

"Boy, were you good!" Paul Truit said, shaking her hand. "Congratulations!"

"You won the cup for us," Mark added.

She turned to him in sudden flushed confusion. How odd, she thought, bewildered, it's as if Mark weren't Mark at all, but an attractive stranger she was eager to impress. Somehow, all the youthful years during which they had played and fought and made up, childish friends and confidants, had vanished, leaving no trace. She was shy with him, she longed for more praise from him, she wished the others would leave them alone. And when Miss Lovejoy rushed over to her, she burst suddenly into tears.

6. Mark had not seen his parents for almost eleven years, and the prospect of their visit to St. Croix in June, 1923, was almost more than he could bear. When his mother stepped off the train, assisted by his father and the porter, he was deeply shocked. She must still be very sick he thought. She was so thin that her beige kasha coat flapped about her emaciated body. Under the carefully applied mask of rouge and powder, her face was gaunt and deeply lined. Months of tedious enforced rest had subdued her spirit.

Tears filled her eyes as Mark put his arms around her and kissed her shyly.

"Darling, you're so grown," she marveled. She stifled a cough and turned to her husband. "Dick, do look at your son. Isn't he wonderful, aren't you proud of him?"

Mark met his father's dispassionate glance and realized there was nothing between them. Dick was a lean, handsome man in his forties with courtly manners and a bored air. He was absorbed in his wife, solicitous of her every move; for him no one else existed, especially an attractive young son.

"Elinor must have two hours of rest before dinner," he said.

"Mark is coming upstairs to talk to me," she said, linking her arm with his. "We've so much to catch up on."

Eben Holmes reflected sardonically that her dramatic interest in Mark had been awfully late in coming, but he remained silent.

They arrived the week of graduation exercises, and having them here made all the difference in the world to Mark. He was cheerful and much more talkative than usual. Old Eben was exasperated by his reverent devotion to his mother. After all, Elinor had neglected the boy for years. Only now when she was ill, did it gratify her ego to have a charming young son dancing attendance on her. Mark was no weakling, but he was young and malleable. Eben feared she would cast her spell over the boy, and transform him in Dick's image.

His dislike for her increased momentarily. And when she asked casually, "Father Holmes, whatever happened to those magnificent pearls belonging to Dick's mother?" he answered coolly, "I still have them."

Elinor shrugged off his rebuff. She could be thick-skinned when it suited her purpose. She had undertaken this long exhausting journey with a shrewd motive. Her son was Eben's heir; obviously the old man doted on the boy. Obviously, it would be to her advantage and Dick's to have Mark with them, in order to mold him into their sort of person, who would use his fortune to indulge his pleasures. She feared rightly enough that if he were left in St. Croix much longer, he would develop into a second Eben.

Coming down to dinner in a red crêpe evening gown, knee-length in front and falling in a fantail to her gilt slippers, her thin corded arms weighed down with diamond bracelets whose sparkle was no less feverish than the light in her blue eyes, Elinor refused to sit down. Instead, she inspected the ornate rooms with an appraiser's eye.

"A Sisley and Pissarro! Father, where in the world did you get them?"

"Bought them in Paris the year Mark was born."

"They're enormously valuable now." They would be Mark's one day, she realized, and he must be educated to appreciate their worth.

"Mark, dear," she said, "next autumn I should like to see you in a good English school. Near enough so you can visit me often." She placed her thin, jeweled hand on Mark's shoulder affectionately.

"I've been a woefully negligent mother, I'm afraid. But you do understand the circumstances, darling? And we'll make up for it now."

"Grandfather feels I should attend college here," Mark began uncertainly. "Not that he's tried to influence me in any way . . ."

"College isn't merely book-learning, darling. It's making friends who can be of help to you in the future. It's brushing off the provincial edges. Besides, if you return to Europe with us—as your grandfather promised when we first sent you here—I'll have a real incentive for getting well!"

Still he hesitated. He didn't want to leave home, his grandfather and Faith. He belonged here. He felt no genuine kinship with his parents—at least, not with his father.

"May I think about it?" he hedged.

"Mark, dear, I need you. I need you very much." She moistened her parched lips. "Darling, don't tell me you have a girl!"

"Yes," he answered candidly, without embarrassment, "and I'd like very much for you to meet her."

Elinor suffered a coughing spasm, and he rushed into the kitchen for a glass of water. Afterwards, she said weakly, "I'm sure she's charming, dear. But at eighteen, you mustn't get entangled."

At the graduation exercises, she met Faith and was offended by her exuberance and healthy animal spirits. And that evening she said feverishly, "Mark, you're young, handsome and rich. The world's ahead of you. Darling, it would break my heart to see you waste yourself before you've even had a chance!"

It was important to take him away. The sooner, the better. She only hoped he wasn't too involved with the girl.

7. Mark walked slowly down Manistee Drive. The trees were sculptured in the purple dusk. A veil hung across the sky, softening the flamboyant sunset, and the air was tranquil and drowsy, smelling of freshly mown grass and flowering shrubs. This is home, he thought. I cannot leave.

But he *was* leaving. Tomorrow. And tonight he must say goodbye to Faith.

As he turned into Ontario Place, he found her waiting on the weather-beaten porch of the shabby bungalow.

"Sorry to be late," he said.

"I don't mind." The sound of her laughter was forced and unnatural. "Sit down, Mark."

They shared the porch swing, rocking silently, the rusty chains creaking in protest. A night insect beat its wings against the screen. A car lumbered by in the darkness. The street lights came on, soft yellow, diffusing the shadows.

She said in a small choked voice, "Paris is so far away."

"Not really, Faith. And I'll be back before you know it."

She stared blindly at the street lights until her eyes ached. "I don't suppose you'll have time to write."

"Of course, I will! Didn't I write you whenever I went away summers?"

"This is different," she said woodenly. "This isn't the same thing at all."

He was conscious of her beside him. There was a healthy fragrance about her, as if she were part of the fresh grass and the flowers.

He said practially, "Senior math is tough—I won't be here to help you, Faith. You want to watch it."

"Yes."

"You'll be captain of the debating team," he continued doggedly. "Don't jump to conclusions too fast—especially in rebuttals."

"I'll be careful."

"Will you visit grandfather once in a while? He likes you very much."

"I'll go to see him."

They were silent. Then he said, "I guess I'd better get back to the house."

They stood up, facing each other clumsily. In the darkening sky, Venus shone clear and luminous.

"Mark."

"Yes, Faith?"

The white hydrangea bushes were ghostly blossoms in the darkness.

"Mark, will you kiss me goodbye?"

He remembered how kind she had been the first day of school. Without her, I'd have been lonely all the time, he thought. Without her, I couldn't have managed.

He put his hands on her trembling shoulders and kissed her on the cheek. "Take care of yourself, Faith."

"I will. And you, too, Mark. You take very good care of yourself."

He said unhappily, "If my mother weren't so ill, I wouldn't be leaving. But I'll be home as soon as I can, Faith. I promise."

8. Mark was gone. She couldn't quite believe it at first. She'd wake up thinking, In a little while, Mark will be over. We'll play tennis in the morning, later, Mr. Holmes will take us for a drive. Then, she'd remember. Mark wasn't here, Mark wasn't anywhere she could see him. He was miles away—with other people and other interests. At first, the shock sickened her. Then she suffered a sense of frustration and anger. Always before, Mark had been there to give the day a special quality. Now, she had only the dreary routine of home to look forward to. I can't take it, she thought wildly. What can I do—until Mark comes home?

She found no solace in the friendliness of her classmates. Several times, Winona Kraus sought to include her in the gang's activities, but she always made an excuse. If only she could talk to someone! Her father might prove sympathetic, he liked Mark, but he was away all day and in the evening, mother was always around. Charlotte was, of course, pleased with Mark's departure. What did I tell you, she seemed to be asking triumphantly. You're best rid of him.

On a sweltering afternoon in July, Faith decided to pay Eben Holmes a visit. She found him in the garden, sitting on a stone bench near the fountain, where a cherubic pixie splashed streams of water on the colored tiles below.

His lined face relaxed in a smile. "I'm glad you've come to see me," he said, making room for her beside him. It was cool in the garden by the juniper hedge; except for the music of the fountain, it was quiet, too. She could pretend Mark was in the house. In a moment, he'd run out to greet her, tennis racquets in hand. . . .

Jacob the gardener came over to consult Mr. Holmes. Putzi waddled at his heels. Impulsively, Faith knelt and gathered the aged dachshund in her arms. Mark had hated to leave Putzi, but she was too old to be taken. Mark . . .

"Don't grieve," Eben said comfortingly. "The year will pass sooner than you realize."

"I don't know what to do with myself," she confessed in despair. "The days drag out so."

She has an odd maturity, Eben Holmes reflected, she is so different from most sixteen-year-olds.

"Would you like to work until school begins again? A job would be good for you, Faith. Take you out of yourself."

"I'd like it a lot! But what could I do?"

He rubbed his fingers against his bearded cheek. "I'll speak to Vrest Macklin tomorrow. Perhaps he'll have something."

The following morning, he arranged with his friend to hire Faith as a copy girl on *The Observer*.

And somehow, between her chores at the paper and Mark's frequent letters, the summer slipped by. Outwardly she was reconciled to her solitary existence. Occasionally, Winona dropped by to jeer, "You're an awful stick-in-the-mud, Faith. Don't you think Mark's having fun in Paris?" But she remained unruffled. Each night, she took out Mark's letters and reread them avidly. He wrote that his mother's health had improved and they were now staying at Antibes. He swam every day, and was as brown as his grandfather. He had met an American boy, a crazy, irresponsible but enormously amusing chap named Phillip Latham.

The inexorable dog days came to St. Croix, and only Mark's letters sustained her.

She dreaded the return to school, which she must face without his help and encouragement. This year she was captain of the debating team, an honor which involved considerable work. The first important debate of the season, between St. Croix and Genesee—winner of last year's Midwest Trophy—took place the week before Christmas in the high-school auditorium.

Vrest Macklin was one of the judges. He was a big man, well over six feet, but he looked shorter because of his stocky frame. The cherubic plumpness of his face was counteracted by the sagacious gleam in his nearsighted eyes. His spectacles were always slipping down his short blunt nose. He was carelessly dressed in an old brown tweed suit, and the collar of his rumpled shirt was wilted.

After the debate was over, and St. Croix won, he spoke to Faith. "Not many of your arguments held water," he said dryly. "But you were so smooth and convincing, you fooled the audience—and even the judges. That's a facile trick, you know. Put the punch in your delivery—and nobody'll bother to analyze the contents. A politician's trick."

She flushed. It was the only criticism of the evening.

"But it helped us win," she said.

"No doubt. However, I held it against you."

The six summer weeks she had worked on *The Observer*, Vrest Macklin had ignored her. "So you're Tod Andrews' girl," he had said the first day. "I hope you're dependable." And since this was obviously a left-handed jab at her father, she made it a point to be on time. She had worked conscientiously, too, hoping to please him. But when it came time for her to return to school, he had let her go without a word.

Now, to her astonishment, he said casually, "If you're interested in a steady job after graduation, come and see me."

"Thank you, Mr. Macklin. I'll be there."

She reported the news to her father and he was delighted. "A chance to work steadily for Vrest Macklin—that's a great privilege, pumpkin. And the best Christmas present you could get!"

She hated to contradict him, but privately she considered the packages from Mark infinitely better gifts: the length of Liberty silk from Selfridge's, the old French map, the Chanel perfume, the copy of *Jean Christophe*. If only Mark himself were home . . .

Spring arrived swiftly. She was acutely sensitive to the beauty of the season, the violets in the last patches of gray snow, the daffodils, the pale-gold forsythia and the creamy petals of the dogwood. She worked tirelessly and lost ten pounds, and there was about her the first promise of potential beauty. In June, she graduated, seventh on the list in scholastic achievement. But under her photograph in the Class of 1924 Yearbook, there were these significant words:

The Outstanding All-Around Student.
Destined for Future Fame: Faith Andrews.

Chapter Five

1. Years later, whenever Mark Holmes thought of Paris, he remembered the quais washed in the pearly morning light; the chestnut vender near the Bois, grumbling to himself in the chill autumn air; and Phillip Latham demanding, astonished, "You mean you take your Baedeker seriously? Boy, you really don't know Paris until you've dated one of those cute American mannequins at Patou's!"

Dick and Elinor Holmes were settled briefly in the apartment on the Avenue Victor Hugo, and Mark re-lived his youth in the ancient gray stone building with its lofty spacious rooms. His mother's exquisite taste pervaded the flat, arranging the delicate French furniture, Venetian chests and baroque mirrors into an elegant pattern.

Except for a short stay at St. Malo, Elinor did not leave Paris again that summer. As a concession to Dick's plea, she consented to remain in bed all morning, a cure whose benefits were erased by her hectic afternoon and evening activities.

Fortunately, Mark's days were his own. He decided not to enter school that autumn, accepting his grandfather's suggestion that he make this a year of self-education. He wandered around Paris, discovering its magic for himself, and making ill-assorted friends of whom his parents would never have approved. In December, they went to Antibes where he met the American boy who was to become his close friend.

His mother had returned to Minneapolis so Phillip Latham was alone in the white stucco villa, with a half-dozen French servants at his disposal. He was of average height and build, and his manners reflected a shocking boredom and cynicism. He had cropped light hair and a loose, undisciplined lower lip. The pale scar on his high square forehead was the result of a racing accident. His friends ranged from the croupiers at the casino to the models sent down by the Parisian couturiers to display the latest fashions.

His great-grandfather had been an immigrant Danish miller who laid the groundwork for the vast mills which were now turning out *Wheat-Pops,* the candy cereal *Pep-Korn,* the source of energy, and

Wheat-Lax, the morning stimulant. His father had died when Phillip was a child, and his mother had taken over the reins of the business.

"She's an energetic woman," he admitted, sadly. "And she loves to reform people—especially me."

The malicious gleam in his guileless blue eyes promised to thwart his mother's efforts. He was still a small boy bent on shocking his elders. Even in his excesses, there was a strain of innocence that modified somewhat the extent of their depravity. No matter how many bistros he visited during the night, he showed little signs of wear, and even managed to drive his red Mercedes roadster home with a reasonably steady hand. He had a vast and expensive collection of pornographic literature, which he shared generously with his friends, and his conversation was limited to Babe Ruth's latest home run, John Held, Jr.'s cartoons in *College Humor,* and Constance Bennett's looks. He thought Mark Holmes was quite a guy, but an awful prude.

"Get wise to yourself, fella," he said. "Time enough to be a little gentleman when you're too old for fun!"

Phillip was dedicated to the proposition that while all men were created equal, only the rich were entitled to mundane pleasures.

Mark found him a gay and jovial companion. Nevertheless, despite his friendship, despite the stimulation of travel, he was intensely homesick. He longed for the tranquillity of the house on Manistee Drive, for the long talks with his grandfather, and most of all, for Faith. His delight in Paris would have been greatly enhanced if he could have shared it with her. Whenever he wrote to her now, describing the view from the top of the Sacré Coeur; or listening to a Bach fugue in the church of St. Genevieve; lunching at the Pré Catelan, or attending a Picasso exhibit, he added a postscript: "I'll be home in August."

In July, as he was making plans for his return, his mother collapsed. And he spent the month of August by her bedside in the Lucerne sanatorium.

2. The first Monday after graduation, Faith started work again at *The Observer.* She got up early, dressed carefully in her neat gray-and-white-striped cotton frock and her good suede pumps. She was much too excited to eat. Since she could not hope for a college education, this eight-dollar-a-week job was to her the first rung of a career.

"I envy you," Tod said, as he picked up his worn blue jacket and work pail. "You're going to make the grade, pumpkin. You've got more to you than your old man."

Faith hugged him impulsively.

"Dad, you're always belittling yourself! I wish you'd stop it!" But today for the first time, she noticed the stoop to his high shoulders, the resignation in his manner. He'd had a hard life. Mother was always complaining because his wages did not keep pace with their expenditures. Their rent had been raised, food was so high, they were always in debt. Faith was aware of their hopeless poverty; they were no better off than the unskilled Polish and Hungarian laborers whom mother always ridiculed on Grant Street.

With a surge of affection, she vowed, I'll work hard—and when I get a raise, we can live more comfortably. Mother won't worry so much, and dad can ease up. . . .

She walked up Main Street, feeling mature and competent enough to take on the burdens of the world. She stopped at the Bon Ton window long enough to admire a gray and yellow flowered dress. Just the thing for Sunday best. She'd save up for it, and for a sweater for dad and a new dark dress for mother, who was partial to black crêpe. How wonderful it was going to be to earn her own money!

The Observer was housed in a two-story narrow red brick building on the west side of Main Street, just below the Lake Shore Hotel. The front windows, piled high with printing matter, were hidden by a large blackboard on which were chalked last-minute news bulletins. Vrest Macklin's scarred oak desk, littered with pamphlets, reference books, and unanswered mail, stood at a point where Macklin, slouching behind it, corncob pipe stuck between his teeth, could keep an eye on all activities.

As Faith came in, he struggled to his feet, spectacles in one pudgy ink-stained hand, pipe in the other. He led her over to Miss Smith.

"We're going to step you up," he said genially. "You'll assist Miss Smith, the society editor."

"Society editor? Gosh, what do I know about society?"

"No less than anyone else in town." He chuckled. "Besides, it's the spot where you can do the least harm."

He was laughing at her, but without malice, as if he liked having her here. He was a strange man. She knew St. Croix was divided in its opinion of him. Industrialists like Lewis Trout, politicians like Big Bob Costello and the Mayor hated him. But the plain decent townsfolk admired him tremendously. He hit out against evil and injustice generally, and against corrupt local politics specifically. He had fought a ceaseless and undiscouraged battle against the unprincipled men in

power; and his blunt, outspoken editorials were often quoted in the
Eastern press. Despite its limited circulation, the reputation of *The
Observer* was so great that reporters who had received their training
under Macklin often graduated to larger and more spectacular papers.

Among Macklin's few close friends was Eben Holmes, who was his
senior by twenty years. They often dined together in the gray stone house
on Manistee Drive or in Macklin's dusty, book-cluttered rooms at
the Lake Shore Hotel. Faith suspected they sometimes discussed her,
for Vrest often questioned her about young Mark of whom he was fond.

She loved her work, and made herself useful not only to Miss Smith
but to other members of the staff. She never balked at staying late or
doing more than was normally expected of her. She responded enthusiastically to the bustle and excitement of the office, to the incessant ring-
ing of the telephone and the monstrous grumbling of the presses, to the
easy camaraderie of the staff. They ate lunch together, thick ham sandwiches on home-baked bread, mustard pickles, coffee in soggy containers
brought in from Willie's Tavern.

"You've got printer's ink in your veins," Steve Pringle, Macklin's
assistant, told her.

She grinned. "I come by it naturally."

3. In September, while Miss Smith was on vacation, Faith was
assigned to cover a garden party at the new Country Club on the
Heights, and Steve Pringle drove her there in a borrowed flivver. A
gaily striped tent was set up on the first green, and white-coated waiters
juggled trays of long cold drinks and canapés. Faith stared avidly at the
women in chiffon gowns and huge straw cartwheels. She realized her
ten-ninety-five frock from the Bon Ton looked its price and not a cent
more. Her nose was shiny. She should have worn a hat.

I don't belong here, she thought wistfully. The office is more
my style.

The Country Club's new publicity man—an anemic fellow with
lank blond hair and no chin—introduced himself, offered them each a
cocktail in a teacup, the guest list, and then retreated.

Steve Pringle mopped his red face.

"There's Lewis Trout and his missus," he said. "Give Lew another
five years and he'll own St. Croix. Let's make his acquaintance, honey.
Even snobs are just lovely to reporters."

She followed him across the lawn.

"Excuse me," she began uncertainly, "we're from *The Observer* . . ."

Lewis Trout glared at her. "Not interested!" And taking his wife by the arm, he walked brusquely away.

Steve whistled. "Mr. Trout doesn't like our boss," he said. "Our boss gets into Mr. Trout's hair."

"Who the dickens does Trout think he is?" she said angrily. "After all, we're just trying to do our jobs."

"Let's make ourselves scarce, my sweet. Cinderella's got her copy to turn out."

This was the only occasion on which she went out with Steve, but he was not sensitive to rebuffs, nor was he one to suffer in silence. The entire staff had a press box on his wooing of Faith, whom he called his handsome Valkyrie, and she lacked the poise and experience to shrug off their amusement. Steve was a good-looking fellow with regular, almost feminine features and a mop of coarse red hair that grew low on his forehead. He was a glib, impressive talker, and most women found his impudent manner irresistible. Miss Smith adored him. And though his efforts were pedestrian, his reporting not always accurate, Vrest Macklin tolerated him. "Every office needs a buffoon," Vrest said wryly.

Several times Steve walked Faith home; brought her boxes of Huyler's chocolates tied with big satin bows; invited her to dinner.

"There's a swell speak on Marquette Road. Serves the best steaks I've ever eaten. Tony Spade's place."

"I wouldn't be caught there dead," Faith replied loftily.

"Then how about asking me home for Thanksgiving?" He moistened his fleshy lips. "I haven't had a home-cooked meal in years!"

"I'm sorry, Steve."

"What's wrong? Don't you like Stevie?"

She flushed. "You're very nice."

"Got a boy friend?"

She made no answer. A boy friend? She'd never thought of Mark in this way.

She still missed him dreadfully, but the acute longing had worn off. She knew that since August, he was living near a sanatorium in Switzerland, watching over his sick mother. His hope of entering the University of Michigan in September was ruined. "I wish you could see how much mother depends on me. . . ." he wrote Faith.

She understood. She was growing inured to the circumstances that kept them apart. Mark's most recent note convinced her that his return was entirely dependent on his mother's recovery.

You may as well get used to it, she assured herself grimly. You'll have to wait.

Then, the day before Thanksgiving, Eben Holmes telephoned her at the office. He had just received a cable from Dick. Elinor had died. Mark would be home for Christmas.

4. As it turned out, Mark's boat was delayed by violent mid-Atlantic storms. Without him, Christmas at the Holmes house was a sorry affair. Faith had tea with Eben Holmes in the afternoon, and they did nothing but speculate about Mark's return. How would he look? Would he have changed? There were other questions Faith needed to ask, not aloud, but to herself.

It was a relief to return to the office the following morning, and to lose herself in the chores Miss Smith assigned to her. At four in the afternoon, as was his habit, Steve Pringle brought in wedges of chocolate cake and steaming coffee, which he placed on Faith's desk.

"Fall to," he urged hospitably.

"Thanks."

She looked up as the door opened. A tall, dark-haired young man in an English coat stepped into the room and stood uncertainly for a moment, looking about him. Then, as he spied her, a smile transfigured his thin face.

"Faith!"

The coffee spilled, unnoticed.

"Mark! Is it really you? When did you get in?"

"Half hour ago. And it's sure good to be back."

They stared at each other, too moved to say more. Steve Pringle turned away, brushing the crumbs from his rumpled shirt.

"Can you leave now?" Mark asked.

"I'll get my things."

In her excitement, she snatched Miss Smith's brown felt hat and had to go back and retrieve her own. She led him past Vrest Macklin's unoccupied desk and into the street, where the whirling snow attacked them furiously. It was treacherous underfoot. Once she slipped, but Mark caught her arm.

By common impulse, they turned down Main Street. A streetcar rumbled by; a snowplow made an unwieldy turn. The dead Christmas bulbs strung in festoons across the street were blurred chips of color.

The snow was methodically blotting out the world. They might be alone, just the two of them, lost on an island, hidden by the curtain of falling snow.

Suddenly Mark stopped.

"Let me look at you, Faith," he said. There was a new note in his voice, which she found immeasurably exciting. He took off his glove and brushed the snow from her short curling hair. "Faith . . ."

She was crying. She didn't mean to cry, but it had been such a long time. Each day she had said to herself, It's a day nearer Mark's homecoming. But now that he was here, she couldn't believe it. She just couldn't.

A woman coming out of the Bon Ton collided with them. "Why don't you look where you're going?" she snapped.

"Sorry," Mark said.

They turned toward Manistee Drive.

"How beautiful the snow is," Faith marveled. The drab world had taken on a radiance, which was reflected in her own spirit.

The heavy grilled door of the Holmes house still wore its green-and-scarlet Christmas wreath.

"Let's go," Mark said.

Holding hands, they ran up the steps together. As if they were coming home.

5. She stayed for dinner. Even her mother's morose answer when she telephoned to explain why she would be late coming home couldn't dim her happiness. She sat at the long table in the ornate dining room, which was being used tonight in Mark's honor, and gazed down its polished gleaming length, at the silver candelabras and the Victorian epergnes filled with purple hothouse grapes. They were all in a festive mood. Eben Holmes wore a serene and contented smile; Mark was grinning boyishly, in spite of the new maturity in his gray eyes. Even Mrs. Hanrahan, passing the roast beef, was beaming. Again and again, her fatuous gaze returned to young Mark. How handsome he was! What a fine young man! All the girls in St. Croix would be setting their caps for him. But not one stood a ghost of a chance, she reflected, looking slyly at Faith Andrews who was not quite at ease in all this elegance. Mrs. Hanrahan had nothing against the girl, except that she came from such common people. Still, she was cheerful, good-natured, and so high-spirited she made other young ladies, even the beauties, pallid by comparison. And she did the old gentleman a world of good.

Eben Holmes raised his glass.

"To Mark's homecoming," he said.

Solemnly Faith joined him.

To Mark's homecoming, she thought. May he never leave again.

Mark was recalling an evening in Paris. "When you were a child," his mother had said, smiling brilliantly, "I always gave you a sip of my champagne. You called it tickly water. . . ."

He mustn't think of his mother. This was today, and he was home, with Faith, and it seemed to him she was a new Faith. She was no longer the plump, rather ungainly girl he'd left eighteen months ago; the kid he'd talked to and argued with, and even occasionally bossed around a bit. This was a ravishing young woman, and he was captivated by the change in her.

She was relating an incident that had happened at *The Observer* recently, and her face was vivid, her hands expressive. In her breathless excitement, the words ran together, and several times, she broke off abruptly.

He said, teasing her, "Finish your sentence, Faith."

Dinner over, they went back to the comfortable sitting room, where Mrs. Hanrahan placed a Tole tray of coffee and liqueurs on the table before the fireplace. Eben Holmes leaned back in his armchair and made a ceremony of lighting the one cigar allowed him each day.

"What is Paris like now?" he asked.

"I was there only a fortnight before sailing. But last summer, it certainly was the Mecca for tourists. The American Express was like Main Street on a Saturday night. The franc was fluctuating, and they were all milling around, waiting for a higher rate of exchange before they parted with their money."

"Did you get to the opera at all?"

"Yes, we heard *Tristan* and *Die Meistersinger* before mother got sick again. And some concerts with a sensational Russian conductor, Serge Koussevitzky."

"Gosh, I'm envious," Faith interrupted. "Do you suppose I'll ever get to see Paris?"

"Of course you will," Mark answered confidently.

Eben went to bed early. "Good night, children," he said. They watched him walk slowly from the room and they heard the muffled sound of his feet on the stairs. They were alone. Faith was conscious of a sense of tension and strain, and she thought nervously, This is ridiculous. We have so much to tell each other, yet we sit here like strangers.

"Mark . . ." She turned to him, her expression vulnerable, waiting.

With an abrupt and clumsy gesture, he took her into his arms. "Faith," he whispered roughly, "all the days I thought of you—and dreamed of being home with you. Darling . . ."

It was midnight when he took her home to Ontario Place. The sleeping streets were transformed by the blizzard into a strange and magical world. The stars were diamond chips in the charcoal sky. The air was brisk and cold.

They lingered at her door. "I hate to leave you," he said, "even for a little while."

"Oh, Mark, it's just too good. It scares me to think . . ."

"You mustn't be afraid, ever." He held her protectively. "It's up to us. We can make it last forever."

That was how he proposed to her. On the night of his return, when they knew almost immediately that only in each other would they find happiness.

She clung to him. "Darling!" Terror blurred her voice. "How can I tell mother?"

"I'll talk to her."

"Couldn't we be married first—and tell her later?"

He shook his head sternly. "We'd better face it right in the beginning. I want our life to start right."

6. St. Croix celebrated New Year's Eve in various ways. The well-to-do young married set drank their toasts at the modern chrome bar of the Country Club. The small businessmen and merchants gathered with their women folk in the Grille of the Lake Shore Hotel, where, fortified by gaudy paper hats, noisemakers and Scotch bootlegged from across the border, they lifted their glasses to Prosperity. The college crowd, home for the holidays, raised the roof at Tony Spade's speakeasy. Workmen from Wolverine Motors, Lane-Crandall, and Trout Celluloid started the evening at the Tavern, known in pre-prohibition days as Willie's Bar—and ended the night in the houses on Grant Avenue. Winona Kraus was having the old school gang over, and she invited Faith to bring Mark and a flask, both being the open sesame to any party.

However Faith and Mark spent the evening quietly with Eben Holmes. At midnight they wished each other a Happy New Year gravely, and then sat down to figure out the way to break the news of

their engagement painlessly to her mother. The very thought of Charlotte's reaction put a blight on their optimism. For how could they make
any plans until she agreed to their marriage?

"I'll be over in the morning," Mark promised. "About eleven."

"Do you think I should talk to her first?" she asked nervously.
"Sort of prepare the way?"

"Let me take care of it." He smiled reassuringly. "Don't worry,
Faith. It'll come out all right."

"You don't know my mother."

She was much too stimulated for sleep. She sat up in bed, striving
to anticipate her mother's behavior. She was so unfair! After all, she had
nothing against him—except that he was Mark Holmes. The old childish
rebellion flared up in Faith's heart. Other parents would be delighted
with Mark. Why must her mother always prove so difficult?

When she awakened from a heavy restless sleep, she was still
tense and had a queasy lump in the pit of her stomach. She tried to
convince herself the fears were exaggerated. Finally she got up, wrapped
herself in an old blue robe and went into the gloomy parlor, where she
found her father slouched in the Morris chair, scanning a copy of *The
Observer*. Impulsively, she blurted out the news to him.

Tod put down the paper, smiling. "That's good news, Faith. You
couldn't pick a finer boy."

"I hope mother agrees with you."

He rubbed the reddish stubble of his beard reflectively. "If she
kicks up a fuss, pumpkin, I'll talk to her. But don't you let anything
she says change your plans."

She had never heard his voice so resolved. Yet it gave her no
assurance, for she knew from bitter experience that, in the end, her
mother invariably won out. She bathed and put on her new brown
woolen frock. By the time Mark arrived, she was sitting with her
father, trying to gain strength from his presence.

Tod stood up. He was wearing the trousers of his good blue serge
suit, a clean shirt, and a brown coat sweater that made him look like an
old man. However his manner was neither old nor wavering.

"Mark," he said, shaking hands cordially, "before you speak to
Faith's mother, I want you to know you have my blessing."

"Thank you, sir." Mark was deeply moved. "Thank you very
much."

"Unfortunately," Tod continued dryly, "my wife is so emotional
she seldom listens to reason. She relies on her intuition, which makes
it tough for all of us. But we'll try . . ."

"Wait here, Mark," Faith said nervously. "I'll get mother."

She hurried into the dark kitchen, where Charlotte was scraping carrots and potatoes for the pot roast.

"Mother, will you come in the other room? We want to talk to you."

Charlotte dried her chapped hands on her percale apron.

"Faith, you have a guilty air," she said craftily. "What are you up to?"

"Mark is here. He'd like to see you."

Charlotte's gaunt face grew secretive. She hesitated; then, warily, she followed Faith. In the doorway she stopped, as if she had changed her mind.

"Please, mother," Faith begged, praying, Dear God, don't let her make a scene. . . .

Charlotte did not look at Mark.

"Mrs. Andrews," Mark said quietly, "Faith and I love each other. We want to be married. Will you give us your consent?"

Even before he spoke, Charlotte knew her long struggle to keep Faith from temptation was over. She had lost. This young man was stronger. There was no way in which she could break the spell he had woven about Faith. Evil has triumphed, she thought incoherently. It has triumphed over my child, because she has inherited my own weakness.

"I will never give my consent," she answered bitterly.

"Mrs. Andrews, please be fair. You have nothing against me."

"Faith isn't ready for marriage yet," she said evasively. "And you're not the right man for her. You have nothing in common. But men like you feel you can buy anything with your money."

Mark was horrified. The woman was out of her mind.

"Mrs. Andrews . . ." he began.

"I will never consent," she repeated in a mocking voice. "And my child will not disobey me."

Faith was pale and stricken, too shocked to defend him. But Tod spoke up for her.

"Lotte," he said severely, "Faith is not a child. She's old enough to know her own mind. She and Mark love each other, and you have absolutely no right to stand in their way!"

Charlotte put her trembling hands to her face. "A marriage built on deceit can never last," she whispered. "It brings only misery and despair."

In her frenzied mind, she saw the pattern repeating itself. The pattern from which all these years she had struggled to save Faith.

7. A week passed. Outwardly Faith was docile. The tension had given way to an armed truce.

The afternoon was gray and somber. As Charlotte dried her hands on the roller towel behind the kitchen door, she noted the sky was the color of pewter. The winter days were dreary and depressing. It looked like snow again, and Faith had gone to work this morning wearing her spring coat. Charlotte had barely spoken to her all week, but when she saw her dressed so lightly, she could not contain herself.

"You'll catch your death of cold."

"I'm wearing a sweater underneath," Faith answered, adding, "my old coat's awfully shabby!"

She had hesitated, as if she wanted to say something more. Charlotte thought, She realizes how much she has hurt me. She wants to make amends. Charlotte forgot her own bitter anger; she longed to take Faith in her arms, to protect her fiercely from the cruel and disillusioning world.

But Faith picked up her worn black bag and gloves and left the house.

The day dragged. The squirrel-gray sky grew more melancholy. Something in the still air made her restive and depressed. She hunched in her old rocker, thinking of her own marriage. What an innocent fool she had been to succumb to Tod. Oh, he'd done the right thing in the eyes of the law; he had married her, but grudgingly. And forever after she had read the contempt in his eyes. How could she explain to Faith that all men were basically selfish? That a woman must always be on guard, never entrusting herself completely to one of them?

Why must she suffer as I have, Charlotte mourned. I must save her from herself. I owe it to her.

She went to the window to draw the shades. In the drained light, the trees were stark and mournful. She had the fantastic notion that on those naked branches dead men hung, their stiff bodies swaying in macabre rhythm. It seemed to her she was kin with all the dying. She put her hands to her throbbing head. Something was wrong. She was drenched with sweat, shivering with a vague, unknown fear.

Footsteps on the back porch. Tod opened the door, stamping snow off his galoshes. The sight of him should dispel this odd mood, but still she felt strange and frightened.

He put down his lunch pail and the folded copy of *The Observer*.

"Looks like a storm is coming up," he said, rubbing his red hands. "What's for supper?"

"Pork chops."

In a daze, she started her chores. The table set, the bread sliced (how strange the knife felt in her cold hands, she was both fascinated and repelled by it), a jar of preserves opened, the chops frying in a heavy iron skillet. She had to enumerate the duties to herself, not just once but repeatedly, so she wouldn't miss up, and go off in space again, cowering and lost before a nameless monster. . . .

Words. Her numb lips must form the words; Tod mustn't grow suspicious. Her mouth shaped a name. Faith. The symbol of her guilt. Faith.

"Faith," she began laboriously. "She is late today."

"She isn't coming home tonight." Tod wasn't looking at her. With a clumsy gesture, he pulled a yellow slip of paper from the pocket of his faded workshirt, and handed it to her.

"Now don't go off the handle, Lotte. Faith isn't sick, or hurt, or anything. The kids just got tired of waiting. So they ran off and got married. . . ."

Abruptly he sprang up.

"Lotte, Lotte! What's got into you! My God," he whispered, frozen with horror. "Oh, my God!"

8. Great Falls.

The yellow taxi skidded on the car tracks, turned the corner of Michigan Avenue recklessly and then stubbed its nose on a huge snow bank.

"James Madison Hotel," the driver announced.

Mark helped Faith out of the cab and paid him. The air was raw and gusty; a few pedestrians scurrying past shuddered under the fierce blasts. Faith was shivering in her spring coat. She was grateful for the sudden warmth of the garish hotel lobby. She lingered behind, while Mark went to the desk.

"A double room and bath, please."

The clerk, a gaunt cheerless man with an egg-shaped head and a sparse yellow mustache, regarded him suspiciously. "Baggage?"

"I'm sorry. We haven't any."

The clerk looked off in space. "I don't believe we have any vacancies at the moment."

Overhearing the words, Faith flushed. But Mark was grinning, as if it were a joke. He pulled a paper from the pocket of his Burberry.

"Will this help? We were married by the local Justice of the Peace a half hour ago."

The man spied the name and address on the license.

"Are you related to Mr. Eben Holmes? Well, then, we will most assuredly find a room for you, sir. It's just that we have to be careful. I hope you understand. . . ."

They followed the jaunty bellhop to the elevators. A few loiterers, sprawling in the overstuffed velour chairs, noted their progress with lewd speculation.

After the boy closed the door on the ornate bridal suite, Mark said, "We'd better wire grandfather and your folks right away."

"I suppose so." Faith pulled off the black felt cloche and rubbed her forehead pensively. She thought the room was handsomely furnished: the ivory twin beds with their spreads and bolsters of changeable green taffeta; the triple-mirrored dressing table; the colored etchings on the gray walls. Even in her excited state, she couldn't help but be impressed.

"We can send dad's wire to the factory," she said. "And he'll tell mother."

Mark sat down beside her. "Try not to worry, Faith. She'll forgive us."

"I hope so."

"It may take a little time, but I'm sure she'll see it our way."

She was silent. The room was hot; steam spouted from the radiator valves. Mark struggled to raise a window, and a gust of cold fresh air rushed in. He looked at his watch. "It's after eleven. You must be starved."

"Oh, I am!" Her voice was much too loud; it sounded strident even in her own ears. "I want an enormous breakfast."

"Shall we have room service?"

"No, let's eat downstairs."

In the dining room, the hostess assured them there was still time to order breakfast, and showed them to a table. Faith sat erect and ill at ease. She opened her bag to hunt for a handkerchief, and knocked over a glass of water.

"Oh, I'm terribly sorry," she said, blushing. "I don't know what's the matter with me."

This time Mark was embarrassed for her.

The waitress brought them platters of ham and eggs and heavy home-fried potatoes. Faith looked at the food with sudden distaste.

"I'm afraid I'm not really hungry," she said miserably.

"I'm not either," Mark said. "I guess we'd better drive home and face the music."

"But this is our honeymoon!"

Her protest broke the strain. Suddenly they were laughing a little hysterically.

"So it is," he said, "and we'd better get you a decent wedding ring." For she was still wearing the cheap gilt band the Justice of the Peace had given them.

At the corner of River and Michigan, they found a jeweler. He brought out a tray of flashing jewels for their approval.

"The very latest in engagement rings," he said with a shrewd glance at Mark's expensive gray tweeds. "Diamonds in platinum setting."

Mark shook his head. "We're looking for something quite plain," he said.

The man shrugged. Faith was disturbed for fear he was thinking Mark was close-fisted. Actually, she couldn't help but consider his request rather odd, too. After all, he came from a wealthy family, he could afford a fine ring, why did he insist on something simple and inexpensive, almost as if he were ashamed of her?

Once they were out on the windy street again, sheltered in a doorway while he whistled for a cab, he said carefully, "Darling, I hope I didn't sound like a prig."

"Of course not," she said, but without conviction.

"I dislike the conventional seals for marriage," he explained. "A diamond for your engagement, platinum for your wedding, bracelets or a fur coat for anniversaries. Heck, I'd like to give you gifts spontaneously, not when convention tells me I have to. I hate getting into a rut, like others. I can't make it any clearer, Faith—but I don't want us to stumble into conventional pitfalls either. We're not like other people. . . ."

We're not like other people. That was Mark's banner, and she was to see it many times during their marriage.

She tried very hard to comprehend. If he felt it was right, well, then it must be. They had never before disagreed, and she didn't want them to begin now. She'd make the best of it.

They were glad to return to their warm room now. "I'd love some coffee," Faith said.

"We both need a drink," Mark answered. "I'll see if I can rustle up some rum toddies. The bellhops are usually obliging."

When the drinks arrived and, shortly afterwards, a tray of club sandwiches and coffee, Mark waited on her.

"Here's to you, Faith."

She smiled tremulously. "To us, darling."

The winter afternoon faded outside the taffeta-draped windows, leaving a pale afterglow. Faith kicked off her slippers and curled up in the easy chair. Mark sat on the arm, looking down at her with great tenderness, enthralled in the wonder of their being together.

"Faith," he said softly, "are you falling asleep?"

She opened her eyes. "Must be the coffee."

"Must be the rum toddy," he grinned. "I believe my wife is tipsy."

"I'd like to nap," she said hazily, making an effort to unfasten the buttons on her white blouse.

"Let me help you."

"Thanks, I can manage."

She stepped out of her black woolen skirt, pushed away the green taffeta spread and slipped quickly under the covers.

He knelt beside her. "Faith. Faith Holmes. How does it sound, darling?"

Her face was illuminated with happiness. "Next to Mrs. Mark Holmes, it's the nicest name in the world."

9. They were driving back to St. Croix the following afternoon in Mark's old roadster. She said blissfully, "Gosh, it's wonderful being married. Do you suppose other people are as complete as we?"

"Nope. They haven't enough to give each other."

Mature words for a couple of kids. Yet, here beside him, she vowed that she'd always measure up to his ideal, that she'd be a wife of whom he could be truly proud. . . .

"Happy, darling?" she asked.

"Happy isn't the word for it."

"That's an evasive answer, Mark Holmes!"

"I think," he said gravely, "we're fools for luck."

"I know. It scares me to think about it."

They drove past the State Hospital, two miles this side of St. Croix. Finally the first factories loomed in sight, the smokestacks of Trout Celluloid bold and ugly against the pale sky.

"Isn't it a beautiful day!" she marveled. "The sun and the birds . . ."

"It's January sixth, ma'am—and cold as hell."

"I beg your pardon, Mr. Holmes. It's April—and there's spring in my heart."

Her gaiety did not last long, for a moment later, she said, "Mark, you'll be patient with mother?"

"I hope she's as patient with us."

Now she grew aware of a dozen obstacles. Really, she should have spoken to her mother first, sort of paved the way. . . .

Mark swung the car down Ontario Place and brought it to a stop at the curb. She was sickened with a sense of foreboding. What words were powerful enough to bridge the gap between her mother's intolerance and her great love for Mark? She must forgive me, she must!

She stepped up to the door.

Tod alone greeted her.

10. They were standing before the heavy oak entrance to the drab brick building. Faith stared numbly at the narrow barred windows. Only an hour ago, she and Mark had driven past here on their return to St. Croix. The bughouse, the kids called it. The State Hospital.

"I can't understand," she said dully. "Mother seemed perfectly well when I left the house yesterday morning. No different than usual."

Words, words, she was hiding behind them, and they made a sorry screen. Everything seemed normal when I left the house. Which implied mother had cracked up when she got the news of their elopement. Mother had tried to kill herself. Hide behind more words, Faith. Here's a brutal truth you can't face.

Mark was silent. He had never felt more helpless in his life. How could he comfort her, what could he say? To remind her of their own future would be utterly heartless.

A nurse opened the door.

"Come in," she said. They entered the brightly lighted office, permeated with a faint antiseptic smell that sickened Faith. Mark gripped her arm, seeking to give her courage. What do you say now, she wondered. Whom do you ask for?

Mark spoke. "Mrs. Andrews—she was brought here yesterday. Would it be possible for us to see her—for just a moment?"

The nurse's lined face revealed sudden comprehension. "If you'll wait a moment . . ."

Shortly, a heavy-set white-coated man appeared. "I am Dr. Cummings," he said.

"About my mother . . ." Faith began uncertainly.

"Yes," Dr. Cummings said. "Oh, *yes*." He regarded Faith intently. "Under the circumstances, Miss—er—Andrews, I feel it would be wiser to wait until later. Perhaps when she herself asks for you. A more auspicious time, yes. Until then . . ."

He shrugged.

Faith closed her eyes. Slowly Mark led her to the door.

11. "They're here!" Mrs. Hanrahan called out. "Mr. Holmes, they've come!"

Eben Holmes put down *The Observer*. A deep frown etched itself on his bony forehead. He was debating his action. Although the boy was very dear to him, he never demurred at reprimanding him when the occasion warranted it. This was a side of Eben's character which few people knew today: the man who in the early days of the lumber camps had kept a mob of rowdies in check. Mark would receive the full brunt of his anger. Not because he'd married the girl, though they were much too young for marriage, but for running away. Elopements were cowardly procedures. And since this was the first time he'd found Mark remiss, he was doubly vexed.

They were coming into the hall now. He listened intently for the sound of their youthful voices. But there was silence. A moment later, the measured tread of their footsteps echoed solemnly on the parquetry floor. The door of the sitting room opened. He looked up sternly.

He saw Faith first.

Mark began, "Faith's mother . . ." and broke off.

Eben Holmes did not hesitate. He stood up and held out his arms. "Welcome home, children," he said.

Chapter Six

1. St. Croix read the news of the elopement on page one of *The Observer*, which carried a photograph of Faith, the one used in the high-school yearbook, revealing her young, life-eager face. Staring at the headline, Vrest Macklin realized how loath he was to lose her. She had vitality, energy and something more—a talent for getting along with people, which made her invaluable to an employer. She had an over-developed sense of fair play which, in a less attractive girl, might be called the trait of a busybody. The staff liked her. She always had the time and patience to listen to another's troubles. Rather a pity she married. Still, Mark Holmes was a first-rate lad. He'd take care of her, too. Eben had told Vrest Macklin he was putting the boy to work in his lumber office, and the young couple would live with him.

From rags to riches, Vrest Macklin thought ironically. If any girl can take such a dazzling ascent, Faith's the one!

He picked up an item from his desk, and reread it. Charlotte Andrews, wife of Tod Andrews, had been committed to the State Hospital.

In town, the marriage evoked curiosity, speculation and plenty of gossip. Mothers with marriageable daughters wondered how she'd done it. Winona Kraus boasted of their friendship, and pictured herself a privileged guest at the Holmeses'. Leah Parker, who was working in the Fashion Shop, assured her best customers, among them Mrs. Lewis Trout, that Faith was practically her oldest and dearest friend.

"How interesting." Madeline Trout opened her jeweled case and took out a cigarette. "I saw her once at the Club—she was reporting the affair for that horrible newspaper. A big ungainly girl. Not the type I'd think a Holmes would go for. Still, you never can tell."

Leah's pert nose climbed an inch higher. Really, it wasn't fair, a girl of her own family background having to work in a dress shop, catering to vulgar women like Mrs. Trout, while Faith struck it rich.

"I suppose she'll be shopping here now," Madeline Trout probed.

"Of course! But she has no style sense. She didn't pay much attention to clothes in the old days."

"Didn't have the dough," Mrs. Trout said shrewdly. "I wonder if
they'll join the Country Club. Old Eben Holmes has never been near
the place."

"I wouldn't know. Madeline, what about this sapphire gown? It's
a wonderful buy!"

Mrs. Trout snuffed out her cigarette. "The new Mrs. Holmes has
an old-fashioned figure. Breasts and a fanny."

Leah said desperately, "We won't bill you until next month. What
do you say, Madeline?"

"Sorry, darling. I'm not interested." Mrs. Trout, like her husband,
was an opportunist. "Some day, you must introduce me to your friend,
my pet. I'm curious to meet her. Make it real soon, won't you?"

2. "Faith Andrews—I mean, Faith Holmes!" Winona Kraus was
phoning her old dear friend. "Gee, I should be mad as hops! I mean,
we've been friends since we were kids—and I have to get the news from
the papers! Honestly!"

"It was rather sudden," Faith replied, embarrassed.

"Well, I want to congratulate you! Listen, I'm going to throw a
party for you—a real shindig! All your friends from school and the paper,
and your husband . . ."

"We're sort of tied up now, Winnie. Maybe later on . . ."

Winona was furious. "Who does she think she is?" Winona ranted
to Leah Parker, "high-hatting her old friends? She should hear what
people are saying about her!"

A new and delicious suspicion struck Winona. "I bet they *had*
to get married," she added.

Faith received a note from Steve Pringle. "*The Observer* won't be
the same without you, Valkyrie. Nor will Stevie. But I've always admired the girl who looks out for the main chance."

Mark cabled his father, who came through with a perfunctory
greeting and eventually a handsome gift. When Faith unpacked the
box, she found an old chocolate pot bearing a huge gilt N, which was
repeated on each of the dozen tiny cups. Privately she considered her
father-in-law rather stupid to send second-hand things. Even the initial
was wrong. When Mark informed her it was a rare set with a Napole-
onic crest, she had the grace to laugh at herself.

Mark heard, too, from his friend, Phillip Latham. "I can't understand how any guy can tie himself down to one girl in a world of beauties," Phillip scrawled. "If she's as good as you say, watch your step."

"He's crazy," Mark said fondly. "But a good guy."

Surely Faith had every reason to be happy. Mark was deeply in love with her; Eben was pleased with the marriage; she was obviously the luckiest girl on earth.

But there were too many nights when she would awaken from a troubled sleep and lying still, in order not to disturb Mark, her hand would creep to her throat, to touch the tiny gold locket she wore all the time now. And in a flash, the radiant happiness was darkened. She thought of her mother crouching in the darkness behind those impersonal and impenetrable brick walls. Would she ever come out in the sunlight again?

"I'll let you know when your mother is ready to see you," Dr. Cummings said.

That was weeks ago. She was still waiting. And in the troubled night, she had a premonition she would be waiting a long long time.

Was I to blame, she asked herself again. Should I have given up Mark to pacify her? But I love Mark. He comes first. I couldn't live without him.

Outwardly she managed to appear at ease and content. But inwardly the conflicts were already stirring like poisons about to distill their lethal brew. Her father knew she was deeply disturbed and sought to comfort her. He never disclosed Charlotte's last sane words—or her agonizing conviction that this marriage of Faith's was a necessity, a tragic repetition of her own mishap.

He closed the old house on Ontario Place, sold the shabby furniture, and moved back to Mrs. Hussar's. Wipe out the past, he begged Faith silently. You have a new life. . . .

"Dad looks much better these days," Faith said to Mark. "And somehow I feel closer to him than ever before in my life."

She invited Tod often to dinner at the Holmes house, but though old Eben and Mark liked him immensely, he was not at ease.

"Pumpkin," he said, "the Holmeses are fine people. I like them. Still, it'd be better if you and Mark came to Mrs. Hussar's."

In the spring, Mrs. Hussar's rheumatism improved, and she prepared her excellent dinners for them. Golden chicken in paprika, dumplings light as foam, flaky apple strudel. Tod usually brought home a bottle of red wine from the Italian speakeasy on Grant Avenue, and they had a fine evening.

3. When she wasn't thinking of her mother, Faith was ecstatically happy. She loved the gray stone house. Eben had built it in 1897, after the elaborate new mansions along the lake shore in Chicago and Riverside Drive in New York. Walls two feet thick; narrow Tudor windows almost blinded by dense English ivy; a slate roof and crenelated turrets; a solarium and an elegant porte-cochere.

The rest of the town had groped its way to adolescence in the late nineties, and its architecture reflected that ugly period. The streets were lined with small neat bungalows sprouting overhanging roofs like mushroom caps; and sprawling, shingled Victorian houses that were decked out in bays, turrets, gingerbread trim like a newly rich woman wearing all her jewels at once. By contrast, the Holmes house was a landmark, and in time St. Croix grow proud of it.

While his wife was alive, the house echoed with gaiety; dinners and balls, guests arriving from Cleveland, Chicago and the East. It took a staff of six to run it in those days.

After her death, Eben closed off the wings, dismissed most of the servants, keeping only the housekeeper, Mrs. Hanrahan, and Jacob, the gardener; and the core of the house was centralized in the great hall, the sitting room, the bedrooms and the kitchen. Eben retired to the simple and unpretentious way he preferred, and a melancholy curtain descended on the place. Jacob still tended the cutting gardens and the rose-beds, but it was a half-hearted and perfunctory gesture to ward off disintegration, a token evidence of ultimate decay.

As children, Mark and Faith had been tremendously curious about the closed wings, and longed to explore them. But Mrs. Hanrahan always managed to frustrate their attempts. Now, on a lazy Sunday morning, they rummaged through the rooms, all ornately furnished, but airless and oppressive. All life was suspended here, and they were glad to hurry back to the inhabited quarters.

Faith was especially fond of the library, where the book-lined shelves stretched from the lofty ceiling to the polished floor; mezzotints of the Atheneum, the Parthenon, and the Colosseum hung on the green walls; the marble busts of Plato, Heine and Byron stood on pedestals. And young Faith and Mark, sitting at grandfather's feet, listening to his counsel.

How could her mother have denied her the chance at such happiness? How could she have been so darkly suspicious of Mark, who was everything a man should be? Why did she warn Faith their marriage would never succeed? Faith tried to analyze her bitter words. She realized that in her new role as Mark's wife, she must assume responsibilities that would test her character. But she was not afraid; armed with Mark's love, she would never be afraid.

Each morning, weekdays, Mark left for the office of the Holmes Lumber Company, and usually Faith walked part of the way with him, up Manistee Drive, cutting through the park to Sycamore; stopping at Town Square, and saying reluctantly, "Well, I suppose I should turn back."

Mark kissed her.

"I'll walk another block—just one more . . ."

And finally, at the entrance to the Lumberman's Bank, "Mark, I hate to go home. I wish I worked with you."

"You'd be more fun than old Miss Peabody."

"Will you be home for lunch?"

"Sure thing."

"Then I'll meet you in the park."

Laughter, and a final quick kiss. "Oh, Mark, darling." How very much she loved him!

She was left to her own resources the rest of the day, and she spent much of the time with Eben, who despite his failing health had no intention of becoming a recluse. She helped him with his heavy correspondence. She read aloud those books in which he was interested, on economics, sociology, current affairs—and what she did not understand he explained to her. He maintained a lively interest in the state of the world, and he punctuated his viewpoint with a wit and wisdom that Faith found reflected, in a less profound way, in Mark's own thinking.

He was particularly outraged by the way in which the late President Harding had brought disgrace on himself and discredit to his electorate.

"We're all responsible for Harding and his Ohio henchmen," he said tartly. "The millions of staunch Republicans who hew to the party line."

He added that he was not as deeply shaken by the actual scandal of the Teapot Dome affair as the fact that the people themselves were prone to dismiss it lightly—a mere tempest in a teapot, he added with a twinkle. "We're too busy jumping on the bandwagon of Coolidge Prosperity. If it keeps up, poverty will become un-American."

They had tea in the afternoon and listened to organ recordings on the new victrola. Here Faith heard Bach's "Jesu, Joy of Man's Desiring" for the first time. She was sitting on the worn crimson velvet hassock by the fire, looking out at the dead garden. The weary dejected curve of her body warned the old man that she was still brooding. He thought, I should have spoken before. There are times when tact is more cruel than a blunt honest word.

"Nature doesn't intend for a young person to take the long view," he said, "but, Faith, I promise you that in time the pain of being separated from your mother will ease. Once you have your own children you'll see the situation objectively. And when you've acquired the long view, you'll find every painful experience will outgrow its immediate anguish."

She listened politely, but she did not believe him. The memory of her mother's breakdown, the knowledge of its cause, would haunt her for the rest of her days. "Once you have your own children . . ." Eben said. That, she realized intuitively, was her hope of salvation. She wanted a big family. And I'll give them a healthy, normal upbringing, she thought. Not a childhood like my own.

But there was still no indication of the hoped-for pregnancy, and meanwhile she fashioned her days to conform to the pleasant, gracious Holmes pattern. Under Eben's patient tutelage, she blossomed, and from him she learned an intelligent approach to life.

Often, on bright afternoons, they took a drive along the lake front. And shortly before Easter, Eben took her on a shopping expedition to the Waycross Shop in Great Falls, where he helped her choose a spring wardrobe, consisting of a gray flannel tailored suit and a brown suede topcoat, several light wool frocks, and a severe and beautifully cut blue silk evening dress.

"I've never had such lovely things before," she said, frankly awed. "You're too good to me, grandfather."

"You deserve it, my dear."

Mark usually came home at five-thirty, which was the high-light of her day. They had so much to tell each other—as if they had been separated for weeks instead of a few hours.

Unfortunately, Mark wasn't happy in his job, but being Mark, he worked hard at learning the lumber business. Faith had visited the offices of the Holmes Lumber Company on the second floor of the Lumberman's Bank Building, and she could readily believe his statement that they hadn't changed perceptibly since Eben started the firm forty years ago. Mr. Pauley, the general manager, was definitely of the old school.

"He's still living in 1890!" Mark fumed. "Show him a stand of pine and he thinks he's got a new forest."

"Well, he's an old man," Faith said tolerantly. "I'll bet he's sixty if he's a day."

"Trouble is he's got no vision. God knows I'm inexperienced. But it's plain horse sense. Great Falls is ordering more lumber for its furniture factories than we can turn out—so Pauley's going to build another sawmill!"

"What's wrong with that?"

"We don't need another sawmill. We've got to replenish timber first—so we can keep feeding this one! Second-growth pine is okay for pulp, but we're growing short of hardwoods. Pauley's blind!"

He was obviously still chafing under Pauley's condescending attitude toward him.

"You're young," Pauley had said. "And every kid thinks his new-fangled notions are gonna set the world on fire. When he grows up, he finds the old ones best, after all. Mark, you're looking *too* far ahead!"

"Isn't that better than being too far behind the times?"

"Nope." Mr. Pauley bit off the end of his cigar. "It's always safer to be a step behind. The pioneer is a sucker."

And that was the end of their talk.

Now, Faith said sympathetically, "It must be awfully hard working for such a stuffy old man. Couldn't you be transferred?"

He grinned crookedly. "Not unless I become a logger."

"But darling, if you aren't happy . . ."

"Happy! If I hang around that office long enough, I'll go nuts! All Pauley sees is a toothpick in every twig and a chair in every trunk."

"Perhaps you don't belong in the lumber business."

"Perhaps you're right."

"Why don't you speak to grandfather . . ."

He shook his head. "I can't hurt him. I may as well carry on."

4. The first time Vrest Macklin came to dinner, Faith was distressed.

"Have you forgiven me for walking out so suddenly?" she asked nervously.

"I have. But I'm afraid Steve Pringle never will."

"Oh, that crazy Steve."

After that, she looked forward to his visits, plied him with avid questions. She admitted how much she missed her work, the friendship of the staff, even the noisy rumble of the old linotype.

"Possibly I'm not cut out for a life of leisure," she said.

"Marriage," Macklin answered tartly, "isn't exactly a prolonged vacation." She should have children, he reflected—a batch of kids—to keep her occupied. She's the kind of girl who needs to run other peoples' lives, in order to make her feel happy and needed.

In the course of the evening, he and Eben usually had a heated and enlightening discussion. Although Eben had been suffering from a severe attack of bronchitis since March, he never allowed his friend to skip a visit. He always said that the most rewarding change in Vrest Macklin was that he'd developed from an erratic Socialist into a true liberal.

Now Eben commended him on the caustic editorial he'd just written on Coolidge, at last President in his own right.

"I've antagonized every Republican subscriber to *The Observer*," Vrest said contentedly.

Eben smiled. "I've known many men who've hidden their appalling ineptitude behind a veil of silence. It always works."

Faith and Mark were absorbed in themselves. Yet some of the talk seeped in and germinated slowly in the recesses of their minds.

5. Spring lingered far beyond time that year, and when summer arrived, it was accompanied by a broiling sun and a breathless humidity. St. Croix, accustomed to bitter winters and scorching summers, settled down for an endurance test.

Faith was packing. Mark's steamer trunks stood agape waiting to be fed the sweatshirts, dungarees, sweaters, mackinaws and heavy boots they would both use during their four weeks' stay at Eben's camp on the northern peninsula.

"We'll be alone up there," Mark said. "Just the two of us. Two against the world. I like the sound of that phrase, Faith. Perhaps we should make it our family crest."

In these heady days, she was inclined to take every word of Mark's for gospel. Two against the world it was!

They left St. Croix after breakfast and reached the lodge at ten o'clock that evening. As Mark drove cautiously along the wagon trail, the headlights of the car blazed a path for them, leaping over the ruts like nervous jackrabbits. A dry branch reached out for the car and snapped back with a groan. A small animal scurried across the road and melted in the underbrush.

"Too bad you can't get your first impression of the place by daylight," Mark said, parking the car. "There're a couple of hundred steps to climb. Think you can make it?"

"I need a stretch first. Mark, this air is wonderful!" She caught his arm. "But it's so dark."

"You'll get used to it."

He kept the headlights on and started unloading the bags. "Follow me, honey. And watch your step. There isn't a doctor within miles."

She was breathless by the time they reached the dark house. Mark opened the door. "I'll light a kerosene lamp. We'll be all set in a minute now."

The flickering yellow light revealed a long rustic room, roughly timbered, the upper balcony at the far end almost hidden by colorful Navajo rugs, the stone fireplace a focal point for comfortable sofas and wicker chairs. Mark stooped to light the fire.

"You like it?" he asked boyishly.

"I love it," she answered. Home is where Mark is. She'd never forget that.

She fell asleep almost immediately, and in the morning, she was awakened by his lusty voice. "Get up, lazybones! I have coffee on the stove. How about a dip before breakfast?"

"A dip!" she shuddered. "Is that the best you can offer?"

He pulled the covers away ruthlessly.

"Mark, don't you dare! Stop it—or I'll yell!"

"Not a soul around," he retorted smugly.

After she conceded defeat, he wrapped her in a flannel robe and led her out on the porch.

"Here's a world, Faith. On a silver platter—and for us alone."

The rambling lodge was situated on a bluff, almost hidden by sentinel fir, pine and spruce which shut out the sun and kept it in perpetual obscurity. Below them, the lake stretched to the distant blue horizon, a faint breeze ruffling its glistening surface.

"It's beautiful," she whispered. "But it makes you feel so small and unimportant."

"I know," he said, holding her close. "But it's nice, being small and unimportant together."

The swim over, they took brisk rubdowns; then, dressed in jeans and warm sweaters, they went down to make breakfast in the kitchen lean-to.

"You fix the grapefruit," Faith ordered. "I'll make the eggs. How do you like 'em?"

"Scrambled."

"Squiggly?"

Mark looked pained. "No. Scrambled. Just like Mrs. Hanrahan makes."

"Okay, darling. I know just what you want." She rolled up her sleeves, tied on an apron, and went to work efficiently. When she brought in the result, Mark stared quizzically.

"I thought I was getting scrambled eggs."

"Darling, I'm sorry!" She was conscience-stricken. "I just wasn't thinking. I'll eat this omelette. Let me try again."

"Never mind." He was laughing at her. "But what must I ask for in order to get what I want?"

"You speak in parables," she said, kissing the top of his head.

In the afternoon, they took a walk in the woods, and in the evening, they read, toasting themselves by the fire. Mark had brought with him *Babbitt,* and *The Man Nobody Knows*, while Faith concentrated on *The Plastic Age* and *The Green Hat*. "Michael Arlen's terrific," she said. Sometimes they worked crossword puzzles and listened to records on the portable victrola—Gershwin's "Rhapsody in Blue," or music from *The Student Prince,* or Paganini's Concerto in D Major, which Faith adored.

Perfect days.

They swam and sunned themselves and went fishing. They took the motorboat down the lake to the general store, where they picked up mail. They lay on the couch before the fire, listening to the music, drinking too much coffee, talking. They never got tired of talking.

Looking at his dear familiar face, at once calm and assured, Faith said impulsively, "Darling, if ever you showed the slightest enthusiasm for another girl, I couldn't bear it. I just couldn't."

Mark propped himself up on his elbow. "What a possessive female!"

"No fooling, darling. I couldn't take it."

"You're too intense, Faith."

"Maybe. But wouldn't you be jealous if I—well, if I were interested in another man?"

"Jealousy would imply insecurity," he said flatly, "and I have complete faith in the strength of our love."

She was beginning to enjoy this.

"But suppose there was evidence. Wouldn't you make some effort?"

His eyes darkened and he looked chill and remote, almost a stranger.

"Not the slightest. You can't keep anyone against his will. Too much like *Of Human Bondage.*"

She grew uneasy. Impulsively, she leaned down and put her cheek against his.

"We'll never allow it to happen to us," she said softly. "We *are* two against the world. . . ."

They savored each moment, knowing that soon they must return to earth, leaving their private paradise far behind. For Faith, this vacation was a reaffirmation of her sacrifice and love for Mark. And it was, incidentally, to serve a secret purpose of her own. Recently, she had gone for a checkup to Dr. Savage, the Holmeses' physician.

"There's no physical reason why you shouldn't become pregnant," he said. "But you're too tense, possibly too anxious. Faith, why don't you and Mark go off for a little trip by yourselves? Forget St. Croix." Meaning, she knew, forget your sense of guilt about your mother.

At the lodge, she was happy and relaxed, and thought of her mother seldom. Dr. Savage's advice was sensible. She had a serene feeling of confidence that she would conceive the child she wanted so eagerly.

Then, at the end of their third week, a guide brought them a telegram received at the general store. Mrs. Hanrahan wired that Eben Holmes was seriously ill.

They reached home the following night, and both of them went directly to the sickroom. Faith knelt and kissed the old man's cheek.

"Fine way to bring us home," she scolded lightly. "Couldn't you just write you were lonely for us?"

"I had nothing to do with it. Mrs. Hanrahan is a hysterical old woman who delights in doing her disagreeable duty!" He smiled contentedly. "But it's good to have you back."

6. They were home a fortnight when Faith heard from Leah Parker.

"We have some beautiful fall clothes in," Leah telephoned. "I'd love you to see them before they're picked over."

Faith wasn't really interested, but she wanted to be kind. After all, it was sweet of Leah to remember her. It really was.

"I'll try to get in during the week," she said.

"Why don't you make it Thursday? We'll have a bit of lunch together."

"Good."

When Faith entered the Lake Shore Grille at one-thirty, she saw that Leah was not alone. Mrs. Lewis Trout was with her, very smart in black crêpe, with a black cloche hiding her hennaed hair, and high-heeled pumps decked with steel-cut buckles setting off her thin handsome ankles.

"This is Madeline Trout." Leah found it necessary to explain elaborately. "We ran into each other. I felt you two should know each other, so I asked her to join us."

Mrs. Trout smiled intimately at Faith. "I do wish Leah would let us go to Tony Spade's, but she is so priggish!"

"I wouldn't be seen in a speakeasy," Leah retorted. "Besides, I'm a working girl. I have just an hour for lunch."

It was a pleasant luncheon, and Faith almost persuaded herself to forget the snub Mrs. Trout had once given her. Afterwards, they sauntered over to the Fashion Shop where Leah showed them the new numbers.

"I'd love to see that navy print on you," Mrs. Trout said to Faith. "Do try it on."

Faith hadn't intended buying a thing, but she allowed herself to be led into the dressing room. The navy print really was stunning, and so was the beige banded with red and black ribbon.

"You certainly can wear them," Mrs. Trout exclaimed. "Better take them both."

"I really shouldn't . . ."

"I'll open a charge for you," Leah interrupted smoothly. "Don't you need some lounging pajamas?"

"I don't think so. And I'd better be going now."

"Can I drop you?" Mrs. Trout asked. "I have the car."

"I think I'll walk home. Thanks, anyway."

"I do hope we'll see you again, Mrs. Holmes. Why don't you and your husband dine with us Saturday?"

"I'll let you know."

She related the incident to Mark that evening, while he was shaving for dinner.

"Grandfather doesn't think much of the Trouts," he said.

"Well, actually she seemed rather nice," she said defensively. "I wouldn't mind going there."

"I would. Better tell her we can't make it."

She hadn't been serious about it until he raised objections; now, suddenly she wanted very much to go, and she found herself resenting his refusal. However, she made an effort to control her irritation.

"By the way, darling, I bought a couple of dresses today. They're rather expensive, but awfully pretty. Wait until you see them."

"How much?" he asked.

"One was fifty and the other seventy-five."

"You shouldn't have done it, Faith." His manner was stern. "You know what I earn a week. How am I going to pay for them?"

She stared at him, astonished. "I don't think grandfather will object to taking care of the bill. I mean, he's bought me things. . . ."

"Gifts are something else!" Mark retorted, and she had never seen him so angry. "You can't keep on sponging! When you buy clothes, I've got to pay for them. You're my responsibility! And that means you must keep within a certain limit! I'm sorry, but that's the way it's got to be!"

She was subdued and hurt. "Shall I send them back?"

Mark picked up his robe. "No. Keep them. I'll find some way to meet the bill."

"I don't understand," she said, bewildered.

"You should. You've known me long enough."

She found his reaction very confusing. It reminded her of his explanation of why she didn't need an engagement ring. She had known him almost all her life. Yet there were facets to his character which she was only now discovering, and which puzzled and antagonized her.

Chapter Seven

1. Phillip Latham arrived for an unexpected visit two days before Thanksgiving. Faith heard the crunch of tires on the blue stone driveway and looked out of her bedroom window. She saw a young man step out of the old station taxi, and her first impression was of a bare sun-bleached head, bold white teeth, a big, expensive camel's-hair coat and foppish brown suede shoes, surrounded by a half-dozen pigskin bags camouflaged by gaudy, multi-colored hotel labels.

She reached the balustrade in time to hear him announce to Mrs. Hanrahan, "I'm Phil Latham—an old pal of Mark Holmes's." Then, as he caught sight of Faith, he whistled. "You're the bride, of course. Mark once described you—but I realize now how limited his vocabulary was."

Mark had told her he was crazy.

"Why didn't you let us know you were coming?" she asked. "We'd have met you at the station."

"I decided at the last minute. Just an impulse. Say, where is the boy?"

"He'll be home for lunch."

"You mean he's working?" Young Latham looked pained. "What makes Mark do these things? Look, we'd better get acquainted. How about a drink for the prodigal?"

By the time Mark arrived, Faith decided Phillip was all he had said—a sort of fourteen-carat Huckleberry Finn. He had had four Scotches which had made no perceptible impression on him.

"Paris wasn't the same with you gone, fella," he said, pumping Mark's hand. "I sure missed you."

"What about the models from Patou?"

"Even they changed."

"Phil, you're giving my wife a wrong impression."

"I know." Phillip turned mournfully to Faith. "Have no fear, my dear Faith. Mark always walked the straight and narrow path. He's a throwback to his Puritan forebears. My ancestors had no inhibitions, fortunately."

"Why don't you grow up?" Mark jeered, explaining to Faith, "Phil's idea of a high time is to take a Folies Bergères girl out in his roadster on a rainy night—jam on his brakes because she likes to spin round and round—and wind up in the hospital with the mark of Cain of his forehead."

"That's true. I have no sense," Phil agreed placidly, "absolutely none."

Mark replenished his drink. "How long can you stay?"

"Well, I'm due home for Thanksgiving. There's to be a meeting of the family lawyers. Now that I've reached my majority, mama can't hold the purse strings any more. I'll be in clover now—more dough than I can spend."

"If I know you," Mark said with dry optimism, "it won't be for long."

Phillip didn't need to be coaxed to make himself at home; he ignored his appointment in Minneapolis and his mother's deluge of telegrams, and stayed on. "I like it here," he said disarmingly. "I like you both, my friends."

Coming down to breakfast the first morning, he squinted at the table. "Something's missing," he announced sorrowfully.

"What is it?" Faith asked.

"Don't bite," Mark warned her, "He's up to some shenanigans."

Phillip ran his fingers over the scar on his forehead. "What is this? No *Pep-Korn*, no *Wheat-Lax!* How can you be so callous, my friends? No *Pep-Korn*, no sales. No sales, no dividends. No dividends—and what will poor Phillip do?"

"Sit down, you clown," Mark ordered, "and eat a man's breakfast instead of that shredded pap."

The following morning, Phillip found his place at the table decorated with a half-dozen boxed Latham Mills products, and a note in Mark's writing: "To keep Phil out of the Poorhouse and in Blondes."

Eben Holmes tolerated Phillip, who, in turn, accorded the old man a charming and unusual deference. But Mrs. Hanrahan was captivated, and soon became a champion of all Latham products, including Phillip. She was not the first woman who felt he needed to be saved from himself.

Phillip considered sleep a sorry waste of time and avoided it as strenuously as possible. Yet his energy was boundless; his need for

gaiety and escape seemed to recharge his spirits whenever they lagged
momentarily. He had brought an ample supply of Scotch with him, and
was also fortified by the liquor in the Holmes cellar, yet on the second
day of his visit, he had already discovered Tony Spade's speakeasy. He
was as unstable as quicksilver, and Faith had a vivid picture of him,
glass in hand, rushing nowhere in a hurry. His day was marked off by a
series of Scotches or martinis, yet she had never once seen him really
drunk.

"Have you ever stayed completely sober?" she asked curiously.

"Being on the wagon violates all rules of etiquette," he said shud-
dering, "like being caught nekkid in public."

Phillip couldn't understand why Mark buried himself in the
gloomy ancient office.

"Do you like it, Mark?"

"God, no!"

"Then for Pete's sake, why do it?"

Mark shrugged. "To please my grandfather."

"You're too damn noble."

"Wrong slant, Phil. I'd like to learn the business. There's nothing
else I'm keen on."

"You were pretty damn keen on the motor engines that day your
dad took us out to the Citroen factory."

"Yeh." Mark was noncommittal.

2. Faith and Phillip were idling before the fire in the sitting room.
Tea over, Mrs. Hanrahan had removed the cart, and they were alone.

"Faith, you know you're really two people," he said idly. "Yourself—
and the girl Mark wants you to be."

She lifted her eyebrows.

"I'm not kidding. Mark has set up the image of his dream girl—and
you're making yourself over to fit the mold. Or maybe he's making you
over. I can't quite decide."

"You're implying Mark is arbitrary," she said defensively.

"Isn't he?"

She wouldn't discuss Mark even with his friend; she refused to
place their relationship under a spotlight.

"Let's not talk about Mark and me," she said restlessly. "It's your
turn. . . ."

He put his arm carelessly at the back of the Chippendale sofa.
"Now, you're about to tell me I can make some nice girl very happy."

"What's wrong with that?"

He lit a cigarette with a quick, impatient gesture.

"Same thing that's wrong with marriage. *You* tell me how two people can stand up at an altar and promise to be faithful forever? How the heck can they see what's around the corner?" A spark of genuine interest illuminated his boyish features. "Okay, a guy falls for a cute little blond number. He swears to love her all his life. At that moment, he means it! But can he help it if after a couple of years, he sees the dark roots in her hair and the spreading fanny. . . ."

"Phillip, you're horrid."

"Nuts. I'm just honest. If nature means you to be faithful, why the hell does she put temptation in your path?" He got up indolently. "That calls for a drink. Where's the Scotch, baby?"

His bland face was like the mask of comedy, she thought, but behind the veneer of undergraduate wisecracks there was a sophistication and weariness shocking in one so young. She pitied the girl who'd fall in love with him.

3. He was grave the morning of his departure from St. Croix; grave, for the first time. He stared intently at Faith and Mark, coming into the great hall, their arms linked possessively. They were self-sufficient and secure. They thumbed their noses at the rest of the world. Dammit, he glowered. They alone had the omniscient power to make him feel he was missing something. Suddenly he was the starved, ragged boy outside the baker's window, his snub nose flattened against the pane, tormented by a hunger never to be sated.

All his life he had been exposed to the tyranny of too much money. A nod—and the world came running, fawning, cringing. Lacking the calm stolidity of his Danish forebears or even the tolerant resignation of his intelligent mother, he was unable to meet life realistically. Instead, his forced maturity plunged him down the path where self-indulgence walked shoulder to shoulder with a search for the great friendship that might prove his refuge. This incoherent search drew him into indiscriminate affairs and impulsive associations which invariably disillusioned him. Then he met Mark Holmes, who already gave indications of the character, self-discipline and reliability which Phillip so sorely lacked. Mark became the sole stable influence in his life.

He put his arms around Mark and Faith.

"Why don't you two run down to Palm Beach in February? It'd be like old times."

"Sorry, we can't make it," Mark answered. "Thanks all the same."

Phillip kissed Faith's cheek. "You kids have really got something," he said. "I think it's bound to last."

Mark drove him to the station. On the way he said casually, "Boy, I'm going to be sunk in a mess of red tape—documents, papers, wills, et cetera. Look, Mark, I'd like you to be one of my executors. You've got more on the ball than all those damn lawyers put together!"

Coming from Phillip, that was indeed a compliment.

4. The day after Christmas, Faith received another call from Madeline Trout. Madeline said quite firmly, as if she and Faith were old friends, "My dear, you and your husband cannot go into retirement for life! You've been married a year—and you haven't stepped out. Everyone's anxious to meet you. I'm giving a party in your honor. At the Country Club. On New Year's Eve. I've already invited dozens of people, so you cannot refuse, my dear."

"You're very kind," Faith said helplessly. "I'm not sure . . ."

"But it's all settled!"

She refrained from telling Mark as long as she could; and when finally she related the conversation to him, Mark said, just as she had feared, "Well, I'm glad you didn't accept."

"But I did, darling. I couldn't help it. I was on a spot—she'd already asked the others."

"She might have consulted us first." He switched on the new radio and she waited unhappily for his decision. "I suppose we'll have to go. But we really have nothing in common with that crowd."

"Mrs. Trout is eager to be friendly."

"Not because of your personality, I fear." He tweaked her ear fondly. "Most likely because of grandfather. They're awful snobs."

She listened, but his words made no real impression. She had deliberately wiped the Trouts' snub from her mind. And she was determined to go to the party, to meet the town's social set. Madeline was right. They needn't go into retirement. They should be making new friends.

New Year's Eve, she dressed painstakingly in the new frock Mark had chosen for her; a white crêpe sheath so simple she considered it too plain. She replaced the tarnished gold locket with the magnificent string of pearls once belonging to Mark's grandmother, which Eben had given her at Christmas.

"Do I look all right?" she asked nervously.

"Stunning."

"I hope the others think so."

"Does it matter what others think? *I* like you."

"Mark, you sound like a Turk!" She laughed uneasily. "After all, you don't want people to consider your wife a dowdy creature."

"I don't give a damn what they think," he repeated.

"Mark, do you really mean that?"

"Darn right, I do!"

She sighed and put her hands to the pearls. "These should fortify my morale. I'm scared silly."

Mark looked as if he were truly sorry for her.

"Faith," he said, "you're better than the best of them. And don't you ever forget it, funny face!"

A half hour later, she wondered what in the world she had been nervous about. They entered the warm, crowded foyer, and the hat-check girl directed them, "Mrs. Trout's party is in the Circus Room at the left." They passed through the ballroom, where the orchestra perched on a dais was playing "Lady Be Good." In the next room, they saw Mrs. Trout rushing toward them, smiling and effusive.

"My dears, how perfectly sweet of you! Mr. Holmes—I'm going to call you Mark—we're all very informal here—I'm going to take your beautiful wife and introduce her to everyone."

Madeline Trout was a small animated woman in her early thirties; her appearance and dress were influenced by Clara Bow and Texas Guinan. Her hennaed hair lay in a feather bob on her heavy skull. The mascaraed lashes of her lids were tiny prongs that guarded her protruding eyes. She wore an expensive red crêpe dress with a tiered skirt, and her armful of bracelets flashed as garishly as her manner. She gesticulated with a Russian cigarette holder.

"Lewis, do come here," she cried, snagging her husband. "Faith, my dear, this is the Better Half. I should warn you, he is crazy for brides!"

Lewis Trout greeted Faith so enthusiastically that she looked around, embarrassed, hoping Mark wouldn't notice. Fortunately he was nowhere in sight. Trout took her possessively by the arm and led her over to the smart young socialites of St. Croix, huddled at one long table. The Alexis Jenkinses, of the Midwest Auto Body Company, two thin, intense young people; the John Norcrofts of Norcroft Gypsum, who reminded Faith of Jack Spratt and his wife; and several other couples whose names were lost in the flurry of introductions.

"You're sitting at my table," Trout said with relish. "We don't allow husbands and wives to sit together—Club Rule. Now, honey, you take a martini and relax. Don't worry about friend hubby. If I know the gals, he'll be well taken care of!"

There were two other guests at his table, busily opening paper hats and trying out the horns. The woman was a brassy blonde, with a wide mouth and the raucous voice of a parrot.

"Mrs. Buxton," Trout introduced her. "The richest widow in St. Croix!"

Her companion, a negative young man with a pretty face, giggled.

Faith accepted a cocktail and looked about for Mark. Finally she spied him in the company of Mrs. Trout. He was too polite to show his boredom. She resigned herself to her partner. It was nine o'clock before the party was seated and the harassed waiters served the shrimp cocktails. Then the Rhythm Boys struck up "Yes, We Have No Bananas." Lewis Trout said, "Faith, honey, let's dance."

She tried valiantly to enter into the spirit of the festivities. After all, the party was being given for her. Yet she felt uneasy, and as they danced past Mark's table, she made a move toward him.

Lewis snatched her away. "No, no," he chided. "No can do."

They danced a few more steps, then Mr. Jenkins cut in.

"Look," Faith said desperately, "I have a husband here. If you don't mind, I'd like to dance with him."

"It isn't done," Mr. Jenkins said, shocked. "The ideas you have, Mrs. Holmes!"

In a moment Lewis Trout was beside her again demanding his turn. Desperately she signaled to Mark. Why didn't he come to her rescue?

Sitting in a corner, Mark reflected he had been to plenty of parties, but never to a brawl like this. In Paris and London, where his parents were popular, he had gone out a good deal, but such social gatherings always had an air of propriety. As he watched now, the crystal chandeliers darkened; spotlights splashed their gaudy reds and blues over the hectic dancers, writhing and swaying, as if they were pulled by strings without pattern or meaning. The entire scene resolved itself in a fantastic kaleidoscope of color and sound. Morty Chambers, assistant to the president of Lane-Crandall, ambled by, jealously guarding a glass of Scotch in one hand, a beer chaser in the other. In one corner, Mrs. Buxton was doing a Charleston with the blond boy, her skirt hiked above her bony knees, her jewels clicking like dice, her ghastly mouth stretched in a lurid smile. He was suddenly conscious of a babble of voices. . . .

The *Vagabond Lover's* out of this world. . . . Come on out to my car, I've got some real stuff there. . . . Didja see my collection of speakeasy cards? Swell joint in New York. Fifty-second Street. Bar's an aquarium, gold fish swimming under your nose. . . . So I said, if I fork out two hundred berries for that little French number, I don't want to see a fourteen-ninety-five reproduction. . . . Don't buy American Tel and Tel. I just got a hot tip from my broker—a mining stock that's got Anaconda beat! . . . Honey, let's get outa here. Okay, but what about your wife? . . . This man Coolidge may be a sourpuss, but he's sure pepped up the country. Prosperity's here to stay. . . . So they bought a castle in Germany for the price of a mink. . . . Tony Spade's brought in some good stuff from Canada. . . . I hear Lane's sunk a million in Miami property, lost every cent. . . .

Mark spent the next hour in the deserted billiard room, smoking one cigarette after another. From behind the closed door, he heard the muted laughter of the merrymakers. What the hell am I doing here, he wondered. He looked at the watch strapped to his wrist. At midnight he meant to find Faith. It would be just a year that they'd pledged their love. Thinking of it, he felt better. With a faint smile on his lips, he returned to the Circus Room.

As he approached Faith's table, he saw Lewis Trout lift his glass in a toast. "Let's drink to the beautiful Mrs. Holmes—a most welcome addition to our little circle!"

The lights went out. After the first hush, there was a burst of hysterical laughter. When the chandelier bulbs flicked on again, Mark saw Lewis Trout ostentatiously move away from Faith. Suddenly he was filled with a cold deadly anger.

"Faith, get your things!" he ordered brusquely. "We're leaving."

"But, Mark . . ."

The others stared, outraged. A wet blanket, a spoilsport, running out just as the fun was beginning!

He made no answer. He turned and strode out. Faith flushed, but without hesitation she picked up her bag and followed him. As they plunged into the darkness, the poignant strains of "Auld Lang Syne" followed them.

"Darling," she cried, "wait for me!" Her thin gold slippers crept over the precarious ice. The chill air seeped through her brocaded evening wrap. The pleasant haze was entirely gone. She was sober and alert.

Mark slammed the door of the car, switched on the ignition. As he backed out, the tires crunched in protest. At the exit of the Club grounds, they narrowly avoided another car swinging toward them crazily. Mark jammed on the brakes.

A hazy face peered out at them, grinning idiotically.

"Happy New Year, folks! Whoopee!"

"Damn," Mark muttered under his breath.

The inside of the roadster was black as the interior of a mine. The glow of the dashboard was a faint glimmer in the distance. Her spirits were thoroughly dampened by his grim silence. She turned her head to the window. The night was a smoke screen, blotting out the evanescent moon, transforming the trees and shrubs, the hillocks and sand dunes into mysterious masses of sculpture, terrifying as the music from *Night on Bald Mountain*.

She couldn't bear the silence another minute.

"Mark."

He kept his gaze on the dark road ahead.

"Mark, why are you cross? You know those people mean nothing to me. It was all in the spirit of good fun. Lewis and his wife . . ."

"They're indecent. Nothing but a couple of alley cats! It made me sick to see how you fell for them!"

"I didn't fall for them!" she cried, thinking, He should be pleased at the fuss they made over me. Why isn't he pleased?

"Besides," she added stiffly, "you didn't show much interest in dancing with me."

"How could I—with all those louts cutting in! How do you think I feel seeing you handed over to any Tom, Dick, or Lewis!"

"But it's the accepted thing. . . ."

"Not to me."

"Mark, I believe you're jealous."

"Is that all you can see about this whole business?"

"Yes, darling. Because it looks to me as if you're making a big fuss over nothing at all."

They reached the house. Usually, she waited while he put the car in the garage, but tonight she went in directly. They undressed in strained silence. When they were lying together, she said hesitantly, "Mark. You do love me . . . ?"

"God, yes!" he answered savagely. "Why do you think I get so damned annoyed? Can't you understand?"

In the darkness, her glance was pleading. She couldn't understand. Try as she might, she couldn't see what he was driving at, why he got so angry with her. If it weren't for him, she'd have enjoyed the party immensely. She loved music and gaiety and people, and she'd never had enough of them. Sure, Lewis Trout had tried to paw her, but he was tight and he didn't mean anything by it. It was all in the spirit of good fun, of New Year's Eve. And she failed to see why Mark felt such behavior would hurt their love. She wanted to explain her viewpoint to him, but when it came to complexities, she knew she'd never make herself clear, and then he'd be apt to grow angry again. "Is that all you see about this whole business?" Mark had demanded. They were looking at it from different viewpoints. As they had on their wedding day in Great Falls, when he was buying her ring, or the day she chose those two expensive frocks at the Fashion Shop. I never know whether he's going to be pleased or annoyed, she thought. It made her nervous. For she realized that although she and Mark loved each other, they were two different entities. This sudden revelation disturbed her profoundly, and it was dawn before she fell asleep.

5. "New Year's Day." She turned her head from the pillow and met Mark's glance.

"Oh, darling," she cried, "I'm sorry I was such a fool last night!"

He grinned. "Forget it."

They went down to breakfast in their robes. Sitting opposite him Faith traced his features with a surge of renewed affection—the deep indentation of his temples, the way his deep-set gray eyes were placed under the thick brows, the wide disciplined mouth over irregular white teeth. She sighed contentedly, "You're such a nice husband."

"You didn't think so last night."

"Oh, that." She shrugged it off, praying silently that he would forget about it.

"Faith," he persisted, "did you like the party?"

She was suddenly wary, afraid that her honest reply would infuriate him. Yet she could not deny the party had made an impression on her. For the first time since their marriage, she measured the confines of their life and found them stifling. She felt rather like a fledgling imprisoned in the nest long after its wings are developed for flight. Her fertile imagination soared; she saw herself and Mark at the long gleaming table in the dining room, surrounded by friends; she pictured the faultless service, heard the compliments of her guests. . . .

"Mark, what do we do now?"

He yawned. "I'm going back to bed."

"I was talking about the Trouts, darling." She was too impatient for tact. "Shouldn't we ask them for dinner? To return their kindness."

Mark finished his coffee. "If we never see those people again, it'll be too soon for me."

She didn't dare tell him that the Trouts had asked them to join the Country Club. She knew what his answer would be.

6. The change crept up imperceptibly, insidiously, like the mists over the lake which obliterated the cliffs and scrub oak yet left the general conformation. The outside world left its calling card. The obligations of new duties beset their private little domain like malevolent intruders. Here, you two lovebirds, they seem to say, you can't evade your appointed place on the social treadmill!

Faith was now the young mistress of the house. She learned to do the marketing, she went over the weekly menus with Mrs. Hanrahan, she checked the inventories of linen and silver and staples, attended the accounts, and generally acquitted herself well. Eben was pleased with her.

But she was young, energetic, ambitious, and she had too much leisure on her hands. And Mark was away all day.

"Mark, do you mind if I join several of the women's organizations?" she asked.

"You're apt to get pretty bored."

"Not any more than I get staying at home," she said. "I'd like to do something. I get so restless."

She needs children, Mark thought again. There was still no sign of a pregnancy, and although Faith fretted, Dr. Savage did not seem too disturbed.

"By all means, find some new interests," he said.

That spring, under the sponsorship of Mrs. Alexis Jenkins and Mrs. Lewis Trout, she was initiated into the fashionable Book and Garden Club, whose members were the wives of the young business executives of St. Croix. Most of the women were in their late twenties and early thirties. They had plenty of leisure which they scattered carelessly, and they waged an incessant and voluble battle against encroaching age and flesh. Just as Mark had prophesied, Faith found the meetings dull, but she refused stubbornly to admit it. However, she made a friend in Mrs. Alexis Jenkins, a slim, dark, hard young woman with a tart tongue and a contemptuous estimation of her clubmates.

"All that Holmes dough," she said to Faith, "and you don't take advantage of it. I wish I were in your boots, baby. I'd show the world how to have fun!"

Recently, Faith had got in the habit of having a martini before dinner with Mark and smoking a cigarette with her coffee. At Mrs. Jenkins' suggestion, she took to wearing black, which was not a becoming color, and she interspersed her conversation with the current catch phrases that were fashionable among the Book and Garden Club members until Mark started teasing her about it.

"'And what have you,'" he would repeat. "Faith, I'd rather you stuck to your old habit of not finishing a sentence than to hear you end every one with 'or what have you.'"

On the surface, he strove to be tolerant of her new friendships, possibly because he feared that their original passionate unity must inevitably wear thin with time. But he was hurt. Because she needed others while he needed only her.

After a while, Faith learned to be diplomatic. Knowing how bored he was with the Trouts, the Jenkinses, the Wiltons, she entertained them only at luncheons or cocktails.

Unlike Mark, old Eben Holmes encouraged her new interests.

"You can't stifle her," he said to Mark. "An energetic girl like Faith must have some outlets."

On their second anniversary, she promised Mark they would spend the evening quietly at home.

"The Jenkinses asked us for dinner. But I told them we couldn't come. This is a special evening, darling."

"You're a pal," he said fervently.

She curled up on the sofa before the fire. "Another year of marriage," she reflected smugly, "and still no pitfalls."

"What's so surprising about it?"

Her smile was wicked. "The more I see of other men, darling, the more I realize how utterly different you are. Things that might rile them wouldn't bother you in the slightest."

"Go on," he said affably. "You interest me."

"On the other hand, your standards are inhumanly high. You expect altogether too much of me."

"You have no appreciation of your capabilities."

"And," she continued blandly, "I do think you're a wee bit possessive."

"Possessiveness is a one-sided affair." He was suddenly grave. "It implies ownership and enslavement. We don't own each other, Faith. What we have to give is given freely and willingly."

"Then why are you so touchy when we're with other people?"

How could he put it in words, without being misunderstood? He couldn't very well say, When we're together, we're one. When you're among outsiders, you give yourself too generously to them. And our unity suffers.

He liked people, too. But he always maintained that protective barrier of reserve. Faith however went overboard in an orgy of friendliness and enthusiasm which elicited a ready response. She had no discrimination.

Perhaps I appear too possessive, he thought.

Yet only in such evaluation lay their safety.

7. In July, Mr. Pauley, general manager of the Holmes Lumber Company, was rushed to the hospital for a serious abdominal operation. His recovery was slow, and the bulk of his duties fell on Mark's unwilling shoulders. Since it was Eben Holmes's wish that his grandson ultimately take over the business, he saw to it that Mark's training was thorough. Nevertheless, after two years' apprenticeship, Mark detested more than ever the musty offices and the obsolete procedure with which Pauley, and his assistants, Feenan and Gibbs, serviced the organization.

"Sure, the company is making money," he said to Faith. "However, that's not due to any initiative or enterprise of its executives, but simply because Holmes lumber is uniformly first rate, and the demand is always there!"

Right from the beginning, he knew he wasn't cut out for the lumber business. He felt it the very first day when his grandfather took him down to the office and introduced him to the staff. "My grandson is coming into the business," he said. And there was a sense of confidence and elation in his voice, as if now all would be well with the Holmeses.

Mark had looked around the old-fashioned offices, shook hands with the old-fashioned man in charge. "I'm glad to know you, sir," he said, and wanted to turn and escape from here. This is not for me, he thought, hating it all, fearing he would be buried here for life. I want to strike out for myself in a field that will be stimulating and inspiring, where I'll want to fight for the future.

The words of refusal were on his lips. But the pride in Eben's weather-beaten face silenced him. He loved the old man more than he did independence. He owed him a good deal. And now, Mark had a wife to support, too. He was disciplined, and he did the right thing without regard for the cost to his young ego. And all the time, he watched himself strictly so Eben would have no inkling of his dissatisfaction. I've got to take it, Mark thought. And stuck grimly to his responsibilities.

Recently at a Lions' luncheon served at the Lake Shore Grille, which he attended at Pauley's request, he met the new engineer for Wolverine Motors.

Allan Griswold was a small, slight young man with sad brown eyes and a shy, vague manner. His body had ceased growing prematurely; nature compensated, however, by providing him with a brain that would continue its development to the end of his life. In a brief, halting speech, he visualized the future of the airplane and stressed the importance of its engine.

Mark was so impressed that afterwards, he stopped at Griswold's table.

"I was very much interested in your talk," he said. "And I wondered if perhaps we couldn't lunch together some time."

"I'd be delighted."

They met the following week for an agreeable and stimulating hour during which Mark learned that Griswold had been graduated from the Massachusetts Institute of Technology with highest honors. He had been working for a Detroit automobile firm, when Zeb Whiting, president of Wolverine, made him a better offer.

"A project I'm really hepped up about," he added, "is an engine I've been tinkering with. An airplane engine."

"I'd like to hear about it," Mark said.

Allan Griswold was living at the Lake Shore while he hunted for a suitable house so his wife, Joyce, could join him the following month.

Before parting, they made plans to meet again. Allan was eager to take Mark through the Wolverine plant and show him the recent innovations for which he was responsible.

Returning to the Holmes office, Mark thought enviously, What a fortunate fellow Griswold is—to know where he's bound for, and to go about his journey so expeditiously. . . .

8. Late one afternoon in mid-August, Winona Kraus approached the iron gates of the Holmes place.

Since Faith's marriage, Winona hadn't seen her more than three or four times, and then by accident—at the Fashion Shop, in Burnside's Drugstore, at the band concert in Holmes Park. Each time Faith had been cordial enough, but it was apparent to Winona she was ducking her old friends. Putting on the ritz.

Winona ruffled up her short blond curls, ran a moist finger over her light eyebrows, cast a critical glance at the seams in her nude silk stockings. Here we go!

A maid in a black silk uniform and a tiny white apron opened the door.

"C'n I see Mrs. Mark Holmes, please? I'm an old friend."

The maid asked her to be seated, and she looked around curiously, at the graceful curve of the staircase, the paintings on the paneled walls, the massive organ at the far end, its pipes blending in the ruby light from the stained windows. Faith certainly had struck it rich!

Then Faith came into the room, and the pert greeting died on Winona's childish lips. Was this the girl she had known, or a stranger born to these surroundings? Faith wore a white linen dress, which was in startling contrast to her deeply tanned skin. She had tied a bright scarf on her head, a fashion Winona wouldn't have dared try, but it looked right on her. How did she do it?

"It's good to see you, Winnie."

Even the way she spoke antagonized Winona, and she decided it wouldn't be such a bad idea to remind Faith of her antecedents.

"My mother was speaking of your folks this morning, Faith. She wondered how your mother is getting along?"

"About the same," Faith said tonelessly.

"Gosh, that's tough on you. How often do you get to see her?"

Faith's features were expressionless. "It depends on the doctor," she lied deliberately. Her hands were trembling and she held them in her lap. Winona isn't cruel, she reminded herself. She is simply voicing the curiosity of the whole town.

And then, having delivered her barb, Winona abruptly changed the subject. "I just had to come and tell you my good news, Faith. Something wonderful has happened! You know, I've been taking voice lessons with a new teacher in Great Falls. Well, he says with my voice and my looks, I should get into the musical-comedy field without any trouble. Can you imagine?"

"That's wonderful, Winnie," Faith said.

"You haven't heard the most exciting part. My teacher used to live in New York—and he'd send his star pupils to John Murray Anderson. For his Greenwich Village Follies. So I'm going to New York with a letter to Mr. Anderson."

She already saw her name in lights. "I've got my stage name picked out, too. *Winnie Cross*."

Mark came in then from the office, and Winona related the entire story again. "If a girl gets a job with Mr. Anderson," she said happily, "there's no telling how far she can go."

"Just how far is that?" he asked quizzically.

Winona's eyes were innocent. "Well, it's entirely up to the girl."

She lingered, hoping to be asked for dinner. But finally she just had to get up. "Mark," she said, not without malice, "it's really to your credit that Faith has settled down. I always figured that when I lit out for the big city, Faith would be right alongside of me."

As they dressed for dinner that night, Faith said, "I never thought . . ." And her words trailed off.

"Finish your sentence," Mark grinned. "What didn't you think?"

"That Winnie would finally make it. I suppose New York is the dream of every small-town girl."

"Including yourself? Faith, do you miss your job at *The Observer*?"

"Darling," she said, "it isn't that I love *The Observer* less, but you a darned sight more."

That should have satisfied Mark. But somehow it didn't.

9. Because of Pauley's protracted illness, Mark could not hope for a vacation that summer. His hours were long and exacting, and often he stayed in the office until late in the evening.

Consequently, Faith was thrown very much on her own resources. Fortunately, her chores took up most of the morning and her afternoon was given over to Eben Holmes. One evening a week she visited her father and Mrs. Hussar, who delighted in plying her with savory Hungarian dishes. Saturday afternoons, she played tennis with Madeline Trout at the Club. Still she had too much leisure.

I'm not being fair to her, Mark thought wistfully. Twice he made plans for a vaction at his grandfather's northern camp, but each time an emergency came up. Finally, without daring to confide in her, for fear she would be disappointed again, he made arrangements for the Labor Day weekend. They would drive to Great Falls and re-live their honeymoon. They needed to be together, to recapture something of their old sweet intimacy.

But Pauley did not return to the office as expected.

Saturday night, Mark was still working, and Faith went to the Country Club dance as the guest of Lewis and Madeline Trout.

When Mark got home at midnight, she was still out. He undressed slowly and got into bed. How quiet the house was. He had lived most of his life here, the place was dear to him—yet tonight, it seemed alien because Faith was missing. For the moment he resented this utter dependence on her which left him so vulnerable. Still, he had no right to be critical. It had been a dull summer for her. Nobody's fault; just circumstances. He turned restlessly between the cool sweet-smelling sheets, acutely conscious of the empty place by his side. The moonlight shining on his worn young face kept him from falling asleep.

The moonlight and his thoughts.

10. Faith was meeting Madeline Trout and her house guest, a Mrs. Schuyler of Chicago, at the Lake Shore Grille for lunch. As she entered the lobby, Madeline greeted her with a new suggestion.

"I know you're fond of this place, dear, but would you mind if we ran out to Tony Spade's for lunch? Jenny Schuyler's been living in Europe for years. She hasn't seen a speakeasy."

Faith hesitated, knowing Mark would be annoyed if she visited the notorious hideaway. Still, she hated to object. Besides, Madeline had spoken so often of Tony's, where she and Lewis dined and gambled regularly, that Faith couldn't help but be curious. They crowded into the front seat of Madeline's Stutz roadster and drove out to the Highway. At Marquette Road, they turned right until they reached a low white stucco building almost hidden in the thicket of pines. They managed to find parking space and Madeline knocked on the door. After they were scrutinized through a peephole, they were allowed to enter.

"Just like a gangster movie," Mrs. Schuyler said breathlessly as they followed Madeline single file through the narrow corridor to a dimly lit room, lined at one end with red leather booths and at the other with a well-stocked, glittering bar. Tony Spade himself greeted them and showed them to a booth.

"How is Mr. Trout?" he asked patronizingly.

Madeline preened. "Couldn't be better! Tony, we'll start with a round of old fashioneds. Then antipasto—veal scallopini—a green salad." She explained in an aside, "Tony has the best chef in St. Croix."

A swarthy waiter brought in their drinks and a huge platter of appetizers. They were enjoying the food when suddenly they were conscious of a commotion in the rear room; a violent commotion. Faith turned her head nervously. Tony was signaling furiously to the bartenders, who began clearing the shelves of bottles, which they dumped into a chute behind them.

"Quiet, everybody!" Tony yelled hoarsely.

A brusque voice ordered, "Stay where you are. This'll be over in a minute."

Tony Spade's was being raided.

"They can't do this to Tony!" Madeline cried, outraged. "Why, he's a pal of Bob Costello's!"

Faith was too frightened to move. She was conscious of the perspiration trickling down her face. The antipasto sat squeamishly in her stomach. She wiped her lips with shaking fingers.

"What will they do to us?" she asked the officer.

"Take it easy, lady," he answered. "It's nuthin' to be scared of."

"Will we be in the papers?" Mrs. Schuyler asked eagerly. "What a pity I photograph so badly."

"I wouldn't know, lady. All we do now is take your names."

Dear Lord, Faith thought in anguish. If Mark hears of this— Or grandfather!

"Don't worry," Madeline soothed her. "I'll call Lewis. He'll have it hushed up. You'll see."

Madeline was right; her husband took care of everything. But for weeks afterwards, Faith was tense. Each time she opened *The Observer,* she cringed, expecting to see her name in headlines.

A fortnight later, Tony Spade's was open for business as usual. However, he never had the pleasure of serving young Mrs. Holmes again.

11. That autumn, Faith and Mark saw a good deal of the Griswolds. Since a strong friendship had developed between the men, the wives were inevitably thrown together. Joyce was not precisely the companion she would have chosen of her own accord but Faith was pleasant to her for Mark's sake.

Joyce Griswold was of medium height and frame, but in contrast to Allan's slightness, she seemed overpowering. She had thick blond hair, which she wore braided in a coronet over her head, and she was flagrantly proud of her plump rounded bosom. It was impossible for her to join in an intelligent conversation, and while the rest of them talked and argued, she found refuge in knitting. Her smug display of wifely virtue irritated Faith.

"After all," she exploded to Mark, "Joyce isn't the only woman so devoted to her husband." She smiled wickedly. "I'm not doing so badly myself."

For on their third anniversary, she found she was pregnant.

CONTINUATION OF HOMER SWEET'S REPORT ON FAITH HOLMES

Fourth Year of Marriage. Sudden return to Vrest Macklin's paper, *The Observer. Reason.* Her disappointment in Eben Holmes's will, which left bulk of fortune to town. Persuaded Mark Holmes to dispose of family lumber business, and embark on fresh venture. Here first indication of her talent for mischief. Tried to break up his friendship with young inventor, Allan Griswold.

(*Source.* Joyce Griswold, wife of Mark Holmes's partner in the now flourishing Holmes-Griswold plant, part of Wolverine Motors.)

Note. Important angle on rabble-rousing. First indications of her potentialities as rabble-rouser. Used minor accident in Trout Celluloid plant as means to repay Trout for original rebuff.

Important. Lewis Trout willing to be of help to us, any time. Charmed aging Vrest Macklin into sponsoring her newspaper column. Beginnings also of her talent for attacking reputable institutions and respectable people—for personal publicity.

Mark Holmes, broke, ill, on the verge of despondency when she deserted him for greener pastures.

Her affair with Phillip Latham, heir to Latham Flour Mills, started at this time. Latham, Mark Holmes's best friend. Double cross.

Special Note: Use her behavior with Mark Holmes in campaign against her.

Early New York Years. Met Corrigan at Democratic convention. Used him mercilessly to get ahead in New York.

(*Source.* Steve Pringle, who was with them at convention. Pringle says, "I first realized how dangerous Faith Holmes could be when I saw the smooth way she handled Corrigan—a woman-hater if ever there was one—as a means for her future. Although she appears to act impulsively, every move is planned well in advance. She never loses track of anyone who can be of use to her. Her affair with Corrigan is of long standing, yet she did not allow it to interfere with her pursuit of Phillip Latham nor her marriage to Harvey

Jessup. And neither did she allow that marriage to disturb her relationship with Corrigan."

Urgent note. Use above material in campaign against her.)

First job in New York with magazine. Fired.

Returned broke to St. Croix. Discovered Mark Holmes in the money again. Tried to make him. Failed.

(*Source.* Joyce Griswold.)

Second job with *Alliance for the Advancement of Women in Politics.*

Fired.

Testimony of Mrs. Reynolds, president of organization: "We refused to become the front for her lust for power."

Wangled a trip to the Palm Beach home of the Lathams.

(*Important.* What happened there prior to Phillip Latham's death?)

Chapter Eight

1. The news was a tonic for Eben's failing strength.

"A great-grandson," he mused. "What more can any man hope for?"

As for Mark, he showed his utter happiness by making Faith's life miserable with his determined and fussy attentions. No matter how rushed he was at the office, he called her at mid-morning.

"Faith, did you keep your breakfast down?"

"Well," she giggled, "just about."

"Don't forget your second glass of milk at eleven."

"Yes, darling."

"What're you doing now?"

"I'm going out for a walk. After all, there are two of us to keep in trim."

"Too cold and damp." He was frantically afraid of an accident. "Stay in until I get home. Then we'll take a walk together."

"Mark, for heaven's sake—who's having this baby, anyway!"

"Sorry," he said sheepishly. "I'll call again after your nap."

She hung up, smiling to herself. Milk, orange juice, calcium tablets. Mark saw to it that she followed her routine rigidly. Mark directed her welfare and the baby's, even by remote control. Well, she couldn't blame him. The child meant so much to both of them. After three years of sterility, she had almost given up hope.

The following months were among the most perfect of their married life. Mark was almost comically devoted, Eben equally solicitous. Mrs. Hussar expertly knitted tiny sweaters and bootees, and sent them by Tod, along with involved directions for looking after Faith's health. Even Madeline Trout offered confidential notes on the problem of bringing up children without having them underfoot.

"Lewis Junior spends his winters in a southern military academy," she said, "and the summers at a Maine camp. The Jenkins girls go to a good finishing school in New York, and spend their summers in Ohio with Alexis' mother. It's the only sensible way to raise a child these days."

"When do you get to see them?" Faith demanded. She and Mark

would bring up their youngster differently. They talked about it long into the night. He would be part of them. He would never suffer the indignities which had plagued their childhood. He would be loved, understood, wanted. . . .

He will make up for the wretchedness of Mark's childhood, she reflected. And for my mother, too.

Despite her inner resolutions, she found herself thinking a good deal about her mother these days. Resting on the chaise in her room, or lolling on a bench in the park, grateful for the pallid February sun, she let her imagination run free, trying to visualize these days as they might have been were her mother a well and normal woman.

One evening she sat down at her desk impulsively, and began a note: "Dear Mother, If only you will consent to see me . . ."

Her pen dropped. She stared at the blue paper a long time. Then deliberately she picked it up, tore it once, then again, and tossed the scraps in the tooled-leather wastebasket.

Oh, what's the use! she thought, biting her lip for self-control. What's the use of trying again?

She knew intuitively the ache in her heart would not be assuaged by the child's coming, but only when her mother finally relented.

2. Late in March, Miss Smith of *The Observer* telephoned.

"Faith, Steve Pringle's leaving us to work for the Rentschler Syndicate in Detroit. The staff's giving him a farewell party. He asked especially that you come. Do bring your husband, too."

Listening to Miss Smith's warm friendly voice, Faith was back in the dusty cluttered office, the smell of printer's ink perfume in her nostrils, the thud of the linotype machine music in her ears.

"Of course we'll come. I wouldn't miss it for anything!"

She couldn't wait to tell Mark. "It'll be a change for me, darling," she said. "I'm beginning to feel like a prize cow."

"Where's it going to be?" he asked, shedding his heavy blue coat.

"At the Fishery. Tomorrow night. You don't mind, darling? I mean, this isn't like going out with the Trouts."

"I'll be glad to go if it makes you happy, Faith."

She hugged him. "I'm really looking forward to it."

Rain fell all the next day, a cold nasty rain. She hoped it would let up, for Mark would never consent to her going out in such beastly weather. By late afternoon, the clouds did lift, the sky shone bright and clear, and a wind came up. She put on a warm light-blue woolen frock, which needed letting out at the seams, and waited impatiently for Mark's arrival.

Mark kissed her expertly. "How's Little Puck today?"

"Couldn't be better!"

He mussed the short chestnut curls on her forehead. "Has he started any maneuvers yet?"

"Mark, you're getting the symptoms confused. It's much too early."

She tagged upstairs and watched him shave and change into fresh clothes.

"Let's not stay too late," he suggested casually.

"Of course not, darling, I'll be in bed by eleven. Does that suit you?"

"It does." He chose a maroon tie and knotted it carefully. "Pringle's a fool to leave *The Observer.*"

"Vrest's always been afraid he'd sell out." It took a while to make herself comfortable in the armchair. "Steve's smart, but he may be getting his signals mixed. Probably looks like the main chance to him." She sighed. "Vrest told me Rentschler's gobbling up all the small papers he can lay his hands on. And pirating experienced men to staff them."

"I'm afraid the day of the individual paper like *The Observer* is on the way out," Mark said regretfully. "But Vrest will go down fighting."

The evening turned out to be pleasant enough, even for Mark. Vrest Macklin was missing from the festivities, but the rest of the staff was there and effusively pleased to see Faith again.

"The place hasn't been the same without you," Steve Pringle said sorrowfully. "No shoulder to lean on, no chum to share a hamburger with. That's why I'm getting out, honey. Some guys rush off to Africa to get over an unrequited love. Me, I go to Rentschler."

"Steve, be serious for a moment. Are you sure you're doing the right thing?"

"Positive." His handsome face crowned with bushy red hair was suddenly scornful and vindictive. "I'll be making twice as much dough for one thing. And I won't have to take any more of the Great Humanitarian's contempt!"

Steve hated his boss. She had never realized it before. This was his means of retaliation. For to lose an employee to Rentschler was a great blow to Vrest's principles.

There was much wine with the dinner, much laughter and many toasts, in which Faith joined enthusiastically. But by ten o'clock, the shadows of fatigue darkened her glowing eyes, and Mark said quite firmly they must leave. Politely they shook hands with Steve, who was a little drunk now, and made their way out to the car.

"Tired?" Mark asked.

"Not a bit. It was fun," she added, as he tucked a lap robe over her. "Really, darling, we should be seeing more people."

He drove along the unlighted dock with extra caution, to avoid the slippery car tracks. "This glare ice is damned tricky," he worried.

As he turned at the Ferry Slip toward Main, he was forced to swerve, in order to miss a switch. The car skidded wildly over the frozen rut, struck a stanchion with a jolting impact, lurched and stalled.

In a daze, Faith saw Mark had flung out his arm to protect her from the windshield.

"Faith! *Faith*—are you all right?"

She stared at him blankly. His words seemed to be coming from a great distance.

"Lord, what a scare!" he said, taking her hand in his. "You sure you're okay, Faith?"

She roused herself. "Of course, darling. Don't be upset. I was just confused for the moment."

Fortunately he was able to start the car again. By the time they reached home, Faith appeared, to his relief, perfectly normal. She speculated a little wistfully on the lucky person who'd get Steve's berth at the paper. Without the usual fuss she drank the milk he heated. He watched over her anxiously until she fell asleep.

What an escape, he reflected. We've been damned lucky.

At four in the morning, she awakened suddenly.

"Mark." She clutched his arm. "*Mark!*"

He was instantly awake.

"Call the doctor," she whispered. "Something's terribly wrong."

3. Mark and the doctor were standing in the white corridor of the hospital, just outside her door. Three days had passed since she had been rushed to the operating room, but Mark was still in a highly emotional state of mind. He had almost lost Faith. The thought of it brought icy terror to his heart. The realization that she was finally out of danger compensated for the loss of the child.

"This miscarriage has been a great blow to her," Dr. Savage said. "But she'll get over it in time. She's an intelligent girl."

Mark longed to believe him. Sure, she'd get over it—if she didn't wear herself into a nervous breakdown in the meantime.

"If I hadn't insisted on going," she had moaned, when she came out of the ether. "If Steve weren't going away, if the streets weren't slippery. If . . ."

"No recriminations," Mark begged despairingly. "This is the way it had to be."

Tears filled her eyes. She turned her head away. "But we waited so long! Three years!"

He wanted to console her, to say, "My darling, we will have other children." But remembering the odd expression on the doctor's face, he was silent.

Tonight as he entered the sickroom, he found her sitting up in bed, pale and listless. He placed a white box containing long-stemmed American Beauty roses on the bed table and handed her an elaborately wrapped package.

Faith regarded it without interest.

He opened the box and held up a very feminine pink-and-lace bedjacket.

A faint smile tugged at her lips. "You didn't pick this out yourself?"

Mark laughed boyishly. "Leah Parker helped me. I said you were the tailored type, but she was sure you'd like this one anyway."

"Thank you, dear."

Her momentary interest lapsed. Leaning back on the pillows, she listened politely to his account of the day's happenings. He ached with compassion. Poor Faith. She didn't deserve this.

But he was too reserved to express his pity, and her very lassitude raised a barrier between them. Finally, still troubled and ill at ease, he kissed her good night and left.

She had been in too lethargic a mood to respond to his presence. Yet once he was gone, she was lonely for him. Her tired body, accustomed to lying beside his, felt incomplete. The days were bad enough, but the nights were unbearable.

She reached out for the bell and eventually the night nurse looked in.

"I can't sleep!" she said. And the nurse saw it was more than the petulant complaint of a sick woman. There was bleak terror in her eyes.

"I'll get you a phenobarbital," the nurse promised.

Even with the sedative, it took her fully an hour to doze off. And that night, she had a dream. She dreamed of her mother. Her mother was running away from her. And no matter how swiftly Faith ran, she could never quite catch up with her.

"Wait for me!" she entreated. "Mother, wait for me!"

But her mother was fleet as the wind.

She awoke, crying hysterically, and the nurse rushed in.

The following morning, she pleaded with Mark to take her home. She'd be safe there. No more nightmares. And that night, lying in his arms, the familiar blue satin comforter drawn up to her chin, the west windows open to the air, she relaxed, confident that he would look after her. He was her talisman.

In the ghostly wash of dawn, Mark was abruptly aroused. He opened his eyes.

Faith was sitting up in bed, terror-stricken.

"I had a dream," she whispered.

The same dream.

On the very first day the doctor allowed her up, she called a taxi and left the house without telling Mrs. Hanrahan her destination.

"The State Hospital," she directed the driver. And then she sat huddled in a corner of the seat, weak and trembling to the point of tears. If only her mother would consent to see her—just long enough to listen to her explanation!

"I'm sorry," the staff doctor at the institution said, "it is still inadvisable for you to see her. It wouldn't do her any good."

4. Spring came. May was a tender month. The sun poured its abundant streams of gold through the budding maples, dappling the fresh sod. The lilac hedges were weighed down with blossoms ripe as clusters of grapes. The bridal wreath was out, and the heady mock orange. The earth was preening under the advances of the sun.

There was no spring in Faith's heart.

Summer came, and dragged on monotonously. Gradually, her health was returning. She and Mark took long walks, went swimming, read to each other, listened to new recordings. But her old sparkle was missing. Mark, acutely sensitive to her moods, recognized the deep-seated turmoil. He took her in his arms and said, "Faith, you mustn't forget that we're two against the world. Together, we can lick any problem." But she smiled evasively and turned away.

He appealed to his grandfather. "There's something going on in Faith's mind I can't figure out."

From the vantage of the bed to which he was now confined, Eben Holmes regarded him compassionately. "She's had a tough time, Mark. You must be patient and tolerant."

Neither of them mentioned the hope uppermost in their minds. Another child . . .

Then one afternoon, Faith paid a visit to Dr. Savage. When she returned home, she went directly to her room and locked the door. By the time she came down to dinner, she was composed once more, and she even managed to smile and joke a little. But both Mark and old Eben sensed the change in her. She was not the same as she had been that morning.

In July, when Joyce Griswold smugly announced that she was pregnant, Faith went to the drawer in the mahogany chest and took out the expensive and unused layette.

After the last visit to Dr. Savage, she knew she would not be needing it again. Ever.

5. In August, Eben Holmes suffered a stroke. His power of speech was stricken, the right side of his body paralyzed. He lay immobile in his old-fashioned walnut bed in the cool darkened room, unable to communicate with the world, but keenly aware of all activity about him—Dr. Savage, the nurses, Mark and Faith, all feverishly intent on sustaining life in his frail worn body.

Time lost all significance. There were no longer seconds, minutes, hours. It was marked off by the nurse's coming on duty, going off duty, the visits of the doctor, or Mark's and Faith's endless and devoted attendance.

Days turned slowly into weeks; a month passed. Dr. Savage was cautiously optimistic about his progress, although he warned Mark the recovery would be slow and tedious.

Faith spent all her time with Eben, relieving the nurses, giving them extra time off, for it was apparent he preferred her care. Since the terrible morning she had found him stricken, she had ignored her own unhappiness, projecting herself into his world—the very limited sphere of a frail old man, mute and partially paralyzed, who was nevertheless conscious of everything around him, every nuance, every word, every gesture. There was deep within her an instinct for self-sacrifice and renunciation which rose to the surface in this emergency. She reached the very peaks of selfless devotion in ministering to him.

She read to him from the books he loved, Thoreau and Emerson and Carlyle. She had the victrola brought in, and she played his favorite Bach fugues. She saw to it that the vases by his bedside were filled with fresh asters and chrysanthemums from the cutting garden. By means of a pencil and pad and some sign language, she worked out a way of communicating with him.

She prayed fervently that his life would be spared. For he was the durable link in her life with Mark. He was always there, wise and kind and tolerant, eager to help and advise, yet he never interfered in their private life. She loved him in a way she had never loved her own father.

"He *is* improving," she assured Mark. "He seems to show more interest. I can tell."

6. It was cooler that evening with a touch of autumn in the air. Faith and Mark were having dinner on a small table in Eben's bedroom. He was propped up against the pillows, watching them, his gaze lucid and content. Impulsively, Faith jumped up and kissed his wrinkled cheek.

"You're looking very handsome tonight, grandfather," she said. Her smile added. And I love you very much.

His deep-set eyes, so much like Mark's, flickered in response. With an effort, he motioned her back to the table, lest her food grow cold. As they talked to each other, he watched them intently. The muscles of his throat ached with the effort to form words. Suddenly his pad dropped to the floor. He gasped, a faint guttural sound.

They rushed to his side. Mark's arm steadied his drooping shoulders. His eyes were still open, a benign and peaceful expression on his face. But his heart had stopped.

7. In the months after Eben Holmes's death, a subtle change came over the great house. A vagrant phantom skittered through the rooms, infecting the very air with loneliness and sorrow. The formal drawing room with its fine paneling and imported marble mantel, the dining room with its Georgian silver and Dresden china, the great hall with its tapestries and organ, all took on a static quality, like the backdrop for Madame Tussaud's figures.

They missed Eben acutely.

"With grandfather gone," Mark said somberly, "it doesn't feel like home any more."

On the fifteenth of December, they gathered in the board room of the Lumberman's Bank to hear the reading of the will. Eben's lawyer, Mr. Sinclair, was present, as well as Mr. Pauley and two directors of the bank who were also concerned with the Holmes Endowment Foundation, and Faith and Mark.

The document was simple and concise. To his son Richard, who was still living abroad, a life annuity; to Mrs. Hanrahan and Jacob, outright sums; to Mark and Faith jointly, the house and its furnishings, except for the works of art, which after their lifetime would revert to the Holmes Foundation. He bequeathed them also the summer camp, a hundred thousand dollars in gilt-edge securities, and to Mark fifty-one per cent of the Lumber Company, the balance to be divided among Pauley, Feenan, Gibbs and other employees.

The bulk of his fortune went to the Endowment Foundation for the benefit of the people of St. Croix.

Eben Holmes had been an eminently just man. He was returning to the town that which he had taken from it.

The following days were bleak and dismal as the winter blasts. Mrs. Hanrahan, suffering from arthritis, decided to move to Florida with her only niece. Another link with the past was broken. Faith hired a new cook, and they went through the holidays perfunctorily. An air of depression settled down on them. Intuitively they both felt they must get out of the house.

"We should get some land," Mark suggested, "and build a house. Something to our own taste."

Faith smiled at him. Since Eben's death, the bonds between them had strengthened, as they found solace in each other.

"I'd love it! On the Heights perhaps. And a modern house."

After a search, they found just what they wanted; five acres on a hilltop overlooking the lake.

As they drove home after a consultation with an architect, Mark said lightly, "I wish I could build a new business as easily as a house."

He had discovered quickly enough that having control of the business did not necessarily mean having control of its operation. The Holmes Lumber Company was going on just as before.

"I wish grandfather hadn't left me stock in the business," he said. "I'll never find it anything more than a grind."

"Then for heaven's sake, get out," Faith suggested. "Find work that'll be more agreeable. This is the time."

He brightened. "I've had a couple of interesting talks with Allan Griswold. In his spare time he's been working on the plans for a new engine."

"Dad says they have a great respect for Griswold at Wolverine. He's considered an engineering wizard."

"Faith, I've been thinking—I'm now in the position to finance the development of this engine. As long as he's tied to Wolverine, Allan will never have the time or money to finish it."

"Well, darling, this looks like your big chance."

In May, Pauley and his associates were pleased to buy out Mark's holdings. They had been waiting for this opportunity a long time.

8. Everybody was making money in 1929—although much of the spectacular profits was on paper only. The new brokerage office on Town Square was a beehive, men and women swarming before the board, growing more and more excited as their stocks soared skyward. Speculation was no longer only the rich man's prerogative. Now the little fellow on the street, the clerk, the postman, the mechanic, was pouring his savings in the torrent, denying himself the necessities of today, a pair of shoes or a shirt, for the probable luxury of a new car tomorrow.

With this heady prosperity, St. Croix got its face lifted. New modern stores on Main Street; an ornate movie palace; a dance hall. Every night was Saturday night, the restaurants jammed, the crowds jostling good-naturedly, anxious to spend the easy money. Everybody feeling hunky dory! Good pay, new car, stocks on the up and up.

It's the Hoover prosperity and we're richer than ever!

New housing developments mushroomed on the Heights; neat white bungalows in the four-thousand, nine-hundred-and-fifty-dollar class with names like Dreamwood Gardens, Cottswold and Lake Vista. A car blossomed in every garage, brightly lacquered Fords and Chevvies aping their richer cousins—the Cadillacs and Lincolns at the Country Club. Wolverine Motors was selling at 205, and Zeb Whiting, the president, built himself a huge English Tudor place beyond the golf links. Lewis Trout enlarged his celluloid plant and imported Negro help from Georgia to replace the arrogant white laborers. His wife Madeline sported the first Russian sable coat in St. Croix.

In the midst of this yeasty industrial expansion, Mark thought optimistically, I can't miss!

He brought Allan Griswold to the bank, where they met with Mr. Sinclair, Eben's lawyer, and Mr. Everett, president of the bank, to outline the proposed new venture. Mark would put up the capital to build a shop for further experimentations on Allan's engine, provide the necessary staff and equipment. If things went according to schedule, they hoped to be in production within a year.

Both Sinclair and Everett approved of the project. After the meeting, Everett asked Mark to wait.

"What are you doing with the stocks your grandfather left you?" he inquired.

"Why, I've just been holding on to them. They're good, aren't they? Railroads and utilities . . ."

"Yes, they're good. Very good indeed. But you are not getting enough return on your investment. You'll be needing money for your business, too. I know of a very good thing. . . ."

Mark promised to consult Faith, and if she were agreeable, trade the stocks for a block of Insull Utilities Investments Corporation.

Everett was pleased. "Smart move," he said. "You won't regret it."

They decided to postpone the building of their own home until Mark had the arrangements for the plant under way. And again, this summer, Faith saw little of him.

But she saw plenty of Joyce Griswold.

Evenings, while Mark and Allan pored over blueprints, Joyce brought the baby over and made herself comfortable for the duration of the conferences. Since the formation of the partnership between Mark and her husband, some of her original awe and admiration for Faith had been transformed into a rather cloying intimacy.

"I do hope this contraption of Allan's makes us the fortune he promised me," she said.

Mark was paying Allan the same salary he had drawn at Wolverine; besides this, he was to share fifty-fifty in the profits. But Joyce felt Allan should be getting more money now. The house on Sycamore Street wasn't nearly large enough to accommodate them in their now station. She needed a maid. After all, Allan couldn't expect her to give the baby all the attention he deserved, and do the housework, too! She had gained twenty pounds since her confinement, and she reminded Faith of a Flemish Madonna, placid and bovine. There was nothing spiritual about her thinking, either. She was a very practical woman.

"We must start saving for Junior's education," she decided. "I want my child to have everything I missed."

At three months, Allan Junior weighed fifteen pounds and looked like an unbaked bun. Joyce carried him with her everywhere. "I don't trust strangers to stay with him," she said darkly. It was apparent that all her devotion was now focused on the child. Allan had sired it, but as far as she was concerned, the baby was completely and exclusively her own.

How can a brilliant man like Allan put up with such a stupid woman, Faith wondered.

Mark had an answer. Mark felt that since Allan lived almost entirely in his own technical world, he was blind to a woman's faults as well as her virtues. He ate what Joyce set before him, slept in her bed, and was blandly impervious to her complaints or blandishments.

The more intimate she became with Faith, the more exacting her demands—in the name of friendship, of course. She was not averse to inviting herself to the Holmes house for the entire day. It was much cooler in the secluded Holmes garden than in the sun-scorched back yard on Sycamore Street. And Faith had plenty of help, a cook and a maid. So it wasn't expecting too much, really, to be asked for lunch and tea, too; and to have the snooty maid heat the baby's bottles.

Occasionally, when she had an appointment at Marie's Beauty Shoppe for a shampoo and blond rinse, she asked Faith to mind Junior.

"You're the only one I'd trust him with," she said, as if this were an accolade.

Although Faith would never have admitted it to Joyce, who was, heaven knew, smug and superior as it was, she looked forward to taking care of the child. He was lumpy and ungainly. He had no personality. But the joy of holding him in her arms was almost more than she could bear.

This is what I have missed, she thought, as they played in the cool garden one afternoon. She had spread a blanket on the grass under the maple. Junior, in shirt and diapers, was lying on his stomach, kicking his plump little legs and cooing like a dove. He was so sweet! She closed her eyes and tried to picture what Mark's child would have been. Dark, probably, with a long narrow body, gray eyes and black lashes. Sensitive, like his father; shy, quick to hide his emotions. She tried to stifle the agonizing pain. There would be no children, dark, intense, sensitive, like Mark. There would be no children.

Dr. Savage had had to repeat it before she would believe him. Before she could make herself face it.

"You're sensible and intelligent," Dr. Savage had said. "You must learn to make a life for yourself without your own children. After all, you and Mark have a most unusual relationship."

Was that enough? Enough for a normal young woman, who had been expecting babies as her birthright? I must make it suffice, she thought. If I show any signs of unhappiness, it will only hurt Mark. . . .

If only she had some absorbing work! Her household chores took up only a small part of her day and left her with time to brood, especially about her mother. She was not in the least interested in returning to her old social routine. So there was no outlet for her abundant energies.

"Mark, isn't there something I can do to help you in your business?"

"I'm afraid not," regretfully.

She sighed. "I do wish I had some kind of a job."

"Faith, why don't you go back to *The Observer*? I'm sure Vrest will find a place for you."

Macklin greeted her cordially. Since Eben Holmes's fatal illness, he had seen little of her and Mark. The past year has made a great change in her, he thought. Two tragic blows have taken their bitter toll. There was a touching maturity about her now, as if the process which nature had so recently begun was coming to premature fruition. She was only twenty-three, but already some of the bloom was gone from her radiant personality.

"Are you serious about a job, Faith? Or is it to be merely another stopgap?"

"I have no idea, Vrest." She was honest. "But I must keep busy. And I was so happy here in the old days!"

"Why?" curiously.

She smiled. "Maybe because it's sort of an inspiration working for you. You never let your people get into a rut."

"What do you want to do this time?"

"Meet people, talk to 'em, write about 'em. I'm still a pushover for people."

"What does Mark say to your taking a job?"

"Oh, he suggested it. I wouldn't have come without his approval."

Vrest sucked on his corncob pipe.

"You're hired," he said.

She had been on the paper four weeks now. And she loved every minute of it. *The Observer* had grown with the town, and its influence stretched far beyond it. The simplicity and logic of Vrest's editorials cut through sham and false ideologies like an acid knife.

Faith knew she was fortunate to be working with him again. This time she created a place for herself. With Vrest's blessing, she turned roving reporter, interviewing newsworthy visitors, hunting out human interest in the daily events of the town. She found the actual interviews stimulating, but the writing an exhausting chore.

Mark was delighted with her absorbing interest in her job, and relieved, too. Since he could spend so little time with her, it was a source of considerable satisfaction to know she was busy and happy. She needed an outlet for her pent-up energies. Particularly now.

Chapter Nine

1. Every first and third Friday of the month, promptly at noon, a group of St. Croix businessmen dropped whatever tasks they were doing and headed for the banquet room of the Lake Shore Hotel.

After checking their coats and hats, they filed noisily into the fraternal chamber, stopping first before a canvas bulletin board studded with round white celluloid buttons lettered O.G.F. Each man snared a pin, speared it on his left lapel, and found his assigned place at the U-shaped table amid much laughter and kidding. But the talk blurred into silence as they remained standing and looked to their Grand Master, Mr. Carpenter, at the place of honor. On the plastered wall behind him hung a black felt banner inscribed with the words in white: *Order of Good Fellowship.* Underneath the lettering, there was an embossed circle with the insignia of a handclasp, like a Victorian valentine.

Mr. Carpenter, head of Carpenter and Smilley, Auditors, nodded his portly gray head. At this signal, each man turned stiffly to his neighbor on the right and gave him the secret salute: a warm handclasp, followed in quick order by 1) a slap on the back, 2) a poke in the ribs, 3) a conspiratorial wink. Then they chanted in off-key voices the pledge of eternal friendship.

This was the Order of Good Fellowship, an organization ranking second only to the Elks in St. Croix. Its members, hell-bent for good fellowship and civic virtue, and hoping incidentally to reap a little extra business on the side, included Joe Simpson, the real-estate broker; Spike Hennessy, manager of the Ford Motor Agency; Alf Chandler, the insurance man; Karl Kraus, the butcher; Doc Pugliese, the vet; Mike Burnside, the druggist; Jack Wertheimer of the Bon Ton; Griffith, Calabresi, Mankiewicsz, and others. There wasn't one called Babbitt, nor one who didn't make fun of his wife's Sewing Circle.

While the waiters cleared the table, Mr. Carpenter rapped for order.

"Fellas, today's the first Friday in December. You know what that means. It's time to take inventory—of the folks who aren't as lucky as us. Now, I happen to know we've all had a pretty good year." He cleared his throat. "The Lord has filled our coffers—and I have the statistics to prove it."

(Much laughter. As chief accountant, Mr. Carpenter knew the extent of everybody's business.)

"Now, don't get upset because your stocks may have taken a drop in the last coupla months. I always say, '*Everything that goes down must come up.*'"

(Applause.)

"Now, fellas, to paraphrase a great poet, 'Open thy heart.' I'm not asking you to open your hearts. All I want is for you to dig down deep in your jeans. The 'filthy lucre's' going for a worthy cause!"

When he had finished, they pushed back their chairs and arose. Each man extended his arms, embracing his neighbors, until they formed a chain. Then, on a signal from Mr. Carpenter, they began to sway in unison, like a group of fat chorus girls who had lost the knack for precision.

"For we're the jolly Good Fellows!" they sang lustily. "For we're the jolly Good Fellows!"

Stuffed with chicken patty, creamed peas, soggy apple pie and good will, they saluted in the final secret clasp. And then filed out.

The white celluloid buttons (manufactured by the Trout Celluloid Company) drooped on the canvas board until the next session.

The annual Christmas party the Order of Good Fellowship gave for the Underprivileged Children of St. Croix was the big event in the lives of the children themselves—the undernourished, sallow kids from the tenement district around the docks.

After a fashion, it played considerable importance in the lives of the members of the Good Fellowship group, too. As Mr. Carpenter always said, it made you think of the Christ Child to see those poor kiddies swarming around the table, shoveling in the turkey and fixings. How they could eat! With sweet humility, the wives of the members served the dinner with their own hands. And afterwards, going home, they kept thinking of those pinched childish faces, suffused with unusual color, the dark eyes sparkling like bits of anthracite, the thin little hands clutching greedily at the cornucopias of candy, oranges and toys. It did your heart good to watch them, the women said, feeling a lot better when they sat down to their own ample tables, surrounded by their own families. It made the tinsel star of Bethlehem burn all the brighter on the peak of the tree, shedding a glow of fraternal love right back in the hearts of the benefactors themselves.

The only trouble, Mr. Carpenter reiterated each Christmas, was that there seemed to be more and more underprivileged children.

Obviously the wrong kind of people were coming to town.

2. Faith covered the Christmas party for *The Observer*. She typed the story, handed it to Vrest Macklin and went over to the hot plate to brew some coffee. How different this Christmas was from the ones when Eben was alive. He had always made it the occasion for true festivity.

Mark was working late tonight.

I've got the blues, she thought.

Vrest Macklin pushed up the spectacles that had slipped down his short blunt nose, and reread Faith's copy. It was good. It was honest, passionate and excoriating. It packed a wallop.

She slanted it through the eyes of Micky Sermalino, aged seven, of lower Ontario Place. His father made twenty dollars a week, and there were eight hungry Sermalino mouths to fill. But the cold, hunger, suffering, and rheumatic fever, were forgotten on Christmas Eve, when the good kind people of St. Croix gave Micky and his brothers a party. When the kids gazed at the star high on the tree . . .

This wasn't the Rentschler brand of sob stuff, Vrest realized with great satisfaction. This merely shows up a society that lets children go hungry and sick all year, then turns paternalistic for one day, and basks in its own benevolence for the other three hundred and sixty-four days.

He relit the corncob pipe and sucked at the stem reflectively. He'd have to talk to Faith. Show her that society was no better than its components. Just as black and white particles whirled in a mixer will produce gray, so each man was a conglomerate of good and evil, integrity and weakness, honor and corruption. No man was a complete villain, any more than an embodiment of complete virtue. A whim of circumstance, and the saint turns sinner!

"Vrest, is the story okay?"

He looked up, still enmeshed in his thoughts. "It's pretty strong meat, Faith."

"It's meant to be."

"You won't change anything by it. And you may offend a lot of well-meaning people."

"But it's the truth!" Her eyes flashed. "And if the well-meaning people can't take it, they should do something for the kids with rickets, adenoids, bad teeth every day of the year—instead of once. It makes me sick to think of it."

"I expect it does. But there's much more in the world that's sickening."

"Then why isn't something done about it?"

"Faith, as you get older, you'll find that shouting from the housetops does absolutely no good. No good at all. You've got to attack injustice in a more subtle way."

Her contempt for his words was obvious. "I suppose that means you won't use the story."

He pulled off his spectacles, without which his heavy face was defenseless and weary.

"Of course, I'll use it. We'll let the brickbats fall where they may."

Vrest was good for her. She was continuously learning from him. He helped her understand that while the world made fabulous strides forward in science, it wasn't doing so well sociologically.

"Here we *do* make progress, too," he added, "but not at the same pace. And not without sliding back. Its a couple of steps forward—and one back. But we mustn't lose heart. The point is that we *are* moving ahead. And in time . . ."

3. Faith's story appeared Christmas Day on the front page of *The Observer*. There were immediate repercussions. The pleasure of the Order of Good Fellowship in having its generosity publicized turned quickly to fury.

Mr. Carpenter reflected the general reactions when he said tartly, "You do your best—and that's the thanks you get!"

"I'd like to give that woman a piece of my mind," he growled to his wife over their hearty Christmas dinner. He had already telephoned Vrest Macklin and told him plenty. "You and your damn Socialist ideas! I'll see that you don't get another line of advertising from any member of our lodge!" But Macklin wasn't perturbed. He said he'd been threatened before.

So Mr. Carpenter marched up Manistee Drive and through the Holmes gate, rehearsing his words. Belligerently he pressed the bell. A maid in a black alpaca uniform opened the door, and he caught a glimpse of a richly furnished hall complete with a pipe organ that belonged in a church. He had never before stepped over the Holmes threshold. Neither he, nor any of his friends. He made a mental inventory; his wife would surely ask him all sorts of questions.

Suddenly he saw Faith Holmes coming toward him. She was wearing a soft green velvet lounging suit, caught at the waist with a wide gold kid belt. Her burnished hair was brushed off her ears, and there was such a vivid aura about her that Mr. Carpenter decided she was much more beautiful than he'd ever realized.

"I'm so glad you're here, Mr. Carpenter. I do want to talk to you. Come in and meet my husband."

Her cordiality disarmed him. He followed her into the sitting room, feeling his anger slipping away. Mark Holmes shook hands with him, then excused himself. Faith filled a silver mug for him from the bowl of eggnog on the low table and cut a slice of fruitcake.

"Mr. Carpenter," she asked earnestly, "do you have children?"

He cleared his throat. "Yes. Two girls and a boy." Then he remembered the reason for his call. "I didn't come to talk about my family."

"I know, Mr. Carpenter. But I'm sure your children have had all the milk, vitamins and food to make them healthy adults."

He made an effort to interrupt, but she continued smoothly, "I'm sure your original motive was most commendable, Mr. Carpenter. But it takes more than a turkey dinner one day of the year to put flesh on those undernourished kids. What you should do is to underwrite a milk fund. Such an act would give your organization tremendous prestige. And think what it would mean to the children, each to receive a pint of milk a day . . ."

"Sounds like a pretty good idea, Mrs. Holmes. I'll be glad to speak of it at our next meeting. . . ."

"May I be the first to subscribe?" she said impulsively. "I'd like to give you my check for a hundred dollars."

"Thank you. I've an idea it'll go through." He decided that if his lodge members raised any objections, he'd ask Faith Holmes to talk to them. By God, she'd make 'em see the light!

Later in the afternoon, when Vrest Macklin dropped in, Faith related triumphantly the results of Mr. Carpenter's visit.

"It's still cold charity," Vrest said, brushing a crumb of fruitcake from his spotted vest. "No wrong has been righted."

"But it's a step in the right direction," she retorted. "Another step forward—instead of one going back!"

4. New Year's Eve, Faith invited Vrest and the Griswolds over for the evening. As the maid showed Vrest into the drawing room, he

saw Mark and Faith standing together by the fireplace, and it was an impression which would stay with him for many years: Mark, tall and lean, his shoulders a little stooped, his face alert and intelligent, his deep-set gray eyes sensitive and kind. And Faith, almost as tall in those absurd French heels, her expression lively but not quite as vivacious as in the old days; the two of them together, safe within the charmed circle that excluded any intruders. Yes, it was a successful marriage; decidedly so. Much better, Vrest mused, than we had dared hope for.

"Hello, Mark," he said warmly. "How are things going?"

"Couldn't be better!" optimistically. "By the time we get into production, I think the stock market will have righted itself. Everett is positive of it."

"I hope you're both right," Vrest answered.

The Griswolds arrived soon after, Allan lugging Junior, swathed in a heavy blue bunting.

"We'll put him on your bed," Joyce announced, to Faith, who led the way upstairs. "He'll go right to sleep."

"He's a good baby," Faith said approvingly.

Joyce slipped out of her white fur jacket with a distasteful gesture. "Next year at this time, I'll be wearing ermine instead of bunny. Allan promised me."

Faith was staring at the placid sleeping child. "How nice," she said absently.

But Joyce was in a cozy confidential mood. "For the first time now, I can honestly say I'm glad I married Allan. I wasn't so sure about it when he was courting me. Another fellow was just crazy about me—his father had a big garage and storage place, loads of money. But he was sort of peculiar. I mean, he thought the girl should do the chasing. So I settled on Allan—even though it didn't look as if he'd be much of a provider." She smiled to herself. "It just goes to show you."

"It may be another six months before any money comes in," Faith warned her.

Joyce ignored it. "Where did you get your beaver coat? Do you think the Fashion Shop is as good as Waycross in Great Falls?"

"Every bit as good. And when you're ready to buy, I'll introduce you to Leah Parker. She's the manager now. She'll look after you."

Dinner was excellent, the roast beef rare, the Yorkshire pudding light, the wines full-bodied, the talk inspired, especially by Vrest Macklin, who was, Mark often said, everyman's intelligent guide to a stimulating evening. Afterwards, they had coffee in the drawing room. Joyce made herself cozy on a petit-point stool, her sturdy back resting heavily against Allan's thin spindly legs. Faith had never before seen her so solicitous of her husband.

Mark switched on the radio.

"Folks," the announcer began, "in another hour it will be midnight. A new year will be born. 1930!"

"The end of the Cockeyed Twenties," Mark said, not without regret.

"Quite right." Vrest put down the crystal champagne glass and filled his corncob pipe with pungent tobacco. "We've finally reached the end of a hectic decade in which we hitched our wagon to the Almighty Dollar. It's been running away with us in a mad race to perdition. We Americans are pretty damn sick now—and we need a purge!"

Inwardly, Joyce groaned. That old windbag. Why do the Holmeses bother with him?

Allan Griswold spoke up suddenly. "It's the women who have gone on a rampage during this decade! Bobbed hair, short skirts, loose morals . . ."

"Why, Allan Griswold!" his wife exclaimed indignantly. "Don't you dare make any cracks about us poor women!"

Mark grinned. "He was discussing the ladies in general, Joyce. I think he'd like them to return to the sensible ways of the pre-war era."

"It's too late for that!" Faith retorted, and found to her surprise she was very much more in earnest than the others. "Women have really come of age, you know. I don't mean in the matter of the vote alone. In general, they are now emancipated."

"Yeh," Allan jeered good-humoredly. "Emancipation! What's it got them? They fought like wildcats for the privilege of voting—and what have they done with it?"

Vrest Macklin leaned forward, his chubby face flushed with wine. "I rather doubt if political equality means nearly as much to the individual woman as the fact that she's become man's equal. The fact truly important to her is the freedom of her sex—the right to stand at a bar, or sit in an office, side by side with men. I think this is purely an aftermath of the war, and has little to do with her gaining the vote. . . ."

"But, Vrest," Faith interrupted, "you do feel women should have the vote?"

"Certainly! They should have had it years ago."

Joyce yawned. "Why all the fuss? Personally, I think this business of women voting is terribly unfeminine. After all, it *is* a man's world!"

Mark replenished the champagne. "Women are entitled to their new-found freedom—if they don't go overboard in their enthusiasm."

"Mark," Joyce began sententiously, "how would you act if Faith were a really modern woman—with a career and moral standards of her own?"

Mark sent Faith a faint wink.

"I'd turn her over my knee," he announced firmly. "And show her who's boss."

Happy New Year! Ring out the old year, ring in the new! Farewell to the gaudy ribald twenties! Hail to sanity, to hope of a Brave New World!

Lying beside Mark, aware of his easy regular breathing and the comforting warmth of his body, Faith was filled with a sense of tenderness and gratitude to him. Still, her mind persisted in mulling over the evening's talk.

Was Vrest right? Did the privilege of being man's equal socially and morally, in a speakeasy, over a business lunch, on an extra-marital couch, gratify women more than the satisfaction of gaining the franchise? Why hadn't women done more with their latent political powers? Vrest's words stung. Yet she knew he was not likely to have made an unfair accusation.

She fell asleep, having solved nothing.

5. Elisha Jones was a Georgia Negro, born and raised in a weather-beaten hovel in a patch of pine woods right on the macadam road, U.S. 17.

Elisha went to the Negro school, and when he fell out after the fourth grade, nobody fussed much except his mother. He did odd jobs in town—busboy in a restaurant frequented by Northerners on their way to Florida.

That's where he got his first inkling of the difference between white folks of the North and South.

At eighteen he went to work in the turpentine mill. He worked hard, never got drunk Saturday night, never got into a razor fight, a nice honest colored boy. His mama should've been proud of him. But she was always nagging. Get out of Georgia. Go up North. You heard what Flora's children said. No Jim Crow cars. No nigger heaven. Chance for a decent, law-abiding Negro to live in dignity and safety. No sleepless nights for his mama when there's talk of a lynching party, or a fiery-red cross burning in the hills.

Elisha's mama was awful insistent, but he paid her no mind till he married Lily. Then Elisha got to listening to his old friends, home on vacation between jobs, sporting fine clothes, a car, a fistful of dollars to shoot craps. When he and mama and Lily went to church and sang "Go Down, Moses," he'd speculate on the Promised Land, and he'd conjure up a vision of himself and Lily in a little house, painted white, like the folks in town had. The white folks.

When the white man came from the North, somewhere in Michigan, it was, to round up men for work in a celluloid factory, Elisha cocked his ear.

Good pay, the white man said. Fifteen bucks a week. A house, the white man said, swell house, all to yourself. Black boy, you'll be sittin' on top o' the world. Right up there in front!

Elisha came to work for Lewis Trout in 1928.

In the beginning, fifteen bucks a week looked like a lot of dough, even though he had to pay Mr. Trout ten for the house they lived in. St. Croix had no Darkytown on the other side of the tracks, which made him and Lily feel real good, until they found out the Darkytown existed right around Mr. Trout's plant.

"I like it," Lily said fiercely. "I like it fine." This was after they had heard Elisha's brother was caught and beaten by a mob near Macon. Lily took in washing to help out.

The celluloid factory was a long building, part weather-beaten clapboard, part brick. The windows on the ground floor were barred.

Elisha worked in a room with five boys from Mississipppi. They used to kid each other about getting roasted—on account of the flash fires. One of the fellows said, "This joint ain't run right. They oughta break it up in small buildings with fire doors. Like the place I worked at in Delaware. An' they oughta git their own fire department. . . ."

The signs read: *No Smoking. Danger.* But they sneaked out for a drag plenty of times. Finally the old white man who checked them in and out snitched. The order came down from the office: five minutes for the toilet morning and afternoon. The boss ordered a watchman stationed in the corridor outside their door, which was locked until he opened it for the five-minute breather. Might as well be in the chain gang, the fellows grumbled.

Elisha never told Lily about it. No use upsetting her, with the second baby coming soon. He worked hard and stoically. Colored boys didn't complain.

At three minutes of ten on the morning of January 19, 1930, the boy from Mississippi leaped from his vat with a frightened shout. There was a spontaneous flash of flame. And instantly the room was ablaze.

"The door!" Elisha screamed. "Open the door!"

They pounded on the heavy door. Ten fists beating hysterically, begging for help.

Where was the watchman who was supposed to guard them? Why didn't he unlock the door?

They groped through the smoke to the windows. They splintered the glass with their bare hands.

"Fire!" they shrieked. "Help, *help!*"

The siren started its piercing wail. Smoke and fumes billowed from the room. Elisha thrust his bleeding hands through the jagged glass in supplication. People were rushing to the building, but they were still far away. Too far away. He strained toward them with all his might. The smoke gagged him but he struggled frantically.

The bars held him back.

6. Vrest Macklin slouched at his desk, drinking his fourth cup of coffee when the call came in. He called to Don Adams, "Fire at Trout's!"

Faith pricked her ears. "Wait a minute, Don. I'm coming with you!" She snatched her tweed coat and rushed out to the Ford, jumping into the front seat beside him. Adams stepped on the gas. They heard the harsh clang of the fire engines, the screaming dirge of the ambulances. Long before they reached the plant, they saw the heavy black smoke mushrooming to the sky.

He parked the car, and they ran toward the burning building. Flames were leaping high in the air. Smoke was black and acrid.

"Stand back!" a policeman shouted brusquely. Adams held out his press card, and they were allowed through. Faith rubbed her smarting eyes with the knuckles of her hand. Firemen were working frantically, hacking away at the brick sills of the groundfloor windows.

She stared, paralyzed with horror.

"Don!" she called hoarsely. "Do you see what I do? Those windows —they're *barred!*"

Men were struggling wildly to get out, their arms spread-eagled against the bars, their hands clawing madly, their bulging eyes glazed with terror. The firemen hacked away, the black smoke poured deadly fumes in the men's lungs.

A dying Negro spied Faith.

"Help me, ma'am," he begged. "Don't let me die!"

She heard him. And lost all sense of reason. Heedless of the mob, she elbowed her way toward the flaming building, guided by an instinct stronger than reason.

A policeman grabbed her roughly. "You nuts, lady?" A strident voice yelled, "Get outa here!"

The screaming grew weaker. Died away.

When finally she dared to look back, the window was a blackened hole.

Adams found her, finally, huddled in the car. The eerie light cast green shadows over her stricken face.

"I'll never forget this," she whispered. "I'll never forget it as long as I live."

"Take it easy, Mrs. Holmes," Adams said, trying to soothe her. "Soon as I've phoned in the story, we'll get ourselves some coffee. Do you good."

He led her across the Highway to the Busy Bee Diner. She sat on a stool at the counter, clutching a heavy mug of coffee in her shaking hands. Her eyes reflected the shock she had suffered.

"They never had a chance," Adams said bitterly. "Door locked. Windows barred. Watchman off duty. They fried, those guys."

He gulped the scalding coffee, and his eyes grew sharp and bitter. "No wonder Lewis Trout can't get white men to work for him."

Faith was still trembling. The memory of the young Negro's frantic appeal obsessed her. She couldn't get it out of her mind. Violent death, needless death, in the Promised Land of Lewis Trout. And Madeline Trout would buy a new platinum fox jacket without a qualm.

When she faced Vrest Macklin again, he realized she was not the same girl who had left the office two hours ago. She had been baptized. Cruelly.

"I saw men die today," she said. "And there was no excuse for their dying." Abruptly her forced calm broke, and she was sobbing. "Oh, Vrest, it was *horrible.* . . ."

He knew he must not allow her to go home in this state. Sensitive though Mark was, he might not be able to give her the comfort and reassurance she so desperately needed now.

So he suggested that she and Mark dine with him tonight, and then he kept her occupied with another task until six o'clock. When Mark arrived at the office, they went over to Vrest's apartment at the Lake Shore Hotel. Faith had scrubbed her face and put on fresh lipstick, but the horror still haunted her eyes and the smell of smoke clung to her beige tweed suit.

"What's wrong, Faith?" Mark asked, as Vrest poured sherry. "You seem upset."

She explained graphically. "I only hope Trout gets what is coming to him."

"In a factory like his," Vrest said, "spontaneous combustion does occur often. It's one of the hazards of the business. However, there is no question that the workers should have been safeguarded."

"Vrest," she began ominously, "did you know Lewis Trout locked the men in—and put them under guard—so he could get the maximum amount of work out of them?"

"No. Not specifically. But I've suspected it. The average white man won't work for him."

"And yet you never spoke up?" she continued relentlessly. "How do you differ from the Rentschler papers for whom you have such contempt?"

Mark touched her arm, warning her. "Calm down, Faith. Vrest is too sensible to tilt at windmills. After all, what can one man alone do?"

"He can speak up—as he's spoken up on other things. Trout mustn't be allowed to get away with this!"

His pride in her was mingled with pity. But Mark realized his girl was growing up, ready to accept what he had never been articulate enough to explain, that a man like Lewis Trout was predatory, and his greed and lust tainted everyone and everything they touched.

"Is this going to end as merely another headline: SIX NEGROES DIE IN FIRE?" she demanded passionately. "Vrest, aren't you going to do anything about it?"

Vrest thought unhappily, I must be growing old. I had almost forgotten how deeply hurt I was at her age. How loudly I protested against injustice in the world. I, too, made each stranger's hurt my own. I, too, gloried in my suffering, and dedicated myself to the hopeless fight. . . .

But with maturity, he had learned. It had taken time, but in the end he was ready to concede that human nature could not be changed overnight. The best one could do was to contribute one's mite to the Good Fight, and hope one day posterity would benefit from the accrued results.

How could he impart this bitterly acquired knowledge to Faith, who was still so young, so zealous, so impassioned? How could he make her see that when youth is replaced by maturity, one still fights on—but less emotionally; riding the current, instead of bucking it?

He arose clumsily from his chair and went over to the sofa, where she was sitting, bewildered and desolate.

"Open your eyes slowly, Faith. The birth of the spirit is every bit as agonizing as the birth of the flesh. Open your eyes slowly, so you won't be shocked by what they see."

She moved restlessly. "I wish I could find it as simple as that."

He sighed. "Faith, do you remember the Sacco-Vanzetti case?"

For a moment she looked blank. "Weren't those the men electrocuted in Massachusetts?"

"Yes. A *cause célèbre* only three years ago. And already you've forgotten."

He took her hand in his. "Listen to me, my dear. Each day, somewhere, there's another Sacco-Vanzetti, another Leo Frank, another Dreyfus—a martyr dying every minute! The woman crucified by gossip—the little guy kicked out of his job for his political thinking—they're forgotten causes, too. Do you believe Great Falls, for instance, gives a damn for our six Negroes burned to death? By tomorrow, they'll be history, not even an item on the back page, buried among the ads."

He was speaking to her as he had not spoken to anyone in years; with some of the passion that went directly into his scathing editorials.

"Sacco and Vanzetti have been sent to the chair. Leo Frank's body is rotting. The act's over, folks. Go home for intermission until the next show. Maybe we'll find a human-interest story in the next Georgia lynching—that the Rentschler papers can whip up into a front-page sensation."

And he added bitterly, "Man learns so damn slowly—and forgets so very easily."

There was silence in the room.

She said soberly, "I suppose these are my growing pains." Then on an impulse, she turned to Vrest and kissed him on the cheek. "Thank you," she said. "But all the same, I'm going to see Lewis Trout."

7. She rang up the office of Lewis Trout the next morning. "This is *The Observer*," she began.

"Mr. Trout is out of town," the switchboard girl said. "We don't know when he'll return."

Ten minutes later, Faith called again. "This is Mrs. Mark Holmes. I'd like to speak with Mr. Trout."

A moment later he was on the wire, flattered that she had rung him up, and very cordial.

"Faith, my dear. What can I do for you?"

"I'd like to see you."

"Good! How about lunch?"

"I'd rather come this morning," coolly.

When she arrived at his office on Town Square, she was ushered into his private room immediately. Lewis, impeccable in a Glen-plaid suit, stood up to greet her, a smile on his handsome anonymous face.

"I'm delighted to see you, honey. Madeline was saying the other night you've been high-hatting us."

"I've been busy."

"Madeline says you're doing some things for the local paper. Fashions?"

"Human-interest stuff."

"Really?"

"Yes. That's why I'm here, Lewis."

"Well, sit down, my dear. Cigarette?"

"No thanks." She remained standing.

He slipped the thin platinum case in his pocket. Behind the bland smile he was watching her shrewdly.

"I gather you're here because of yesterday's unfortunate accident? Well, you can quote me as saying I am deeply shocked. And grieved. But such things do happen in spite of all our precautions. The human element." He shrugged eloquently. "We'll take care of the families, of course."

"Why were all exits barred?" Her eyes blazed. "Why did you watch those men like prisoners? And why was the guard away from his station?"

He watched a smoke ring dissolve in thin air.

"Where did you hear this?"

She made no answer.

Trout snuffed out his cigarette. His eyes were cold and dangerous.

"I mean to make this perfectly clear to you, Faith. That accident need not have happened. It was the result of plain carelessness on the part of those men. We do our best to warn them. *No Smoking* signs all over the place. But one damn fool sneaks a cigarette—and we get the blame."

"Six men burned to death."

Trout made an impatient gesture.

"Look, Faith. You're a swell kid—I've always liked you. So I'm going out of my way to put you wise to the facts of life. You barge in here—mad as hops—intimating I'm all kinds of a heel. That's beside the point. . . ."

He sat on the edge of his desk, faintly amused and very sure of himself.

"What does matter is this: There's no room for sentiment in my business or in my way of life. Right now, the town's seething with talk of locked doors and guards off duty. Well, I can promise you it'll remain just talk—and nothing else. Too many of the influential people in this town owe me favors and more!"

"I wouldn't boast of such contemptible power."

He slammed his palm on the desk.

"For God's sake, grow up! It's the only way to get along in the world. Remember the time you were caught in that raid at Tony Spade's? How do you think I managed to hush it up? Through personality? Nuts! Five hundred smackers in the right palm did the trick!"

"Had I known it, I'd have preferred arrest."

"What're you trying to do? Show up the ills of the world? Better people than you have tried—and flopped!"

"Vrest Macklin won't let you get away with this!"

"Oh, Macklin." He shrugged scornfully. "He's never touched me. And he never will."

"I used to think injustice was an abstract word," she said angrily, "but *you're* injustice, Lewis. Men like you poison humanity with your corrupt stench!"

He touched the buzzer on his desk. "As a reporter for *The Observer*, you're not welcome here again."

His secretary came in and Trout nodded brusquely. The interview was over.

But going home, Faith was conscious of a bitter elation. She wrote the story of the fire. Not as a straight news feature, nor as an emotional editorial. Instead, she wrote a factual interview with Lily Jones, Elisha's wife. Lily said she would manage somehow. The man from Mr. Trout's had had her sign a paper. Then he gave her fifty dollars. Of course, she'd have to get out of the unpainted shack—another batch of boys were coming up North to work for Mr. Trout. But she'd taken in washing and done day work before. She'd look after the children, like Elisha would have wanted.

Faith's stark, simple story had repercussions. There was talk of an investigation. There was talk of revising the fire laws. There was talk. . . .

That's what it remained. Talk. Just as Lewis Trout had prophesied.

But a change had come over Faith. Up to this time she had been fighting with her intellect. Now her heart was in it. And intuitively, she knew that she had begun a climb which promised neither rest nor surcease nor inner happiness until the very pinnacle came into sight.

Chapter Ten

1. In April, Mr. Slavery, the contractor, began work on the new house. He was less busy this year. People weren't putting up any more expensive houses until the depression was over. Somehow, during the summer of '30, Faith didn't mind living in the old Holmes house as much as she had feared. For she was working hard and Mark also was engrossed in his business. The factory was finished and in the process of being equipped with machinery and tools. He expected to be in production by Labor Day. Getting this far had drained the entire sum he had realized from the sale of the lumber company. But once Holmes-Griswold was turning out engines, the bank would give him a loan.

He had asked Tod Andrews to leave Wolverine and come in with him.

"I like having your dad with me," he told Faith.

Tod was proud of his new affiliation.

"Dad, what's your opinion of the new engine?" Faith asked him confidentially.

Tod rubbed his out-jutting nose reflectively. "It looks good to me, pumpkin. But like any new motor, it's got to go through a testing period. Don't worry though. Mark knows what he's doing."

Her father's confidence reassured any doubts she might suffer.

Each morning after breakfast, Mark drove her to *The Observer.*

"I'll call you in the afternoon," he would say, "and tell you how the rest of the day shapes up."

"Do try to get home for dinner, darling. Even if you have to go back to the plant at night. You've been living on sandwiches and coffee. That's not good for you."

"We'll get back to normal soon," he promised, kissing her on the cheek. "You're a good sport, Faith. I realize how tough it's been for you."

"I suppose in the beginning every business is a jealous mistress."

"We'll make up for it," he promised.

2. Faith was working hard, too, on a new project of her own. She was revamping the Woman's Page, the only section of *The Observer* to which Vrest was indifferent. Consequently, it was no better, no worse than the woman's pages in a hundred other papers: a column on Advice to the Lovelorn; Society Notes; What to Do on Wednesday with Last Sunday's Roast; How to Improve Your Game of Bridge; Hollywood Beauty Secrets.

"It's obsolete!" Faith complained. "There's absolutely nothing on this page to appeal to an intelligent woman."

"Perhaps not," Vrest admitted. "But I've never taken an interest in it primarily because I think women are sheep. They've done nothing to throw off the yoke of tradition."

Stubbornly, Faith disagreed with him. Yet after he had gone, she remained at her desk, mulling over his words, as she had done so often in the past. Sheep, he said. Women are sheep.

She thought of Madeline Trout, who was representative of the affluent Country-Club set. What did Madeline demand of life? Clothes, jewels, new motor cars, good private schools for the children, material things, anything and everything money could buy. That, and nothing more. If Madeline had ever had a soul, it was swaddled in mink at birth.

And Winona Kraus? Winnie's voice might prove the open sesame to a new world, but Winnie's spirit was infinitely smaller than her commonplace ability, and she readily bartered her talents for what she considered the Good Things in life.

"Too many women follow the line of least resistance," Vrest had said. "They're like corks bobbing on a wave. That's the reason it is so easy to standardize them."

Perhaps he's got something there, she thought. Cloche hats, for example. Every woman wears them, girls with round faces, girls with bony faces. Because it's the style. Small mouths, big mouths—a gash of orange lipstick, like a Picasso clown. It isn't your mouth, but Joan Crawford's!

The line of least resistance, of letting somebody decide what you're to wear, what you're to eat, how you're to behave. Oh, the comfort, the blessed anonymity of being a sheep among a million sheep!

That's one of the things I'll write about, Faith decided. Ideas began to crystallize in her mind. She'd write a column. A column for women; a column to be called *As the Woman Sees It.*

As one sheep to another.

And yet—she went a step farther—if women are sheep, who is

basically at fault? The men, perhaps, who have until recently considered them pariahs, totally unfit to take their rightful place in the scheme of life.

I know just where to start, she thought excitedly.

And on August 17, 1930, *The Observer* carried her first column.

"Your name is Mary Smith or Susan Meggs or Penelope Van Dusen. Your birth certificate may carry a date that marks you sixteen or sixty. But in either case, it lies. For you have just come of age. And are, I hope, rarin' to go!

"You're determined at last to take your rightful place in the world. You know the going will be hard. No man's going to help you in the fight. Not when he's kept you enslaved so long. 'Come out of the Kitchen' should be more than a mere musical-comedy title. Let's make it our slogan for going places and doing things—for the betterment of Women!"

The feminine readers were delighted with her article. Even Vrest admitted it had possibilities. True, it was young, clumsy, impassioned, even a little arbitrary and absurd, but it was honest and stimulating. It carried a barb. Her words brought up images most women could grasp easily. After the first column, she never sermonized again so obviously. Like the description of the Christmas party for the underprivileged children, she let the cold facts speak for themselves.

As a result, hotel lunches were served to school children at cost; a Visiting Nurses Association was formed; playgrounds were kept open all summer and supervised. And the women in town became conscious of themselves as a united force for good.

Vrest Macklin said she was the best mouthpiece the women of St. Croix had.

She still struggled with the actual writing, for she found it difficult to string words together, a fault doubly exasperating because she was such a fluent speaker. After dinner, she slaved over her column while Mark worked on his business reports.

Since she read the *A.P.* and *U.P.* stories coming in, she had a realistic picture of the business slump. But Mark was not too pessimistic.

"If you have a good product," he repeated stubbornly, "you can always sell it."

3. Their new house, a modern whitewashed brick, was completed in September and they made plans to move on October first. There was so

much for Faith to do; shopping for new furniture, drapes, accessories; closing the old Holmes place.

"I wish I could help," Mark said apologetically. "But I'm tied up."

"I'll manage, darling."

She sandwiched the chores in between her work at the paper. Most of the tapestries and paintings were sent over to the library, but Faith kept a Sisley landscape and a Renoir nude for the new living room. A good part of the collection of Georgian silver, linens and china she packed in huge cases to be put in storage.

The old house would be closed and boarded up.

The final night of their stay on Manistee Drive, she said thoughtfully, "I'm afraid I'm going to miss the old place."

"Habit or sentiment?" he asked.

But she knew he was even more deeply touched for his roots were here and it was not easy to say goodbye.

Late the following afternoon they drove to the Heights, and when at last they saw their new home silhouetted against the brilliant sunset, they were filled with great pride. It was their very own, and their future would lend it personality and character.

They had a leisurely dinner on a card table set up in the living room, and afterwards they went out on the terrace and watched the evening star winking in the dark sky.

Mark put his arm around her shoulder. "Happy?"

"Unbelievably so."

"We've a lot to look forward to. Once business gets going, we'll blow ourselves to a trip. You've always wanted to see Paris. . . ."

Upstairs, the new maid was turning down the beds.

4. Within a fortnight, the house was in order, the modern pieces arranged side by side with the antiques; the books stacked in the small handsome library; their large collection of records in place; the routine well organized, so she could leave for her job each morning confident the house would be clean, the meals well cooked and served on time. It was all very efficient and pleasant.

Yet as the year progressed, she wondered why dreams were always so much sweeter than reality.

For one thing, she found herself disturbed by the change in Mark's attitude. She would come on him, sitting in his easy chair, utterly preoccupied. He spoke little of his plans these days, and even less of the future.

There had been setbacks, she knew. The completed engine had been approved nine months later than they had anticipated. And now that they were all set for production, new problems loomed up. Mark needed money. Mr. Everett, president of the bank, hedged. Business was bad. They dared take no more chances. However, once Mark showed him bona-fide orders, they would grant him a loan.

Mark went to New York, seeking to interest aviation plants in the motor. Everywhere he received the same answer. We've heard of your engine. It sounds okay. But right now, we're retrenching. When business picks up, get in touch with us.

He tried to dispose of the old Holmes place, but there wasn't even a nibble. Finally he said, "Faith, I'm going to have to sell our Insull stock."

"But, Mark—our nest egg!"

This was the first time she'd ever questioned his decisions.

"I've got to keep the plant running until conditions improve."

"What about the northern camp? The timberland must have some value."

"Not these days. But I'll try. I'm supposed to see Everett again in December."

Under such unhappy circumstances, the new house was a burden. And she felt curiously cheated.

5. The news that Wolverine Motors was laying off men came on the morning Mark was due at the bank to see the board about the new loan. He drove downtown with considerable misgivings.

Precisely at eleven o'clock, five directors' chairs were drawn out from the long polished directors' table in the board room of the bank, and five men sat down. They might have been turned out of the same mold: conservative dark suits, white shirts, starched collars, subdued four-in-hand ties.

They were waiting.

Five minutes later, a nattily dressed man strode in, an urbane smile on his good-looking anonymous face. The chairman of the board, Lewis Trout. He was a man to cultivate, he was always in a position to do you a favor. He had an "in" with Mayor Breedon, not to mention Big Bob Costello, the political boss.

The five men smiled in return.

"Gentlemen," Lewis Trout began briskly, "the first matter before us . . ."

They decided against the renewal of John Dulaney's note; they approved of the matter of new capital for the Bon Ton Department Store; then they came to Mark's application.

Lewis Trout unbuttoned his cashmere jacket, looked at them confidentially. "Gentlemen, much as it distresses me, I should like to say this: At a time when old firms are collapsing like kingpins, we've got to be mighty cautious about lending money to a new business."

"I don't agree with you, Trout," Mr. Everett said. "There's no hazard. Mark has a good product. And this recession can't last much longer. Once buiness itself is on the upswing . . ."

"Even then," Lewis retorted, "I doubt whether young Holmes is a good risk. Why didn't he stick to the Holmes Lumber Company? What right did he have to build himself a forty-thousand-dollar modern home in these times? I call that a sign of irresponsibility and poor judgment. He's squandered a fortune!"

"I consider that beside the point," Everett snapped. "He's got a good engine."

"Besides," Mr. Sinclair, the lawyer interrupted, "we mustn't forget Eben Holmes founded this bank and was the first chairman of its board. We owe young Mark every consideration we can give him!"

"Gentlemen," Lewis asked cynically, "is this a bank, or a charitable institution?"

The next day, Mark turned in the Insull stock as collateral. The loan gave him a breather. He cut his personal expenses to the bone, and reduced the force at the plant to a skeleton crew. It was a matter of hanging on. All over the country, they were pleading, *Don't sell America short!*

6. No wild festivities ushered in the new year of 1932.

The unemployed of Wolverine Motors, Lane-Crandall, Trout Celluloid, flung their last pennies in the blind tigers, on cheap gin that would bring momentary surcease. At the Country Club, they drank out of sheer bravado, out of a hysterical need to recapture the Good Old Days—only three years past—when U.S. Steel reached 260, and life was a rich gaudy merry-go-round.

The hyperthyroid activities which had made St. Croix a boom town were at a complete standstill. True, Main Street was still jammed Saturday nights. But it was crowded weekdays as well; flowing over with the Unpossessed, men not accustomed to leisure, baffled by it; frightened by empty pockets, shamed by the mute look in their wives' eyes,

a portent that credit was running low; mumbling in unhappy under-
tones, "I heard they were takin' men at the cannery, but I got there too
late. . . . Midwest Auto Body's folding. . . . Kraus won't carry me
any longer. . . . Miz Hussar's gonna get my watch soon. . . ."

That man, Hoover.

The hunger, the frustration, the bewilderment, the fear all found
a scapegoat in one man—the man with a mild plump face, so easy to
caricature, who had made the mistake of promising them a chicken in
every pot and two cars in every garage.

They say conditions will right themselves soon. Business is always
slow in an election year, though that's no sop to empty bellies. They
say veterans are selling apples on the street corners in New York.
There's talk of a bonus march, a hunger march. . . .

Down on Ontario Place, the kids on the street grew more pinched
and scrawny. And the grocer on the corner was torn between pity and
survival.

Mrs. Hussar's pawnshop was the Mecca of St. Croix.

"My business is good. Too good," she complained bitterly to Faith,
who was doing a human-interest story on the store. "I hate it! The
town's starving. Why doesn't the government do something?"

The Bon Ton advertised a slashing clearance.

The fashionable Chatterbox Café announced: *All You Can Eat
for 75¢!*

The Odeon offered an Early Bird Matinee; a dime before noon.
And it was jammed by the men who escaped reality to its comforting
darkness.

Alexis Jenkins, head of the Midwest Auto Body, used his expensive
hunting rifle on himself.

7. For the first time in her marriage, Faith was plagued now by
money problems. Until recently she had used her earnings for inci-
dentals, hairdos, luncheons, gifts for her dad, Mrs. Hussar and Mark.
But now her salary must go for household expenses. And only last
month, Vrest had been forced to slash the pay of the entire staff. Instead
of forty, she was drawing thirty dollars a week.

She taxed her ingenuity for ways in which to earn extra money.
She wrote an article, "Can Love Survive in Our Time?" and sent it off
to a New York magazine, which returned it promptly. Discouraged,
she, nevertheless, mailed it out again.

Their social life was limited these days to an occasional visit from the Griswolds. Joyce was always petulant and grumbling. Allan had promised her the moon, but she was still chained to an awful house on Sycamore Street. Privately, she confided to Faith her doubts about Allan's invention.

"It'll never amount to anything!" she wailed, "and neither will Allan. I should have known when I married him . . ."

"Don't blame Allan," Faith said. "We're in the midst of the worst depression in history."

As much as she loathed Joyce's fair-weather behavior to Allan, there were moments when she, too, feared she was losing faith. Perhaps Mark was showing too much bulldog tenacity. The times were hopeless. She wondered if it might not be wiser to face reality, to shake loose from this aborted venture, even to admit defeat—and start fresh. Mark was young, intelligent, energetic. In another field, a more active field, his talents might very easily assert themselves and bolster up his waning self-confidence.

She wished she dared suggest to him this sensible and logical way out of his troubles. But she lacked the courage.

During these difficult months, her own work was going extraordinarily well. Her column, *As the Woman Sees It,* had developed into one of the most popular features of the paper. There was plenty to write about, and she wrote with passion and simplicity. But no matter how extravagant the praise she received at the office, she lost her air of happiness whenever she returned to her home.

Mark was so moody and taciturn.

"Darling," she would say tactfully, "don't let this get you down. Please! After all, the depression can't last forever."

"Neither can we," Mark answered with grim humor.

This was the moment for her to offer sympathy and encouragement. But what she really longed to say was, "Darling, chuck this business before it ruins your health and your morale. Write it off as a bad loss!"

"If only we can hold on till conditions improve," he repeated stubbornly. "We must!"

Obviously even to him, this was no longer the great adventure with which he was going to make his name in the world. The vast plant, lying idle, demanding every dollar he could lay his hands on, was a cruel octopus, slowly crushing his body and spirit. But he refused to give in. His steadfastness was the only thing left him.

"I wish there were a way you could wipe the slate clean—and start over again," she said.

"With what? Every cent I had is tied up in the plant. And it isn't the money alone. . . ." He stood up, so gaunt and worn that her heart ached for him.

"I sink or swim by this project," he said resolutely.

Although his attitude exasperated her, she was wise enough to hold her tongue. She only hoped the article she had written, in which she stressed the fact that the economic factors of the country determine the success or failure of its people's marriages, would not, ironically enough, apply to her and Mark.

8. For St. Croix, the winter '31–'32 dragged out like an interminable nightmare. There were no longer queues before the Odeon and the Palace. Now the long line of shabby men shivered before the Soup Kitchen.

Only Mrs. Lewis Trout went to Miami that winter.

Life for the young Holmeses was no easier than for any other family in town. Mark had trouble meeting taxes on the new house and the old place. Without consulting him, Faith let the part-time cook go. After work each evening, she hurried to the market and then home to cook dinner. Afterwards, she tidied the house, did a few chores and sat down for an hour's preparation of her next column.

Marked helped with the dishes and the beds, but quietly, almost sadly. There was nothing left of his old gay humor. He was a silent stranger for whom she dared show no pity.

These were no days for self-pity, anyway, for all the world was in the same boat. Leah Parker came into the office to see Faith. She had been let out of the Fashion Shop. "They're not selling any merchandise," she said miserably. "They might as well close up."

She was still well dressed, but painfully thin and extremely nervous. She reported that Mrs. Alexis Jenkins was hoarding her husband's insurance, almost starving herself and the children in order to stretch every dollar. She added that she'd spoken to Madeline Trout before the latter left for Miami, asking if Lewis couldn't use her in the office. But she'd had no luck. And she had no idea how she'd manage. . . .

Faith lent her enough money to pay her rent. And the next week, through Mark's efforts, Leah found temporary work at the Holmes library.

"At least I'll be able to eat regularly," she said. And Faith realized with dismay that she had been going hungry.

She heard from Winona Kraus regularly, too. Winona wrote there were no longer openings for showgirls these days. And her old boy friends were so worried about business, they had no time for fun. She decided to settle down; at a bad time, however, for there was little choice. Her new husband was a bond salesman. Only he wasn't selling bonds now, he was working in a men's haberdashers', and they had a cute flat on Perry Street, in the heart of the Village. Winnie expected to land a job any day, and then she'd take her mink out of hock.

Faith read her letter to Mark, hoping it would amuse him.

"Winona Kraus, or Winnie Cross," she laughed. "Our little friend will get along!"

Mark, bent over the bank statements, made no answer.

9. In April, Samuel Insull's financial pyramid collapsed. The Lumberman's Bank immediately called for new collateral on Mark's loan.

"I've offered them grandfather's house," he told Faith worriedly, "but they say at today's values, it's almost worthless."

Without a word she went into their bedroom. When she returned, a small white satin box rested in her hand. She opened it and took out the pearls.

"These should help, darling. They must be worth a good deal."

He was too moved to speak. He shook his head. They belonged to Faith and he would never touch them.

"But what will you do, Mark?"

"I don't know," he cried despairingly. "I don't know!"

She wanted to help him. If only she could borrow some money. Vrest was the only person she could turn to. But things were not going well for *The Observer*, either, although no one had ever seen Vrest down-hearted or heard him complain. Both advertising and circulation had dropped off sharply. People weren't spending three cents for a paper to be told times were getting worse. They damn well knew it!

Faith heard Rentschler had made Vrest an offer. Rentschler had seized in his tentacles a number of small newspapers unlucky enough to be pushed against the wall.

"Rentschler's turned enough papers into rubber stamps," Vrest said bitterly. "He's not getting mine. He'll never get it!"

10. Then the bank put a lien on the new house and all its valuable furnishings. The Holmeses were given sixty days to vacate it. The town buzzed with the news. The Holmes aura hadn't saved Mark. No one was immune.

Vrest commiserated with Faith.

"Our dream house has gone sour," she said wryly. "You know, all the years Mark and I lived with Eben Holmes, we thought we needed privacy. So we finally built ourselves a ten-room, four-bath house. Now we'll find real privacy—in two rooms at the Lake Shore Hotel." She smiled impishly. "From rags to riches—and right back again."

"You're a good sport, Faith."

"It's the fashion, these days."

Meanwhile, Mark went to the plant every day, and sat around, waiting, hopeless. He knew what the condemned man walking the last mile must suffer. Day after day, the same disheartening routine. Mark, getting up gloomy and taciturn, going to bed, white and beaten. Faith couldn't take it any longer.

"Darling, I can't bear to see you like this! You've taken such a frightful beating—and you keep coming back for more! How long can it go on? The time's come when you've got to admit you're licked. . . ."

Slowly, almost clumsily, he put on his blue robe. His awkward, half-hearted movements broke her heart. All youth, all resilience, all spirit, seemed erased from his blank tired face. He stared at her vaguely. She realized he hadn't heard her.

"Mark, it hasn't been easy for me to stand by—to see this happening to you. You aren't your old self. You haven't been for months. You never think of us—of the two of us—but only of this business!" She caught his arm. "Suppose conditions don't improve? Suppose nobody wants a new airplane engine? Face it, darling. Let's start fresh."

"I've got obligations," he whispered. "Your father . . ."

"Dad's my responsibility, not yours."

"And Griswold. He's married. . . ."

"So are we!" Impulsively she knelt beside him. "Darling, do you remember *two against the world?*"

His thin face was tortured.

"Darling, let's try it my way. We'll start fresh. New York, Chicago, anywhere. The world's ahead of us, as long as we're together. I don't mind being broke. Heck, I was born poor. I don't mind anything, just so you get a second chance! I'll work with you. I'll do my share!"

"You can do your share by staying right here." His face was stern now. "I belong here, Faith. This is where my roots are. If I flop in St. Croix, I'll never be a success anywhere else."

She stared at him.

"I'm seeing it through," he repeated firmly.

11. The last week in June, Vrest sent her to Chicago to cover the Democratic Convention.

"Do it your own way," he suggested. "Lots of human interest. Give our readers a peek behind the scenes—how our presidents are chosen." He smiled wryly. "You may find it an eye-opener, yourself."

She was eager to go; the change would do her good. The business of closing the new house, storing the packing cases, and then setting in order their two small rooms at the Lake Shore Hotel had proved a great strain on her.

Then, too, she was deeply concerned about Mark. In March, he had caught a severe cold and couldn't throw it off. His normally healthy brown skin was pallid. He coughed a good deal at night. When she suggested he see Dr. Savage for a checkup, he retorted there was nothing wrong with him. He was abrupt, absent-minded, indifferent. Their relations grew more strained, and Faith found herself in a groove of depression.

The trip was something of a release. She was twenty-six years old, and she had never been outside of St. Croix without Mark. Indeed, she had never traveled farther than Great Falls or their northern camp.

At the convention in the sweltering Chicago Stadium, she ran into Steve Pringle.

"Well, bless my heart! If it isn't Faith Holmes!"

"Hello, Steve."

"What're you doing here? Delegate from Michigan?"

She smiled. "I'm covering the convention for *The Observer*."

"Don't tell me! Working *and* married?"

"Why not?"

He was considerably heavier than the last time she had seen him, four years ago, at the farewell party of *The Observer* staff. She was reluctant to remember that tragic night.

"I got hitched myself. And is she a cute little devil! Here, let me show you." He reached into his breast pocket for his wallet.

"Your wife?" politely.

"Hell, no. My kid. Look at that baby. Isn't she just like her old pappy?"

Faith saw the image of a blond chubby two-year-old with a heavy lower lip.

"She looks as if she enjoys her food, too."

"And how! Speaking of food, how about having dinner with me t'night? For old times' sake. I know a place that serves the best prime beef and bourbon in Chicago."

She refused his invitation, but it was through him that she met Corrigan, the political reporter of the New York *Record*. Corrigan was a tall, cadaverous individual, no more than thirty, with a long head crowned with a shock of coarse black hair, and the lugubrious face of a hound who has never caught up with the hare.

During the grueling all-night session on June thirtieth, he was the only reporter to remain calm and unperturbed, as if the spectacle were nothing but a gigantic puppet show.

Sitting beside him in the press box, Faith found his acidulous comments, shouted above the incessant clicking of the typewriters, a relief from the monotonous tension.

Steve wandered in with a half-dozen bottles of Coca-Cola.

"Some fun, eh, keeds? Shouldn't be long now."

At last dawn straggled in. Everyone was hot, exhausted, irritable. Strident brass bands abused the eardrums. Delegates shuffled wearily around the floor like marathon dancers about to collapse. Their raucous voices croaked like bullfrogs in a pond.

"It's about time the bigwigs made up their minds," Corrigan said impatiently. "Mrs. Holmes, have you ever attended a shindig like this before?"

"This is my first."

He lit a cigarette and held it negligently between his stained fingers. His long angular jaw was in need of a shave.

"This is merely window dressing. Backstage, the horse-traders are bartering. They're a shrewd gang. They know how to crack the whip— and no one is giving up anything without getting something in return. The Lone Star Rangers are doubtlessly holding out for a prize plum for their man, Garner. And this Roosevelt . . ."

Faith yawned shamelessly. "I've got about all the human-interest stuff I need. Personally, I don't even feel human any more. I'm off to bed."

Steve Pringle watched her departure with obvious regret. "Damned attractive number, eh?"

Corrigan snuffed out his cigarette and stood up, stretching. "She's nothing in my life."

12. On her return to St. Croix, Faith and Mark settled into their new routine. Compared with the old Holmes place and their new modern house, the hotel quarters were appallingly cramped. They brought with them only their clothes, a few cherished books, the old victrola and

records. In the Bon Ton basement, Faith purchased an electric hot plate on which she cooked their simple breakfasts. They ate dinner in the Grille, and she invariably ordered the cheapest blue plate on the menu.

"I'm not very hungry," she would say. "I had a substantial lunch."

That backfired, for Mark, too, ordered little, and she suspected he often did without lunch, as well. She brought in milk and fruit for a bedtime snack, but Mark had no appetite. She tried to hide her concern over his health. Recently he had begun to resent her solicitude. I mustn't act like mother, she warned herself. I mustn't nag at him.

Even when he ordered the storage firm to sell for a pittance some of Eben's fine possessions in order to settle their hotel bill and share with Allan Griswold, she schooled herself to keep quiet. For she knew any words of hers might start another misunderstanding. They quarreled so often and so bitterly these days! And over such inconsequential matters. One word led to another; trivial, insignificant remarks touched off the fuse of another explosion. Once, in the midst of such a violent denunciation, she left the room abruptly.

We sounded exactly like my own parents, she thought horrified. Like dad and mother, screaming at each other hatefully. Are we following in their footsteps? Where is this leading to . . . ?

Watch your step, she counseled herself. Don't talk out of turn. Placate him. And perhaps we can still save our marriage.

He slept badly. He tried to hide it from her. But one night she awakened suddenly to find his bed empty. Her heart started pounding. She thought of the news items about men who had found the simplest way out of their difficulties. But not Mark! Dear God, Mark wouldn't be so weak. . . .

She padded into the other room. He was standing by the window, looking out at the sleeping street. There was such weariness and defeat in the sag of his young shoulders that she felt the hot tears burn her eyelids.

"Darling," she whispered, "I can't bear to see you like this."

He turned around stiffly, his face in shadow.

"I'm sorry I disturbed you. Go back to bed."

His voice shut her out as completely as a stone wall.

Another night she was aroused by a strange sound. She sat up. Mark was missing from his bed. There was no light in the adjoining room.

Then she heard it again. The awful sound of a man sobbing.

She found him huddled in a chair, asleep. He was having a nightmare.

"Darling." She shook his arm. "Darling, wake up!"

She sat with him, holding him like a child, until the first muddy streaks of dawn filtered through the windows.

In the morning, he told her Wolverine Motors was suing him and Allan, claiming that the latter had been in their employ when he first conceived the idea for this new motor.

"They're getting an injunction," he said bitterly. "But they have no real case—and they damn well know it!"

However the lawsuit had nuisance value, since it would involve the services of lawyers, and additional money to fight the case.

Mark reminded her of a fighter down for the last count, but stubbornly refusing to concede the knockout.

How much can a human being take, she wondered sorrowfully.

That night, without consulting him, she sent to various New York magazines copies of her column, together with letters of application.

13. Conditions did not improve that sultry August. The hotel rooms were stifling. Sleep was impossible. They sat on a park bench or the beach until past midnight, each lost in his private thoughts. They might still be on their island together, but they were as far apart as the poles.

Toward the end of the month, Faith received a reply to one of her letters. It came from *Feminine Appeal,* the magazine which, earlier in the year, had purchased her article, "Can Love Survive in Our Time?" The editor, Jeff Lundquist, was sufficiently impressed by her column, *As the Woman Sees It,* to make her an offer as assistant to the back-of-the-book editor.

Salary to start: seventy-five a week.

With considerable trepidation and a vestige of hope, she showed Lundquist's letter to Mark. He read it and handed it back to her without comment. His gray eyes held the remote and rather sleepy look which invariably antagonized her, since it meant he was shutting himself away where she could not possibly reach him.

But she would not allow herself to be rebuffed. This was too crucial a moment for them both.

"Mark, this is really a break! With one of us assured of a job, there's no reason why we can't strike out for New York!"

Then, aware of the stormy shadows on his face, she added swiftly,

"I know we've been over this before, darling! But this offer puts a different light on everything! Mark, I *do* admire your loyalty and doggedness. But it's been so woefully misplaced! You've got to be big enough—and wise enough—to admit the venture was a flop and write it off as such. Other men have failed in one business and then gone on to great success. You mustn't live in the past. It's bad for you. It's bad for both of us. . . ."

Never before had she spoken so bluntly.

"In some marriages," she continued, "it's the Other Man or Woman who causes the trouble. In ours, it's been the business. And that's another reason it's so darned important for us to start fresh!"

More than anything, she thought—but this she would not tell him—it would restore his morale. It would extricate him from this dreadful lethargy, this deadening passivity, and restore him to his former dignified status, the Mark she loved and admired. For his sake, she was doubly grateful for this offer. The chance to begin again, in both his career and their private lives . . .

Mark shook his head.

"I haven't lost faith in our product. I've told you before, Faith, I've got to make good here. Don't you see—if I give up and start over again, I'll be jinxed right from the beginning? I'll never believe in myself!"

We're on the merry-go-round again, she thought. The same words. The same defenses. He had lost all perspective. He had gone off the deep end. If this opportunity didn't jolt him into action, they were sunk.

"Mark, an offer like this isn't likely to come our way again."

"I won't stand in your way."

"What do you mean?"

He said with great weariness, "This is a decision for you to make, just as it is your opportunity." His gray eyes mirrored his icy contempt. "I realize that more than the offer of a job for you is involved."

"I don't know what you're talking about!" she flung at him angrily. "Besides, there aren't many such jobs floating around. Seventy-five dollars a week isn't to be sneezed at these days! We haven't seen as much in ages!"

He repeated tonelessly, "I won't stand in your way."

"Well," recklessly, "then I'd better take it. It's about time somebody in this family showed a little gumption!"

The words were out; she couldn't retract them. Mark withdrew again into a shell, where she could not reach him. She busied herself with small tasks. She sorted her clothes, packing those she would need,

the simple tailored frocks and suits still in good condition. She retained
the small tarnished locket of her childhood, but insisted that Mark put
the pearls in the vault. She had a long earnest talk with Vrest Macklin
and she said goodbye to the staff, her dad, and Mrs. Hussar. And all the
while, she was waiting expectantly. . . .

Surely he would say it. "I'm coming with you, Faith. Under any
circumstances you and I belong together. Your words have shown me
the way."

But he remained silent.

14. It rained that September afternoon. And it was still storming
when they drove to Union Station that night. Sheets of rain, as if
buffeted by a wind machine; a wet dirge, the first tragic warning of
autumn.

Mark parked the car under a protecting roof. Faith stepped out
hurriedly, followed by her father, who had come at her specific request
to see her off. Shrugging the raindrops from her tweed coat, she hurried
through the hot waiting room to the outdoor platform. She already had
her ticket.

Standing beside her, Tod wondered wretchedly what had come over
them. They had no business separating, even temporarily. It was dangerous.

"I'm gonna get me a cup of coffee," he said.

Faith stared after his bent, shuffling figure. His faded red hair was
heavily streaked with gray; now that he'd lost his upper teeth, his
clown's nose was more prominent than ever. At fifty-two, he was old
and defeated. She wanted to speak to him about mother. She knew he
went to visit her once a month, but there was never any encouraging
news. No change; no improvement. Perhaps if she concentrated on her
father's problems, she wouldn't have to think of herself and Mark. She
paced the platform restlessly. She hated static moments, just as she hated
passivity in general. Waiting, marking time drove her frantic. "If only
you'd get out and do something," she had cried to Mark. But as always,
he misunderstood her motives. What she termed "passivity" he stubbornly translated as "the strength and guts to see a problem through to
the end." This had loomed up as a vital issue, and finally, as the insoluble
one. They no longer agreed on either major or minor ones. They no
longer agreed at all.

Mark was approaching with her bags. She looked away from his tall
lean figure to the big clock on the wall. The figure of Fate in a black

robe. The minute hand crept on, cruel, inexorable, ticking away its solemn warning. Soon—soon—soon.

Why didn't he say something? Why didn't he throw that stubborn male pride to the winds and cry, "I won't let you go alone. We'll conquer new worlds together!"

It was not too late. She turned to him and he met her supplicating gaze. His eyes were level, gray without light, heavy as the storm-swept sky.

The station master ambled in.

"Overnight Limited—Detroit, Cleveland, Buffalo, New York—coming in on Track Fouurr!"

"Well, dad." She kissed her father on the cheek, clinging to him. Mark picked up the heavy bags again, waiting beside her for the train to come to a stop. They walked toward the coach. On the lowest step, she hesitated.

"Mark . . ."

Nearby, a young couple were kissing in wild desperation. But Mark did not kiss her. Mark did not even touch her. There was so much she wanted to say. This moment was a tragic surprise to her. She hadn't meant it to happen this way.

With a convulsive jerk, the train started. The conductor slammed the door. Faith remained in the corridor, her face pressed to the cold, rain-washed window.

She saw Mark walking, slowly at first, his pace increasing in order to keep abreast of her coach. Now at last, he was speaking. She saw his lips form the words. She strained to catch them, but they were lost in the air.

She was leaving Mark.

How had it happened?

"Mark!" she cried. *"Darling!"*

His upturned face was a ghostly blur. The train gathered speed. She heard its lonely wail.

And Mark was one with the rain and the darkness.

15. Her berth was made up. She lay there, pillows propped behind her head, listening to the brisk patter of rain on the window; shut off from the world by the green baize curtain. The train plunged into the night, sounding its plaintive cry over the land. Here and there, the glimmering light of an isolated farmhouse flickered briefly against the monotonous black backdrop, and was gone.

She closed her eyes, as if the simple gesture would help shut out the miserable memories of the past week. But the scenes remained vivid in her mind, with all of the pain and humiliation, and her own stiff-necked pride that equaled Mark's.

Now that she was gone, perhaps he would come to his senses. He must finally admit she was acting for both of them, and wisely.

And yet, was she doing right, she wondered, heartsick and bewildered, when with each turn of the wheels, she was leaving him farther and farther behind?

Chapter Eleven

1. Through the September morning haze, the towers of the metropolis rose in the distance, reaching arrogantly to the sky. They seemed fantastic and illusory, like the pictures in a fairy tale, of a delicate and improbable beauty, which might at any moment dissolve in the iridescent mist.

These spires were the focal points for a million youthful dreams and aspirations. To the Dream City which they represented, there came in daily hordes, from every part of the country, the unworldly young, brimming with ambition, optimism, faith, and drawn by the magnet of Success.

These grandsons of the pioneers of the covered wagon and the Gold Rush were reversing the Great Migration.

Go East, Young Man. Go East.

Here is buried the hidden lode, to be mined by your will, your ability, your application. The successful play, the great American novel, the first million—maybe you'll be the lucky one!

City of triumph and success; the market place where talents are bartered for fame and power and riches.

It's here for the taking.

Every man for himself.

Come and get it!

2. Now the train was deserting the tranquil, sparkling Hudson for the gloomy caverns of the city. Absently, Faith gathered her possessions, the brown tweed coat, the fur scarf, the alligator bag. She was a thousand miles away from Mark, yet she saw his face clearly, as he strode beside the slow-moving train. There had been anguish and terror written on his face as he called out to her. What had he been trying to say?

The train stopped with a series of small jolts. She looked up to the grin of a redcap.

"Youah bags, ma'am."

She followed him up the ramp and through the crowded station to the taxi stand, where she directed the driver to take her to the Barbizon. After registering, she sent Mark a telegram announcing her safe arrival. Then she bathed, changed into fresh clothes and went down to the magazine office. Despite the unhappiness that attended her coming to New York, she was raring to go.

Feminine Appeal, begun originally as a pattern book, had developed into a highly popular magazine, dedicated to Woman in all her ages and phases. Jeff Lundquist, the editor, was a spare, scholarly man with a perpetually haunted expression on his sensitive face. He had a great fear of meeting strangers.

His assistants were a group of thin, clever women of indeterminate age, all exceedingly well dressed and well armed with the weapons of self-preservation. They copied each other's ideas, pirated each other's beaux and were ready to knife each other with wicked suaveness. They were known as the Assassins.

For once, they were all united in the very articulate conviction that the Boss was out of his mind to bring on a young woman fresh from the cornfields, simply because he'd been impressed by some ghastly little column she wrote for a hick paper.

Nevertheless, they were outwardly charming to her, especially after they noted the taste and quality of her clothes. But what gave away her origins were the rouge on her round cheeks—no truly smart woman would ever look more than anemic—and her exuberant good humor. She was completely wholehearted, a trait which they were confident would soon wither on the vine. Her disarming sincerity amused them no end, until they saw how exceedingly well she got along with the male members of the staff, including the shy and reticent Lundquist.

Her work consisted of a one-page article in the back of the book, sandwiched between the food and beauty pages. The first week of her arrival, Mr. Lundquist summoned her into his office for a talk.

"I wish you'd go over the book with a critical eye," he said. "You're fresh here and I'd like your reactions."

Taking him literally, she pored over the last issue, scribbled innumerable notes and brought them in.

As he read her criticism, a gleam of amusement touched Lundquist's scholarly face.

"We seem to be off on the wrong track entirely."

She blushed at her presumptuousness, but stuck to her guns.

"I've given you my honest opinion, Mr. Lundquist. The fact that you gave me a job on the strength of my column proves you believe women will accept more of the truth than you're accustomed to giving them."

He stared at the notes which tore his magazine apart: realistic fiction, instead of frothy escape literature; hard-hitting articles; an approach that would treat women as if this were 1932, instead of 1890.

He was both pained and beguiled.

"I'm afraid your suggestions are a bit radical," he said. "We're in the midst of a depression. I'm primarily interested in maintaining our circulation."

"You might even increase it," she said, "if only you'll stress the potential power of women—not in the home alone—but in the sphere of world affairs!"

He showed no enthusiasm, nor did he encourage her to follow this trend. Nevertheless, she projected all her fervor into her first article, which she called "Fair-Weather Wives," and in which she lashed out at the women who in adversity bit the hand that had pampered them in prosperity.

Lundquist decided to run it, with some editing, despite the united protests of the Assassins.

"You'll get hundreds of indignant letters," they warned him. "And cancellations."

The first week was most difficult for her. She could lose herself in work, but the hours afterwards were a sore trial. The lonely and impersonal hotel room, the blue-plate special in the small tearoom frequented by other single women, the ocasional movie she almost never enjoyed, the sleepless nights tormented by the image of Mark. Yet she was determined to hold on, convinced that eventually Mark would come to her. For their united good, she must be strong.

She sent half of her first pay to Mark.

The money was returned three days later, accompanied by a brusque note assuring her he could manage without her help. She would not allow herself to be hurt; she tried valiantly to understand his male pride. If he wouldn't accept it directly, she would get around it somehow. She'd send her father twenty-five dollars a week, and thus relieve his burden somewhat.

3. After she had been in New York a fortnight, she looked up Winona Kraus, who was now living in Sunnyside. Winnie was almost tearfully pleased to hear from her, and invited her out the following Sunday. Despite her directions, Faith managed to get lost among the rows and rows of small houses, all depressingly alike.

Winnie flung open the front door of a pseudo-Tudor, semi-attached house, and hugged her extravagantly.

"Gosh, Faith, am I glad to see you!" There were tears in her pale-blue eyes. "And do you look wonderful!"

Winnie herself was not looking well. Her formerly silky hair was coarse and touched up with peroxide; there were shadows under her thickly mascaraed eyelids; her once willowy body strained at the seams of the short black crêpe dress.

"Welcome to my penthouse!" she cried, and then added wistfully, "I did have one, you know. Not so long ago."

The boxlike living room into which she led Faith was a reflection of the present Winona, blowzy, cluttered with empty cocktail glasses, ashtrays spilling over with cigarette butts, long-legged, foolish dolls propped on the taupe sofa, the Sunday *News* open to the comics.

"How long have you been in the big city, Faith?"

"Several weeks."

"Where's Mark?"

"Home."

"You here for a visit?"

"Not exactly."

"How long you going to stay?"

"That depends," Faith hedged. "Tell me about yourself, Winnie."

"Come into the kitchen while I fix us a drink."

Back in the living room, Winnie curled up on the sofa with a martini and gave Faith a résumé of her life in New York.

"I didn't have much luck with my voice. But everybody loved my legs—I really did look wonderful in the front row! So I had me *some* fun."

She'd made friends, loads of friends, all men of course; and they were perfectly darling to her. Like Bob, who was *so* considerate about investing in the market for her. Of course, when the stocks flopped, he did, too. And Schuyler, who'd given her a simply gorgeous mink four Christmases ago. It was a little worn now, but still stunning.

She was down on her luck now. She had married, and her husband was a flop as a meal ticket. He spent Sundays with his family in Brooklyn. He was a model son, but a lousy husband.

"Can't you get back on the stage?" Faith asked.

Winnie shrugged.

They spent the afternoon together, and then Winnie invited her to dinner at a steak house down the block, adding candidly, "You're going to be stuck with the bill, dear. Henry left me with two nickels and a thin dime."

Afterwards, walking Faith to the subway, she said impulsively, "Look, Faith, why don't you move in with us? We're just a half hour from your office. And it'd be a lot cheaper than your hotel."

In the end, Faith agreed, despite her inner reluctance. Even Winnie was better than a bleak hotel room, and every penny counted. Of course, there were disadvantages. Winnie had grown sloppy and careless; obviously, she meant to sponge on Faith, and to use her as a sounding board for her irritation with her husband.

Henry Nielson was eminently suited to his present post as a haber-dasher. Even in his straitened circumstances, he fought to remain the model of the well-dressed man. He spent an hour each morning in careful grooming. The precise part in his sleek black hair; the knife edge to his trousers; the perfect knot in his cravat, the high polish of his shoes. Just before leaving, he would survey himself in the dingy hall mirror, black Homburg tilted at a jaunty angle, and fall in love with himself all over again. In the evening he pored over the sports pages and the comics, or gave Winona a detailed report of the clothes he had sold. He had married her when she was still glamorous, and he was fond of her in his limited way. But Winnie, no mental prodigy herself, was already bored with him. She inflicted her pouting confidences and woes on Faith, who learned to take them with equanimity.

4. When she had been living in Sunnyside for several weeks, Faith met Corrigan, quite by accident. He had asked her to look him up if ever she got to New York, but she had hesitated to do so, thinking that he had probably forgotten her by now. It was inevitable that she should see him one day among the luncheon crowd at the Athenaeum, a restau-rant which was the gathering place of a group of writers, columnists and critics banded together in the spirit of Samuel Johnson and his cronies. There they dispensed the wisdom of today which they hoped would become the literary gems of tomorrow.

She was eating alone, and when he spied her, his long dour face lightened. He excused himself to the men at his table and loped over.

"Did you ever find out who was finally nominated?" he asked solemnly.

She laughed. "By the time they came up with Roosevelt, I was sound asleep."

He took the seat beside her, and his sad brown eyes scrutinized her. "What're you doing so far from home?"

"Didn't you once tell me New York was the only place for an ambitious young woman?"

"Not if she's happily married."

She was silent. He brushed back the coarse black hair from his deeply lined forehead with a nervous gesture.

"Where are you working, Faith? I'll call you soon."

Her growing friendship with Corrigan compensated for the emptiness of her leisure. She was greatly drawn to this lean, loose-jointed ugly young man with his dry, caustic wit, his almost intuitive understanding, and his brutal, cynical commentaries. Right from the beginning, she was completely at ease with him. He never mentioned her marriage again, he never probed; nor did he make any overtures to her. He was honorable to an almost prudish degree, and she loved him for it. He was her only true friend.

She wrote Mark regularly, but his answers left her frustrated. They were brief to the point of curtness, and never mentioned his affairs. He had not flown to New York, as she had hoped. And she realized that as time progressed, the chances of his coming lessened. The business venture had won out, she thought bitterly. It was stronger than his love for her.

Still, she was determined to resolve this misunderstanding between them before it dragged out and proved disastrous. If she were to come home, if he saw her again and held her in his arms . . . Yes, that was the answer.

A week before Christmas, she wired she would be home for the holidays.

5. A day later, she read on the society page of the *Herald Tribune* that Mrs. Norwood Latham, and her son, Phillip, were at the Plaza for a week before going to Palm Beach for the season. She and Mark hadn't seen Phillip in three years, since the time he had dropped in casually for a day, and spent a week. For months they did not hear from him. Then she would receive a box of roses with a card, "Love and kisses from the *Pep-Korn* boy." A case of Scotch at Christmas, as well as a huge carton of assorted Latham products, enough to feed the guests of the Lake Shore Hotel. "For good health, kiddies, and Latham dividends!"

Impulsively, she telephoned the Plaza, and got Phillip on the wire.

"*Faith!* What're you doing in town?"

"I've got a job here."

"Where's Mark?"

"In St. Croix."

"You're here *alone?*"

"Yes."

"And Mark's home *alone?*"

"That's right."

"I don't get it." His indolent voice quickened. "Where are you? How about lunch? I'll pick you up in a half hour."

When he arrived, she was waiting for him in the magazine's reception room. He kissed her on the cheek enthusiastically.

"Faith, you look wonderful!"

"Thank you, Phillip. So do you."

He had changed surprisingly little; his excesses left no mark on his bland face. The light cropped hair, the baggy tweed jacket and flannel slacks, the worn old raincoat, the unpolished brogues, all carried out the undergraduate air. As they came out on the windy street, he put his arm through hers. "Tell papa everything," he said cajolingly. "But *everything.*"

"There's nothing to tell. We're broke, so I got a job."

"What's Mark doing?"

"Sitting on the ruins. And trying to salvage what he can."

"It's that bad?"

"Worse."

"I'm sorry. I hate to see Mark in a jam."

He took her to Clare's, a speakeasy off Park Avenue, where the tenor of the headwaiter's greeting was in direct proportion to the patron's rating in Dun and Bradstreet's.

After they had ordered, Phillip said bluntly, "I don't understand why Mark let you go off alone. I know that guy. It isn't like him."

"Phillip, you don't know what it means to be broke."

"Why didn't the damn fool tell me he needs dough? He knows I've got plenty!"

She smiled quizzically. "I thought you knew Mark."

He rubbed the scar on his forehead absently. "Faith, is everything okay between you?"

"Of course."

"That's good. I'd sure hate to see you two go on the rocks." His deep regard for Mark was not lessened by the fact that they seldom saw each other. He knew also that Mark was too steadfast to fall out of love easily. Phillip had regarded this marriage as something precious and rare, and in spite of his basic cynicism, had been deeply impressed by it.

"Look," he said, abruptly, "why don't you and Mark come South with us?"

"It's not that simple, Phillip. I've got to stick to my job—and Mark won't leave St. Croix."

"I'll call him. Maybe he'll change his mind. . . ."

"He won't," flatly. "Besides, I'm going home for Christmas."

"And after Christmas?"

She shrugged.

"You worry too much, both of you! If Mark wants a job, the mills can give him one. And when you see him in St. Croix, tell him the Latham latchstring is always out."

"Thanks, Phillip."

He could not concentrate on misfortune for long, even a good friend's.

"Will you dine with us tonight?" he asked. "My mother's always been anxious to meet you."

He drove out to Sunnyside for her that evening, and Winnie greeted him with a shaker of martinis. Henry Nielson shook hands with him, thinking, His clothes look as if he didn't have a cent in the world.

"Why don't you wear my mink coat?" Winnie said to Faith. "There's nothing like a mink to give you the old *savoir faire!*"

"I couldn't get into it," Faith answered. "But thanks all the same, Winnie."

Driving across the Queensboro Bridge, Phillip said, "Whatever made you pick that rabbit hutch for a home?"

"Winnie's an old friend," she said, as if that answered everything.

Phillip led her into his mother's apartment. "You two gals should hit it off," he said. "You've got so darned much in common."

Faith took an immediate liking to Mrs. Latham, a small spare woman who didn't resemble her son in the slightest. Her lively blue eyes were remarkably youthful, her finely lined face animated by a friendly curiosity. She wore a plain black evening frock, sensible low-heeled shoes, and a magnificent diamond brooch and earrings.

"I feel that I know you and Mark very well," she said. "You've been a shining light in my son's eyes."

"Darned near blinded me," he said blithely.

It was a pleasant evening. When Mrs. Latham learned the nature of Faith's job, she plied her with intelligent questions. She was an active woman herself, since she took a hand in the running of the Latham Mills, and she agreed with Faith that women in general had not taken advantage of their new-found freedom.

"Now look, ma," Phillip interrupted amiably, "Faith is too young and good-looking to concern herself with what's ailing her sex!" He leaned down and kissed his mother. "If you'd been born poor, you'd have been some little reformer!"

"Might have been to your advantage," Mrs. Latham answered dryly. "Heaven knows, you need plenty of reforming."

After Faith left, she reflected wistfully, Phillip needs a girl like Faith. She could do a lot for him.

6. Phillip escorted her to the train when she left for St. Croix.

"It's been swell seeing you, Faith. You're the only girl I can take for more than a day." He grinned. "Mark sure brought you up right. Ma's crazy about you."

"I like her, too."

He put down the white box of orchids. "You kids keep in touch with me. Tell Mark to get off his high horse. Now's the time a fella needs a friend."

"I'll tell him."

He added lightly, "Don't forget me."

"I won't," she promised absently. But already her mind leaped forward to her meeting with Mark.

7. When she entered the lobby of the Lake Shore Hotel at eleven in the morning, the clerk handed her a note from Mark. Her hands shook as she read the message:

"Sorry I'm tied up. I'll get back to the hotel just as soon as I can."

A fine welcome. Ever since she had stepped on the train at Grand Central, she had been consumed by a fierce impatience. She had pictured Mark waiting at the platform, straining for the sound of the engine, hunting eagerly for her among the passengers, and finally sweeping her into his arms with an ardent embrace, whispering, "Darling, I couldn't wait. . . ."

That was how she had pictured it. Reality was a rude awakening.

I won't let it upset me, she cautioned herself, following the bellhop to the elevator. The rooms were the same, yet they looked alien; she could not believe they had ever been home to her.

She unpacked her bags and took a shower. She was sitting at the window, brushing her hair when the door opened and Mark came in. For a moment, they stared at each other in silence.

Then he said gravely, "Welcome home."

Her excitement gave way to a sense of depression. She had the sudden ominous conviction that she had been foolish to come.

How long, she wondered desperately, as he put down his briefcase and took off his tweed topcoat, could they keep up this polite pretense? How could she face him day after day when his manner was so cool and distant? What hope was there for tomorrow when they could scarcely be civil today?

Mark muttered an excuse about business and left abruptly. She let him go without protest. She sat numb, unable to think, her morale shattered. An hour passed; and she made no move.

Mark returned at six, and he seemed to have himself in better control. They went down to dinner in the Grille, and sat opposite each other, complete strangers.

"How are things going?" she asked with an effort. "Your letters didn't tell me much."

He waited until the waiter removed the soup plates.

"There wasn't much to tell. It was pretty rough sailing until this past week. But yesterday, we finally closed a deal with Wolverine Motors."

"I thought Wolverine was suing you!"

"Zeb Whiting was using the suit as a ruse—thought he'd scare us into selling out. When he was finally convinced we wouldn't bite, he put the cards on the table. Wolverine was anxious to have our engine. So he made us an offer to join him—a damn good offer."

She said guardedly, "Does this mean you'll get out from under?"

"Hell, no! I wouldn't think of selling out. Zeb's taken us in as a subsidiary to Wolverine Motors. But we keep our plant and business intact. Now," a faint smile touched his big mouth, "we're Big Business."

She should be pleased, if only for his sake. He had won out. He had stuck to it and won out. He deserved success. But it certainly put another light on her homecoming.

"Mark, let's quit sparring," she said. "We've always been honest with each other before."

He made no answer. He was slouched in an easy chair in their bedroom, a cigarette in his mouth. In the diffused lamplight, his face was rough hewn, the flesh drawn too tightly over the strong, narrow bones. The set expression gave him a worn maturity that reminded her fleetingly of Eben Holmes.

"You've put up a wall against me, Mark. You've shut me out. You even refuse to admit to yourself that I've been trying to save our marriage."

Her words fell hollowly on the quiet air. Even her sincerity could not give them an authentic ring in the face of his disbelief.

"Don't just sit there," she said angrily, "putting me on the defensive!"

She can't help it, he thought sadly, knowing no desire for retaliation, but only a bitter sorrow. During the months of enforced and humiliating inactivity, he had hungered for a reassuring word from her. A sign that she believed in him, if not in his purpose. He had needed her faith so desperately then. But she had let him down. It wasn't her fault. He realized now that she couldn't have helped herself. It was the way her personality functioned. She was both impatient and impulsive.

"If you don't start again," she had kept repeating until the phrase sickened him, "you'll be licked forever."

He saw how much she took after her father. Perhaps her natural optimism that success was just ahead, her instinctive pursuit of the will-o'-the-wisp made it impossible for her to appreciate his devotion to self-discipline and duty. It was easy for her to cut loose from a failing project, admit it was a flop, and rush on to fresh fields. He couldn't. To him, such defeat would be humiliating and final. This was to him an indication of the differences between them—and love no longer brought them together on common ground.

"I'm not reproaching you," he said.

" 'Reproaching me!' " she repeated. Her tension exploded in sudden indignant fury. "You have no right to talk to me like that! Ever since we were married, I've done my very best to please you. Because you hated people, I gave up friends, stayed home with you, took a job—for your good, even though you were blind to it!"

"And sent me money as if I were kept. How could you be so insensitive?"

"That's just like you—twisting my motives, putting me in the wrong!"

"It's no use, Faith. I shouldn't have forced you to stay with me as long as you did. I should have seen . . ."

"Mark, stop it!"

They were both shocked by the bald naked words, the ugly tone, the way they were tearing each other down.

"I'm sorry," he said abruptly. "Forget it."

Forget it? "I guess I'd better go back where I belong," she said wearily.

He did not stop her. The magic circle was broken. And neither of them knew how to make it whole again.

She left St. Croix the following morning. The savings she had so proudly brought home she sealed in an envelope for her father. As the train rushed along the shore line, she caught a brief glimpse of the red brick walls of the State Hospital.

Her mother should be pleased. The marriage hadn't lasted.

8. Mark glanced at his watch. He stood up from his desk and went to the window. He watched the train roar by, to lose itself in the gray mist. How many times he had stood here, watching the trains fly past, listening to their lonely cries.

Today, a part of him was rushing away, already lost beyond the next curve.

9. She returned to her office the following morning. The staff was surprised to see her but she offered no explanations. She meant to tackle her new assignment with determination, but somehow her mind wouldn't function. She sat before her typewriter, staring stupidly at the words she had written, ". . . women or mice." Her hands fell to her lap. She stared out of the window. It was impossible to focus on the blank paper in the machine. Yet tomorrow was the deadline for the April issue.

"Women of the world . . ."

That was as far as she could go.

Time was a ball of yarn, unwinding slowly, with no beginning and no ending. She loved Mark dearly, but she could not go back to him. She must go ahead. But how—and where?

In order to give her life some semblance of meaning, she had to concentrate on her work, find a purpose, a goal. Else, this would be exile, her own private St. Helena.

10. Corrigan had the jitters. He was glad to step off the train. The incessant clacking of the wheels had set his nerves on edge. Last night hadn't helped, either. It was getting so you couldn't trust even the best bootlegged stuff.

Tipping the porter a half buck, he plowed up the long crowded ramp into Grand Central station. The murky air chilled him to the bone. He was damned tired. Nine weeks on the go, from one hick town to another; food like fried cotton mush; lumpy beds; lousy liquor—he just couldn't take it any more. The survey of business conditions rested in his pocket, ready to be typed and sent to Hastings-Pitney, the investment brokers who had commissioned it. And he was set for a job that would never take him farther north than Fifty-seventh Street.

New York sure looked swell to him. He sauntered crosstown to the West Forty-eighth Street brownstone, sandwiched between two skyscrapers, that served as home and office. He let himself into the airless room, opened a window, stripped off his coat, and hunched himself before the typewriter. He had just completed a trek through Ohio, Pennsylvania, Indiana and Kansas. Business was whistling frantically in the dark. The worst is over. Happy Days Are Here Again! Roosevelt will fix everything! Men clung hysterically to this ray of hope, as financial and economic structures tottered.

Well, today was March 4. The Great Day.

He had been working an hour when the telephone rang.

"Corrigan, this is Faith Holmes."

"Greetings!" The concentrated lines between his sad eyes eased. "I just got in from the sticks."

"I know. I called your office during the week."

"What's on your mind?"

"Corrigan, have you any money?"

"Sure. How much do you need?"

"I'd like a small check cashed. The banks are closed this morning."

"I saw the headlines."

She hesitated briefly. "I've been fired."

"I'm not surprised." His voice was oddly gentle. "It's a wonder anybody is keeping a job these days." Then he added casually, "How about lunch?"

"Well, I'd like to listen to Roosevelt's inaugural address."

"There's a radio at Tony's."

When he showed up at the speakeasy, Faith was already waiting. She was wearing a brown tweed suit, and the streamers of her beige silk blouse were tied in a ridiculous bow under her round chin. Her short chestnut hair was curled up over a brown skullcap. She looked healthy and vital, and not the least downcast.

"Hi!" He slid into the chair beside her, tossing his battered gray felt on the empty chair. For so gaunt a man, Corrigan's movements were remarkably fluid. He opened a pack of Luckies and offered them to her.

"What's the lowdown?"

She managed a rueful smile. "I wrote an article that backfired."

"You're a damn fool."

They were alone in the big room; even the early drinkers hadn't shown up as yet. The bartender struggled into a fresh starched coat and switched on the radio. The feeble bravado of "Who's Afraid of the Big Bad Wolf" filled the air.

He ordered a couple of martinis.

"What's the piece about?"

She grinned. "Are women people—or appendages?" she said with mock solemnity. "And how long will men continue to exploit them?"

"Good grief! Why must you do such things?"

"Well, it got by the editor. As a matter of fact, he considered it controversial enough to stimulate circulation. But when the publisher got a look at it—whoops! He said it was inciting women to riot. He said wasn't the divorce rate high enough, what with their new-found freedom? I suspect he added, 'Get rid of that troublemaker—fast!' "

The waiter wheeled in the hors d'oeuvres cart.

"But I told them off anyway!" she finished with a chuckle.

"What're you going to do now?"

"I'm not worried. I'll find another job."

Gradually, the room was filling up; the crowd listening to the voice of the radio announcer, reeling off the names of the politically famous who were gathered on the platform. A middle-aged man hunched over the bar looked into his beer.

"These are uncertain times, all right," he muttered.

"Yeah," the bartender said, "they sure are."

"What we need is a leader. A real leader!"

"Yeah. You got something there."

"They can't do any worse than those damned Republicans."

Corrigan looked at Faith with mock sorrow. "They don't want a leader," he said. "They want a whipping boy."

Abruptly, there was a dramatic hush. Then they heard Franklin Delano Roosevelt take the oath for his first inauguration. In solemn and measured cadence that resonant voice rang over the air, inspired and inspiring:

"President Hoover, Mr. Chief Justice, my friends . . ."

The room was hushed; the glasses untouched, as the listeners heard his confident and reassuring convictions. ". . . so let me assert my firm belief that the only thing we have to fear is fear itself."

Sitting here, intent on the words, Faith could not help but recall the late Eben Holmes's outspoken faith in his country. She thought also of Vrest Macklin, and what the new President's words must be doing for him and for his town, which was dying not only of starvation but of apathy and despair. And Mark—no, she dared not speculate about Mark.

It was over. The first brassy strains of the "Star-Spangled Banner" struck the air. The bartender picked up a cocktail shaker. The crowd settled back to serious drinking. Faith wiped her unashamed tears.

Corrigan finished his martini. "Don't be sentimental," he growled.

"I'm not. But he was wonderful! He inspired such confidence!"

He shrugged. "Any new broom."

"Don't be flippant. You spoil it for me."

"Roosevelt may turn out okay. But Hoover was no devil, you know. I'm all for giving the guy on the ropes a pat on the back, instead of a kick in the tail. I'll be around with a kind word for Roosevelt—when they begin damning him. Corrigan, the great humanitarian, embraces all factions and all parties!"

Faith was vexed. "You're too cynical for me."

"Nope. I'm merely analytical." He poured fresh coffee. "Let me give you a few pointers. Sort of a Primer for Politics. Politics is run precisely like any other big business. Executives, business managers, office help, are translated into party bosses, district captains, ward-heelers. It's got a product, too: the man put up for public office on a few set ideas called the Party Platform, which must be sold to the ultimate consumer—the voter."

She stared at him. She had never seen him so bitter.

"Faith, do you vote?"

"What a question! Of course, I do!"

"I suppose you vote like your father?"

"No. Like my husband."

"And he goes straight Republican?"

"As a matter of fact, we considered both Coolidge and Hoover good men."

"Wasn't Al Smith a good man—a man of the people?"

"I'm sure he was."

"But we don't really vote for the man—we're influenced by race, religion, sectionalism. The South's still fighting the Civil War. And as Maine goes—Faith, what's the political setup in your home town?"

"I really don't know much about it. Except that my old editor, Vrest Macklin, carried on an unceasing fight with Big Bob Costello. Why . . ." she straightened up, astonished. "Why, Costello must be the party boss in St. Croix!"

He nodded.

"Let me give you an idea of how the machine works. It's pretty much the same everywhere. Take my case. I was a mick on the East Side. Corlear's Hook. That's where the East River turns up from the Battery. Outside the Church, the first saint I ever knew was a big, red-faced guy named Maloney. When my old man was out of work, Maloney sent up a bag of coal. At Christmas, we lined up at party headquarters for the basket Maloney handed out. If we got behind in the rent, Maloney saw to it that we weren't evicted. In the summer, he chartered an excursion boat for a ride up the Hudson—where I saw grass for the first time, by the way. He was the boss of our district—our patron saint."

He offered her a cigarette and lit one for himself.

"We were weaned on the system. I used to hang around the local headquarters. All the kids did—it was our clubhouse. We rushed the growler, delivered messages, swept up, shined up to the boss—until we were regular little wardheelers ourselves!"

The bitterness had faded from his voice, leaving it colorless, as if this were a purely objective recital of facts.

"Before election, the ward captain and his henchmen paid a visit to each tenement. They'd knock at the door and ask, 'How many votes in this flat?' There were four in ours—so the henchman would take eight bucks out of his wallet and toss them under the table. Two bucks a vote. Two bucks bought a helluva lot in those days for poor slobs like us. For the bosses, it was chicken feed. When their stooges got into power—boy, what a rakeoff! Sewer contracts, paving jobs, school supplies. A take on everything!"

"Why didn't someone speak up?" she interrupted. "Why wasn't something done about such corruption?"

There was a strange flash of emotion in his face, one she did not recognize.

"Here and there, you'd find a couple of dissenters. My older brother was one. A good kid, but an idealist. He voted the Socialist ticket. Then when he heard they had dumped the Socialist ballot boxes in the river, he got mad and joined the Honest Voters Committee. Next election, he was a watcher at the polls."

Corrigan's eyes grew deadly.

"For his good intentions, he died of a fractured skull. The thugs got off scot-free. Because Maloney, our patron saint, had ordered the beating."

He added wearily, "The political machine flourishes best in a democracy because the people are apathetic. They're too damn lazy to do anything."

She was to remember his words many years later.

11. Through Corrigan she found a few odd jobs in the following months: reading proof for a publisher and manuscripts for a playbroker. Corrigan also took her to dinner twice a week, making sure she was properly fed, although he was skating on thin ice himself, stretching the money made from his survey. Then, one day in May, she read in the *Times* that Mrs. Horace Reynolds had been re-elected president of the Alliance for the Advancement of Women in Politics. And she recalled her interview with Mrs. Reynolds when the lady had toured the Midwest.

"If you're ever in New York," Mrs. Reynolds had said cordially, "do look me up. We need girls like you in our organization!"

Faith wrote her a note, and received a reply almost immediately. Yes, the Alliance would find a place for her. Unfortunately, however, they couldn't pay much, for the Alliance was always running short of funds.

Besides, the work wasn't hard, Mrs. Reynolds added, striking a shrewd bargain when Faith arrived at the office. Only a bit of typing, filing and transcribing notes. And Faith would be meeting many noted women who were throwing themselves wholeheartedly in the fight for women! She could make fine contacts.

Faith listened docilely. But in the ensuing weeks, she wondered just how much the Alliance had actually done. How did the women's achievements rate in proportion to the efforts they expended?

There was so much talk. Too much talk. And so pitifully little accomplished.

"Women have had the vote for twelve years now," she said. "What have they done with it?"

"What have they done with it?" Mrs. Reynolds was horrified at this sacrilege! "After all, compared with the time men have held power, women are babes—just beginning to crawl. In time . . ."

"What I object to," Faith said, "is the endless talk. Why, if women really got together and acted as one, they could move mountains. I bet they could change the entire pattern of American life! But at the rate they're going . . ."

"You're too young and impetuous, Faith," disapprovingly.

She should have kept silent, grateful for a berth in these troubled times. But it was characteristic of her to speak out, even when it was imprudent. Singlehanded, she sought to inspire the Alliance to immediate and drastic action.

Really, Mrs. Reynolds reflected in the privacy of her own office, that girl might well talk herself into the presidency of the Alliance!

Corrigan was a good proselyter.

In October, she was fired.

12. When she admitted being jobless again, Winona said, "Faith, what's the matter with you? Can't you get along with anybody? Do you always have to shoot your big mouth off?"

Obviously Winona was losing her admiration for her old friend. Corrigan, on the other hand, approved warmly.

"Honey," he said, "you've got more guts than any man I know."

"Guts won't pay my keep," ruefully.

"I'll stake you till you find something."

Each morning at nine, she left the house in Sunnyside to make the rounds of the magazines and newspapers, reading more want ads, applying, and never getting a break. Here and there, a word of encouragement, but nothing concrete. The city was struggling in the maelstrom of the depression; thousands of girls like herself were hunting desperately for jobs, making the last good outfit do, resorting to dozens of petty tricks to save pennies. Doing your own hair and nails; walking miles to save busfare; bringing your own sandwich to the Automat and buying a cup of coffee; choosing the cheap nourishing foods that stayed with you a long time: hard-boiled eggs, cheese, peanut butter. A package of Latham products would have come in handy now, she thought ironically, and more welcome than Phillip's frequent letters.

One Sunday morning, a fortnight before Christmas, she received a telephone call.

"Guess who this is!"

Faith recognized the coy feminine voice; there was only one like it.

"Surprise, surprise!" Joyce Griswold chirped. "I'm here in New York. Can you believe it!"

"Is Allan with you?"

"No, Allan's much too busy to leave the plant. And Bobbie—that's our new baby—is home with his nurse. But Junior is with me." She added smugly, "I just came on for a little shopping trip."

"How nice."

"Faith, do have dinner with me today. I'm dying to see you!"

"I'm sorry, Joyce. But I'm busy."

"Then what about lunch tomorrow? I'd like you to help me with my shopping. After all, you know the town."

In the face of Joyce's determination, Faith decided it was wiser to give in. They met at the Commodore, where Joyce was stopping, and she greeted Faith effusively.

"Here's Junior, darling. Hasn't he grown? Junior, say hello to Aunt Faith!"

Junior held out a pudgy hand.

Joyce led the way to the dining room. The birth of her second son had left a halo around her blond head and fifteen extra pounds on her hips, which the expensive beaver coat tried to disguise.

"Faith, I'm simply dying to hear all about your career. I bet you run the magazine by now."

"I'm not with *Feminine Appeal* any more."

"Really? Then what are you doing?"

"Oh, various things."

There flashed in Joyce's pale-blue eyes the recognition that all was not well with Faith. Come to think of it, she did look a bit seedy. That brown tweed suit was at least four years old.

"Faith, you haven't asked me a thing. Aren't you interested in the news from home?"

"I've been getting it," noncommittally.

"Then you know how well things are going with our husbands." Efficiently, Joyce mashed the potatoes, peas and liver on Junior's plate, and shoveled it into his rosebud maw. "We finally got out of that awful dump on Sycamore Street. We've put a down payment on a house on the Heights—a beautiful place, and a wonderful buy! I'm really sorry for the people who had to give it up."

Faith said nothing. The chef's salad was sawdust in her mouth.

"Allan has been so good to me," Joyce continued. "Do you know what he said? 'Joyce, you've been such a *good* sport during our bad times, you deserve a real nice present. You take a trip to New York and buy yourself some real pretty clothes.'" Her eyes glittered. "He gave me a thousand dollars—and I'm going to spend it all on a mink!"

Faith thought desperately, How can I get out of here, fast?

"Are you coming home for the holidays?" Joyce asked bluntly.

"I don't know."

"It's kind of interesting," Joyce said, hunting down the last cake crumbs on her plate, "the way you and Mark lead separate lives. Sort of a companionate marriage, I suppose you call it. Allan would never stand for it. He wants me beside him all the time."

And just before they parted, she added lightly, "Don't stay away too long, Faith. Not that you can't trust Mark. But the way some of the St. Croix girls are eyeing him, you'd think he was a bachelor again."

That night, Faith sent a wire to Phillip Latham in Palm Beach. IF YOUR INVITATION STILL HOLDS GOOD I WOULD LIKE TO ACCEPT IT.

Chapter Twelve

1. When Faith stepped off the plane at the West Palm Beach airport, Phillip was waiting for her. He was clad in a faded blue pullover, stained canary-yellow slacks, a pair of disreputable sandals. His light hair was clipped to the roots, his skin beet-red and peeling, the livid scar on his forehead prominent. Faith thought he looked like a hard-boiled character in one of those *Wanted! Reward!* placards hanging in the post office.

He hugged her exuberantly, then held her off at arm's length, his raffish head cocked.

"A little too pale—a little too wan, I'd say. But I'm sure glad to see you, honey chile."

She flinched under the brash intimacy of his greeting.

"Right now, I feel like an icicle. I've been frozen so long I don't think even the hot sun . . ."

"The sun and I," he promised affably. He picked up the bags and led her to the station wagon. "How's Mark?" he asked impulsively, and very much against his better judgment. He had meant to keep Mark out of it.

"Okay, as far as I know."

He helped her into the front seat. It felt good having her beside him. He was easy and relaxed, and a little superior, too, as if he'd stepped out of character and into a new role—a role he had visualized whenever he thought of Mark.

As he drove the station wagon across the Royal Palm bridge, Faith caught her first glimpse of the island: the stately rows of royal cocoanut palms; the deep rich green of the turf; the vivid pinks and reds of the oleanders, hibiscus, and bougainvillea; and then as they turned right on Ocean Boulevard, the resplendent sweep of sea, streaked with aquamarine and purple. He parked the car in the walled courtyard, and a stocky, hawk-nosed Negro in a starched white coat came out for the bags.

"Come with daddy," Phillip said, smiling boyishly. She followed him through the white door into a cool marble hall, where classic sculpture was displayed in niches, and from there to the wide veranda facing the circular pool, outlined by masses of lilies and poinsettia. Thick vines crept around the colonnades, spilling profuse pink and scarlet blossoms.

Mrs. Latham was bent over a small bamboo writing table, and two Belgian griffons were nuzzling at her feet.

"Ma," Phillip shouted, "here's our prize captive!"

Mrs. Latham greeted her warmly. "I'm very happy to see you, my dear. We'll see to it that you get a good rest."

They had cocktails on the terrace, and then Mrs. Latham said, "You've time for a nap. Dinner is at eight."

"Faith isn't tired," Phillip protested. "I thought we'd play some tennis."

"Don't be greedy," Mrs. Latham answered, as if he were a small boy.

When Faith was shown to her cool, spacious room, she sighed contentedly. Her old black evening gown had been pressed. The maid was drawing her bath. She stretched out on the chaise, conscious of a sudden pang of guilt. Only yesterday, she had been part of that sluggish and pitiful mob on Sixth Avenue, staring without hope at the placards: Seamstress, cook, nurse, counterman; fifty a month, thirty a month and living quarters below basement, a roof over your head, that was about all you dared expect these days. After she scanned the Help Wanted column in the paper, she turned back to the headlines: In Massachusetts, the mills were closed; in Michigan, the conveyor belts had come to a standstill; in Pennsylvania, the mine pits were boarded up. And it was the worst winter in years, Long Island Harbor froze over, t.b. and pneumonia stalked through the hungry land. The Hunger March had ended in frustration, and even the proud and mighty were looking to the W.P.A. . . .

I have no right to this luxury while others like me are cold and hungry, she thought. Her innate sense of fair play continued to plague her, until finally she was forced to remind herself this unexpected vacation was heavensent, just what the doctor ordered.

She came down to dinner, served on the terrace.

"You're looking better, Mrs. Holmes," Phillip said gravely. "Just give us a little time, and we'll restore the bloom to your cheeks and the come-hither to your eyes."

Mrs. Latham, in a dowdy printed chiffon frock and a priceless string of pearls, sat at the head of the table, the griffons whining softly at her comfortably shod feet. She poured mineral oil on her salad, wheat germ on the grilled pompano; then, for dessert, she took Yogurt and Melba toast. Faith and Phillip were served the same avocado, but with a rich dressing, the same fish with a heavy sauce, and then, for dessert, a strawberry mousse. Mrs. Latham looked on disapprovingly.

"You'll never gain your strength on such foods," she said. "Tomorrow, Faith, I'll take charge of your diet."

"I warn you, ma's a food faddist," Phillip groaned. "She prescribes hay, straw, and no red meat."

After dinner, he announced blithely he was going to show Faith the moon over the ocean.

"No thanks. I've seen the moon," she replied sedately.

"Not the tropical moon," he grinned. "I'm counting on it to send your blood pressure up. It's more effective than ma's vitamins."

The moon was a platinum disk in the deep-black sky; the dark, hypnotic ocean was cleft by the path of its shimmering silver. They walked along Lake Trail, and the griffons pranced serenely at their heels. They lingered in the shadow of a ceiba, whose interwoven branches guarded it jealously from the intruding light.

"I got a letter from Mark last week," he said abruptly.

Her heart leaped.

"Faith, why aren't you home with him? There are no longer any financial problems to keep you in New York."

How could she explain? Conventional excuses for the break in their unconventional marriage would fall flat.

She said in a low voice, "I was the girl on the pedestal."

"And the air was too rare up there?"

"After a while I fell off."

"No one to pick up the pieces?"

"No one."

"That means you're washed up?"

"I don't know, Phillip. It's all so muddled."

He tossed away his burning cigarette. "Not as muddled as you think, sister. It's simple arithmetic. If you're still in love, why aren't you together? If you're through, why don't you call it quits—and try again? It's being done all the time, you know."

"I couldn't, Phillip. I just couldn't live with anyone else! That's what Mark's done to me."

"You haven't the guts to admit defeat."

She was astonished by his intensity. It wasn't like Phillip to turn so serious.

"Phillip, you don't understand. I don't quite understand it myself."

"Well, what're your plans?"

"Please, Phillip. Right now, I'd rather not talk about it."

They retraced their steps in silence. He realized she was no longer aware of him. She had fled to a world of her own, populated exclusively by Mark Holmes. Suddenly an image focused on the screen of his mind. He saw Faith and Mark standing together in the great hall of the house in St. Croix, their arms linked, their bodies close, their compelling oneness shutting him out in the cold. In that moment, he was sickeningly envious of Mark. For he saw, with a sense of intuition rare in him, that the integrity and purpose in Mark's character had brought him fulfillment. Phillip did not dramatize this merely as a great and enduring love affair, or even the ideal marriage. The picture of Faith and Mark together haunted him far less because of a desire to possess Faith than for the fact that she was the symbol of Mark's successful search for happiness.

He had said, "If you two ever smash up, I'll lose whatever little faith I have in humanity."

They had broken. Faith was here in the South with him, and he dared imagine a future with her. An end to his casual, puerile affairs, to the emptiness and frustration of his life. Through her, he meant to find the answer that had eluded him for so long. Through her, he might even learn to identify himself with Mark, and thus realize the dream that had plagued him since they were both boys together.

2. She slept surprisingly well, and woke up tranquil and refreshed, all thought of last night's talk with Phillip banished. She sat up as the mulatto maid brought in her breakfast on an enormous pink tray set with Spode china. Mrs. Latham had made good her threat. Faith stared at the bowl of sliced oranges in lemon juice, the whole-grain cereal topped with raisins, dates and figs, the pitcher of unpasteurized cream, the whole-wheat bread and honey, the pot of decaffeinated coffee. And in the center, beside the single red rose in a narrow silver vase, stood a small box of *Wheat-Lax*.

"All for me?" she gasped.

"Yas'm. Miz Latham look after her people."

Mrs. Latham, Faith learned, was a devotee of the health stores. Whenever she arrived in New York, her Lincoln could be seen parked outside a Health Bar, where she sampled with a judicious air the bilious concoctions, and listened deferentially to a pallid clerk weighing the merits of Vitamized Prunes over Bran Yum-Yums.

She kept her staff in a dither of embarrassment, for she checked their morning habits, insisted that they take their quota of brewer's yeast and Yogurt. She kept complicated calory charts, and she was familiar with the theories of the nutrition experts, from Fletcher to Gaylord Hauser.

Phillip teased her mercilessly; after all, her fortune came from refined-flour products. But Mrs. Latham saw nothing amusing in his attitude. Like most reformers, she lacked a sense of humor.

3. The first two weeks were pure heaven. Gradually, Faith became acclimated to the penetrating heat of the sun, the enervating opiate of the warm salt water, the languorous effect of the sultry air. She played tennis with Phillip, swam in the pool, but most of the time she lay on the chaise, indolent and free of all care. New York and its worries were forgotten. Never before, even in the early days of her marriage, had she known such sybaritic luxury, and it was proving a marvelous tonic. Her fine color returned, glowing through the smooth tanned skin. She gained weight. Her mind was taking a sabbatical; for once, her bodily senses reigned.

Afternoons when Phillip drove over to Gulf Stream for polo, she spent with Mrs. Latham, who was tremendously interested in the problems of the modern woman, and was eager to discuss them with her.

"I'd like to see a woman leader arise in this country," Mrs. Latham said. "Then we'd see some action!"

"The words of a militant suffragette!" Faith teased.

"Why not? Women have been passive far too long. That's why the world is in such a sorry state."

"You've had enough rest," Phillip announced blithely. "You've grown brown and sleek, darling. How about stepping out for a change?"

"Faith will be bored to death by your friends!" his mother retorted.

"With a buildup like that," he groaned, "how do you expect me to make a good impression?"

Although he enjoyed having Faith to himself, he did want to show her off to his friends. He took her to lunch at the Bath and Tennis, to dinner at the Everglades. And to his gratification, his friends did admire her, possibly because she was different. Often, they took a drive along

the shore, and he would park the car, and they would talk idly. Recently, the pattern of Phillip's speech had become a little more personal
and intimate. He even spoke of his childhood in Minnesota, of his
father who had died when Phillip was still a small boy. At first, it did
not occur to Faith that there might be a deliberate plan in these revela-
tions. She still saw him in the old light: Mark's friend, who was somehow not quite worthy of Mark's affection. His adolescent, undergraduate
charm amused and flattered her, but she realized she had come here to
Palm Beach only because she had no other place to go for a rest. And
she did like his mother. Actually, she liked Mrs. Latham far more than
Phillip.

One evening, he took her dancing at a local nightclub, and afterwards, they drove home and had a drink on the terrace. Then, without
a preamble, he pulled her roughly into his arms and kissed her. She
made an instinctive effort to resist him, but he held her fast. She was
appalled by the torrent of emotion, and she struggled resentfully.

"Faith," he whispered, "if you and Mark are finished, do give me
a break! You must know I love you. . . ."

"Please, Phillip." She turned her head away. "*Please!*"

His hands dropped to his sides before her anger. She left him and
ran into the house. In her room, the French doors opened on a balcony
smothered by bougainvillea. Standing there in the darkness, she thought,
I'm such a fool, I should have seen this coming.

She had seen it. But she had closed her eyes. Because she was discouraged and desperate, she had compromised with herself.

I'm here under false pretenses, she thought.

Before going to bed, she wrote Corrigan.

4. She dreaded meeting Phillip the next morning. But, to her relief,
he was his usual cheerful and amiable self. He reminded her of their
date on his friend Edward Dennen's yacht.

"Eddie reeled in a seven-foot sailfish yesterday. We've got to beat
him, honey!"

Perhaps, she reflected, she had taken him too seriously last night.
Nevertheless, she was heartened to find a telegram from Corrigan
awaiting her; apparently, their messages had crossed.

LANDED SNUG BERTH WITH HOMER SWEET PUBLIC
RELATIONS STOP CONVINCED HIM I NEED ABLE ASSIST-
ANT STOP COME HOME IMMEDIATELY CORRIGAN.

She waited until dinner was over before she broke the news.

Phillip, badly sunburned from the day's fishing trip, was showing the effect of his martinis. He made no protest, but his mother spoke quickly.

"Faith, you can't leave now! You're just beginning to perk up. I was hoping you'd finish the season with us."

"You are awfully kind. But I have a chance to get a job if I return to New York now."

"At least stay the weekend. I insist, my dear."

Finally, Faith agreed.

When she came down after breakfast the next morning, she learned that Phillip had taken a plane north, unexpectedly. Well, she would spend the last three days at the Lathams' in peace.

5. It was snowing in St. Croix, and the violent wind whirled the flakes into a blinding barrage. Leaving the office of the Holmes-Griswold Company, Phillip put up the collar of his camel's-hair coat, and rushed down to the waiting taxi.

"To the airport," he said. "And stop at Western Union on the way."

As they sped out to the Heights road, he calculated how soon before he would see Faith again. He pictured her surprise when she learned where he had been and what he had accomplished. He certainly could make plans now!

At the airport, the pilot was warming up the engine.

"How does it look?" Phillip shouted above the noise of the motor.

"Not so good."

"We've got to get out!"

Once air-borne, he settled down to his exhilarating thoughts. When had he decided to confront Mark? The night he had spoken to Faith of his love, and begged for a chance? Or last night when Faith had announced suddenly that she was leaving for New York?

Early this morning, without any explanations, he had chartered a private plane and flown to St. Croix, where he phoned Mark immediately.

"What're you doing here?" Mark demanded, astonished.

"I just flew in. To see you."

"The unpredictable Phil! Well, for Pete's sake, come on over. It'll be good to see you again!"

As he entered the factory, he was aware of the hum of activity. Mark's secretary led him into a private office. "Mr. Holmes is on the floor," she said. "I'll tell him you're here."

He paced nervously back and forth in the large, sparsely furnished room. For the first time since he had embarked on his impulsive trip, he was keenly conscious of a qualm. Should he have come? Had he taken too much on himself? Was it the fair thing to do?

"Phillip!"

He wheeled around. Mark was striding toward him, a warm smile on his lean face. Abruptly Phillip was conscious of the great difference between them, much more apparent now than in the early years. Suddenly he regretted the reckless decision that had brought him here. He wished they were on the old footing again, with nothing to mar their friendship.

"You're looking well," Mark said.

"Thanks."

"Sit down, Phil. Cigarette?"

"Thanks."

"Sorry I haven't a drink around."

Phillip grunted, "I didn't expect you'd have any."

Mark grinned at him affectionately. "Loquacious as a clam, aren't you? What're you doing up north in this lousy weather?"

Phillip was flustered, without his usual flippancy. Regarding Mark unhappily, he managed to communicate to him some of his own wretched tension.

He said abruptly, "Faith is at our place in Palm Beach."

Mark's gray eyes grew alert. "Is anything wrong with her?"

"Oh, no. She's fine."

Mark showed his relief. He came over to Phillip, put his hand on his shoulder.

"You're a damn good friend, Phil. But a poor emissary. This matter is entirely between Faith and me—and we've got to solve it in our own way!"

"Just a minute, Mark. You've got it all wrong!" Good Lord, he thought horrified, Mark was under the impression that he was bearing an olive branch. He couldn't have been more wrong, and it was Phillip's fault for muddling, instead of coming right out with it.

"Look, Mark. We've known each other a helluva long time. You know how I feel about you. If there's anybody I want to play fair with, it's you." There were beads of sweat on his forehead now, and he was struggling with the words. "I'm in love with your wife. Now, wait a minute—if you're planning a reconciliation, I'll step out, with my humble apologies. But if you're washed up, I want to marry her!"

Mark looked sick. Then after a moment's silence, he said carefully, "If Faith has made any plans, you can tell her this again: I won't stand in her way. . . ."

Phillip stared at the pilot's rigid body. They had been in the air for three hours, constantly fighting vicious headwinds. This meant they would land later than Phillip had anticipated. He was impatient to see Faith again. He was confident that now her attitude toward him would change, for Mark was definitely setting her free.

He moved restlessly. The plane was flying low. The cold mist enveloped them.

6. At sunset, Faith and Mrs. Latham took a walk along the Lake Trail, the griffons dancing at their heels. When they returned to the house for tea, the houseboy handed Faith a telegram. She tore open the envelope. It was dated this morning, signed by Phillip, and sent from St. Croix.

St. Croix! she thought, dazed. There must be some mistake!

HAVE SEEN MARK STOP GOOD NEWS STOP WILL BE BACK FOR DINNER LOVE PHILLIP.

There was no mistake. Phillip was in St. Croix. He had actually seen Mark. What did he say to Mark? She was torn between anger and anxiety. Should she call Mark? No, she had no right to. No more right than Phillip had to . . .

She'd have a showdown with Phillip tonight. Then she'd leave for New York.

When she came down to dinner, Phillip had not yet arrived. "I imagine he'll call from the airport," Mrs. Latham said. "I do wish he wouldn't take these impulsive jaunts to New York."

Obviously his mother had no idea of his real destination.

They sat idly listening to the radio. The evening was tranquil. The golden glow faded in the west and the first star glimmered in the pale-blue sky.

At seven o'clock, the news came on.

"An hour ago," the announcer said, "a private plane flying across the Smokies in a storm, crashed. The pilot and his passenger were both killed. From his luggage, the passenger has just been identified as . . ."

CONCLUSION OF HOMER SWEET'S REPORT
ON FAITH HOLMES

The Years of Fame and Treachery. Through Corrigan, landed berth
with Homer Sweet. Insinuated herself into Sweet's confidences.
Absorbed his famous principles of public relations in her work for
the Christine Ostbergh campaign for Congress.

Influenced Eric Ostbergh to give her spot as radio commentator on
Ostbergh Symphony Hour.

Broke up Harvey Jessup's happy marriage.
(*Important note.* Use this in campaign against her. Testimony of
Harvey Jessup's first wife.)

Used notoriety of Ostbergh broadcast for immediate self gain. Persuaded Mrs. Latham to sponsor new radio program. Went overseas
to become "Our Faith" for gullible G.I.'s.

On return, subverted famous Homer Sweet principles to launch
new political organization for women.
(*Note:* Under peculiar circumstances impossible to discover, she
encountered Mark Holmes in Paris. Scandal still to be uncovered
here.)

Her notoriety now so great, a campaign of personal attack is certain
of success. Cover the following:

a) Cruelty to mother.
b) Indifference to first husband; treachery to Harvey Jessup.
c) Betrayal of Christine and Eric Ostbergh.
d) Calculation behind her new organizations, especially
   The Women's National Committee.
   Plan to put women in key positions?
   Where does she place herself in this picture? White House?

Chapter Thirteen

1. Corrigan arranged for her interview with Homer Sweet the following Monday morning at eleven.

She arrived in New York Sunday night, to discover that in her absence, Winona had quarreled violently with her husband and walked out on him. She had found a job in a burlesque house and was living alone in a dingy hall bedroom.

So Faith checked into the Barbizon again. She was showing the effects of the past four days. On the train coming north, she had been unable to rest. The fragments of a dozen scenes lingered in her tortured mind; the news of Phillip's death, Mrs. Latham's collapse, the arrival of Mr. Steelman, the family lawyer, who took charge of the funeral arrangements. Nor could she forget about Phillip himself; she was sick with self-recrimination. And Mark; she was desperately worried about what Phillip had said to Mark. As Phillip's friend and executor, Mark must have attended the funeral. If he had a talk with Mrs. Latham . . .

She must stop fretting about it. She took a sedative and went to bed. In the morning, she kept her mind resolutely on her appointment. For the interview, she dressed carefully in her old but still good navy blue suit, a white blouse, her worn beaver greatcoat. The shock had left its marks under her eyes and around her mouth. She looked tense and tired.

She took a Madison Avenue bus and then walked over to Fifth. Entering the reception room of Homer Sweet's offices on the thirtieth floor of a Rockefeller Center skyscraper, she found it the replica of the library in an old English manor house. The pretty blonde at the switchboard, protected by a sheet of plate glass, was an anachronism.

"I have an appointment with Mr. Sweet," Faith said.

"About a job?"

"Yes."

"Then you'll have to make this out." The girl handed her a printed form. "Every applicant must fill out the entire questionnaire. Mr.

Sweet's orders. You'll find pen and ink at the desk." A mocking smile flitted across the painted mouth. "Make yourself comfortable. It'll take quite a while."

Reading it over, Faith thought, Heavens, this is practically a third degree! Besides the conventional routine questions, there were innumerable others, referring to the applicant's background, personality, aspirations and private life.

Where have you worked previously?

Why didn't you continue there? Fired? If not, give reasons for leaving.

Do you drink? If so, why? a) To be sociable?

b) To build up ego?

c) To combat loneliness?

The last page, half blank, was headed by a request: *What have you to offer this organization? Write your answer in not more than fifty words.*

A discreet footnote added: *All ideas, slogans, suggestions remain the property of Homer Sweet.*

She returned to her easy chair. Paper in hand, she waited. Fifteen minutes passed, a half hour. Messengers rushed in and out of the reception room; a postman staggered by with a huge bag of mail; the switchboard hummed with activity. Finally she got up and tapped on the plate-glass partition.

"How about my appointment with Mr. Sweet?"

"He's busy."

"Does he know I'm here?"

"I told Miss Kelly, his secretary, when you came in, miss."

"Will you remind her, please?"

"It won't do any good."

A tall young woman with hyperthyroid blue eyes and a receding chin looked into the room.

"Mrs. Holmes? Will you come with me, please?"

Faith followed her through a long pine-paneled corridor to a door which the woman opened reverently.

"Mr. Sweet," she said, "this is Mrs. Holmes."

Faith had the impression of a spacious room, at least thirty feet long and handsomely proportioned, its large windows festooned with curtains of beige raw silk; of paneled walls hung with English hunting prints and two eighteenth-century oils; of Chippendale chairs upholstered in green and scarlet leather; of a fine Aubusson rug. And at the farthest end of the room, a massive mahogany desk was placed at an angle between two windows, leaving in shadow the figure of the short stocky man who sat behind it.

"Come in, come in!" he ordered in an impatient didactic tone, holding out his plump hand for the application blank. "Sit down, sit down."

While he scanned it, Faith regarded him curiously. His round head was outlined by a fringe of neutral brown hair; his eyes were pale and moist, his skin the color of putty. His compact body was squeezed into a gray sharkskin suit, with a fawn-colored vest. He wore a striped pink shirt, a turned-down white collar, a maroon knit tie. A white carnation decorated his buttonhole.

"So you're the young lady Corrigan recommended." He looked up briefly. Then he chose a pipe from the half dozen in a rack on his cluttered desk, and bit the stem reflectively.

"You didn't complete my questionnaire. Why not?"

"Much of the information wouldn't concern you, Mr. Sweet," she said. "I answered the questions I considered pertinent."

He leaped up, gripping the edge of his desk, as if he were about to address a seminar.

"Young lady, your attitude is ill advised!" He cleared his throat nervously. "No detail is so minute that it does not have some bearing on the matter under consideration. Much time, effort, and—uh, shall we say erudition?—has gone into the preparation of this questionnaire. My good friend, Professor VanCleve—a great student of psychology—contributed to its contents. It is an instrument designed to gauge the intelligence, the acuity, the latent capabilities of the prospective candidate! It gives me the opportunity to weigh his merits and pigeonhole his talents."

One of the three telephones on his desk pealed, and he muttered an excuse as he picked it up. When he finished the lengthy conversation, he scrawled a few words on the huge memorandum pad before him.

"Now, take *yourself,* Mrs. Holmes," he continued, teetering on the balls of his feet. "The very fact that you rebel at the nature of the questions gives me the index to your character. I gather you are a) independent, b) given to speaking your mind candidly, c) poised and courageous! These are qualities I greatly admire. Used with discretion, these qualities can be made to cement efficiently relations between our organization and our clients—and between our clients and their public. It is evident to me that you evoke a ready response in people. In due time we shall give you the opportunity to show us what you can do along these lines."

Faith found herself mesmerized by the flow of words. Nevertheless, she wasn't sure whether she was hired or not. She summoned up the courage to ask baldly, but he gave her no chance to speak.

"Have you had any experience in the field of public relations?" he asked. "Do you know anything about our profession which in so short a time has become a most decisive factor in establishing good will between industry and consumer, capital and labor?"

He paused at last for breath, and Faith wondered if this were her cue to applaud. But again, he rushed on.

"May I clarify for you the needs and potentialities of our profession?" He sat down abruptly, dwarfed by the thronelike chair, the tips of his shoes barely touching the rug. "The office of public relations is the leaven to the dough, the spark to the kindling, as it were. When times were prosperous, industry thought, foolishly enough, it could dispense with our help. Then when conditions deteriorated, banks, investment houses—even industry—became anathema to the people! So the public-relations counsel has come to their rescue. He is indeed the friend in need! He reinstates them into the good graces of the common man. And in turn, he shows the little fellow that he needn't fear the bankers, industrialists, etc. They are no villains. For what constitutes big business is merely a group of decent, hard-working men like himself. Men who have reached the pinnacle of success *through their own efforts!*"

Miss Kelly came in silently, bearing on a tray a glass of milk, an apple and two graham crackers.

"Your lunch, Mr. Sweet."

"Thank you." He turned to Faith. "That will be all, Mrs. Holmes. Thank you very much indeed."

She stood up uncertainly. "Am I hired?"

"Yes, yes, of course. Miss Kelly will attend to all the details."

He cleared his throat again. "Just one thing more, Mrs. Holmes, for you to bear in mind. It is my precept to all new members of my family: *Make public opinion your personal opinion!* That is all."

2. Corrigan was waiting for her at Tony's. It was no longer necessary to be scrutinized through a peep-hole before entering; the doors were wide open now.

"I'm sorry to be late," she said breathlessly.

"I didn't expect you any sooner," he answered. "How long did the Great Illuminator keep you waiting?"

"How do you know about it?"

"Common procedure." Corrigan helped himself to the bowl of cheese-coated popcorn. "The longer you cool your heels, the more deflated your ego. That's Sweet's policy with people who want something from him."

She smiled impishly. "I think I put one over on him. I didn't complete the application."

"My dear girl, that's a flagrant violation of protocol! But he'll see that you fill it out properly before long."

"What makes you think I've got the job?"

He regarded her dolefully. "Did he make a speech on the high ideals and notable obligations of public relations?"

"Why, yes. He did."

"Then you're engaged. He doesn't waste his breath needlessly."

"Corrigan, I couldn't get a word in edgewise. He didn't stop talking until his secretary brought in his lunch."

"You mean the graham crackers and milk? Don't let the milk fool you—it's spiked with brandy!" He finished his own whisky sour. "What did you think of his spiel?"

"I couldn't help but be impressed."

"Yeh, he affects everybody that way. The first time." He speared a clam and swallowed it with relish. "Public relations, of course, is merely propaganda with a gilded halo."

"Still, I'm darned glad to have this job. I don't know how to thank you, Corrigan."

"We'll see how you feel six months from now."

It wasn't the future that mattered, but the present, this moment. She would live from day to day, and after a while, perhaps she would forget.

3. Homer Sweet never confided to his coterie of admirers how he stumbled on that hidden treasure, the Miracle of Publicity.

Homer hailed from Ossawachee, a small town in Iowa. His father, principal of the local public school, was a vain, pedantic man given to the sort of flamboyant rhetoric and Bible quoting which his son found invaluable, years later, in coining slogans for a great tobacco concern.

At seventeen, Homer entered the Iowa College of Applied Sciences, where he soon developed into the least-liked student on the campus and fast acquired one of the most flourishing inferiority complexes on record. But this sorry state did not last for long. Homer took stock of himself, and after a brutally revealing self-diagnosis, he evolved a plan that was to bring him if not popularity then at least, notoriety. He would get himself talked about. Good or bad, it didn't matter. The important thing was the publicity!

He worked hard in his special and oblique way. By senior year, he was the best-known man on the campus—manager of the basket-ball team, cheerleader, guiding genius of *Campus Chatter*. He always managed to insinuate himself prominently into any outstanding group.

During the snake dance after a victorious football game, Homer was in the vanguard, prancing up to the goal post. Once there, however, he stepped nimbly aside, to allow a six-footer the privilege of rooting it up. That was the theory he had evolved. Let some poor dub do the dirty work, while you get the glory—via publicity.

If the Iowa College of Applied Sciences had had a river and a crew, he would surely have been coxswain. As it was, the only sport he excelled in was tongue wagging.

The girls he admired never paid any attention to him. But he was popular at bull sessions and smokers, for he had an inexhaustible fund of stories, fortified by a little black book to which he referred whenever a point eluded him.

He knew everyone on the campus and everyone knew him. By the time he was ready to graduate, *Homer Sweet* was a byword on the campus, and one of his more astute teachers said sourly that if he hung around much longer, they'd rename the college after him.

Years later, he confided to Hank Jessup, president of the Jessup Advertising Agency, "Psychologists aren't taught. They're self-made!"

He was born one; he was the finest example of what exploitation could do.

It was inevitable that the sign on the door of his first small office should read: *Homer Sweet. Publicity.*

Five years after he opened his New York office, he was on familiar terms with the buxom, middle-aged woman president of Stay Young, Incorporated, his first big account. His name began to appear in the national magazines, over articles entitled, "How Women Can Influence Public Opinion," or, "Who Is to Blame for Our Rising Divorce Rate: A Symposium."

And finally, after he signed a contract with the Ace High Packing Company to make the American housewife conscious of their new tinned product, *Ham Mélange*, at a retainer of fifty thousand a year, he rented a suite of offices on Madison Avenue.

One of America's foremost public-relations counsels had come of age.

His Alma Mater never forgot him. After all, he was the only alumnus to become so prominent. He had worked industriously for his first degree, a B.A.S. (Bachelor of Applied Science); but after that, it came easy.

Every few years, his Alma Mater showed its pride by conferring a new degree on him until finally he had enough initials after his name to compete with an English baronet.

4. Nothing in Faith's experience had quite prepared her for the unique privilege of working for Homer Sweet.

The layout of the offices, for example, was suggested by Mr. Sweet himself. There was the impressive English reception room from which you stepped into the adjoining General Operations Room. Here stood twenty desks in serried array for the use of the clerks, stenographers and lesser assistants. The filing cabinets against the walls bulged with voluminous correspondence, brochures and pamphlets. A half-dozen mimeograph machines stood on plain tables. And at the outer rim of the room, segregated in glass-enclosed cubicles, slaved the contact men, the account executives and Homer's personal aides.

The conference room which separated Homer from his staff was spacious and elegant, with a long polished table around which were arranged a dozen leather-upholstered armchairs. In the corner towered a huge Spanish chest, converted, like the one in his office, into a private bar.

And finally, there was the last entrance to what the staff called the "Sanctum Sanctorum."

Homer Sweet was addicted to referring to the staff as his "Happy Family" and they in turn called him "the Little Father," though never in his presence. He usually hired brilliant graduates from Yale and Harvard, the Phi Beta Kappa boys, and he made it clear to them that a job with Homer Sweet was a sacred trust. He demanded the best, and paid well for it. He was an indomitable worker and expected as much from his staff.

Indeed, his intense absorption in his career had ruined his marriage. For although he felt he was chosen to shed light upon this earth, his wife found it difficult to reconcile his prophetic destiny with any semblance of a domestic life. She was a public-relations widow.

After their separation, Homer took a small flat near his office. No longer hampered by the exigencies a domestic routine might inflict on him, he was up at five each morning to scan the newspapers, blue-penciling any items of interest. By eight, he was at his desk. He worked longer than the staff, and often returned to the office after dinner.

At the time Faith came to work for him, he numbered among his clients representative industries, motors, foods, fashions, cosmetics, several banking houses, among them Hastings-Pitney, which Corrigan had brought with him.

But the outstanding account on which he lavished his personal attention was, of course, International Petroleum. This organization had for years been involved in nefarious dealings which had given it a dubious reputation until its mysterious head, Eric Ostbergh, awarded Homer the privilege of presenting the company to the public in a more palatable light.

The campaign proved an extraordinary success. Among the projects with which Homer had whitewashed the company, was the one given nation-wide publicity:

"Aware of its obligation to the hungry peoples of the world, the International Petroleum Company has put into operation a plan for feeding the needy families in the Far East. Eric Ostbergh, philanthropic head of the International Petroleum Company, conceived the idea. It is his hope that other companies will follow suit, each assuming a share of responsibility in this humanitarian project."

Faith was deeply impressed. "That's a very generous act," she said.

Corrigan scowled at her. "Don't fall for it, Faith. Ostbergh isn't posing as his brother's keeper unless the results warrant it. Homer probably said to him, 'Bread cast upon the waters inevitably comes back in the form of dividends.'"

Faith's desk was in Corrigan's office. She did the clerical work on the Hastings-Pitney account, took care of the correspondence, kept the clippings up to date. For these duties, she received fifty dollars a week.

She returned to the office after dinner one evening in order to finish the extracts on a survey which had been sent out to a mailing list of people notable in their fields, college professors, scientists, ministers, sociologists, industrialists. Homer Sweet had studied the methods of the pioneers in public relations, and emulated them. He dictated the foreword to all such surveys:

"Dear Mr. ——:
"We are soliciting your help in a survey to be used as an index for ——. We feel that you, as a leader in your field, can be of in-

estimable aid to us in formulating the proper conclusions. What is your opinion on ——? May we use your name in our final reports?

"Cordially yours,

"Homer Sweet."

Three thousand questionnaires had been mailed out; more than ninety per cent were returned with all questions answered in great detail. Before her was a gold mine of information, ideas, suggestions. Many of the writers even sent along their photographs and biographies.

Why should they be so generous? Faith sometimes wondered, until Corrigan reminded her bluntly that *Who's Who* was the greatest sucker list in the world.

Occasionally, however, a few replies were brusque, the writers refusing to be inveigled. One response was especially caustic. "You have an infernal nerve, Sweet. I'll provide you with the information—for my regular fee."

She was staring perplexedly at this note when the door of General Operations opened, and Homer strode in.

She approached him hesitantly. "Mr. Sweet, there is an answer here from a Dr. Ellis Cairns. . . ."

"Disregard it! He should not have been included on Corrigan's list. We've had trouble with him before—a most unco-operative man!"

"Mr. Sweet," she began quickly, hoping to hold his interest. "I wanted to talk to you. I've been here a month now. Of course, I do like my job—but it doesn't really require much initiative."

"We'll take care of it," he promised vaguely. "In the future."

"Wouldn't this be a good opportunity to try me out?" she suggested eagerly. "Let me see this Dr. Cairns. Perhaps I could persuade him to answer the questions."

"Very well, very well. See what you can do. But I warn you—he's an irascible old codger!"

Dr. Cairns, Dean of the School of Business Administration, was tart and short-tempered. He informed her with a wintry smile that he admired Sweet's gall, if not his character.

Faith sat at the edge of her chair. "But Mr. Sweet has done so much," she said earnestly, "to mold public opinion in a manner advantageous to the people themselves."

"And why shouldn't he?" Dr. Cairns snapped. "With the very best brains in the country at his disposal—without charge."

"Dr. Cairns, have you ever met Homer Sweet?"

"Is it necessary?"

She ignored his sarcasm. "Yes, it is! Because once you'd met him, I'm sure you'd change your views. I know you'd be impressed by his sincerity—you couldn't help it! You mustn't confuse him with those publicity men who're in business only to exploit their clients' products. There's a spirit of altruism in all of Mr. Sweet's operations. I know that sounds stuffy and pretentious. But it's true!"

He appeared to be impressed by her sincerity. He leaned back in his chair. Any girl who spoke so wholeheartedly deserved a chance.

"Tell Sweet I'll call him soon. Give him a chance to talk for himself!"

Homer was of course enormously pleased with her success. He resolved henceforth to use her as a liaison between himself and those recalcitrant few who needed persuasion.

Finally he entrusted her with the new campaign for Stay Young, Incorporated.

"I am especially sentimental about this account, Faith," he explained, filling the pipe-of-the-day with a special blend of tobacco. "And I see it as a challenge to your resourcefulness. On its results will depend your future here with us."

"I'll do my best," she promised.

He puffed at his pipe, cuddling the bowl in his pudgy, manicured fingers.

"I wish to emphasize," he began, "the fact that we handle this account not merely to increase the prestige and sale of its products— what we're trying to do incidentally is to *benefit womankind!* There are too many tragically unhappy women in the country—women who, as they turn forty, feel they have been relegated to the back seat in life, as it were."

He looked to Faith for approbation.

"It is absolutely our duty to persuade every woman over forty to acquaint herself with the Stay Young way of beauty! We must build up the esteem of the mature woman—elevate her spirit! And if we succeed, who can tell what beneficent results may accrue?"

Faith scribbled industriously, "The tragedy of the American woman is that she worships the young instead of Youth."

"That will be all, my dear. Good luck."

She went to work, using all his methods. "A campaign," Homer had once told her, "is composed of innumerable details, none of them too small to ignore. Personally, I always attack a problem with my own

SCA approach. That is 1) Be skeptical. 2) Be critical. 3) Be analytical. Once you've explored every angle and exhausted every possibility, you are master of the situation!"

She saturated herself in the study of the Woman After Forty, her problems, her outlook, her aim in life. She wrote articles, begging these women not to lag at the end of the procession, but take their rightful place among their younger sisters in the vanguard.

She arranged for promotion tie-ups with the magazines, including *Feminine Appeal,* which proved especially co-operative. And everywhere she went, she found the name of Homer Sweet an open sesame. He had a great reputation even among the press.

Once a week, he sent out a capsule pep talk "For My Family," in order to spur the staff on to greater efficiency and achievement. In this mimeographed sheet, he always cited an outstanding performance by some fortunate member, which reminded Faith of the tiny gold stars Miss Lovejoy used to hand out every Friday to the good little children.

More than once, she was singled out in the sermon as the star of the week. She came in for her share of praise from the staff, too.

At a cocktail party given by Stay Young, Incorporated to launch a new lipstick, Pink Dawn, Harvey Jessup, head of the Jessup Advertising Agency, cornered her.

"Mrs. Holmes, I do want to congratulate you on the wonderful job you've done. Homer is certainly lucky to have you on his staff!"

"Thank you." She smiled wanly. "By now, it's got me down."

"Then there's no use your hanging around here. Much too noisy. Let's find a bar where I can congratulate you quietly."

She had met Harvey Jessup in the office several times, for he and Homer often worked on campaigns together, and she had found him affable and attractive. She was quite willing to steal away with him; the party was pretty dull. As they entered the elevator, she tried to stifle a yawn.

"What a day! I'm sick and tired of Pink Dawn lipstick. If I hear it once more today . . ."

"What you need," he said capably, taking her by the arm, "is a good nourishing dinner. And I know just the place."

He helped her into a cab and gave the driver the address of O'Mara's Chophouse. They found a booth, and he ordered broiled steaks, baked potatoes, salad, apple pie and coffee, and made no attempt at conversation until Faith had eaten.

"Feel better now?"

"Much, thank you."

"Cigarette?"

"Please."

He touched his thumb to the expensive silver lighter. He was a handsome man, not yet forty, and remarkably successful in his attempts to retain a youthful appearance. He was five feet ten, and of wiry build, though a little overweight now. His brown worsted Brooks Brothers suit disguised the onset of a paunch. His thick, neutral brown hair was parted in the center and brushed down ruthlessly. His face was square, the eyes small, deep-set and lively, brimming over with contagious optimism. And his talent for spontaneous friendliness was his greatest asset. He was a born salesman. He was proud of his wide circle of first-name friends, though actually he had few intimates. The string of clubs after his name in *Who's Who* began with the Advertising Association of America and ended with the Yale Club.

He ordered another pot of coffee.

"You've sure put a lot of energy into the Stay Young campaign."

"Let's not talk about it," she begged wearily, "or I'll be having nightmares about christening lipsticks."

"I'm sorry. I have no business keeping you up. You need a good night's sleep."

She smiled gratefully. "Do you mind if we leave now?"

"If you promise to let me take you to dinner again."

"I promise."

In the taxi, he said curiously, "Where are you from, Mrs. Holmes? Somehow, you don't strike me as a professional New Yorker."

"I come from a small town in Michigan. St. Croix. You've probably never heard of it."

"Oh yes. Isn't that the place Wolverine Motors is putting on the map?"

My home town, she thought. And once upon a time, my own people.

5. She worked hard. She was friendly and honest. In a profession noted for its flagrant practices, she built up a reputation for solid integrity.

All around the town, in newspaper, magazine, advertising, radio offices, she met girls like herself, who had climbed to success by sharp intelligence and sheer tenacity. She joined the ranks of the career women with their own apartments and private lives. She leased a small furnished flat in a brownstone on East Seventy-seventh Street. The night she prepared her first solitary dinner, she recalled how passionately she and Mark had longed for a room of their own in the old Holmes place. What, she wondered, had Mark done with the belongings they had stored? Was he making use of them again? And did they remind him of his life with Faith?

Strange. She could go on for days, absorbed in her job, driving herself with abnormal intensity, reasonably content, the past forgotten for the time being. Then, she would pick up a new Sinclair Lewis novel, or a Bach recording by Stokowski, or she'd come across a reproduction of a Rouault clown, and the scar of memories would be torn wide open again.

Fortunately, her capacity for hard work, her natural affinity for people came to her rescue in this crucial transition period. She disciplined herself to live in the present: the interview with the famed sociologist on the status of women in the New Deal; cocktails with Amy Stockton, the perennially youthful actress, who had promised a testimonial for Stay Young cosmetics; luncheon with a brilliant young braintruster, to whom Corrigan had introduced her; dinner at the Institute for the Dissemination of Information for World Peace, as Homer's guest; and once a week an evening with Corrigan, who had been recently transferred to Sweet's Washington Bureau, and came directly to New York on his day off.

She heard regularly from her father, who was working for Mark. Conditions were improving daily for the business. The airplane industry had proved its faith in the new Holmes-Griswold engine by an avalanche of orders. There was talk of a new plant adjacent to Wolverine. Tod added he was well, but Mrs. Hussar was ailing. The new doctor said it was arthritis.

Invariably, he finished on the same note: "When are you coming home for a visit? We miss you."

He never mentioned her mother. Or, directly, Mark.

6. Once a month, Winona Kraus dropped in to see her, usually at dinner time. She was still at the Forty-second Street burlesque house, and apparently content to be there. During her last visit, she admitted unhappily she was on the wagon. The company manager warned her that while he liked the girls plump, he wasn't running a beef trust. So she'd better lay off the bottle.

"Winnie," Faith said impulsively, "why don't you go home?"

"To that store dummy? Another day with Henry, and I'd go nuts!"

"I was thinking of St. Croix."

Winona popped a chocolate-covered cherry into her mouth and licked her fingers.

"What about you?" she parried. "Why don't you go back?"

"It's not exactly the same with me, Winnie. I like my work."

"What have I to go home to? Can you imagine if my folks saw me now?"

"It doesn't seem possible so many years have gone by," Faith said. "We're almost thirty."

Winona's glance measured her—the tall, well-rounded body, the chestnut hair softly waved in a long bob, the face nicely modeled now that the youthful plumpness was gone, the brown eyes sparkling with enthusiasm and vitality.

"You don't look it," she said enviously.

"Still," Faith persisted, "there are times when I think how nice it would be to be a kid again."

Winona refused to bite. "Not me. Not *my* family," she retorted.

7. Miss Kelly said, "Mr. Sweet wants to see you. Right away, Mrs. Holmes."

Faith got up and followed her into the Sanctum. Homer was standing by his desk, his round face in shadow. The fresh anemone in the lapel of his Glen-plaid suit proclaimed the news that spring was finally here.

Sitting back in a high Chippendale chair by the desk was a massive, heavy-set man in a neat conservative blue serge suit, whom Faith recognized from Corrigan's description.

"Mr. Ostbergh," Homer said, rising to the balls of his feet, "allow me to introduce Faith Holmes—the most efficient and charming member of my family."

Mr. Ostbergh acknowledged the introduction with a brusque nod of his massive head. He did not rise. And now Faith realized why he was known as the Sphinx. He was, she surmised, in his late forties or early fifties; his sandy hair, thinning over the high bony temples, was streaked with gray. His brows formed a promontory over the pale, deep-set eyes, giving the terrifying impression of empty sockets. This suggestion of a death's head was further emphasized by the short blunt nose and the prognathous jaw.

"Sit down, Faith," Homer suggested and from his manner, she knew he was on edge.

Mr. Ostbergh's pale-blue eyes, without shadow or highlight, were measuring her shrewdly.

"Faith, what is your personal opinion of women?" Homer asked with the indulgent smile of a fond parent questioning a precocious child. "I am referring to their status in this modern world of ours. Socially, economically, and politically."

She rose swiftly to the bait, for this was a subject dear to her heart since the day she had been fired from the Alliance.

"We women are still living in the dark ages," she said. "If we could only make full use of our latent powers, the repercussions would bounce the men in power right out of their sacred thrones. And we'd have the beginning of a new era: The Age of Woman."

Almost imperceptibly, Eric Ostbergh nodded to Homer.

"It's obvious women are heading for political power," she continued, but Homer interrupted blandly.

"Faith, how would you like to be instrumental in helping a fine woman become the new spokesman—or should I say spokeswoman—for your sex?"

"A new account?" she asked curiously.

"No, no. Let us say, rather, a mission, a supreme effort to contribute something vital to our American way of life."

"Who's the woman?"

The antique chair creaked under Eric Ostbergh's weight.

Homer cleared his throat nervously.

"Christine Ostbergh," he said. "Mr. Ostbergh's wife."

8. When Corrigan got in from Washington late that afternoon, he went directly to her apartment, where, over cocktails, she related the story of the afternoon's session.

"So Christine is to be America's gift to politics!" He whistled. "That's a mighty tall order."

"Homer's the man who can do it."

He regarded her sardonically. "I guess it's time for his Alma Mater to knight him with the final degree. Master of Double Talk."

"Corrigan, don't laugh at the idea of more women in politics!"

A twinkle lightened his brooding eyes. "Far be it from me to jeer. Actually, women should be better in politics than men. For one thing, they're superior as deceivers. You know how one woman sizes up another and tells at a glance the value of every garment, from hat to shoes? Suppose a female politician had some boodle to sock away. Do you think she'd hide it in a little black box? Not on your life! She'd blow herself to a mink. And right away, her loyal constituents would know there's something rotten in Denmark!"

She choked on her drink. "Corrigan, stop it. You aren't funny."

"Imagine a woman President," he continued with enormous relish. "She'll run a contest for the most original hat—and fifty million women will vie for the prize: a weekend at the White House!"

"Corrigan, you're a misogynist, and there's no hope for you," she said severely. "But you just wait and see what a couple of women can do!"

9. Thursday, Faith received a note from Christine Ostbergh, inviting her to spend the weekend at Twilight Hill, their place on Long Island.

Since Homer had also been asked, they drove out to the North Shore in his Cadillac. It was late Friday afternoon. In the soft spring twilight, the country reflected the luminous glow of a Sisley landscape.

"Faith," Homer Sweet said, patting her hand paternally, "I am glad to see you looking so well-turned-out, yet so inconspicuous, which to my mind is psychologically correct. Christine needn't be envious of another woman. Still, you are cognizant of my dictum: the minutiae create the whole."

She was abruptly impatient with him. "I wish you'd tell me something about Eric Ostbergh," she said.

"He's an extraordinary man," Homer answered obliquely. "Extraordinary. He came to America penniless. Today he is one of the most powerful men in the world." He added with rare candor, "Oil is his god."

"I cannot understand why his wife should want to go into politics."

Homer was silent.

The Cadillac swung off the main road, passed a small English gate house and drove along a private lane guarded by Lombardy poplars until it reached the vast gray Tudor house, almost hidden by shrubs and evergreens.

"The Ostberghs generally use this place in spring and autumn," Homer offered. "His empire in oil has ramifications in every corner of the globe, so, he maintains homes everywhere—London, Paris, Cairo—completely staffed and ready for occupancy at all times."

The man is a myth, Faith thought.

When they were shown into the drawing room, Ostbergh was seated by the fireplace, a bottle of Irish whisky on the Pembroke table beside him. He nodded deliberately.

"My wife will be down shortly. There are drinks on the table."

Homer poured two martinis and handed one to Faith; he was strained and ill at ease, his eyes wandering to the door. He relaxed slightly when Christine made her appearance, and Faith mused, He's afraid of Ostbergh, but he knows he is stronger than Christine. . . .

During the introductions, Faith observed Mrs. Ostbergh intently. She was slight and rather pallid, a shadowy creature in contrast to her massive, dictatorial husband. She was, Faith judged, anywhere between thirty and forty, for while her white skin was unlined, it had a preserved texture that was faintly repelling. Her oval face was outlined by dark hair, combed back in a thick chignon, the center part as ivory as her skin. Her well-spaced eyes were dark, too, and without expression, her mouth was thin-lipped and unrouged. Except for the jet embroidery on the yoke of her black chiffon frock, she wore no jewels other than a simple gold wedding band.

"It's good of you to come," she said pleasantly to Faith. Homer interrupted, with an appeasing glance toward his host, "Faith is most anxious to get started on the job."

Dinner was served in a baronial hall at a table so large Faith had the notion an amplifier was needed for them to communicate with one another.

Ostbergh sat at the head, impassive as granite, saying little, yet aware of every move, every nuance about him. He remained aloof from his wife and his guests, as he was deliberately aloof from all people. For long ago, he had learned how easy it was to manipulate humans and bend them to his will, and the knowledge left him slightly contemptuous of humanity.

Few people in America were aware of his origins, for Homer was paid well to keep such information out of the press.

The hulking, raw-boned young giant who had worked his way from Sweden to South America on a cattle boat, and from there to New Orleans and beyond to the Texas oil fields, was no star-struck youth, following the line of his destiny westward. He was inordinately ambitious, and the seeds of ruthlessness took root easily in his mind. For he discovered from the very beginning that both pioneer and wildcatter were gullible folk, easily duped and taken in.

He developed inevitably into a lone wolf, wily and alert for the stray sheep. The first step was the hardest, to acquire the first million took the longest. After that, it came easy. In Oklahoma, he gobbled up a small oil firm in straitened circumstances. Soon he added a couple of others and formed a holding corporation. Under each company, he leased or bought huge tracts of oil land, pyramiding his holdings by juggling the assets of the three firms, robbing Peter to pay Paul, and then having Paul disgorge to make good for Peter.

After that, he manipulated to gain control of the largest company in the state. As a majority stockholder, he formed a committee to gain existing control, then lined up a number of lackadaisical stockholders on his side. Finally, he called for a showdown, accusing the controlling group of mismanagement and inefficiency—a duplicity of which he was able to convince his cohorts, who thereafter backed him up solidly as he wrested control of the voting stock.

Before long he was active head of the organization. That was his real beginning, and from that time on there was no stopping him.

At forty, he was the uncrowned potentate of an empire in oil stretching to the very corners of the earth. Now, he saw again a great opportunity, and once more he decided to use his singular weapons to grasp it.

He looked around the festive table at the pawns in the game he always played alone.

Watching him shrewdly, Faith noted he had not spoken once to his wife during the entire meal. Mrs. Ostbergh puzzled Faith, too, for she did not give the impression of a likely political figure. Indeed, she seemed negative and withdrawn, a colorless and submissive woman who, in spite of her position, was not at ease in her surroundings.

Finally, she stood up, and Faith followed her, leaving the men to their talk. Mrs. Ostbergh led the way to the garden. The tranquil night air was saturated with the fragrance of spring flowers; the dark sky was hung with glittering stars.

"What a beautiful place this is," Faith said.

Christine smiled. "The house comes from Surrey, you know. Mr. Ostbergh had it dismantled and brought here. It has quite a history." She linked her arm through Faith's and added impulsively, "But it's rather ghastly to have to live up to a house, don't you think? Could anything be more dull or devastating?"

Faith was surprised and a little impressed by her candor. Still, a kernel of doubt lingered in her mind, for this was surely too iconoclastic an opinion for such a wealthy woman.

"I suppose the reason I grow so impatient with most women of leisure," Mrs. Ostbergh confessed, "is that I've worked very hard most of my life. I was Mr. Ostbergh's confidential secretary for five years before we were married. I've been on my own since I was eighteen. So I've had ample opportunity to see how much women are exploited in business—overworked, underpaid, with little chance for real promotion. It made a deep impression on me. 'Some day' I promised myself, 'I'll do something toward improving the lot of all women.'"

"I know just how you feel," Faith said warmly.

They sat down in the bamboo chairs.

"Recently, I've given it considerable thought," Christine Ostbergh went on. "I said to myself, 'Now you have money, position, leisure. Now is the time to help your sisters.' I turned to Mr. Ostbergh for advice. 'What can I do?' I asked him."

She paused delicately.

"When he suggested politics, I was horrified. What do I know about politics? Mr. Ostbergh laughed at me. 'What does anybody know about politics?' he said. 'You've got common sense and a level head. That's enough.' So I thought, Well, if I can get into politics, perhaps I can help promote laws to foster women's rights."

As she listened, Faith was unable to shake off the odd feeling that while Christine Ostbergh might be sincere, there was a subtly complex origin to her ambitions.

"That's the reason you and Homer Sweet are here today," Christine said and added with sudden and unexpected passion, "Do you think people will listen to me?"

Faith cast all doubts aside.

"We'll make them listen!" she promised fervently.

They held a brief conference Sunday night, just before Homer and Faith left Twilight Hill. It took place in the library, where the logs in the huge stone fireplace sent out a reassuring blaze against the cool April night.

Homer picked his way cautiously. "We must call upon all our inner resources, our past experiences to launch this campaign. We must approach it as a glorious experiment. True, there are a few women in politics. But who hears of them? Who knows of them? What have they done to date?"

A log sputtered in the fireplace and he scowled at its impertinence.

"Our task is to make this country conscious of what Woman, given the opportunity, can really do. Specifically, we will apply our efforts toward putting Christine in Congress, where she will serve as the first important exponent of woman's power. Faith will work closely with me on the project, for it is a matter dear to her own heart."

Christine lowered her eyes. Ostbergh sat in the tapestry chair, stolid and impassive.

"I shall devise the method of procedure," Homer continued blandly, "and apprise you in the near future."

"Good," Ostbergh said. The start was indeed auspicious.

Chapter Fourteen

1. Because she had an affinity for causes, Faith approached the new job not as a challenge but as a divine mission. The first important conference took place the following week. Since Homer was giving this campaign his personal attention, none of the brilliant young men on his staff were present. Only Faith, the Ostberghs and Miss Kelly, who recorded the proceedings.

"Our first and foremost task," Homer announced, "is to demolish the opposition. That is, the suspicion of the average voter toward a rich, affluent candidate. The strongest point in our favor is this—Christine will be groomed to hold office in the current party in power, the New Deal. Inasmuch as Christine will be running from Long Island, she'll be branded a traitor by the North Shore gentry. We'll turn this to our advantage—and capture the imagination of the average voter. Don't forget, Roosevelt is considered a traitor to his class, too."

It was Faith who suggested the slogan for Mrs. Ostbergh's eventual campaign for Congress: *A New Deal for Women.*

"Well taken," Homer conceded, "but a bit premature. The entire year—all of 1935—must be dedicated toward bringing Christine's name before the public. Making Christine Ostbergh synonymous with liberalism, a symbol of true democracy!"

Faith applied Homer's SCA formula for the campaign. As one of the first steps, she sent out a questionnaire for a survey to hundreds of men and women well known in public life.

How in your opinion can modern woman contribute to our political structure?

Homer Sweet found the replies stimulating. He ordered Faith to analyze them and integrate them into a comprehensive article, which he sent out gratis to the women's magazines, with a photograph and caption: *Christine Ostbergh, wife of the famed industrialist, who is an ardent advocate of women's active participation in the American political scene.*

Faith then mailed out two thousand releases to newspapers throughout the country of an interview with Mrs. Ostbergh on *The Destiny of
the American Woman.*

Here Faith credited Christine with her own ideas: "Women must
take time off from their homes and families to exert a refining influence
on matters pertaining to their government—a field until now unfortunately dominated and corrupted by men."

She wrote innumerable human-interest stories, mentioning Christine
prominently in all of them. She arranged for interviews. She dispatched
photographers to Twilight Hill for pictures of Christine in the Tudor
house, in the formal gardens, at the pool with her two black French
poodles, in the paddock with her hunters. She sent Christine's recipes,
concocted by the Ostbergh chef, to the women's pages of the newspapers.
And as the season blossomed, Christine was seen at the opera, at concerts, exhibitions, charity balls, political dinners, often accompanied
by Faith and always by a photographer.

Despite the intimacy into which this prelude to the campaign had
thrown them, Faith found it difficult to like Christine genuinely. Beneath
the well-mannered poise and charm, there was a core of frigidity. Nevertheless, Christine was a docile student. When Faith suggested the attentions of a voice teacher to eradicate the remnants of a Western accent
and develop her tonal qualities, Christine took the tiresome lessons without a sign of temperament. She agreed just as easily to wear the simple
black suits and white silk blouses Faith chose for her. And she did
develop in poise and stature, gaining confidence from the assurance that
whenever she faced a new situation, Faith would be standing by, alert
for any distress signals, and ready to step into the breach.

This was building up Christine Ostbergh, the Woman.

Finally, as a tryout, Homer arranged a brief informal talk before a
group of clubwomen on the New Deal for Women. Faith wrote the
speech, chose the suit and hat Christine was to wear, and stood in the
wings, listening attentively, while Christine spoke.

It was a success. In the second speech, Faith grew bolder, weighing
woman's new-found freedom, speculating on what the new moral code
would do to the future of marriage.

"We must never forget that one out of every two persons in this
country is a woman!

"Socially, the American woman has progressed far beyond her sister
in the harem. But spiritually, she still wears the veil of the seraglio!

"Men have sought to divert women's minds with material comforts and luxuries, thus blinding them to matters of vital importance. Well, that's like dangling a rattle before a hungry child.

"Before your child is born, you have no idea whether it will be the governing—or the governed, master or underling. That will depend on its sex!"

This speech, too, was reprinted on the women's pages, interpreted in editorials, expounded from the pulpit.

This was building up Christine Ostbergh, champion of women's rights.

Shortly, Christine, accompanied by Faith, went off on a lecture tour, which Homer had arranged through the Grover Lane Booking Bureau. He wrote to the heads of the women's clubs, "Christine Ostbergh, whose brilliant comments on matters of feminine interest have been given extraordinary attention in the nation's press, has consented to speak informally at a woman's club in your vicinity. While there, she would consider speaking to your group as well—on a subject of vital interest to you: How the Woman of Today Can Improve Her Position in the World of Tomorrow. Her fee will be returned to your coffers as her contribution, for Mrs. Ostbergh is interested only in awakening women to their great future. . . ."

"Now," he announced, "we are ripe for the final step. Christine is going on record as the champion of the Disinherited, the Underprivileged, the Minorities!"

There appeared shortly in various gossip columns the information that Mrs. Eric Ostbergh would be drafted to run for Congress.

"During your campaign," Homer tutored her, "you'll promise to vote for those measures giving the common man a break."

Christine Ostbergh listened humbly to her mentor, and learned her lessons diligently.

As for Faith, she was working harder than ever. And all the while, she was absorbing information she would never forget. Here was a woman of scarcely better than average looks and intelligence, of whose type there must be millions in the land. Yet from the mind of one man, out of his knowledge of exploitation and human weaknesses, a new political figurehead was being created, one whom the nation would eventually worship.

Could Hollywood, grooming a star for fame, have done any better?

2. Just before Decoration Day, Faith received two cards, one from her father, the other from Mrs. Hussar. Were it not for these reminders,

she would have forgotten her thirtieth birthday. These days her life was identified exclusively with Christine Ostbergh's.

Now, more than ever, Corrigan's weekly visit was the highlight on which she depended for relaxation and diversion.

Whenever she related a new phase of the campaign, he repeated cynically, "And that's how a stateswoman is born!"

"Actually, it doesn't matter how she's created," Faith said heatedly. "The important fact is that she's intrinsically honest in her convictions. She means well. She'll make a good member of Congress—good as most of the men."

"Nevertheless, the Homer Sweet assembly line is manufacturing a Great Woman out of very commonplace raw material."

"You're always deriding Homer," she said, a bit exasperated. "I know he's pompous and a windbag. But he's anxious to do the right thing. That's why I, for one, can forgive all his petty foibles."

"Quite right, quite right," he mocked.

"Oh, hush up! You'll never admit what a force for the common good public relations can be!"

"Yeh. Just look at the public-relations job the Kingfish did in Louisiana. Honey, I'm going to send you a copy of the best treatise on public relations the dumb world has ever read. It's fairly recent. The guy who wrote it operates on the theory that if you make a statement often enough—and make it sound true—people will accept it no matter how much of a lie it is. It's a German best-seller called *Mein Kampf*."

3. The Ostbergh name soared like a comet through the sultry summer sky.

Christine Ostbergh, the Woman, the Humanitarian, the Liberal. There was always some member of the National Democratic Committee underfoot, for Christine had been nominated for Congress on the democratic ticket.

The month of October, 1936, was a jumble of speeches, meetings, rallies. Homer had arranged with Harvey Jessup, whose agency handled the International Petroleum account, to buy radio time for a series of talks in which Christine would address the women voters of New York. And Faith had new speeches to write in the late hours when she came home, weary and spent.

At one political rally, Mrs. Ostbergh gave a particularly fine speech, arousing a wild response in her audience. Afterwards, a young reporter from the *Record* began firing questions at her. Instantly, Faith moved to her side and assumed the brunt of the barrage.

The reporter looked quizzically at Christine, carefully turned out in an expensive black suit, a hand-made white blouse, her dark head bare. Then he turned to Faith, in a casual gray flannel skirt and jacket, a brown beret pushed back on her thick chestnut hair, her nose shiny, her mouth badly in need of lipstick.

Funny, he thought. The Holmes girl knows all the answers. Why isn't she running for office?

4. Christine made her most important broadcast the Saturday before election, and when it was successfully over, she remained at the station a few moments, receiving graciously the congratulations of her retinue which, that afternoon, included Harvey Jessup.

She turned to Faith. "I'm driving out to Long Island for the week-end. Why don't you come along?"

"Thanks, but I can't make it. I have an appointment with some interviewers later this evening. Incidentally, Christine, we've arranged to have our own photographer at the polls Tuesday. So we're sure to get good pictures."

Harvey Jessup helped Christine into her Persian lamb coat. The elevator doors flew open, and the royal party descended to the street, where the Ostbergh Rolls, with a uniformed chauffeur, was waiting. Christine thanked them all charmingly and then entered the car. Harvey Jessup covered her knees with a fur lap robe.

Faith thought wearily, I want to go home and sleep a lifetime.

Turning away, she caught a fleeting impression of the ingratiating smile on Hank Jessup's handsome face. He had promised to call her, but had not done so. She was too exhausted to care.

5. No matter how late she'd gone to bed the previous night, Christine always arose at seven. This habit harked back to her working days, when she allowed herself ample time for all chores before going to the office. An extra ten-minute snooze was no recompense for missing a nourishing breakfast or failing to iron a fresh blouse. Christine liked everything just so; she was born precise and methodical.

Now she rang for her maid, did her exercises, showered and dressed in a neat black woollen frock. She wore no jewels except the wedding band that never left her finger. By eight-thirty, she was at the desk in her sitting room, ready for Miss Knowles, her secretary, who was available at all times. Together, they combed the papers for any news items Faith could whip into a speech. Then, with calm and impersonal assurance, Christine answered the mail, letters from men and women who derided, admired or criticized her. Any notes with political significance, she ordered Miss Knowles to dispatch to Homer, who would handle them himself. She turned down requests from four charitable organizations, but sent a check for five hundred dollars to the Orphanage for Children Born Out of Wedlock, as Homer suggested. Graciously, she allowed her name to be included on the list of patronesses for one cause, but tactfully refused another, in accordance with Homer's advice. As she signed the monthly check for one hundred dollars that went off to her widowed mother in Napier, Ohio, she wondered dryly what the old lady did with all the money? Why, only last month, in answer to an urgent appeal, she'd wired an extra fifty. . . .

Miss Knowles brought in a sheaf of clippings, each displaying an expertly retouched studio portrait bearing the caption: *The beautiful and talented Christine Ostbergh, who is running for Congress from Long Island on the Democratic ticket.*

"I'm sure you'll win, Mrs. Ostbergh!" Miss Knowles cried. "And that'll be the opening wedge for another career for women!"

"There have been women in Congress before."

"I know. But you make it appear so dramatic—like a crusade. Before this, I'd always thought politics dull and questionable—well, a man's game."

Since there were no guests present this weekend, Christine lunched with Ostbergh in the smaller dining room. Usually, when they were together, she refrained from ever taking the initiative in conversation. But today she broke the silence.

"Do you think we stand a chance?" she asked.

Robert Grosvenor Hewlitt, the Republican nominee running against her, was putting up a valiant if well-bred fight.

"There'll be a Roosevelt landslide," Ostbergh answered coldly.

Christine was cheered. "I'd like records of the speeches I've made," she said. "I must ask Faith to get them for me. She's done a pretty good job, don't you think?"

"I am pleased with her."

Such praise from him was rare; he expected superb service because he paid well for it. Indeed, he availed himself callously of the talents and efforts of his servitors. His insular climb to the pinnacle of success was strewn with the ruined careers of men broken in body and spirit, events which left him indifferent and untroubled. For he knew the race *was* to the swift, the battle to the strong. . . .

He finished his black coffee and pushed back his chair. Even in the surroundings of his own home, the air of mystery and malevolence clung to his massive figure.

"Call Stewart in Washington," he ordered. "Tell him I want him in New York Tuesday night."

Christine nodded. She obeyed, thinking resentfully, I wish he'd remember I'm not his secretary any more.

6. Christine cast her own vote early Tuesday morning to the edification of a half-dozen photographers. Then she drove to her apartment at the Pierre, which by late afternoon, was jammed with reporters, politicians, well-wishers and hangers-on.

Faith was kept busy answering the phone, seeing that drinks and sandwiches were replenished, placating those admirers whom Christine ignored. She kept looking toward the door, for Corrigan had promised to drop in.

It was after seven when he finally ambled into the room.

"Looks like congratulations are in order," he growled. "Where is our glamorous new Congresswoman?"

Flushed with excitement, Faith pointed out Christine, standing in a corner, talking to Eric Ostbergh and a heavy-set stranger in an expensive gray tweed suit.

Corrigan's inky black brows lifted over his sorrowful eyes. "Well, look who's here!"

"Who do you mean?"

"That fellow gabbing with Ostbergh is one of the kingpins of the lobby gang in Washington. I'm beginning to get it. Damned convenient for Ostbergh—having a wife in Congress."

Faith paid no attention to him; after all, Corrigan was always griping.

7. A fortnight later, she saw Harvey Jessup again. She called him at his office about the transcription of Christine's speeches.

"She'll be back from Nassau by the end of the week," she explained, "and would like to have them then."

Harvey promised to take care of it immediately, and then asked if she would lunch with him. He'd been meaning to call her, he explained, but he knew she was working hard on post-election details, before Christine took office. "Incidentally," he added, "you've rung the gong again. I do wish I had an assistant like you."

She agreed to meet him at "21" and during the two-hour luncheon, he regaled her with stories of his troubles with clients.

"Considering what we have to take, it's no wonder we're known as the Ulcer Brigade," he said. "In our business, no man's a success until he's been put on a bland diet."

They spoke of Homer Sweet, whom Hank admired in an indulgent, tolerant way.

"Advertising and public relations are practically first cousins," he said. "Though we have a concrete product to sell, while Homer peddles hot air."

"You're underestimating him," Faith said.

"Oh, he has his points. But he's a funny little gent. Have you ever heard him decry what he calls the lower forms of publicity? I've heard him say quite seriously that when a girl shoots her lover to make the tabloids, the end doesn't justify the means."

Faith laughed. "Sounds just like him."

"In our office," Hank added, "we call it a 'Homerism.'"

Before parting, he invited her to the première of a new radio program the following week.

"I'd like to have your reaction," he said, flattering her.

Actually, she found the program no better, no worse than a dozen others. A sad-eyed comedian and his fat stooge pelted each other with verbal custard pies which they alone found hilarious. A huge, balding baritone bellowed "On the Road to Mandalay." The Harmony Sisters, who belied their name, crooned a new tune about the tired old moon. And the announcer shouted the commercial with the fervor of an evangelist.

"What do you think?" Hank whispered.

"It's been done before," she answered.

He grinned. "I didn't really bring you here for your opinion, Faith Holmes. That was an excuse. Now let's scram before we're hooked for the sponsor's party!"

Months later, when she knew him better, Faith realized how very much he must have been impressed with her that evening. To walk out on a sponsor was in his eyes the greatest crime of all!

When they reached the windy street, he said it was too late for the movies and anyway, he was too keyed-up to sit through a picture.

"Would you like to drop in at my place?" Faith said. "I'll fix some coffee, and we can talk."

"Fine!"

He stood in the tiny kitchen while she prepared ham sandwiches and poured a glass of milk for him. Then they sat in the living room, smoking and talking. At first, they spoke of Eric Ostbergh and Christine, but gradually they drifted into a more personal vein. Before he knew it, Hank was telling her about his youth, and his parents, to whom he had been deeply attached. They were decent, honest, hard-working folk, who saved what little they could through years of drudgery for the great day when they could retire.

"That dream kept them going all their lives," he said quietly. "Through all the bad times—they never had it easy. Then, just as they were ready for it, my mother died suddenly. Her body was too tired to keep pace with the dream. And in those days, I couldn't help them the least bit."

She leaned back against the gray cushions of the sofa, absorbed in his revelation, curiously moved by it, and wondering, too, what had impelled him to break through the façade of his suave and polished self, to reveal the turbulence and insecurity underneath. His broad, handsome features no longer bore the feverish glow of excitement and stimulation which had carried him through the radio première, but were rather intense and introspective.

"You see before you," he said, "the living example of how far a guy can travel on a pigskin."

"I thought all football heroes wound up in Wall Street."

"I was the exception. The Old Graduate who sponsored me was chummy with Mansfield, head of Quincy, Quigney, Abernathy and Mansfield Advertising Agency. I got a job there through him. Then one day when I was lunching at the Yale Club, an old gentleman came over. 'I'm Sanderson '99,' he told me. And invited me to his table. He asked what I was doing, and when I told him—well, he said of course nothing was too good for Hank Jessup, All-American Boy, so I came out with a juicy new account."

"How long have you had your own agency?"

"About ten years. When I left QQA&M, I took International Petroleum with me. The Ostbergh account has been bread, butter and caviar to me ever since."

He got up and paced back and forth. "I followed the pattern right to the end," he said bitterly, "even to marrying the daughter of my biggest account." He seemed to take a sadistic pleasure in displaying the weakness which had motivated his life.

"That's the story. Not much of an inspiration to future generations, I'm afraid."

She was moved to sudden pity. "Oh, I'm sure you've left out some mighty pertinent facts."

"Such as my wife?" he retorted. "I could tell you quite a story about my marriage. . . ."

"Please, don't," she interrupted. "I'd rather not hear about it."

He took her hand in his. "What about yourself? You're Mrs. Holmes, yet I've never heard you mention your husband."

She flushed. "Mark lives in St. Croix," she said cautiously. "And I —I prefer to live here."

His mood changed. He grew cheerful again. "Faith, this has been the most pleasant evening I've had in an age! May I come again?"

"Of course," she said. "Do call me."

After he had gone, she undressed and got into bed. But she couldn't sleep. She was puzzled, wondering what had prompted his strange confession? Her original estimate of him was changing. She suspected that his poise and affability were a veneer for the world, and she was conscious of a new understanding of him.

She didn't criticize him for snatching at the main chance. But his methods were rather shoddy. And, just before she fell asleep, she wondered what made him so confident that in divulging his past, he would unquestionably appeal to her emotions.

8. The Ostberghs gave a cocktail party at their hotel suite to celebrate Christine's return from Nassau. Both Faith and Hank Jessup were among the guests, but they managed to slip away early.

"You're really the star of this production," Hank assured Faith, "even if you don't get star billing."

She shrugged. "Grooming Christine was part of my job. I got a real kick out of it. I'd like to see more women in public life."

"You'd do right well there, yourself," he said gallantly.

Tonight he had chosen a small quiet restaurant instead of the well-known spots he usually frequented. He had had several drinks, and his handsome face was flushed, his manner audacious. He appeared to have forgotten the revealing conversation in her apartment at their last meeting. He was in an altogether different frame of mind.

Over coffee, he said easily, "Faith, isn't it a pity when two normal, intelligent people who need each other badly keep on pretending . . ."

Perhaps because she had been expecting it, she was not disconcerted; on the contrary, she was very much in control of the situation.

"Hank," she said lightly, "are you leading up to a proposal or a proposition?"

He looked boyishly hurt.

"You know I'm married."

"How very convenient for you!"

"Aren't you being rather unkind?"

Faith leaned against the stiff back of her chair, enjoying his discomfiture.

"Hank, I do like you! You're attractive and loads of fun. But you're putting yourself on the spot. I've heard all this before, you know. Shall I tell you what you were going to say next? As Homer Sweet would put it: *One,* your wife doesn't understand you. You've grown up and left her behind. *Two:* But you can't hurt her and the children. *Three:* Why can't we be civilized? We'll be discreet, and nobody will be hurt. *Four:* I want you so much, darling. You mean so much to me!" She was laughing openly now. "That tired old gag has grown a long beard by now!"

He was embarrassed and angry, "Now, Faith!"

"I'm not frigid, either. I've heard that one before, too. It's just that I haven't had any affairs. And I don't intend to start now, thank you."

His face remained expressionless for a moment, then suddenly relaxed in a sheepish smile.

"Faith, you're wonderful! You're the smartest gal I've ever met, much too smart for me! I'll be honest with you. It isn't a line. As a matter of fact, my wife doesn't give a hang for me. She's as bored with me as I am with her."

"That's tough on you. But why bring me into it?"

He was baffled.

Dammit, he thought, How can I make her want me?

9. The day Christine Ostbergh was scheduled to make her maiden speech in Congress, Faith was in the gallery, accompanied by Corrigan. She had arrived the previous night to put the finishing touches on the speech, and then she had dined with Corrigan and heard much of the Washington gossip.

Now he said glumly, "Greatest Little Show on Earth."

Christine, in simple, expensive black, made a slight and attractive figure on the floor. She spoke appealingly and emotionally for the nation's submerged third.

". . . caught between industry and labor, there is the unorganized group, the disinherited—the white-collar worker, the unskilled laborer, the teacher, the postman, the cop on the beat . . .

"Who will speak for him?"

She finished to a burst of enthusiastic applause.

Corrigan bowed to Faith. "You've got the stuff, honey. Damned shame you couldn't spout the words yourself."

On the way out, they met several correspondents, hard-bitten men with the stamp of Washington on their cynical faces. Corrigan made the introductions.

"What does La Ostbergh want in Congress?" the younger man asked. "And why has the Sphinx turned New Deal? What's he trying to hush up?"

Faith laughed. "Sorry. No answers."

After the men were gone, Corrigan said, "If they were to spill some of the off-the-record stuff they know, what fireworks there'd be!"

10. Immediately on her return to New York, she was called into conference in Homer's office. Harvey Jessup was present and, to her surprise, Eric Ostbergh himself. The purpose of the meeting was to assemble a new radio program for International Petroleum. Ostbergh, massive and inscrutable, listened stonily to their suggestions without committing himself in any way.

Hank snuffed out his cigarette and turned to Ostbergh.

"I'm convinced a program built around a popular comedian and a name band—say, Benny Goodman . . ."

"But, Jessup," Homer Sweet interrupted, "you must bear in mind the type of program that is properly suited for International Petroleum. First of all, it must have dignity!"

"What about a musical program?" Faith asked, and seeing Hank's pained expression, she added swiftly, "No long-haired stuff, just light music. Gershwin, Jerome Kern, Grofé."

Ostbergh stirred, something akin to approval in his cold eyes. "Suits me," he said. "Go ahead with the idea."

"Fine, fine." Homer sighed with relief. Thank God for Faith. "An hour's program. Fifty minutes of music—and the intermission talk. We mustn't forget that the sole purpose of the entertainment is to engage the listener's ear—so he will be receptive to our message."

"Mrs. Holmes," Ostbergh said abruptly, "I want *you* to give the talk."

"Me? I know nothing about radio."

"You're much too modest," Hank Jessup interrupted, quick on the uptake. "I think . . ."

Homer wouldn't allow him to finish. "Mr. Ostbergh should be commended on his excellent judgment," he said unctuously.

Jessup retrieved the ball. "Faith has a priceless talent. She can take a complex subject and reduce it to its simplest common denominator—so anyone can understand what it's all about."

"Thank you, gentlemen. You're very kind," Faith said, "but I'm not up to it. I've never been on the air."

"You'll learn quickly," Hank assured her.

"I have confidence in your ability," Eric Ostbergh said, with finality.

She wondered if he had decided on this as a suitable reward for the thorough job she'd done on Christine's campaign.

11. The groundwork for the International Petroleum radio program was laid in the offices of Homer Sweet and the Jessup Advertising Agency, which were both allied for this project. Hank suggested they buy time on Sunday night, preferably just before Winchell's broadcast. The series would begin early September.

Homer Sweet gave Faith explicit directions.

"Remember, you have only five minutes, so every second must count, every sentence convey a thought. You must convince the listener that it is because of industries like International Petroleum that the standard of living in our country is the highest in the world."

For the subject of her first talk, Faith decided on *A Gallon of Oil*, from the time it gushed forth from the earth to its ultimate destination, the tank of an automobile—and all in terms of the human element.

Necessarily, she saw a good deal of Hank Jessup that summer. The radio program involved many problems and she sat in on all conferences. The more she saw of him, the more she learned to appreciate his genial good-nature, his affable tolerance, and his uncalled-for loyalty to her.

She found herself accepting his invitations eagerly, generally for lunch. She found him a good companion, gay, humorous, considerate, never demanding. He did not refer again to the evening he had so rashly declared himself. Now he was proving that he could be reasonably satisfied with her friendship.

Nevertheless, she played safe, keeping on the alert.

12. Harvey Jessup learned an important lesson from his parents' poverty, one he was never to forget. If you had to start a career from scratch, by the time you amounted to anything you were too old to reap the benefits.

There must be a shortcut to success. He was determined to find it.

He was a handsome lad, good-natured and likable, a Boy Scout in spirit and deed. He was always eager to do a favor, and as he grew older, his vanity fed on the appreciation of the recipients, and he grew even more determinedly helpful.

Among his friends was old Anthony, gardener for the J. B. Bentley Reid summer home. When Anthony fell sick, it was characteristic of Hank to step into the breach. He weeded the garden and cut the lawn, and when Mr. Reid offered to pay him, he refused.

"I'm just helping Anthony," he said sunnily.

The Reids, accustomed to New York service, oiled by tips, were visibly impressed. Their only son lived in California, and they soon found themselves taking a parental interest in this personable youngster.

In his freshman year, Hank made the football team; he played quarterback, for his agile wiry body possessed both speed and endurance. He was the outstanding player on the high-school team for four years. His folks were proud of him and bemoaned the fact that they couldn't give him a proper education, which they were certain was the key to security.

The Reids persuaded him to go to college instead of hunting for a job.

"You'll get bids from the Big Three," Mr. Reid said confidently. "A good football player's worth a dozen scholars. Now, my advice . . ."

Those days, Mr. Reid was always advising Hank. Somehow, he had more of a voice in formulating the boy's future than his own parents.

Still, Hank loved his folks. He wanted desperately to be of help to them; he felt as if he were the father, and they the weak, helpless children. That was what poverty had done to them.

He did get bids from the colleges, and he chose Yale. In his senior year, he made All-American. Mr. Reid felt all his efforts in the boy's behalf were fully justified.

Hank met Mr. Mansfield, the advertising man, through the Reids.

"Come and see me after graduation," Mr. Mansfield said. "There'll be a job waiting for you."

A job—and finally, a girl.

The girl was Peggy Flawless, whose family owned the Flawless Copper Mines. She was slight; her head was too large for her thin spindly body, and her forehead was too large for her head. She had a small nose and prominent white teeth. Hank was scared to death of her. But after a while, he gathered the courage to propose, and when she accepted him, he couldn't believe his luck. The Flawless Copper Mines. If only his dad and mother had lived to see this day!

They were married at St. Thomas' and they went to Bermuda for their honeymoon; on their return, they settled in a Fifth Avenue duplex owned by Peggy's family. Since Hank had started working for QQA&M, his salary had been substantially raised, but it was trifling compared to their expenses.

Five years later, underwritten by Peggy's money and fortified by an automobile account from a close friend of the Flawless family, he went into business for himself. To his surprise, International Petroleum came along with him, which set him off to a successful start. He couldn't have chosen a more fertile field for his talents. His boyhood friendliness was paying off in golden dividends, for most of his friends were influential people in a position to help him inestimably. The advertising agencies always reminded him of a pack of dogs fighting over a bone. No agency had more to offer intrinsically than another, since there was no monopoly on talent, no corner on popular phrases and slogans, no exclusive rights to an idea. But the man who brought in the account— ah, there was the difference between agencies, there was where the Jessup organization had the edge on the others. For Hank was the Personality Kid, himself!

Still, he had to keep on his toes, for there was the constant fear that a competitor might seduce a prize client. That was the reason for his ulcers, the gnawing fear that the easy money, the fifteen per cent of a million bucks would be snatched away. . . .

When he was interviewed for *Success Magazine*, he said in his forthright manner, "I'd rather see a young fellow make ten dollars a week for himself than a hundred working for somebody else. The big man of tomorrow will be the little guy of today who has the guts to buck the line, and the initiative to carry the ball around the end!"

Privately, he knew damn well that if he'd had to start from scratch, without the help of the Reids, the Old Graduate, the Racquet and Tennis Club and the Flawless family, he'd probably be running his old man's general store in Millbridge, Connecticut.

13. The summer was a pleasant one for Faith. She was marking time until the International Petroleum radio program got under way in September. Meanwhile, she relaxed, shopped for new clothes, attended the Stadium concerts, saw Harvey Jessup frequently.

Many weekends, Christine asked her out to Twilight Hill. Eric

Ostbergh was in South America on business, so Christine felt free to surround herself with guests: key men from Washington with their placid, motherly wives; officials from Great Britain; noted refugees from Germany and Austria; and always a number of newspaper and magazine writers who were in a position to enhance her growing reputation.

She was always charming to Faith, even friendly. Yet Faith was conscious of an undercurrent of reserve, as if Christine did not wish to be reminded of her beginnings and the part Faith had played in them. Although she still accepted Faith's advice, there was already a tinge of authority in her manner, and she uttered Homerisms as if she had created them.

Faith thought wryly, Homer must be proud of this modern Galatea.

Chapter Fifteen

1. The first broadcast of the Symphony Orchestra sponsored by International Petroleum took place the first Sunday in September, 1937. It was a gala affair. Tickets had been sent to people notable in the social, artistic and business worlds. And Homer Sweet had done such a superb exploitation job that the listeners anticipated a great cultural event.

By seven-thirty, town cars and taxis congested West Forty-fourth Street, as the guests filed into the theater reserved for the broadcast. Most of them would have considered it indecent to appear on time for a first night, but even they succumbed to the rigid time limitations of radio.

Faith was tense all day. She refused Hank's invitation to an early dinner, and spent the last hours resting. By seven o'clock she was dressed in a new frock of black crêpe, with a high neckline, long tight sleeves and a skirt that fell in Grecian lines. She had had her hair cut short, for the long bob did not become her, and a golden rinse added luster to her sun-bleached curls.

Almost surreptitiously, she took out the tiny gold locket and clipped the chain around her neck.

For luck, she thought. I'll need it.

When Hank appeared, bringing a box of white camellias, he whistled boyishly. "Faith, you look stunning. You'll wow 'em, all right!"

She was still fortified by his words a half hour later, when the orchestra finished the ballet music from Goldmark's *Queen of Sheba*, and it was time for her to go on. She stood before the mike, head high, but the copy trembling in her hands. She began to speak, her voice low and intimate, her manner warm and friendly. She traced the story of a gallon of oil from its crude beginnings to the time when you drive up to a station with the Sign of the Revolving Globe, and say, "Fill 'er up."

After the concert, Hank was the first to congratulate her. "You put it over beautifully!" he said. "No one else could have done as well!" He grinned. "I'm proud of you, Faith Holmes."

They gathered at the Ostbergh suite after the broadcast, where photographers kept them busy posing for pictures, and Eric Ostbergh told Faith he was well satisfied.

"I train my staff well," Homer Sweet said, taking the credit for himself. "Faith, a glass of champagne?"

"I'm quite drunk with excitement, Homer."

Harvey Jessup drove her home and followed her into the apartment. This evening there was no idle talk. Without a prelude, he took her into his arms, and said, self-consciously, "Faith, I'm in love with you."

"Hank, let's not go through this again."

"Faith, you've got me wrong."

His debonair air was crumbling. She moved away, embarrassed before his awkward sincerity. I shouldn't have let him come in, she thought. Why do I let myself in for these situations?

"I've never really been in love before," he admitted haltingly. "Not like this. I could be happy with you, Faith. If you'd only give me half a chance."

She was moved in spite of herself.

"I won't listen to you, Hank," she said quietly, "because it puts me in a very difficult position. I have nothing but the deepest contempt for a woman who comes between a man and his wife."

"But Peggy and I have been washed up for years!"

"I'm sorry, Hank. You'd better go now."

He hesitated, perplexed by inner conflicts. If she were another woman, he could have been facile and persuasive, and presented his case convincingly. But she was Faith, and he was oddly shy and inhibited with her. These were new and baffling reactions, which had never cropped up in his other love affairs.

He realized she would be offended by almost anything he could say.

"Forgive me," he whispered, and had the wisdom to leave on those words.

She sat up long after he had gone. The French clock on the desk pointed reproachfully to four. Occasional footsteps reverberated hollowly on the dark street below. She might as well face it. As far as a love life was concerned, she was in a strait jacket. What's wrong with me? she cried out in silent despair. How have I blundered?

Going over the errors of her past, she wondered whether another girl in her place might have stayed happily married to Mark. Or, having broken with him, gone on to an ambitious life with Phillip Latham? Or, finally, compromised with Harvey Jessup? She had done none of these things. Why? Had some deep subconscious striving propelled her out of the snug cushion of her domestic life with Mark into the sphere of worldly affairs? In that case, why didn't she react like a typical career woman—either carry on a love affair discreetly, or marry conventionally? Since she refused to compromise, did it mean she was unalterably in love with Mark?

She didn't know the answer.

2. She did not go out of her way to avoid Hank in the ensuing weeks, but she was grateful that their meetings were infrequent, and then always in the presence of Homer or the staff. She refused to admit how much she missed his gaiety and good humor. She told herself it was propinquity and nothing more.

Early in December, Homer invited her to the annual banquet of the Council for Industrial Management, at which he was to be guest speaker. As they entered the Grand Ballroom, she caught sight of Hank Jessup and a woman whose petulant face she recognized from the photographs on the society pages of the *Times* and *Herald Tribune,* as his wife. Mrs. Jessup was an unfinished blonde of uncertain years, and her lanky body was swathed in an expensive and unsuitable pink chiffon frock. Her light, shoulder-length hair was the color of the dry skin over her bulging forehead. Her insolent blue eyes refused to concede the possibility that she, Peggy Flawless, would meet her equals at this stupid gathering. When her husband made the introductions uncomfortably she did not appear to notice Faith beyond a bored nod.

Fortunately, Faith was not seated at the same table with the Jessups, and during the tedious dinner, she concentrated on Homer's garrulity, ignoring the appealing glances Hank Jessup sent her way. After the coffee was served, she left the table and proceeded to the powder room. Almost immediately, she realized Mrs. Jessup was following her, and she suspected that a scene was inevitable.

Unfortunately, the dressing room was empty except for the attendant. Faith took out her gold compact and powdered her nose. In the mirror, she saw Mrs. Jessup beside her, and heard the cool, self-assured voice.

"Mrs. Holmes, your meetings with my husband are growing quite indiscreet. Really, I don't approve of them."

Faith flushed.

"Mrs. Jessup, my meetings with your husband have been business conferences for the most part."

"Conducted at all hours of the night?"

"I am not in love with your husband," Faith said angrily. "And even if I were, it's not my policy to step between two married people."

Mrs. Jessup regarded her contemptuously. "How simple and gullible you are, Mrs. Holmes. Don't you realize what I represent to my husband? No matter what his personal feelings, he's much too ambitious to relinquish his most valuable asset—my position and my money!"

Only then did Faith understand how serious Hank was about her.

3. Faith stuck rigidly to her resolve; now, even at conferences, she deliberately avoided Hank. One afternoon, during the gay, pre-Christmas week, he sent her a note, "Faith, you won't be violating any of your principles if you see me now. Peggy and I are no longer living together. I'm at the Yale Club."

So they had quarreled over her! The knowledge troubled her deeply, for she had never consciously been unfair or predatory in her life, and she didn't intend to begin now. She decided she could do very well without Hank.

Meanwhile, the Symphony program was doing very well. The Hooper rating was high; the press commended it. Music for the millions, music they could love and understand. And the friendly, informative intermission talk. An unbeatable combination!

After a broadcast, late in January, Faith went directly home. She had been suffering from a heavy cold, and the anticipation of a hot drink and a rest in bed comforted her. Shivering, she let herself into the apartment. Her head ached and she felt feverish. She dropped her fur-lined cape on a white chair and went into the bedroom. On the night table, at the base of the green Chinese lamp, lay a telegram that the maid had left for her.

She tore open the envelope. It was signed by her father, and read:

MOTHER VERY ILL COME HOME AT ONCE

4. Calling the office of the W.A.A., she got a reservation on a plane leaving at seven in the morning for Great Falls. She was up at five. She took a shower, dressed in a heavy gray tweed suit and a brown cashmere sweater. She made herself a pot of black coffee and left a note for her

maid. She carried her bag downstairs and walked toward Lexington Avenue until she found a taxi.

"Newark Airport," she said.

She huddled in the back seat, her beaver coat insufficient protection against the raw penetrating cold. She was trying to remember her mother, but the image wavered and eluded her. How old was she? Fifty; yes, she had had her fiftieth birthday last summer. Fifty wasn't old. . . .

The plane landed on schedule in Great Falls at two in the afternoon. She hired a car to drive her to St. Croix. The trip took over an hour, for traffic was congested, and she fidgeted all the way.

Why didn't he speed it up? As the car swung along the lake road, she caught sight of the new buildings adjacent to Wolverine Motors. This must be Mark's new plant, she mused, and felt numb at the thought of seeing him.

At last the car stopped before the State Hospital. She put her finger to the bell. After a moment, the heavy door opened slowly and a white-haired nurse stood before her. Behind her uniformed figure she saw Tod.

"Dad!"

He came out to her. He took her hands gently without speaking. And she knew she hadn't made it in time.

5. Tod took her to Mrs. Hussar's.

He had been holding a vigil at the asylum since noon, expecting that she would go directly there. "It's good to have you home, pumpkin," he said, "only I'm sorry it has to be like this. . . ."

They turned down Sycamore to Ontario Place. Snow lay in the frozen ruts in the street, streaked with soot and littered with refuse. How squalid it all looked. Yet it was home; she used to play on this street. She saw the cracked pavement where she had played hopscotch. And there was the lilac hedge near which she used to meet Mark. Now its naked branches stretched plaintively above her head.

The anesthesia of shock was wearing off, and she ached with the anguished awareness of the moment.

Walking beside Tod, hunched and old-looking in his heavy mackinaw, his cap pulled down over his forehead, Faith was conscious of a surge of pity for him and his aborted dreams.

"Did she suffer much?" she asked.

"I don't think so. It happened very suddenly, yesterday afternoon. Her heart . . ."

"Did you see her before . . . ?"

"Yes. The doctors called me after her first attack."

"Was she conscious, dad? Was she rational? Did she say anything about me?"

"Pumpkin," Tod said gently, "she didn't say a thing. You see—she was in a coma."

6. Mrs. Hussar was very kind; she welcomed Faith affectionately, and did her best to make her comfortable and at ease.

"You're too thin, Faith," she fussed. "You don't eat enough." Mrs. Hussar always maintained that good food and plenty of it was the answer to all ills of the spirit and the flesh. She was determined to ply Faith with eggnogs, custards and fattening foods.

"Tonight, you shall have wiener schnitzel and spaetzle and apple strudel and a stein of beer. You've been eating too many salads in your New York!"

Faith thanked her politely, and Mrs. Hussar shuffled heavily into the kitchen. Tod was taking a nap. The house was very quiet. It was the sort of quiet she had never known in New York. Her mother's sudden death brought the past into sharp relief, especially her impulsive marriage to Mark and her mother's rejection of any reconciliation. For years she had been burdened by a sense of guilt that she had gained Mark at the loss of her mother. And now, in the end, she had lost them both.

She was alone, desolate and remorseful.

7. When Tod and Charlotte Andrews stepped off the *Lady Marquette* that May morning in 1906, Wolverine Motors was just opening its doors, and its smokestacks darkened the limpid blue sky and soiled the neat little white houses of the Dutch farmers.

By 1938, there was little left of the village Eben Holmes had founded. Wolverine Motors was the new St. Croix; the main artery through which flowed the life blood of the town's commerce.

Mark Holmes was vice-president of Wolverine Motors, in charge of production and labor relations. The engine Allan Griswold had perfected and Mark had so doggedly promoted was contributing richly to Wolverine's international reputation. The workers respected Mark. He played fair and he expected the same from you. You got a square deal without fighting for it, as if it were your due as a human being. An honest mistake he'd condone. But God pity the guy who tried wilfully to play both ends against the middle. Like that union official who'd harangued the men last year, in an effort to spread the gospel of hate!

Consequently Wolverine's dealings with its five thousand employees was a model of fair practice. For Mark was profoundly influenced by his grandfather's teachings; Eben Holmes had pioneered in many fields. And the more experience Mark gained in his dealings with the workers and their problems, the more he realized that while labor produced the maximum for industry, it had not yet received a fair share of the profits.

"Gentlemen," he said quietly at a board meeting, "the American worker has been liberated by the New Deal. Labor now has a definite voice in politics—and darned soon it will become a power in the government. Now, gentlemen, if we don't want eventual government control of industry, we'd better give labor its rights. That means not only a fair share of the profits, but a voice in management!"

Old Zeb Whiting, chairman of the board, rose to his feet, sputtering.

"Holmes, you're out of your mind! It's nothing less than Socialism!"

"That's what we're trying to avoid," Mark interrupted. "It's common sense and good business. We need labor. Labor needs us. Okay, let's make it a real partnership. And we'll stay in the lead, a step ahead of our competitors!"

Irritably, Zeb Whiting recalled the good old days, when he first organized Wolverine Motors, and the Hunkies and Polacks had flocked in droves to St. Croix, eager to work twelve hours a day for ten bucks a week.

"Whatever labor has achieved," Mark ended, "it's had to fight for, tooth and nail. Right now, the writing on the wall is damn clear. Why don't we meet it with a good face?"

"With a good face?" Zeb Whiting snorted. "If we give in now, there'll be no stopping the bastards!"

But Mark's foresight and sincerity favorably impressed the younger men on the board. They overruled the Old Man and his few satellites.

Mark left the meeting, elated. Eben would have been pleased with him; he was hitting out in the right direction.

8. In 1938, Mark was thirty-four years old. He worked hard at Wolverine, yet found enough time to devote to the many civic works in which he was interested, another manifestation of his grandfather's precepts. He was head of the Eben Holmes Endowment Fund; active on the Community Chest drives, and president of the Chamber of Com-

merce. He spent considerable time directing the Boys' Club, which was
such a strong force for combating the juvenile delinquency which had
developed during the depression years.

He lived in a small comfortable flat in a new apartment house on
Erie Street, overlooking Holmes Park; it was furnished with pieces from
the old sitting room in his grandfather's house, together with his books,
paintings and records.

He was attractive, successful, and most eligible. Many of the new
residents of St. Croix, who were ignorant of his broken marriage, specu-
lated on the reasons for his bachelor state. He had never joined the
Country Club, although he dined there occasionally with Allan and
Joyce Griswold, who were enthusiastic members. And he still saw Vrest
Macklin, at least once a week.

By keeping busy, he managed to have no time for a private life.

In the beginning, the efforts to lose himself were of dire necessity.
He could not bear the loneliness; he longed for the sound of Faith's gay
voice, the sight of her lovely body. But gradually, the routine he had so
deliberately charted became a part of him, and he even managed to find
a sense of solace in it.

Whatever information he obtained about her came from her father.
He often visited Tod and Mrs. Hussar, of whom he was extremely fond.
He followed with great interest Christine Ostbergh's campaign for Congress, knowing Faith had ghost-written her speeches. And later, he made
it a habit to stay home Sunday nights for the International Petroleum
broadcasts. He sat by the fireplace in the wing chair that had once belonged to his grandfather, smoking his pipe, listening intently. Those
precious five minutes were his rendezvous with her; he felt she was
beside him, and he thought proudly, How she has matured!

He knew that no other woman would ever supplant her in his
heart. In time, he hoped he would become reconciled to his loss.

9. The funeral was over. Saddened and chilled, they returned to
Mrs. Hussar's, Tod, Faith and Vrest Macklin. Mrs. Hussar made sand-
wiches and coffee, and Tod finally persuaded Faith to have some food.
She was white and drained.

"Now, you go to bed," Mrs. Hussar ordered capably, "with an
aspirin and a drink of whisky. Tomorrow your cold'll be better."

Faith shook her head. "I can't sleep."

Vrest Macklin sat at the fumed-oak table, drinking his coffee
absently. "How long do you expect to be here, Faith?"

"I don't know."

"Don't leave before we have a little talk. I want to hear all about your job."

He was gentle and kind. She looked at him mutely, and then saw how shockingly he had aged in these past five years. The flesh of his jowls seemed to have melted away, and his clothes were baggy on his thinning body; his hand, holding the yellowed pipe, shook a little.

"I'll be in to see you," she said.

After he had gone, she remained in the parlor. She should be packing for the trip back to New York, but she was trapped by a strange lassitude that drugged her will. What was she waiting for, why was she stalling? Was she lingering in the hope that she might meet Mark?

Her father had told her of Mark's extraordinary success, with great pride in his voice.

"Not many men would have had Mark's courage in the face of such odds," he said admiringly.

Now she could not stifle the longing to see him again. In New York, it had been less of a temptation; she was a thousand miles away from him. But here in St. Croix, with so many poignant memories haunting her, she was finding it infinitely more difficult to contain the hunger.

"He is a remarkable young man," Tod added shrewdly, waiting for some gesture of contrition from her, wanting to show her how eager he was to act as conciliator.

She thought feverishly, Suppose I say "Dad, bring Mark here," and he comes . . .

She stood up with an effort. "I'm going out," she said abruptly, and her father nodded in understanding. She slipped into her beaver coat and tied a silk scarf over her head. She hurried through the familiar streets of her childhood, blank and unheeding. Her mind was in a turmoil as she found herself re-living moments of their early happiness. Her only happiness, she amended, honestly.

It was dusk when she returned, chilled and weary, but resolved that the only possible move was to return East immediately.

She entered the house and went into the small dark parlor. And found Mark there, waiting for her.

She hesitated, shaken, afraid to take another step for fear he would vanish in the mist before her eyes. "Mark," she wanted to cry, "is it really you, my darling?"

"Faith," he said, "I am deeply sorry to hear about your mother."

She was impressed by his air of inner calm and strength, reflected by the self-control and authority in his lean, distinguished face.

"Oh, Mark!"

There was so much she wanted to tell him, and so pitifully little she could say. Their eyes met, and under his compassionate and intense gaze, she felt her frustrations, her pitiful egotism wash away, as the innate purity of her love for him emerged, lucid and durable.

"Faith, you've changed," he said, puzzled.

How simple it would be for her to waver, to deceive him by admitting she had changed, and for all time. Then she could have him again, and this time forever.

And hamper him again, she thought, possibly hurt him again. He had made himself into the man he was in spite of her. She had neither inspired nor helped him. Indeed, she had very nearly ruined him.

She thought sorrowfully, We are still woven of different patterns, you and I, my darling. We are still different, and I dare not hurt you again.

"Faith," he began, obviously disturbed by the conflict mirrored in her dark luminous eyes, "I'd like to talk to you."

Her fettered emotions broke their chains. You're still young, Faith. You deserve another chance at happiness. And Mark is here; with a few adroit words, you can change the picture of your future.

She tried valiantly to smile. It was essential to smile. The first step. The barrier broken. But she could not dismiss from her heart the knowledge that their future would be made up of the tangled skeins of a tragic past, and therefore could denote only danger for him.

With a stifled sob, she turned from him, and fled.

10. Her New York apartment was sanctuary. But not for long. The fog which had descended with her mother's death, and her return to St. Croix with its fateful encounter with Mark, persisted, like a dense curtain shutting her off from normal life. There was an odd strain in her mental behavior, one quite alien to her generally cheerful self, which pulled her down to the depths whenever tragedy struck, and kept her entrapped for an abnormally long spell. Possibly, it was the superstitious, and ominous tendency inherited from her mother, which she knew might prove disastrous, unless she pulled herself together.

There were moments when she looked back wistfully to her youth; how vivacious and irrepressibly gay she had been then, how lightly she had shrugged off problems. In recent times, with the recurrence of new trials and torments, this talent had grown less positive until now there was a real danger of her growing morose and introverted. She knew now how much that last meeting with Mark had cost her, what a deep scar her impulsive sacrifice had left on her being.

It was important to change her way of living. She set out deliberately to cultivate new friends and new interests. Hank Jessup had once told her she was too intense. "You don't know how to play," he said. And during this strained period in the early months of 1938, she resolved to face life in a lighter manner. In this way lay deliverance.

11. Homer Sweet was distressed about her.

He decided on a heart-to-heart chat.

"I'm a wee bit disappointed, my dear. You haven't been among the stars on our bulletin for several weeks. I appreciate how much your mother's passing has unnerved you. But life must go on, you know. *Vive ut vivas*, as it were."

Homer was right. She forced herself to take a keener interest in her appearance. She went to Antoine's for a new hairdo, and was persuaded to touch up the first strands of gray over her temples. She began using more make-up, a brighter lipstick, and she ordered new frocks which were much more sophisticated than the old classic tweeds that Mark had helped her choose. He'd never approve of these dresses, she thought.

Gradually, the depression lifted, and she emerged again, a little more animated and vivacious, but with less of her old simplicity. The luster was artificial, like the highlights in her hair.

At a conference, early in March, Homer said maliciously to Hank Jessup, "I see you couldn't keep it out of the press. Now the whole world knows your wife is in Reno."

Hank looked at Faith.

"Yes," he said, "I'm practically a bachelor again."

Chapter Sixteen

1. They were married in August 1938, at Twilight Hill.

The wedding party was small, just the Ostberghs, Homer Sweet and his staff, several executives from Hank's agency. The ceremony would take place at high noon in the formal garden, and after the wedding breakfast, Hank and Faith would leave for a fortnight's honeymoon. All very efficient; everything planned in advance, and according to convention. Almost, Faith thought, like an advertising prospectus.

In the spacious bedroom that was hers whenever she visited Twilight Hill, Faith was dressing now, an hour before the wedding. Christine's maid was helping her, and Christine herself was stretched out on the white chaise, smoking and watching avidly.

Faith sprayed her body with gardenia perfume from a silver atomizer, and stepped into the beige silk frock the girl held out for her.

"I rather suspected you would finally marry Hank," Christine said idly.

Faith brushed her hair in place. "You knew more than I did."

Mrs. Ostbergh allowed a skeptical smile to touch her thin lips. "Really? Then whatever possessed you to marry him?"

"I think Hank will make a good husband," Faith answered evasively. Inwardly, she was mocking her words; an ambiguity; a Homerism.

For the truth was both simple and pathetic. She was lonely. She needed desperately to cut herself off from the memory of Mark. And a man like Hank, jovial, gregarious, an extrovert, was just what she needed. A therapeutic measure.

She picked up the faded satin box containing the pearls Mark had sent her shortly before the divorce to which he had made no protest. She had put away her mother's gold locket; she meant never to wear it again. A new life, she promised herself determinedly.

Christine glanced at her jeweled watch. "Time to go down," she said. "Nervous?"

Faith shook her head, absently.

The ceremony was brief, and when it was over, she was curiously surprised and shocked. I am Mrs. Harvey Jessup, she thought. How can that be, when I've been Faith Holmes for so long. Faith *Holmes*. For a moment, she was panic-stricken; what was she doing here, beside this good-looking, smug stranger?

"Faith," Hank Jessup called jovially, "the photographers are here."

Homer came over, holding a glass of champagne. "I've arranged a good press," he assured Faith. "Thank heavens, you're photogenic."

"I wish you wouldn't."

"Why not?" Hank interrupted.

"My dear," Homer said pompously, "there are three important events in a man's life—his birth, his wedding, his death. If he is fortunate enough to be in the public eye, he owes the world a record of those events."

At three o'clock, while the guests were still toasting them with Ostbergh's rare champagne, Faith and Hank slipped away in his new roadster.

"Damned decent gesture—the Ostberghs giving us this wedding party," he said. "I bet we're in with them for life. Invite them to dinner as soon as we get back, Faith."

"Yes. I must see Christine, anyway. She'll be up for re-election in November, and she wants a rewrite of her old speeches."

Neither of them considered this an odd conversation for a newly wed couple.

The fortnight they spent at the fashionable Connecticut Inn proved pleasant enough. The weather was perfect, and the place was swarming with successful and important people, several of whom Hank knew when they arrived, and all of whom he met within the next twenty-four hours.

Faith had every obvious reason to be pleased and flattered. Hank was charming and devoted in a conventional fashion that occasionally grated on her nerves. Every gesture was so correct. The expensive, rare orchids, the fine champagne, the orchestra playing special music—the Hit Parade songs that were the only sort Hank enjoyed. And the gifts— a Russian sable cape from Revillon Frères, a square-cut diamond from Cartier.

There were times when Faith couldn't help but think, Emily Post must be a great source of inspiration to Hank, just as Shelley and Keats were to Mark. . . .

Then she remembered the two kids who had eloped to Great Falls, and the room clerk who was so cynical until he recognized the Holmes name. She remembered their shyness, and Mark's remarkable mature tenderness.

How utterly different was the present! She reminded herself, however, that she should be grateful. A new life, remember? Understand the limitations of this new union, do not expect the impossible. . . .

Hank was very much in love with her, but fortunately he was a gregarious soul, who continually restored himself on the response of people. Mornings, while Faith read or took a sunbath, he rushed out to the golf links, and when he returned for lunch, he announced contentedly that he'd made a new contact. Nothing appeared to give him greater satisfaction than the combination of business and pleasure. He was in daily communication with his office, and there were times when the fortnight proved so hectic that Faith forgot it was her honeymoon.

They had leased a brownstone house on Gramercy Park, of her own choosing. Hank would have preferred a Park Avenue apartment with an imposing doorman, but he acceded amiably enough to her wishes. She resigned from Homer's office, but agreed to continue on the Symphony program. She insisted also on paying her share of the household expenses, which rather surprised and antagonized Hank, although it did relieve his financial status somewhat. For all her money, Peggy had exacted pretty stiff alimony as the price of a divorce!

2. They gave a housewarming the first Sunday in October. The rooms were decorated in exquisite taste, the antiques they had chosen from the Madison Avenue shops appropriately displayed. Faith arranged the great clusters of yellow and white chrysanthemums in old vases against the dark-green walls of the foyer, and helped the maids set up the buffet in the dining room.

"I do hope the party is a success," she said to Hank, who was mixing himself a highball.

He smiled genially. "It will be. Everything you touch is a success, darling."

She had made him happy; she knew it. The very first week of their marriage he had boyishly confided, "I'm so proud of you. Every man I know is envious of me."

"I won't disillusion you," she said.

By five in the afternoon, the double drawing rooms and the dining room were jammed with guests; waiters were passing drinks, and the maids were busily serving the lobster salad, sandwiches and finger rolls.

"I didn't dare invite all my friends," Hank boasted. "The house isn't big enough."

He was, she saw, a superb host, who dedicated himself unselfishly to the welfare of his guests. He moved from one to the other, friendly and ingratiating, and incidentally having a fine time himself.

For a moment, Faith was left alone, isolated in the eddy of noise and laughter; a friend of Hank's, an advertising man, was approaching with tipsy dignity, and, looking around for an escape, she spied Corrigan coming into the room.

She moved swiftly to him, a radiant smile on her face. She was visibly pleased to see him, for he had ignored the note she had sent announcing her marriage to Jessup.

"Corrigan, how nice of you to come! I was afraid you were angry with me."

He made no answer; his long cadaverous face seemed more mournful than ever.

"Come and have a drink, Corrigan," she said happily, taking him by the arm. "You haven't wished me luck yet."

Ignoring her words, he stared at the crowded room, his glance rapier-sharp and contemptuous.

"What sort of shenanigans are these?"

"Corrigan," she began placatingly.

His face was black as a Jeremiah's. "The lady who was so fighting mad at injustice seems to have lost her old rancor entirely."

If Hank sees him here, she thought. And in this mood . . .

"Come on, Corrigan, tell me what's biting you."

He regarded her with scathing pity. "Don't you read the papers? Don't you realize what's going on in this wretched little world of ours? Or have you gone the way of all flesh—piddling while Prague burns!"

"Christine feels this mess in Czechoslovakia will blow over."

" 'Peace in our time,' eh? Nuts! And since when has Christine Ostbergh become an authority on the state of the world?"

Hank approached, overhearing his last remarks. "Nice to see you, Corrigan," he said suavely, conquering his dislike of this gloomy individual whom Faith adored. "But for God's sake, lay off this war business. I don't see why it should concern us. . . ."

"Excuse me," Corrigan muttered and turned away.

"Corrigan," Faith followed him pleading, "don't go away. I haven't seen you for so long. I want to talk to you."

"I guess I'm in the wrong pew," he retorted icily. "And this seems to be where I came in."

The door closed after him. She stood there a moment, very close to tears. For suddenly he had taken on Mark's mantle; he was the only man she knew with the mordant power to hurt her.

3. Faith forced herself to dismiss Corrigan's caustic reproach from her mind. She shut it away, deep in her subconscious, and she kept busy. She went out a good deal, for the nature of Hank's business demanded a good deal of entertaining. His first wife, Peggy, had always been bored by the visiting firemen, but Faith proved to be a charming and gracious hostess. His clients were both impressed and delighted with her, and usually ended up firmly convinced the Jessups and the Jessup Advertising Agency were tops. Why change?

They attended all first nights; Hank had a standing order with his ticket broker. Monday evening, they went to the opera, Thursday to the Philharmonic, Friday to prize fights or hockey games at the Garden. Usually, they took their guests to the Stork or El Morocco afterwards and finally wound up in their own home for a nightcap.

Hank loved her all the more because she made such a definite hit with his friends. Nevertheless she suffered from too much leisure, and she made it a point to discover new causes that might occupy her during the day: the committee sponsoring China relief; raising a fund for the children of the Spanish Loyalists. Hank once suggested casually, "Do be careful, Faith, before you allow your name to be used on any committee indiscriminately. Some of these charities are merely fronts for the subversive elements. And your actions do reflect on my business, you know."

Hank was easy to live with, unruffled and amiable. He was beginning to put on weight, which worried him. He bought himself a complicated Exercycle, which he used each morning, and once a week he went to a Turkish bath, usually with an out-of-town client. To her innate relief, they had practically no private life. Hank belonged to his business and to his friends.

The only time he grew impatient with Faith was when he felt she was cultivating unimportant people.

"Life's too damn short," he said, "for such peculiar self-indulgence!"

4. During this time, Faith received an unexpected call from Winona Kraus, whom she had not seen in several years. Impulsively, she

invited Winnie home for lunch. But when her old classmate arrived, she knew she had blundered; she should have suggested Schrafft's or Mary Elizabeth's, where the contrast between them would have been less painful.

For Winnie, slouched in the Queen Anne chair, looked more tawdry than Faith remembered.

"You sure have come through," she said enviously. "I knew you'd land another rich one even after that Latham guy died."

Faith felt her nerves growing taut; she was embarrassed by the cringing attitude and hurt by it, too. Fortunately, the maid came in with a tray of martinis and hors d'oeuvres, and Winona's washed-out blue eyes came alive. Her puffy red fingers snatched a glass avidly.

"It's sure cold out," she said. "This is just what I need."

They ate at a small table in the dining room, overlooking the rear garden, bleak in the gray November air. The little stone figure poised over the tiny fish pond looked desolate amid the dead foliage.

"I didn't know you'd married again until I saw your picture in the *News*," Winnie said, "leaving the opera."

"I tried to get in touch with you," Faith explained hastily, "but you had moved, and the landlady didn't know where."

"I've been around," vaguely. "Say, do you ever hear from St. Croix?"

"I was home last spring. My mother died."

"That's too bad. I haven't heard from my folks in ages. I suppose if they saw me now, they'd close the door in my face." She looked down at her shabby lavender suit. "But you know, I'd kinda like to see the old burg again."

A surge of compassion swept through Faith; she ached for the young Winona who'd started out so confidently to lick the world.

"Winnie."

"Yeh?"

"Winnie, is there anything . . ." Faith stopped, afraid she was doing it badly, afraid Winona would be offended.

The afternoon dragged on, and her friend showed no signs of leaving; she had another coffee and a third brandy. She wasn't talking much now; her face was flushed, her hands unsteady, and she appeared lost in her own moody reflections.

Finally, Faith said uncomfortably, "I'm awfully sorry, Winnie, but I must leave. I have a committee meeting at four."

"Okay." Winona finished her drink and stood up without protest, as if she were accustomed to being pushed around. Her once lovely eyes were bloodshot, and a lock of bleached hair fell over her lined forehead. She struggled into her thin coat, and Faith noticed that the hem was kept in place by a safety pin. She managed to slip a bill in Winona's moist palm. "Perhaps this'll tide you over," she said awkwardly. "Keep in touch with me, Winnie."

"Thanks," coldly. "Well, I'll be seeing you."

Faith stood at the window, watching her wander down the street, and hesitate at the windy corner. She looked so cold and forlorn that Faith's heart ached for her. She thought, Winnie came to me for old times' sake, and I was restless and impatient with her, I soothed my conscience with a fifty-dollar bill.

She was sickened by her own behavior; bitterly ashamed of herself. The thing to do was to make amends instantly. She'd talk to Hank, she'd call Homer Sweet. Surely there was a job somewhere for a girl like Winona!

She snatched her coat and hurried out of doors. But Winnie was already out of sight. And she realized there was no way to get hold of her, no address . . .

The incident gave Mrs. Harvey Jessup a good many sleepless hours that winter.

5. Harvey Jessup hailed a taxi at the foot of Lexington Avenue.

"Park and Forty-seventh," he said, swinging into the musty interior. He lit a cigarette, inhaled, and patted his expensive briefcase. A fine morning! The warm December sun matched the glow in his heart. Mrs. Latham was due in his office at twelve o'clock to pass on the merits of the model campaign he and his staff had outlined in the last three hectic days.

What luck, he gloated. It was part of the general good fortune that had come his way since his marriage to Faith. Last Sunday morning, Faith told him her old friend Mrs. Latham was in town and was coming for lunch.

"Latham?" he repeated. "Not the Mrs. Latham of the Latham Flour Mills."

Yes, Faith had said. The very same, and a lovely person.

Hank could barely restrain his excitement. Was this a break, or was it a break? "Why didn't you tell me about your friendship with her before?"

The Latham Flour Mills were a QQA&M account of long standing.

And because of the Latham loyalty, the agency had begun to take the account for granted; the advertising was routine and commonplace, the slogans still old vintage.

"Darling," he sounded out Faith, "do you think you could help persuade Mrs. Latham to change agencies?"

"I'm sorry, Hank," she said pleasantly. "You'll have to do your own dirty work."

Obviously, she didn't subscribe to Hank's philosophy of give and take. But he could manage nicely by himself. He found Mrs. Latham a small spry woman in a plain black suit, a shapeless felt hat, and the sort of oxfords a social worker might wear. But her jewels were real enough, and behind the pleasant demeanor was the regal assurance of a woman born to wealth and position. After lunch, they got on the subject of Latham products casually enough, and Hank's words were casual, too.

"I used to work for QQA&M," he said.

"Really? Did you handle any of our accounts?"

"In a small way. If I'd stayed on, *Wheat-Lax* would have been my baby."

Mrs. Latham smiled benignly.

"It's an extraordinary product," he continued glibly. "Both Faith and I use it all the time. Pity it doesn't receive the proper exploitation. They're a pretty conservative group over at QQA&M, you know. I'm afraid their reputation has outdistanced their initiative. . . .'"

When he arrived at his office early Monday morning, he called a conference. "Top importance," his secretary announced, as she summoned the art director, copy men and others to his office.

After they settled themselves, Hank picked up the Webster dictionary on his desk, and flipped it to a page his secretary had marked.

"'Bran,'" he read, "'The coarse, outer coat of wheat, or . . . as separated from the flour by sifting or bolting.'"

They listened, puzzled. They watched curiously, as he took from his drawer a flat, bilious green carton, and held it up.

"Fellows," he said, "this is known as *Wheat-Lax*. It is put out by the Latham Flour Mills. It is considered a 'by-product.' Now, what I'd like to do is to convert it into a 'buy-product.'"

He waited for their approval, which came automatically.

"The Latham account has been in the hands of QQA&M so long, it's gathering moss. The company is ripe for a change. Yesterday, Mrs. Latham lunched in my home. I've got her interested to the point where the account is practically on our threshold." He paused. "The rest is up to you."

As they digested this revelation, he added, "Here's the product we're going to concentrate on. *Wheat-Lax.* We'll start from scratch. Redesign the container, and so on. You boys know what I want!"

"Okay, chief."

"Data, layouts, copy, everything must be on my desk by 9:30 A.M., Thursday. Mrs. Latham will be here at noon. If we can sell her, the account is in the bag."

"That gives us only three days," Magnus, the art director, pointed out.

Hank Jessup smiled, man to man. "It's a tall order, I know. If it's a flop, I'm afraid you boys better be prepared to park your ulcers elsewhere. If it clicks—and I know it will—it's up the ladder for all of you."

And now it was Thursday morning, and the material was neatly placed on his desk, stacks of it. When Mrs. Latham was ushered into his office three hours later, he was ready for her. He showed her to a comfortable chair from the vantage of which she could see the color photographs on the wall of products advertised by his agency. Then he picked up a cylindrical box, bright yellow with gleaming white lettering.

"First of all, Mrs. Latham," he said, "we must disassociate from the public mind the idea that this product is merely another laxative. It isn't. I'd like to think of it as the All-Purpose Food with One Purpose. The Internal Cleanser! We are *not* out to compete with commercial cathartics. So I suggest that the name *Wheat-Lax* be changed to *Wheat-lix!*"

Mrs. Latham nodded her head; she listened intently as he outlined the campaign, beginning with a new design for the container. Why resort to cathartics and purges when you can buy a health-giving, life-prolonging food to make you healthy and happy, he pointed out. Stress the psychology of good health as the key to success.

Mrs. Latham beamed.

"In the exhaustive tests we made," Hank continued smoothly, "we found innumerable new uses for the product. In soups, on salad, in practically everything"—he smiled boyishly—"except ice cream, and we're working on that now."

Then he read the doggerels with which he meant to fill the ads.
"Start the Day
    Nature's Way."
"Stay Clear and Bright
    From Morn to Night."

Mrs. Latham interrupted then, inviting him to lunch with her at the Health Bar in Grand Central.

"We'll continue our talk there," she said.

"Good," Hank agreed. He felt fine; he had made it.

6. That tense, jittery summer of 1939, America was ostensibly at peace. But its people snatched the extra editions and hugged the seat by the radio. On the surface, America continued its normal way of life, concerned with the new car, two weeks off with pay, Clark Gable, hot dogs, suntan, the World's Fair. But on the public beaches and in the country clubs, in the supermarkets and the newsreels, there lurked an air of uneasiness, as if nothing could convince the people now that the Jap aggression in China was too far away; that the rape of Ethiopia by Mussolini's Black Shirts didn't concern the Smiths of Sioux City; that the stench of the Nazi Storm Troop barbarities wouldn't reek across the dividing ocean. There was no doubt. The war clouds were rapidly approaching.

Though still at peace, America was divided into two factions: the interventionists and the isolationists, and among the latter were the rabble-rousers who brewed an evil potion to poison public opinion. . . .

Faith remained in town. Her radio program was off the air until September, and to her relief, Hank was out of the city a good part of the time on business. She lost herself in the papers, weekly magazines, and radio news which grew daily more disturbing. Since the day the umbrella had stopped being the symbol of peace and turned instead into a twig of appeasement, she had been dejected and heartsick. How right Corrigan had been when he charged them with piddling while Prague burned!

Probably Corrigan was right, too, in his sardonic comment, " 'The meek shall inherit the earth.' Yeh, six feet of it!"

During one of the rare evenings when she and Hank were dining alone, they discussed the growth of the American Isolationists, and she burst out angrily, "There's only one emblem for those misguided people —an ostrich with his head in the sand and his rear exposed!"

"What're you so het up about?" Hank asked blandly. "It doesn't concern us."

"But it does! It concerns every one of us! What right have we to live in security and happiness when people are being starved and beaten and robbed of their human dignity?"

For the first time since their marriage, he was annoyed with her.

"For God's sake, get off your soapbox!" he ordered curtly.

"I'm not on a soapbox. I'm merely repeating what is in everyone's heart these days."

"I don't agree with you. And I wish some of those noble souls who are always worrying about their neighbors would think of the welfare of our own country for a change. We're just coming out of our own depression. Charity begins at home. Those damn European bickerings got us into trouble before. This time, let 'em fight it out among themselves!"

"That's a very small-minded attitude, Hank."

"Oh, lord," he groaned with distaste, "lay off, will you?"

He got up from the table and switched on the radio.

"This is Berlin," an American voice announced. "There is great tension in the German capital tonight. . . ."

With a muttered oath, he shut it off.

7. By the end of August, Hank was working feverishly to stir up new accounts. Business was sluggish. The ten-year non-aggression pact between Russia and Germany had knocked the wind out of everyone, and there was even greater confusion and uncertainty as all eyes turned to Europe.

During that week, he sat in on two important and secret meetings with Eric Ostbergh and Homer Sweet. Only one other man was present, a Mr. Emerby from Detroit, who spoke vehemently and at great length on the sorry state of the union.

Hank brought Mr. Emerby home to dinner. And during the entire meal, the guest accentuated his hearty appetite with a monologue on neutrality, isolationism and the absolute necessity of keeping America out of the impending war. To Faith, his blank, guileless face was an evil deception, for his feverish eyes reminded her of a Torquemada. Only with the greatest difficulty did she refrain from speaking her mind.

When he finally left, she took a deep breath. "Hank, where in the world did you pick up that mongrel?"

He flushed. "That mongrel, as you call him, is one of Black's most trusted men."

"You mean the head of the American Isolationist movement? What's he doing here?"

"Making contacts," evasively.

"Hank, you aren't going overboard for those crackpots?"

He managed a smile. He put his arm around her, and said cajolingly, "Darling, I'm not going overboard for anything or anybody. And I hope you won't, either. We mustn't get involved in something so distant it doesn't even exist for us."

She stared at him in faint surprise. She couldn't stay angry with a man whose soul was reflected in the slogans he created and the products he advertised. She could neither quarrel with him nor reason with him, for she saw him as he was, a man happily bound by his own narrow limitations, a man whose God and goal were success. He was a good fellow, an easy touch, a grand host, a swell friend, but she felt that if the world had to depend on the justice in the hearts of men like him, it was sunk, now and forever.

She remembered a song popular several years back. "The Music Goes Round and Round."

That's what's happening to us, she realized with dismay. I am married to Hank Jessup who cannot help thinking as he does. It serves me right. For obviously, I deserve no more.

8. The first of the new series of concerts sponsored by International Petroleum was scheduled for Sunday, September third.

On Friday, Faith was working in her library, putting the finishing touches to her talk, when she heard the announcement over the air that Hitler had marched into Poland.

She dropped her pen, and sat there, momentarily stunned. The strident gong of the telephone aroused her.

Hank was calling, his voice crisp and urgent. "Faith, get some things packed. We're driving out to Twilight Hill immediately. Ostbergh just called me. Homer's coming, too. Your speech is out. We'll have to draft a new one!"

After he hung up, she wondered curiously why the revision of her talk should entail a trip to Twilight Hill.

She found no other guests at the Ostbergh place this weekend. A cloud of secrecy enveloped the three men as they gathered in the library. Faith was not called in for the first conference, but Saturday afternoon, both she and Christine were summoned to the room.

"Christine," Hank asked bluntly, "how do the men on the Hill feel?"

Christine gazed into her highball as if it were a crystal globe. "I don't believe Congress will ever give the President all the powers he demands."

"That's our answer." Ostbergh heaved his great weight out of an easy chair and stood facing them, icy and dictatorial. "The Neutrality Act."

"Quite right, quite right!" Homer's fawn-colored weskit quivered with excitement. "That's the theme for Faith's talk: *America at the Crossroads!*"

They mulled over it during the evening, examining it from all angles. Ostbergh said bluntly, "The President is determined to force us into a war with Germany. Homer, it's up to you to present the facts—so the people can judge for themselves. After all," he added with heavy cynicism, "you're paid to mold their opinion."

Listening, Faith stirred uneasily; she could not put from her mind the memory of Corrigan's contempt for Homer's "double talk." Finally, armed with their suggestions, she went to work on the new version. She worked through the morning, that never-to-be-forgotten morning when Neville Chamberlain announced sorrowfully that Britain was at war. She came down to lunch, blue and disheartened, keeping herself aloof from the animated conversation at the table, which included discussions of what the war would do to Ostbergh's empire in oil.

Then, as dessert was being served, she was summoned to the telephone; her houseboy, Jim, told her that Mr. Corrigan had been trying to reach her all morning. He had left a number for her to call.

"Thank you," she said. After a wait, the operator at the Hotel Pennsylvania connected her with Corrigan.

"How soon can you get into town?" he asked, abruptly.

"I'll be in at seven for the broadcast."

"Can't you make it earlier? I want to see you."

She hesitated briefly. "I'll meet you within two hours. Where?"

He named a small restaurant near Penn Station.

Returning to the table, she explained casually that an old friend had arrived unexpectedly for the day, and they planned to have tea together. She packed her bag and put on a dark-blue silk suit and a small faille hat, and went out to the car.

Although this was the first broadcast of the season, Christine and the men were remaining at Twilight Hill, doubtless for further conferences. Hank kissed her on the cheek. "It's a good speech, darling. Put it over with a bang. Don't forget it's our bid against war!"

"Goodbye," she called.

She left behind three men who were much too concerned with their private affairs to worry about the abysmal tragedy into which the world was plunged.

9. Seven-forty-five. Ushers were herding the stragglers into Studio X. Now every seat was taken. The doors closed silently. A strange rest-

lessness pervaded the audience, like a cold wind through a field of wheat. They felt out of place; they should be home, near the radio, listening for news.

What was happening in Europe?

The orchestra was seated; sixteen men soberly garbed in dinner clothes, looking like so many penguins. The orchestra was tuning up.

How far had the invaders plunged into Poland?

The studio clock was a tocsin of doom. Five minutes before eight. The second-hand moved around the face slowly, inexorably ticking off another building bombed, another batch of lives snuffed out. There was something terrifying, something demoralizing, about the hands of the clock going round and round.

The audience was tense. Each man was loath to face his neighbor, yet took solace from his neighbor's proximity. Nerves were raw; fears dark and foreboding. The aggressor was on the march of death. We'll be drawn in like last time, there's no doubt of it. Hasn't the President said that in case of a war, our frontiers would be in France?

Two minutes to eight. The announcer lifted his hand wearily for silence.

"Ladies and gentlemen, this bulletin has just been received in our newsroom. Hitler's *Luftwaffe* has bombed Warsaw. This broadcast will be interrupted for any further developments." The young man's voice was hoarse; he had been on the air all day.

The conductor, a small tense Spaniard who had fled his country when Franco came into power, marched out with a quick, mincing step. He lifted his baton, and the first gay notes of the Scherzo from Mendelssohn's *A Midsummer Night's Dream* lilted over the air.

Seated in the wing, Faith was not conscious of time. She was oblivious to the music. Her mind was in a turmoil, for she was back in the tiny restaurant near Penn Station, listening incredulously to Corrigan's terse revelation.

"This morning," he said, "I heard about a meeting that took place in a Park Avenue office last week. Two leading members of the American Isolationists were present—they're here to establish Eastern headquarters for their party—and three other men. Ostbergh, Homer Sweet, and your husband!"

She hadn't lost her composure.

"What about it?" she asked. "Personally, I dislike those American Isolationists intensely; Hank and I have quarreled about them. But they're entitled to their opinions. I fail to see why a meeting of theirs should be considered such a flagrant . . ."

"Don't be a fool!" he interrupted angrily. "Those men are doing their damnedest to tie the hands of our government. And to mislead the honest, well-meaning Americans who have been fooled by them. Faith, you know Ostbergh! Why do you think he's a prime mover and contributor to this movement? For love of humanity? Hell, no! Selling oil—that's all he's interested in! It's to his advantage to keep America neutral—so he can sell oil to the aggressors through his subsidiary companies in Argentina. Now, do you understand why he wanted his wife in Congress? When the Neutrality Act comes up for revision, she'll fight against it." He paused.

"At this meeting, Ostbergh put up the dough for a prodigious publicity job. Before you know it, thousands will be picketing the White House, millions will be petitioning their congressmen to keep the U.S. out of war. You know what a job Homer will do!"

"Corrigan, what proof have you?"

"You met a couple of my pals in Washington," he said significantly, taking a paper out of his billfold, and handing it to her.

It was a photostatic copy of a canceled check.

"Pay to the order of Hans Emerby fifty thousand dollars," she read. "It's signed by Eric Ostbergh. Why, Corrigan, Emerby's the man Hank brought home to dinner!"

Did this mean her husband was involved, too? No, she assured herself, Hank was just a good businessman.

Corrigan lit a cigarette. His face was somber and intense. "I'm not working for Homer any longer. My resignation's in the mail."

And, his eyes demanded, what are you going to do about this?

Sitting in the wing, Faith remembered how often Eric Ostbergh flew to South America; she remembered the Senator who had often been a weekend guest at Twilight Hill, a man who was the most rabid isolationist in Washington; she remembered Christine's words, spoken only yesterday, "I don't believe Congress will ever give the President all the powers he demands."

And she, Faith Holmes, had worked to put Christine in her present position, where she could exert her husband's evil influence.

She, Faith Holmes, had been the unwitting stooge of these selfish predatory people.

Suddenly she came to life. The men in black were no longer playing the gay melodies above the dirge of a world on the brink of disaster. The announcer turned his head to her.

"And now, our intermission speaker, Miss Faith Holmes."

She stood up, and approached the microphone in a slow measured tread. Her fingers were gripping the typed script. The announcer stared at her, puzzled, his brows raised, signalling, for Heaven's sake, snap out of it!

And she heard a voice, it must be her voice, saying,

"It is September third in the Year of Our Lord, 1939.

"In Europe, once again, the hands of Mars are steeped in blood.

"In our own land, we stand at the crossroads, uncertain, bewildered. We still have blessed peace, and it is our duty to guard that peace."

What am I doing, she wondered dazedly, betraying my own convictions?

"At this perilous moment, we need level heads and sound minds.

"We must heed the warning of our first President, who advised us, 'To keep the United States free from political connections with every other country, to see them independent of all and under the influence of none.'

"We must hold fast to the words of Thomas Jefferson, who said, 'I deem it fundamental for the United States never to take active part in the quarrels of Europe.'

"It is for us to decide on the justice between the opposing forces on the other side of the world!

"It is for us to keep ourselves free to follow the star of our own destiny. . . ."

She was looking at the audience, and she spied Corrigan in an aisle seat. Her voice died. Her eyes stared at the printed words, but her lips would not function.

But abruptly, the paralysis lifted. She started again, and this time the very impetus of her emotion lent a dynamic fervor to her tone:

"Ladies and gentlemen, America is *not* at the crossroads!

"As a nation passionately devoted to fair play, we have only one choice: to align ourselves on the side of Right and Justice!"

Her impulsive words were not part of the speech. She hurried on:

"There are groups in our land, motivated by greed, selfishness, hypocrisy, who are trying their best to blind us!

"But we must not be blin—"

The announcer rushed to pull the microphone away.

But she was already cut off the air.

10. At Twilight Hill they finished a buffet supper and were sitting by the radio. The butler brought in a pot of fresh coffee, and Christine refilled the large Spode cups.

Hank Jessup lit a fresh cigarette. For once he was listening to a program from the outside, instead of hearing it in the studio.

Homer Sweet added sugar to the brew, and sipped it contentedly. In his lapel, the miniature chrysanthemum which Christine had picked in the garden winked like a yellow light.

"America at the crossroads," he mused sonorously. "Tonight these words will sink deep into the troubled nation's consciousness. It will dissipate all doubts. It will crystallize a credo for these perilous times."

Eric Ostbergh stalked across the room to the side table and opened a bottle of Irish whisky. During the day, he had been in constant touch with Buenos Aires. There was nothing more to be done now, but his shrewd mind leaped ahead, making plans for any contingency.

The antique clock over the fireplace chimed eight. The announcer came on the air. They listened dispiritedly to the music, but when finally they heard Faith's voice, they perked up.

"In our own land, we stand at the crossroads. . . ."

Hank thought, What the devil's the matter with her? She sounds like a school kid giving a recitation. He saw Ostbergh glowering, and he tried to signal. It's nothing, she'll warm up.

She's warmed up, all right, he thought the next minute, horrified. But what was she saying? Those words were not part of her speech, they had not been rehearsed.

". . . America is not at the crossroads!

"As a nation passionately devoted to fair play . . ."

Eric Ostbergh's powerful hands clenched in his pockets. His death's-head features were suddenly distorted with fury. The treacherous, double-dealing . . .

"Of all the insolent, impudent creatures!" Homer screamed, struggling from his chair to get to the radio.

"Leave it alone!" Ostbergh ordered harshly.

"What's wrong with the control room?" Hank Jessup shouted. "Where'n hell is the monitor? Why hasn't she been cut off?" He pounded one fist against the palm of his other hand. "Dammit, she's out of her mind!"

The radio went dead.

Twenty seconds of silence, eternity, during which they were rooted in their places, like wax figures. Then the Brahms music broke the spell.

Eric Ostbergh gripped the telephone.

"Get me the broadcasting station," he ordered.

11. Corrigan sat on the hard seat in Studio X and felt he was on a cloud. He had made no mistake. Faith was a fighter, all right. That fool marriage hadn't ruined her, as he had originally feared. The crowd was aroused. Damned shame, the way the announcer pushed her away. There'll be hell to pay, all right!

Meanwhile, he couldn't wait to clasp her hand, to tell her how proud he was.

12. The switchboard of the broadcasting station was jammed with outside calls. What had happened? Why had Faith Holmes been cut off the air? Why had she suddenly changed sides in the middle of her speech? Had she stumbled on some information she wasn't supposed to reveal? And who were the people she was trying to denounce?

City editors snapped, "Get hold of Mrs. Harvey Jessup. Get a statement."

Radio vice-presidents mopped their brows. What a horrible precedent!

Telegrams were pouring in for Faith, from hotheads, crackpots, admirers. The American Isolationists threatened to boycott the station.

In his dusty, book-lined apartment at the old Lake Shore, Vrest Macklin listened, too. At first, he was deeply disappointed, saddened that she had so deeply compromised with herself that she could mouth this false credo.

But his mood swiftly changed to one of pride.

Yes, this was Faith, the real Faith, still impulsive and foolhardy, still staunch in her cry for justice. He was too deeply moved to rationalize, to question the motive behind her abrupt change.

You'll be hurt, he thought sorrowfully. You'll be hurt time and again. But how proud I am of you.

He dialed Western Union.

13. During the autumn and winter, Mark Holmes never went out to dinner Sunday night. For at eight o'clock, he awaited his weekly meeting with Faith. Tonight, he was disturbed. She isn't herself, he thought. Something's happened.

He didn't like the introduction to her talk, either. It was a compromise, spoken dully, without conviction or sincerity.

Unexpectedly, then, the change of content, of pace. Her voice came alive, grew urgent, pleading. He leaned forward, mesmerized, to catch every word.

"There are groups in our land, motivated by greed, selfishness, hypocrisy . . ."

Yes, that was Faith; those were her words!

"But we must not be blin—"

The radio went dead.

He whispered tenderly, "Finish your sentence, Faith."

14. Damn her! Hank Jessup fumed, as he faced Faith in the brightly lit drawing room. She had plunged him into a mess. The worst mess in his life!

He tried to strike a match, but his hand was trembling. He tossed the cigarette in the fireplace with a furious gesture. He turned back to her, savage and vindictive.

"Have you any idea what you've done to me?"

She stood with her back to the window in the elegantly furnished room where they had given their most successful parties, and she returned his gaze, quietly, almost objectively. The reporters who had been waiting for her were gone. The telephone was silent. This was the showdown. She knew. It had been a long time in coming, but it had been inevitable.

She said nothing. Her passive silence drove him to greater fury.

"Ostbergh's ripping mad! Have you no idea how dangerous a man he is when crossed? Why did you do this—what in hell ever possessed you?"

"Hank . . ."

"You left me holding the bag!" he lashed out violently. "Your mad act will be my ruin. You're nothing but a publicity-crazed, demented woman!"

She regarded him with acute distaste, as if he were an objectionable stranger.

Aloud she said carefully, "Hank, quiet down, please. For your own sake. If Ostbergh turns on you, shift the blame on to me. After all, you're not your wife's keeper."

"Yeh, I'm still the fall guy!" He strode over to her, and she saw the bloodshot film of his eyes, the tiny purple veins at his jowls. "What made you go off the deep end this way? You were okay when you left Twilight Hill. God, what a damn fool I was to place my trust in you! The little woman, the helpmate . . ."

She would not allow his ire to soil her. As for his injured innocence, she knew bitterly it was nothing but a farce. She hadn't the slightest desire to defend herself. Let him hate her; let him think what he liked. But he could not blind her to the truth.

"Hank, I was a gullible fool too long. But now I have the facts. Ostbergh is underwriting the American Isolationist party. And you've been tied up with him."

"What about it? What affair is it of yours?"

"It's my affair if it spreads ill will and hatred through this country. It's every decent citizen's affair."

"And who set you up as a crusader?" he demanded in disgust. "You were paid to do a job. Well paid! Instead, you knifed your sponsor in the back. And damn well ruined your husband. Even Peggy wouldn't have been such a louse!"

She listened to him and felt nothing.

"Hank, I don't want you to be hurt because of me. Truly I don't. I had to say what I did—and I make apologies to no one! However, I do think your behavior is ridiculous. Worse than that, it's blind and stupid. Still, I'll take the full responsibility for my deed."

"Damn little good it'll do. I've already lost the Ostbergh account—thanks to you. And it probably won't be the last."

15. It had been a short marriage, and for the past six months, a miserable one. Clearly now she saw that her ties with Hank were only an escape. She had been running away from herself.

She couldn't possibly remain under the same roof with him. The sooner she got out, the better!

She went up to her room and packed hurriedly. Hank had gone out, his anger still blazing. She left a note for him, saying that she could not justifiably live with him any longer. By the time he returned at dawn, she had already registered at a residential hotel near Gracie Square.

Chapter Seventeen

1. The incident of the Symphony Hour program exploded into spectacular repercussions. It appealed to the popular imagination. Here was a woman in a safe berth, who possessed the courage to speak her mind, even when it meant the sacrifice of her home life and career. To some, she was indisputably a heroine; to others, a hysterical female who had betrayed her employer. She was the subject of much gossip and speculation. Newspapers and magazines scheduled stories about her. She was denounced by fascist organizations as a demagogue; she was acclaimed from many pulpits as a woman of courage. She received indignant letters from women who assured her she didn't know what it meant to be a mother, otherwise she wouldn't encourage this war talk.

Homer Sweet sent her the most scathing blast. "You are a creature of perfidy," he wrote bitterly, if floridly. "I accepted you into my family without reservation, and when I think of your treachery, words fail me. You will undoubtedly receive all the publicity you were angling for. But I repeat: The end does not justify the means. . . ."

She turned down offers from two lecture bureaus and one theatrical producer, who wanted to capitalize on her sudden prominence.

Corrigan dropped in to see her. "You've sown some pretty sound ideas," he said.

She smiled ruefully. "And reaped quite a whirlwind."

"Sorry?"

She shook her head serenely. "No matter what happens, I'll never be sorry."

"You've made bitter enemies."

"Better than false friends."

Corrigan told her he had been offered a job in the Attorney General's office. He had found a niche. But she was at loose ends.

At this time, Vrest Macklin wrote her, asking if she would lend her name and active support to the Committee for the Revision of the Neutrality Act.

"Unless we wish to see the end of our civilization," he wrote, "we must throw in our lot with the Allies. The fight will not be easily won, for under the cover of patriotism, many evil men are aiding the forces of aggression. We need volunteers, Faith, for this is a crusade in which women like you can be invaluable to us."

She put all her energy into the new task. She traveled from one town to another, addressing women in auditoriums, clubs and churches, pleading with them to resist the influence of the Isolationist movement, and to demand that Congress revise the Neutrality Act.

It was a task neither simple nor encouraging, for she was often heckled, denounced and vilified. But many women heeded and did bombard their Congressmen. And early in November, the cash-and-carry plan, to aid the Allies, became a law.

She had done a good job, as thousands of men and women like her had done a good job. But her elation held a note of personal triumph. For this was her first step in making amends for the injudicious years that began with Christine Ostbergh and ended with Harvey Jessup.

2. When Mrs. Latham arrived in New York for her annual visit, she called the Gramercy Park home of the Jessups, and was astonished to hear the telephone had been disconnected.

She rang Hank at his office.

"What's wrong?" she demanded. "Where's Faith?"

"We're not living together," he admitted uncomfortably. In New York, the news was common gossip. Indeed, one columnist quipped that the co-respondent in the case was a man named Hitler.

"What have you done to Faith?"

Too many people were reacting as if Faith could do no harm, he thought irritably. His habitual good humor was wearing thin under the strain. He must watch his step with Mrs. Latham. With the Ostbergh account gone, it was essential to nurse every client.

Hanging up the receiver, he turned to his secretary. "Send two dozen roses to Mrs. Latham at the Plaza."

Damn Faith! Would he ever hear the end of her?

3. "Thank you," Faith said. "I'll be there at seven."

She replaced the telephone on its cradle, and remained there for a moment, uncertain. Then she moved across the small room to the window overlooking the East River, where she stared, motionless, lost in bitter thought, until her vision blurred, and the fat tugs riding sluggishly with the tide seemed no more than clumsy childish toys.

Mrs. Latham's brusque, friendly voice had released the devils she had been trying so desperately to shut away. This, she thought, is finis to another chapter in the Life and Loves of Faith Holmes. Watch for the next installment.

Only, there won't be one. That's all there is; there won't be any more.

The healthy and radiant flush, so characteristic of her, was drained from her face, leaving her skin ashen as her spirits.

"Faith, whatever happened between you and Hank?" Mrs. Latham had asked. "I thought this was to be a marriage of maturity!"

Of maturity, Faith repeated silently to herself. What a farce! And here, in this impersonal hotel room, she was at last able to examine herself and the motives for her tragic errors. She faced the problem of her own insufficiencies; she saw how very much her reckless and impulsive actions had shaped her life, to her utter misfortune.

I've always been so darned sure I was right, she thought wretchedly. And each time I've made a mess of things.

The moment of revelation was cruel, but she forced herself to face it unflinchingly.

You thought you'd escape yourself by fleeing to Hank. You were afraid you'd hurt Mark again—and this you needn't have feared at all, if only you'd possessed some of Mark's inner grace and strength. What an idiot you've been! How thoroughly you've managed to ruin your life! There's nothing left for you now—no hope, no faith, no way to recant the past. The only token to your credit is that you've broken with Hank Jessup over a question of moral right. Let this give you what little solace it can. . . .

It was growing late. The room lay in shadow. Mechanically she bathed and dressed. Slipping her black Persian jacket over her shoulders, she went out to the elevator.

At the Plaza, Mrs. Latham was awaiting her for dinner.

She resolved not to think beyond that moment.

4. Mrs. Latham, however, would not allow her to forget her plight.

"I cannot understand you, Faith. You're no child. How could you allow political differences of opinion to break up your marriage?"

Faith leaned back in her chair. She was tired and depressed, and she resented the post-mortems that would do nothing to assuage her anguish. But she could not repulse Mrs. Latham, who had been her staunch and admiring friend for so many years now.

"It went much deeper than a difference in political opinion," she admitted reluctantly. "It's a difference in a fundamental way of life. To Hank his business means everything. He'd sell his honor for it without a qualm. That's why he's been stringing along with Ostbergh all these years. Well, I couldn't take it any more. I couldn't go on violating my beliefs. Not if I wanted to keep on speaking terms with myself."

She spoke so intensely that Mrs. Latham grew concerned.

"What are your plans?" she asked.

"I really don't know. I haven't thought about it."

Mrs. Latham sipped her sherry. "I'm not referring to your marriage," she said crisply. "If you're certain it's over and done with, forget about it as quickly as possible. Don't allow it in any way to interfere with your career!"

Faith was silent.

"You started something with that denunciation over the radio," the older woman continued shrewdly. "Aren't you going to follow it up?"

"There's nothing I can do."

Nevertheless, despite her denial, a faint note of interest quickened her voice. "I'm convinced, however, that some action should be taken—immediately—to counteract the dangerous influence of men like Homer Sweet and Eric Ostbergh. If one could show up their evil intentions by broadcasting directly to the people . . ."

Mrs. Latham nodded.

"Radio is one of the most powerful mediums in the world today," Faith went on. "Just look how Father Coughlin's using it for his own ends! I suppose if someone could address the listening audience . . ."

"Who better than you?" Mrs. Latham suggested slyly.

For a good many years, she had admired Faith extravagantly; not only because Phillip had loved her, but because she considered the young woman a counterpart of herself. Mrs. Latham nursed a secret conviction that were it not for her wealth and position, she, too, would have been a restless and adventurous girl, eager for the fray. She thought, Why shouldn't there be a spot in radio for Faith, so she could project her ideas to millions of listeners?

After all, in these days, it was most imperative to interpret and clarify for women the troubling events of the times.

That was how Mrs. Latham explained it to herself. Before the board of directors of the Latham Flour Mills, however, she pointed out realistically that Faith might possibly sell more flour than the soap operas.

A month later, Faith had her own program.

5. At noon every Monday, Wednesday and Friday, the announcer faced the mike, like a high priest before a sacrificial altar, and intoned solemnly:

"Ladies and Gentlemen, Eiderdown Flour presents *Not by Bread Alone*—with Miss Faith Holmes."

It was a half-hour program, which Faith filled wittily and adroitly with subjects pertinent to women's interest, and bringing to the microphone as her guests those men and women of national importance, who spoke freely and informatively on current political events.

She refused to compromise by holding out bait in the form of beauty hints, cake recipes, household shortcuts and gifts in return for box tops. The times, she felt, demanded serious consideration. And she offered her listeners the courtesy—regrettably rare in radio—of treating them like adults.

The highlight of each program was a trenchant character sketch, either of a "Man of Good Will" or a "Man of Evil Intent." Here, without mincing words, Faith called names and named facts.

The tragic day Paris fell to the Germans, her guest speaker was a former ambassador to France. In a harrowed manner, he described to his unseen audience the tragedy of the Paris all men loved and revered, the beacon of culture and liberty. The death knell of Paris, he added solemnly, would reverberate to every corner of the earth.

After he finished speaking, Faith painted for her listeners a caustic picture of a "Man of Evil Intent":

"Today, in every country across the ocean, there's a man looking out for the main chance—a national Judas, whose thirty pieces of silver are his personal power. Norway has her Quisling, Austria her Seyss-Inquart, France her Pierre Laval.

"We've got one here in our own country.

"His name is Percival A. S. Scholles, and he boasts he's a third-generation American. His great-grandfather, Johann Schultz, fled from the yoke of Prussian militarism to America. It is ironical that his descendant has turned out to be the spearhead for intolerance and bigotry in our free country.

"Percival A. S. Scholles is the active head of a group of faceless renegades known as the Night Shirts!

"He is a *Man of Evil Intent!*"

"In the name of Democracy, he must be silenced!"

Percival A. S. Scholles brought suit for libel against Faith Holmes and the Latham Flour Mills. The Mills were also bombarded with hundreds of letters demanding Faith's removal, and threatening a boycott against the Latham products. A vicious smear campaign was spread against Faith, the origins of which she immediately suspected. Homer Sweet, the Great Illuminator, did not easily forgive.

The board of directors wavered. But Mrs. Latham stood firm. Faith was in the right, and she was supporting her to the limit.

6. President Roosevelt's second term was running out. And the foes of democracy took heed. A third term would break tradition. Here was their opportunity to foist one of their own kind on the country, a man who believed that the Americans and the Aggressors could do business together. We need a man who will keep us out of this foreign imbroglio, they shouted. Never again shall American youth shed its blood on foreign soil!

During this crucial period, there flashed across the political horizon a meteor of extraordinary brilliance and power. Strangely enough, he, too, was of German heritage, like Percival A. S. Scholles. He was a self-made man, a fighter who would never compromise with right, who scorned the professional politicians and refused any concessions toward getting votes.

He was Wendell L. Willkie.

All through her broadcasts, Faith had applauded the President for his foreign policy. But now she was in a quandary. There was something about Willkie's blunt, undeviating integrity that fired her imagination, as it did that of millions of other Americans. Here was a man untrained in political maneuvering, contemptuous of it; a man possessed of such an impassioned sense of humanity that he stood out like a colossus among the venal politicians. Ignoring his political mentors, he appealed directly to the people, barnstorming through the land, and won them over with his simplicity and honesty. And there developed a phenomenon rarely witnessed, and possible, only in this country. The spontaneous Willkie Clubs.

Even after Willkie went down to victorious defeat, Faith could not forget the reaction of the people themselves. When a great man rose in their midst, they fought valiantly for him. There was hope.

The day after the election, Vrest Macklin wrote her: "I believe our guardian angels were watching over our destiny in this time of crisis, for both candidates were dedicated to the cause of Democracy, and no matter which has won, the evil-mongers have lost."

7. Fortified by Mrs. Latham's loyalty, Faith spoke more bluntly to her audience that autumn of 1940. With the help of her guests, she gave her listeners an illuminating description of world conditions, yet she managed to keep the tenor of the programs simple and homey, like a chat over a tea table. During these days, Corrigan often proved of inestimable help to her. He brought her the news that Christine Ostbergh meant to run for re-election.

"She'll make it," he said glumly. "The voters have been impressed by her much-publicized abilities. Thanks to the job you did, my dear."

Faith flushed. "I'm not very happy about that chapter in my life, Corrigan. I wish I could do something to make up for it."

"Quite possibly you can," he said, and gave her one of his rare smiles.

When she went on the air the Friday before Election Day, Faith set off a bombshell.

She announced that Eric Ostbergh was chief backer of the infamous No-European-Wars Committee, which had the tacit support of the Klan, the Bund and the Night Shirts. Then she described to her radio audience a photograph which had just come into her possession. There were three men in the picture: the Argentine head of the International Petroleum subsidiary, a notorious Nazi official, and Eric Ostbergh, who was supplying the Nazis with oil.

"And it is Ostbergh's wife who is asking the constituents to return her to Congress, where she can carry out the malevolent bidding of her husband."

Then, with Corrigan's permission, she released the print to the press.

When the Democratic party returned to office, Christine Ostbergh was missing from the halls of Congress.

8. "Will you close the window, please?" Vrest Macklin asked his nurse. He was shivering under his heavy robe. The chill winds penetrated the walls of the cluttered room which had been his bedroom and study for almost forty years.

With an effort, he pulled himself out of the chair and shuffled over to his desk.

"Mr. Macklin," the nurse protested, "the doctor ordered bed rest."

He nodded impatiently. He took a deep breath and was instantly tortured by a coughing spasm.

"Mr. Macklin, if you please." The young nurse was annoyed as she led him back to his bed.

All this fuss about a cold, he grumbled. Lord, he'd had plenty of colds in his seventy years!

"Where's my pipe?" he demanded.

"You're not supposed to smoke, Mr. Macklin."

He remembered now where he had lost his pipe. Three nights ago, rowdies had broken into *The Observer* office. They had beaten the watchman and demolished the plant. On Vrest's overturned desk, they left a hastily scrawled note:

"THIS IS WHAT HAPPENS TO WAR MONGERS! BE-WARE!"

The police summoned Vrest. As he knelt beside the interne who was working desperately over old Mike Halloran amid the frightful wreckage, he was sickened with despair. Not for the loss of material possessions, but for the wantonness, the wickedness, the sadistic cruelty of men who struck, like rats, under cover of darkness.

He lifted his weary head to the gray dawn, and he thought, Why bother? Why keep on fighting? It's a losing battle.

Justice. Fair play. All men are brothers. A break for every human. All his life he had fought for these principles, and now he was licked.

A cold rain was falling. The interne stood up and brushed the dust from his knees.

"How is he?" Vrest asked.

The interne shrugged. "It's a bad head wound. And he's old."

Yes, Vrest mused when he finally returned to his rooms, wet and chilled, Mike is old, I am old, and it is no fight for the aged. The evil men are rising over the world like a miasma over the lowlands, and only the young can meet the challenge of their wickedness.

When finally he fell asleep out of sheer exhaustion, the telephone awakened him.

He was ready to quit. But the world wouldn't let him. There were letters and messages from Great Falls, from Detroit, from Chicago, from New York, offering help, money, the use of presses. We're back of you, Vrest Macklin. The good fight must go on.

Mark Holmes came to see him. "I've arranged credit with the Lumberman's Bank, Vrest. There'll be ample to cover your needs. You must carry on!"

He was making tentative plans for publication that evening when he collapsed with a high fever. He refused to stay in bed; but grudgingly, he promised the doctor not to leave his rooms, which were, however, cleared of his staff and his friends.

As soon as she heard the news, Faith had wired him that she would come to St. Croix to be with him. He longed to see her, but he answered by asking her to remain where she was. He knew she was busy, fighting in her own way, and that was sufficient for him.

The following day he listened as was his custom, to her broadcast. The profile of the Man of Good Will was a newspaper editor. She related the story of his life, picturing his unending battle against greed, bigotry, corruption. She spoke admiringly of his refusal to sell out to a syndicate in the tough years. And how, at a time of life when most men retire, he girded himself for a new battle—only to be routed by the hired minions of his enemies, and the enemies of his country.

"But Vrest Macklin's valiant head is unbowed," she ended, "and it is our duty to give him courage. For what happened to him, can happen to us. Like the Nazi Storm Troopers who come in the dark of the night, they can destroy your home, your very way of life. . . ."

After she had finished, he sat silent and brooding in his chair. He was too deeply moved to speak, and the nurse was tactfully silent. Then a coughing spasm overpowered him. The nurse started the steam kettle and offered him a sedative, which he brushed away impatiently. He picked up his pencil and pad and began writing. His face was damp and pallid, the flesh hung loosely around his stubborn old lips. But he wrote on steadily, his hand as firm as his heart.

9. Two days after Vrest Macklin's death, Tod sent Faith the copy of *The Observer* containing his last editorial, written just before the pillage. From the front page, his photograph, outlined in black, leaped out at her. My good friend, she thought. The mentor of my youth. Oh, Vrest, the world can ill afford to lose a man like you. . . .

She read his final words.

"In Europe, the lights of civilization are flickering, which is all the more reason why we, in the cradle of democracy, must keep our light eternal. For one day, the survivors of a ravaged Europe will sorely need this last beacon of hope."

Closing her eyes, she recalled another day, long ago, almost in another world, when she had returned to *The Observer* office, crushed and weeping, after the fire in Lewis Trout's plant.

"Vrest," she had sobbed wildly, "men have died needlessly! They never had a chance! Why should such things happen in a civilized world?"

And Vrest had said compassionately, "Open your eyes slowly, Faith.

The birth of the spirit is every bit as agonizing as the birth of the flesh. Open your eyes slowly, so you won't be shocked by what they see."

Now she cried silently, "My eyes are open, Vrest. And they do see the danger that is imperiling the human spirit!"

Her task would be to carry on where Vrest had left off.

10. On that fateful day in December, the blow fell. And the misguided, who were the tools of the foes of democracy, were suddenly robbed of their most persuasive arguments. Many of them repented, hastily donning the cloak of patriotism like sackcloth and ashes. Others scurried to their holes and then came out again, transformed into quasi-patriots. The foes of democracy are adept at changing their disguise.

11. "Talk's not enough!" Faith told Mrs. Latham. "I must do something more active! I'm going to see the Red Cross."

"Take it easy, Faith," Mrs. Latham soothed her. "You're reacting like everybody else. We've had more difficulty with the key men in our mills who want to throw up jobs in which they're irreplaceable in order to enlist! My dear, your program is invaluable. We wouldn't dream of releasing you from your contract."

Faith was not placated, but she was forced to compromise. During the first year of the war, she went off on an extended tour of the East and the South, selling War Bonds. Since each of her broadcasts originated in a new spot, she visited innumerable camps, canteens, Red Cross Centers, defense plants, and she reported in vivid and moving detail the magnificent response of American women in all walks of life to the war effort. For the first time, she thought proudly, the world sees what women can really do.

While traveling through Virginia, she received an invitation to do one of her programs at a Marine boot camp.

"We've had plenty of stage and screen stars," the director of the USO told her, "and I think the boys would like a program of yours for a change. Something to remind them of home."

On a sleety afternoon in January, she wandered into the PX, escorted by a handsome young officer, who was making the most of his enviable duty. The place was deserted except for a couple of boys, and on an impulse, she went over to speak to them. The chubby youngster was no more than eighteen, with a child's bland face; the other was older, short and thin, with a shock of curly black hair standing high over his sallow face, and a sullen morose manner. Both looked ill at ease, and homesick.

"Where are you from, fellows?" she asked.

Dark Hair regarded her impassively, without answering. And as if to make up for his friend's lack of manners, Chubby said quickly, "Michigan."

"Really? What a coincidence, I'm from Michigan, too. Ever hear of St. Croix?"

"Yes, ma'am!" Plump cheeks gleaming like polished apples, Chubby stuttered a little in his excitement. "I—I sure did! Got an aunt living in St. Croix. On South Sycamore—know where that is?"

Faith grinned at him. "I lived a street away. On Ontario Place." She sat down beside him and accepted a coke.

"Gee, it's sure a small world!" he said happily. "I used to visit St. Croix. Plenty of times."

"Did you ever go skating on the pond above Ontario?"

"Sure did!"

"Ever listen to a band concert at Holmes Park?"

"Yes'm. My aunt used to take me Saturday nights. And the Casino on the lake. Boy, those hot dogs!"

They forgot the bored officer and the surly boy. She was twice Chubby's age, yet they were talking on the same level, lost in their happy reminiscences. The old home town—a link the world over.

When the officer finally reminded Faith she must leave, the boy thanked her profusely.

"Miz Holmes, it's been swell talkin' to you. Makes me feel a lot better. I wish some of the other guys could hear about St. Croix."

That evening, on her program, Faith re-lived her girlhood. She described Main Street on a Saturday night, and the frankfurter roasts at Lake Michigan, the Christmas Party for kids at the Elks Hall, the Senior Dance at the Gym. In retrospect, the scenes were tender and nostalgic, and typical, and many of her listeners thought fondly, Why, my home town's like that, too.

The broadcast was a sensation. She was swamped with requests from the boys.

"Mrs. Holmes, why don't you visit my town and tell us guys what's going on there? Why, it'd be like a letter from the folks."

From this casual beginning, originating with a boy's homesickness, there developed the series of broadcasts which, within a year, became a national byword.

Home Town, she called them. *Home Town, U.S.A.*

The USO screened the requests and arranged her itinerary. She barnstormed through the country and loved every exhausting emotional moment of it. All her tremendous energies were focused on her work. Blithely, she ignored the great physical strain. She could weather it. She had always been robust.

However, when Corrigan saw her in the autumn of 1943, he realized that the tour wasn't exactly a jaunt, as she insisted. At last, Faith was beginning to show her age. There were bruises of fatigue under her dark glowing eyes, and strands of gray in her short curling hair. But her smile was contagious, her manner as cheery and entertaining as ever.

"I'm being useful, Corrigan. That's quite enough for me."

"You've changed all right," he growled. "And I'm inclined to think I like you better this way."

Her face was suddenly radiant. "Do you, Corrigan?" she said. "So do I."

In every town, she found the women's clubs of tremendous help in gathering the essential, advance information she wove into her broadcasts.

"I took a walk down Main Street today," she often began. "And stopped for a double malted at Nick's Sweet Shop. The old gang that used to hang around Nick's has thinned out considerably. Freddy Simpson's a sergeant in the Air Corps. He married Barbara Mackey before he shipped out. They had quite a wedding—over a hundred guests— and Barbara looked awfully pretty in her grandmother's wedding gown. She's packed all her gifts away in the family attic, and has taken a job at the Aircraft plant until Freddy comes home. Billy Sykes is in the South Pacific. He sent his mother quite a souvenir last week—she refuses to show it to her friends. There's a new soda jerker taking Jim Norris' place. . . ."

She told them about the new movie at the Strand; about the Church Social that netted fifty-three dollars for the Parish Fund; she gave them the score of last Saturday's game. "The Home Town won! Now, they're runner-up for the lead." She told them about their friends in service and the girls who were married before their boys shipped out; she gave them messages from their families.

The boys listened avidly. Her descriptions of the old familiar scenes reassured them, strengthened their waning sense of security. No matter how rugged it got, they could still dream of home; and they loved her for her contribution to the dream.

Faith was spending most of her time with the enlisted men. She lost contact with many of her old friends, except for Mrs. Latham, who was spending most of her time in Minnesota. Occasionally, she heard from her father, who wrote that Mrs. Hussar was bedridden, her arthritis was so bad they had to get a woman to look after her. Recently, he had seen Winona Kraus on Sycamore Street. For a minute, he hadn't recognized her. She looked awful. He was fine, and working hard. Wolverine Motors was on three shifts; they had received an E. Mark was flying to Washington soon—an advisor to the government; he told Tod only the other day that he might have to go to Europe any day.

In March, 1944, the USO sent her to England. Here she would reverse the pattern, bringing news of the boys to their families in America. England, she found, was an arsenal, making ready for the invasion. Its people, still stunned from Coventry and the blitz, were being tried now by an unearthly missile hurtling from the enemy shores. Everyone she met was tense and on edge, knowing that on the success of the invasion rested the outcome of the conflict.

After D-Day, she spent all her time in the English hospitals, moving from wards to rest camps, always maintaining her high spirits, kidding the boys and being mercilessly kidded in return. She was bringing them not only news of home, but the very essence of home. Whenever she arranged for a wounded boy to appear on her program, a reward that gave him the opportunity to talk to his folks, all the Joes got a kick out of it. She was better for them than the pin-up girls. The very fact that she was older made her somehow more endearing. They were at ease with her. She was like one of the family.

The brass hats recognized her value as a morale builder, and fought for her services. And as more towns and villages were freed, Faith followed the liberators into Paris.

Chapter Eighteen

1. Mark Holmes arrived in Paris two days before Christmas. The Commission of which he was a member had spent a hectic fortnight in England, and planned to rest in Paris several days before flying to the Near East, and then back to Washington to report to the President. The Commission consisted of four men: a Midwestern Senator, who had an extraordinary grasp of the enemy's economic potential, a Princeton economist, a Quaker and Mark Holmes.

The war years had churned up the American scene, bringing to the fore the gallant and durable character of the home front, the courage and endurance of the American fighting youth, and the resourcefulness and ingenuity of the supermen of production, who were turning out the planes, tanks and ammunition for the insatiable maw of war.

Mark was one of these brilliant young men. The Holmes-Griswold engine was being used by the Air Force; Wolverine Motors was expanded for wartime production, and Mark himself was requisitioned by the administration for his extraordinary talent in gearing up production.

Like old Eben Holmes, Mark found self-expression in his work, and had no interest in accumulating money for money's sake. Even after his income had increased perceptibly, he lived in Spartan simplicity. Although he possessed a capacity for deep passion and great tenderness, he had learned to stifle these emotions ruthlessly. They had no place in his life. After the breakup of his marriage, he grew more reserved than ever before. When he approached another woman in the urgency of desire, the need burned out swiftly, leaving an ash both bitter and degrading.

"Why don't you marry again?" Allan Griswold asked. "You've got so damned much to give a woman!"

Marry again? The very thought offended his sensibilities. For in his heart, Faith was still his wife; he was still dedicated steadfastly to their union. He had hoped that after Charlotte's death the inexplicable bond between mother and daughter—a bond which exerted such an evil influence on Faith—would be severed at last. But when he met Faith at Mrs. Hussar's the day of her mother's funeral, he had been shocked by her behavior. It was as if Charlotte's fanatic domination had reached out from the grave.

Nevertheless, the announcement of Faith's marriage to Harvey Jessup was a bitter blow. How could she have done it, he wondered wrathfully. Was she so insensitive?

After that, he told himself bluntly it was over, and he'd better learn to forget her once and for all time. He tried hard; yet despite his resolution, he found himself drawn to the radio as to a magnet Sunday night. And when the announcer still introduced her as Faith Holmes, he told himself wryly that something of their marriage had remained with her.

The night she was cut off the air so dramatically, he was filled with admiration for her courage. She'd always been outspoken—impulsive and erratic, perhaps—but absolutely forthright. He was reminded of the time she had denounced Mr. Crandall, the music teacher, for his injustice to Winona Kraus.

He wished he could write her. But when he thought of the circumstances of their final parting, he could not bring himself to it.

A week later, he read in the Chicago *Sun* that she and Harvey Jessup had parted.

2. Early December, the world was breathing a bit more easily. For it was apparent now that the aggressor nations were doomed to defeat. Their cities pounded to destruction, they became the victims of the devastating forces they had unleashed.

Then as the dawn of victory began to break, a heavy thundercloud darkened the sky. On the western front, the enemy was pushing back the American forces into Belgium and Luxembourg. The German attack had the convulsive force of a beast in his death throes, lashing out with wild and destructive fury.

The news shattered the hopes of the world waiting for a Christmas bearing the overtures of peace.

In Paris, especially, the gloom was a pall; the spirit of its people, cold and hungry, clinging to the dignity so recently restored them, plunged once again to the depths of depression. The first Christmas free of the Occupation—what sadness, what disappointments! The reassurance of the General Staff did not alleviate the people's fear. The enemy was forging ahead.

3. On the morning of Saturday, December 23, Faith arose early. She was living in a small pension on the Boulevard Raspail, and since her bedroom was unheated, she never lingered there in the morning. Shivering, she washed and dressed swiftly and then hurried out into the chilly street.

To her the beauty of Paris was all the more poignant this gray morning when the disheartening news of the Battle of the Bulge hung over the city. In the café around the corner, the garçon who served her croissant and hot chocolate muttered, "If the Boche returns, God pity us. . . ."

"The Boche won't return," she replied with a conviction she did not quite feel.

To her dismay, the depression appeared to have infected the canteen workers. They had been preparing a happy weekend for the boys arriving in Paris on forty-eight-hour passes. But the leaves had been canceled, and the hostesses were sitting, aimless and uneasy, waiting for news. Would this never end?

Faith was unable to shake the feeling of presentiment that enveloped her. She sat down at a desk and sorted her mail. Thank heavens, her broadcasts for the weekend were canceled! How could she possibly have gone on the air, pretending to be cheerful and optimistic when her spirits were down to zero?

I've taken about all I can, she thought drearily. I'm tired.

She was always tired now. Her sleep was fitful. She suffered nightmares, and awoke, shaking, her skin clammy, her heart racing. She was going on nerves alone. Recently a young doctor at the base hospital had warned her to slow down.

She had thanked him politely for his advice, and then hurried out to catch a jeep going to her next destination. How could she even consider going home when so many of her good friends, doctors, nurses, Red Cross workers were carrying on in the face of utter collapse?

Restlessly, she pushed the letters aside. She looked around the spacious room curiously, seeking a friendly familiar face. She hated being alone today; too many persistent memories nagged at her.

She stood up idly to watch a couple of G.I.'s playing table tennis, their voices boyish and breezy, their movements swift and sharp. Then she noticed a group of correspondents gathered around the fireplace. Perhaps they have news, she thought, and joined them, warming herself by the flames. But their brusque and cynical conversation was not encouraging, and she wondered dejectedly what she could do to forget the bleakness of the day, the disconcerting news, the awful and despairing sense of doom.

I must get out of here, she decided. She picked up her greatcoat, as the big door opened, allowing a gust of wind to rush in. She turned her head, conscious of the cold air on her flushed cheeks. Then abruptly, she grew rigid.

I'm more tired than I realized, she told herself wildly. I must be seeing things!

It couldn't be Mark coming toward her. It couldn't be—and yet it was!

"Mark," she whispered, still unbelieving, "Mark—what are you doing here?"

He reached her side, his hands outstretched, a warm smile on his sensitive lips. She put her hands on his shoulders, clinging to him, and her dazed expression told him she did not believe her luck, she feared this was only another dream.

He saw then that even her appearance had suffered a change; it was no longer vital, robust and extravagant. The allure of the flesh had been transmuted by sacrifice and suffering into a rare spiritual quality she had not possessed before, and which moved him more profoundly than her physical beauty.

All that he wanted to tell her and could not welled up in his heart.

"I had always hoped," he said, "that I would be the first to show you Paris."

She smiled tremulously.

"It's not too late," she said.

4. Afterwards, they never remembered leaving the canteen, they never remembered where they walked, or the words of explanation he had spoken. They sauntered down the hazy Boul' Miche, their footsteps echoing in an unfamiliar beat on this foreign pavement so far from home. And yet, they might have been strolling down Manistee Drive, the two of them, young, passionately in love, with the world ahead of them—their own lovely secret world! It seemed to them that the years between had never happened. Miraculously, all the old conflicts vanished. They were together again. Nothing else mattered.

"Mark, how did you know I was at the canteen?" She was suddenly appalled by a new idea. "Was it by accident that we met?"

"It was not by accident, Faith."

Her emotions strained at the leash of self-control; for she saw that Providence was holding out to them what it so seldom offered—a second chance! Oh, she thought in new humility, I don't deserve this good fortune. I don't deserve it.

They walked on, arms linked. A gendarme passed them incuriously. One by one, the cafés were closing, and the darkness was intimate and concealing. They turned into the courtyard of an old stone house. Faith searched for her key.

The concierge greeted them civilly.

"Emilie," Faith said, "this is Monsieur Holmes."

The concierge looked after them, climbing the uncarpeted stairs. So Madame had a husband! One would not have thought it. Only yesterday she had been so dispirited and sorrowful. But now—surely there was something more than connubial devotion in her manner. There was an aura of youth, of gaiety, of a kind of happiness unfamiliar even to an old Frenchwoman who had experienced much and seen even more.

Ah, these carefree Americaines!

5. She was dreaming.

She was racing back through the dark tunnel of the past, propelled by the urging of her subconscious, running swiftly, until finally she emerged on a brightly lit scene. It was a damp morning, early September in a bedroom at the Lake Shore Hotel. Sleepily she had opened her eyes to find Mark standing at the east window, silhouetted by the rays of the rising sun. He was looking down at the street, his shoulders drooping, his head bowed. . . .

The morning of their last bitter quarrel.

The morning Mark cried, "I won't stand in your way!"

The morning that marked their first separation, the prelude to their final disruption.

She awoke with a start. She opened her eyes slowly. The thin winter sun touched the frayed carpet with pale-gold fingers. Mark—where was Mark?

She saw him standing by the window in silhouette, his shoulders drooping, his dark fine head bowed.

She sat up, terrified. Her heart raced sickeningly. For the two images were superimposed as one, and she was weighed down by the terrible premonition that they were setting out on divergent paths.

She sat in her bed, in the chilly room on the Boulevard Raspail, twelve years and four thousand miles removed from that agonizing scene in St. Croix. And she burst into tears.

"Faith!" Mark wheeled around. He came to her, and took her hands in his, seeking to reassure her. Finally she lay back on the high pillows, weak but sweetly relaxed, watching him intently. The morning light revealed the gauntness of his narrow sensitively modeled face, exposed the deep lines around his gray eyes. The old proud and stubborn air had been tempered by understanding. My darling, she thought, I've never loved you as I do now.

"Twelve years," she whispered, "twelve years out of our lives, never to be recaptured. Oh, Mark, all the days we have lost!"

"We'll make up for it," he promised. "The future will be doubly sweet now."

She turned her head away. "For the first time in my life, I know pure happiness. I don't deserve it, Mark. I've been such a fool!"

"Please, Faith. Recriminations are only for the very young."

"I know. But I can't forget how much harm I've done us. And there's no way to undo it!"

"You mustn't blame yourself, Faith. You must understand that in the early days you were the victim of too many inner conflicts."

"That's no excuse, darling."

No, she could not let herself off so easily. Her own restless spirit had been at fault. For she lacked the single-minded devotion that motivated Mark. She loved him, but she could not shut out the world. She had coveted both. Not once had she shown the strength to cry out, "Mark is my world—and I need no one and nothing else! Whatever he does, however he acts, I'm with him!"

"Darling," she said sorrowfully, "I'm afraid my greatest fault is that I lacked the qualities that make for a good devoted wife."

Mark shook his head. "But see how far those qualities have carried you, Faith. By your very own efforts, you've become a great woman—a public figure."

"That's no justification!" she denied passionately. "Because I was too stupid to understand that a woman's work must never conflict with her wifehood. That's where I was blind, darling. That's where I missed up!"

"I was to blame too," he confessed. "I expected the impossible."

He saw now that although there had been a fine patina of harmony in their youthful marriage, it was a harmony born of youthful attachment; it could not possibly blend the basic differences in their characters. Another couple, though less enchanted with one another, and having lesser standards, making less subtle demands on each other, might have found it smooth sailing, never once encountering the obstacles which had plagued them. But they tortured each other unwittingly; their natures chafed against the confines of the immature love which was to make them one. And when that love foundered on the rocks of ego and personal pride, they were tossed into a sea from which each struggled to a different and lonely shore.

They could not live together; yet they suffered living apart. Only now, many years later, were they able to free themselves from the bonds of their individual differences and disunity. Now they were only too eager to compromise, for in submitting to the compromise which maturity engenders, they would find a richer, more enduring love.

"Perhaps if we'd had another child," she said. "Oh, Mark, I let you down so badly!"

He took her into his arms and silenced her lips. What does the past matter, he thought exultantly, since we are together again at last, with so much to look forward to.

Later in the morning, Faith suggested they have coffee in her room. She had some Nescafé, and the concierge would bring up a pot of hot water. But Mark insisted on a hearty breakfast.

"You're much too thin. I don't think you eat enough."

"I haven't had much desire for food."

Nevertheless, she found herself eating heartily of the scrambled eggs and bacon, toast and coffee served them at the G.I. mess. When she had finished her second cup of coffee and Mark lit a cigarette for her, she sighed contentedly. This was like old times, only better. She'd never before possessed this rich capacity for happiness.

"Mark," she asked, "what's happened to *The Observer?*"

"Vrest's heirs sold out to the Rentschler Syndicate."

"How awful! Vrest would have hated that! He'd been fighting Rentschler for years."

"The staff tried to buy it and keep it going on Vrest's principles. But the heirs—a couple of cousins from Ohio—sold out to the highest bidder. Unfortunately, I was in Washington at the time. I didn't hear about it until it was too late."

He added, "Rentschler put in Steve Pringle as editor."

"Oh, no! What a pity a man like Corrigan couldn't get the job!"

"Corrigan?"

She smiled. "He's a newspaper chap, a good friend of mine. In a way he's always reminded me of Vrest—and even of grandfather Holmes —except that he has so little faith in humanity. Or so he says. Actually, he's a cynic of high purpose, and I do hope you'll like him."

"If you like him," Mark said confidently, "I'm sure to."

He went on to tell her about St. Croix, the expansion of the plant, and his post-war plans. He spoke enthusiastically of Allan Griswold and Joyce, adding that they were the parents of three now.

"Remember Junior?" he asked with a grin. "Joyce always babied him, but he finally broke away from her apron strings. He isn't a lump of dough any more, either. He's almost six feet and skinny as a rail. He towers over Allan who hasn't gained a pound or grown an inch since you last saw him. The middle boy, Bob, can't make up his mind whom to take after—he's really like Joyce. But Eddie, the youngest, is Allan in miniature. And smart as they come!"

The affectionate gleam in his eyes sent a sharp pang through her. Mark should have had sons—he'd have made a fine father! I've deprived him of so much, she thought.

"Darling," she confessed, "the night I fought with you about Joyce, I was sick with jealousy. I'd have given anything in the world to be like her—to be able to give my husband a child." She lowered her eyes so he would not see the tears. "Whenever I've thought of it since, I've been so ashamed of myself."

"Let's skip it," he said. "Let's skip everything in the past."

"You know, darling, someday I'd like to see St. Croix again."

"Of course, you will," he said, as if it had already been decided.

6. After breakfast he said he had to get back to the hotel for a meeting of the Commission. He put his hand to his shadowed cheek. "I'd better shave first."

His words reminded her of their old domestic life, and she smiled delightedly.

"When will I see you then?"

"About two."

"Good. I'll wait at the canteen."

When he left, she prodded time to keep it moving. Fortunately, there were letters to be answered, notes to be elaborated, and as she worked, she tried to ignore the watch strapped to her narrow wrist. She was lightheaded and giddy, and it took the most resolute self-control to keep from confiding in the girls at the canteen. By the time Mark finally returned, she was sitting by the fire, outwardly composed, her eyes luminous, her lipstick bright. He helped her into her greatcoat, and as they got out of the building, she said soberly, "These two hours have been worse than a month of Sundays. I hate time when we're not together—and I'll hoard every precious moment when we are."

"We'll turn into misers," he promised cheerfully.

They strode past the Luxembourg Gardens on the Boulevard St. Michel. The streets were strangely quiet, robbed of the impudent taxi horns and the rumbling of the Métro. Bicycles, the only means of transportation, jammed the boulevards, among them an occasional vélo-taxi. The low buildings on the Boul' Miche had been scarred by gunfire; a small German tank lay inert, like an overturned turtle. But children were playing in the Gardens, and lovers sought the privacy of its paths. However, under the gay veneer, signs of the German occupation were still obvious; the malnutrition as well as the moral humiliation.

"They must be the bravest people in the world," Faith said emotionally.

They turned into the Boulevard St. Germain, crossed the Seine, and continued along the quai to the Avenue Henri Martin. When they arrived at its intersection with the Avenue Victor Hugo, Mark pointed to a low gray stone building with a classic façade and shuttered windows.

"That's where I lived as a child," he said.

"Oh, Mark, really? How exciting! Do you suppose we could get in?"

"We can try. Perhaps I can find out something about Yvette—she was my mother's maid for many years. She was with my father when he died during the Occupation. She was awfully good to me when I was a child."

He tried the bell. They waited. Finally, an old woman opened the door. She shook her head to his inquiries. She knew nothing of a Mlle. Yvette Destampes, who had been in the service of M. Holmes. Brusquely, she closed the door.

Mark shrugged. "It's as if my childhood never existed," he said somberly.

She pressed his hand. "You mustn't be sad, darling. The only part of your youth that mattered was Manistee Drive and your grandfather, and," she added softly, "a crazy kid named Faith Andrews who adored you."

"And you're the only one left. The one who matters."

They had apéritifs at his hotel, and dinner at a G.I. mess, a very festive dinner during which they reminisced endlessly about all the Christmases in St. Croix. Do you remember, Mark? Do you remember, Faith?

At midnight, they went to mass at Ste. Geneviève, the beautiful old church Mark had loved. They knelt, offering silent prayers of gratitude for their great good fortune, and promising fervently to make up for the lost years. The emotional mood still clung to them when they returned to her rooms, but it was rudely broken by the appearance of the concierge with an urgent message. M. Holmes was to call the Ritz immediately.

"Thank you," Mark said.

Faith grew pale. She waited nervously for his return.

"I'm sorry, Faith," he said.

"Must you leave now?" she asked haltingly.

"I've got to be at the airport by seven."

"Oh, Mark! All our plans . . ."

He put his lips to the palm of her hand. "We'll have many more Christmases together. We'll have the rest of our life together."

She had no recollection of their return to the hotel, nor of her efforts to help him pack. They were talking quickly now, a little incoherently, trying to crowd in all the things left unsaid. There was so much to say—where had the time gone? How could they arrange for their future?

"Faith, when will you be back in the States?"

"Soon, darling. I'm due for a rest."

"How soon?"

"I'm not sure. In a month, perhaps."

They had to say goodbye. They clung together. I mustn't cry, Faith thought. If I cry, Mark will feel worse.

"Don't lose heart," he begged. "It won't be for long. And as soon as you can get a divorce . . ."

The lobby was dim, deserted except for the men in Mark's party, who were moving toward the door.

"Well, Faith . . ."

"Darling!" she said huskily. And found herself inarticulate. She simply couldn't continue. For once again, they were parting. And there was something about this timeless moment, in the bitterly remembered expression on his thin, intense face that brought back, poignantly, the memory of another parting. Union Station in St. Croix on a rainswept autumn night, and Mark, white and strained, walking beside the slow-moving train.

"Mark, that time I left home to work for *Feminine Appeal*—what were you trying to say as the train pulled out?"

" 'Faith' "—very softly he repeated the words—" 'Faith, don't leave me.' "

7. She returned to the States in February.

As the giant four-motor plane circled the field, and she caught a glimpse of the New York spires, she found herself trembling with excitement. She had been away a year. All she had seen, the sufferings of the fighting youth, the anguish of the subjected and uprooted, would remain in her heart forever. But she was being selfish today. As she walked down the ramp, breathing deeply of the fresh morning air, she thought, I'll call Mark. In a few minutes, I'll hear his dear voice.

She turned toward the administration building, and was instantly surrounded by reporters, photographers and newsreel men, who greeted her with more genuine warmth than they usually accorded an assignment. For this tall, slender graying woman in her rumpled tan suit was the idol of millions of G.I.'s and their families.

"Have you a statement, Miss Holmes?"

"When's the war going to end?"

"What're your plans?"

"Going to the South Pacific now?"

"Boys, will you excuse me?" she begged. "I'm pretty done in."

By this time, Kimball Evans of the QQA&M agency had made his way through the mob. He placated the newsmen by promising them an interview in the afternoon, and he led her to a waiting car.

"I'm afraid, Miss Holmes," he said, "that this is nothing compared to what's in store for you."

She was to stay at the Plaza, as the guest of Mrs. Latham, who had closed her Minnesota and Florida estates and made her permanent home here. Mr. Evans took her up to a suite overlooking the Park. The living room was filled with flowers, packages, letters and telegrams.

"We've tried to screen all calls," he said, "but it's quite a chore."

"I wish you wouldn't," she objected. "There may be inquiries coming in from the families of the boys I've met. I'll take care of those myself."

She picked up the telephone on the French desk.

"Please get me Mr. Mark Holmes in St. Croix, Michigan. Person-to-person call."

While she waited, she leafed through the messages. An invitation to be guest of honor at the Women's Press Association dinner. Marvin LeBlanc, the lecture manager, wanted to sign her for a series of lectures. Kirby and Wales made her an offer for a book on her experiences. King Features wanted the syndicate rights. There was an urgent call from Hollywood. . . .

She pushed them all away with a conclusive little gesture, and waited impatiently for the sound of his voice.

At last it came through.

"Faith, is it you?"

"Mark, darling . . ." her voice broke.

"When did you get in?"

"A few minutes ago."

"How do you feel?"

Her red lips curved into a smile. "Just wonderful."

His tone deepened. "When are you coming home?"

"Tomorrow, darling. I'm taking the morning plane."

"I'll be waiting."

She dined with Mrs. Latham that evening, and before they parted, she asked for a release from her contract, explaining quite simply that she was giving up her career for Mark.

"Very few people get a second chance at love," she added earnestly. "I won't strain my luck this time. Mark is all that matters to me, now and forever."

Reluctantly, Mrs. Latham agreed. She kissed Faith on the cheek tenderly. "I do want you to be happy, Faith. But I can't help thinking what a big price you're paying for it!"

She stood at the door, a small erect old woman in her unobtrusive black frock, her tranquil manner hiding the void in her heart.

"We need women like you, Faith," she added. "The world is the loser for Mark's gain."

8. Faith was up early the following morning. She spent an hour with Kimball Evans, then penned notes refusing all business offers. She packed her duffel bag and looked at her watch again. Two hours before the plane left. There was still one important matter to attend to. She must see Hank Jessup.

It was not a meeting she anticipated with any pleasure. Yet, as she was ushered into his office, and Hank greeted her with cautious civility, she thought, Perhaps it won't be as difficult as I anticipated. . . .

"Hello, Hank."

"Hello." He stood up, handsome and self-possessed, the half-dozen martinis he had drunk at lunch giving his jowls a moist flush and his eyes a wary gleam.

"You're not looking well," he announced, not troubling to hide the cool satisfaction in his tone. His small round eyes, like chips of anthracite, measured the thinness of her figure, noted the unbecoming shadows under her cheekbones, the streaks of gray in her chestnut hair. *You're old!* his insolent stare shouted, *You're old and finished. And no man will want to look at you again!*

"I am rather tired," she admitted casually.

His vindictive glee did not disturb her. She found it simple to regard him objectively, a stranger of whom she must make a request. She had no feeling at all about him. She could not even believe that he had been part of her life. This meeting was a mere formality. Once over, she'd never have to see him again.

"Hank," she said directly, "I'd rather tell you this myself than have you get it first from my attorney. We've been separated for five years. But we're still tied legally, which is a farce. So I feel a divorce . . ."

"A divorce?" He leaned back in his leather chair, outwardly relaxed, but alert inside, figuring out the angles. She had often seen that intent suspicious expression on his face when a big account was threatened.

"Why so sudden?" he asked curiously. "Have you picked up a young officer on your patriotic travels?"

Her cheeks colored and she appeared quite young again, young and vulnerable.

"I'm going back to Mark."

Immediately she realized that her candor was a mistake, a grave mistake. Lord, why had she been so impulsive? Why couldn't she keep her mouth closed, or dole out a few ambiguous words which wouldn't have antagonized him?

For now the bland indifference had disappeared from his handsome, self-indulgent face. His mind was preparing to strike a bargain.

"I'm satisfied," he said suavely, "with conditions as they are."

"But I'm not, Hank! That's the reason I've been honest with you. I want to be free—and you should, too. We should have been divorced years ago."

Her cajoling words left him unperturbed. He busied himself briefly with the papers on his spacious desk. When he looked about again, his eyes were cold and inimical.

"You walked out on me," he reminded her venomously. "I still have the letter you wrote me that night. I'm the aggrieved party—and I'm damned certain that no court, hearing my story, will ever grant you freedom without my consent!"

He stood up, the bland mask stripped, the bitter resentment and malice he bore her, revealed. Doubtless, he had been anticipating some moment like this, rehearsing it in his mind, hoping it would one day become reality. He was paying her back now—and he meant to make the most of his revenge.

"That's the way it stands, Faith. Far as I'm concerned, it'll never change. Never! That's the message you can take back to your Mark Holmes. You'll never get a divorce. I'll fight you tooth and nail!"

It was useless to plead further.

On the plane flying westward that night, she could not rest. What could she tell Mark? How could she tell him?

9. When she greeted him at the St. Croix airport, Mark read the news in her benumbed manner, her trembling lips. He listened, head bowed, while she related the story of her meeting with Hank.

"I don't see how he can hold you—against your will," he said.

Mark, who had been too proud to hold her against her will; who had stood by, sick with despair and longing, yet refusing by word or gesture to sway her decision.

"I deserve this," she whispered. "But why should you be made to suffer?"

Mark's lips set stubbornly. "We're not giving up. We'll get a good lawyer. Meanwhile," he added, "you need a rest, Faith. The most essential thing is your health."

"I'll perk up soon enough, darling. Just being with you."

She was home again, in St. Croix, among her friends, her father and Mrs. Hussar, but she found it was Mark and Mark alone who gave her days their rich and exquisite significance. The blustery March weather did not matter; for her each day was cloudless and rare.

Mark came to the hotel to lunch with her at noon, and they dined together, too, and walked along the Drive or took in a movie. Sundays were their special treasure.

For Mark she allowed herself the luxury of sleeping later, of facials and hair treatments and new clothes. As she gained a little weight, her nerves relaxed, and her mood was cheerful and ebullient once more. She was still confident Hank could not keep her and Mark apart for long.

They would find a way out! Meanwhile, her own newly discovered maturity lent greater meaning to her love, and her reward was Mark's utter happiness.

Her father told her she hadn't looked as well in years.

"You're twenty-five again," Tod said, and she smiled gleefully. Love had touched her beneficently with the magic fingers of youth.

Now indeed, she was prepared to accept as gospel the precept that a woman's bulwark against insecurity, despair and age lay in her husband's love. Yes, Mark was truly her hope and her salvation. With Mark, she could face with equanimity all the long years stretching beyond the thirties and forties; and loving him without reservation, she was at last able to accept his philosophy of living without reservation.

She saw how richly he had fulfilled the great promise of his youth. Calmly but tenaciously, he had clung to his course, and now he was such a great success with his fellow men because he had always been true to himself. In his reserved, yet resolute manner he had always aligned himself steadfastly with right and honor.

She was ready to concede that even in their old relationship, he had known intuitively what to expect of the perfect marriage and what factors each must contribute to it. He had never wavered. She had been the weak one. And she knew that in spite of the popular acclaim, she was fundamentally a failure. But the recognition of her shortcomings did more than humble her; she was determined to profit by them, as she dedicated herself to making Mark happy.

She found time to read a good deal; to visit her father and Mrs. Hussar, who was confined to her bed. Tod was older, a little more stooped, but, surprisingly enough, more spirited than she remembered him.

He still punched the time clock each morning, although he was a respected old timer, and few at the amalgamated Wolverine-Holmes-Griswold Company outranked him in seniority. Mark would gladly have retired him, but this act would have offended Tod's pride, so he saw to it that the older man's tasks were eased.

Tod loved to recall that May morning in 1906 when Wolverine Motors first opened its doors. "I'm a charter employee," he was fond of saying.

Faith found herself looking forward to their little talks. Before her amazed eyes, her father grew in stature; she was impressed by the clarity of his mind and the soundness of his reasoning. What a pity his life had been so wasted! Under different circumstances, he might have found himself, for he possessed curiosity and imagination. She reminded him of the time she had been chosen for a Halloween pageant—she couldn't have been more than seven or eight—and mother refused to make a costume for her. "We'll figure out something, pumpkin," Tod had comforted her. That afternoon, they gathered oak leaves, glued them painstakingly on cheesecloth. Faith looked like an autumn sprite in the outfit, and for their pains and his ingenuity, she was awarded first prize.

"Dad," she confessed simply, "I'm so happy; I feel regenerated."

It was good to see her in this exhilarated state; it reminded Tod of the early years of her marriage to Mark. Of course, he was curious to know their plans, but with his customary tact, he refrained from questioning them. Mrs. Hussar, however, fretted.

"Why aren't they married again? What's holding them up?"

Neither Faith nor they mentioned her second husband.

Mrs. Hussar was not alone in her curiosity; the town was equally inquisitive. Here was a woman known throughout the world, a national figure whom they wanted naturally enough to honor and acclaim. Yet she persisted in demanding absolute privacy. The only person she was seen with was Mark Holmes, who was obviously devoted to her. Why, then, didn't they remarry?

Everyone had a different theory. Joyce Griswold's friends pestered the life out of her. What was the lowdown? Surely Allan must know—being so close to Mark Holmes!

Joyce was furious, because she, too, was in the dark. The first week of Faith's return, she invited both her and Mark to dinner, and then when she cornered Faith alone, she demanded quite bluntly when they were getting married.

"I'll want to do a good bit of entertaining for you, dear," she added generously.

Faith smiled enigmatically and said nothing.

Joyce turned to her husband later in the evening, when they were alone. "Do you mean to say Mark hasn't told you *anything?*"

"We don't discuss his personal life," Allan answered. "It's none of my affair."

Joyce's baby lips tightened, and her double chin quivered indignantly.

"Honestly, I don't understand men. The worse you treat 'em, the better they seem to like it. You'd think Mark would have learned his lesson by now—and taken up with a decent woman!"

"*Joyce!*" The fury in Allan's voice silenced her as abruptly as a slap in the face.

10. Faith and Mark were impervious to the town's speculation. For the sheer blessed joy of being together again held them in a spell that conclusively shut out the prying world. They gathered happiness from every shared experience, no matter how trivial. Without admitting the subconscious fear to each other, they treasured each day as if it were their last. There was a tenor of richness and abundance in their companionship that had been absent in the earlier, ardent days. Time lost all meaning, daily life had no substance; only in each other did they find reality.

They came down to earth when Mark heard again from their lawyers, who were involved in long, drawn-out negotiations with Harvey Jessup. The news was discouraging. They were getting nowhere. Harvey was adamant.

Faith refused to face the gloomy facts. Harvey was the only obstacle to their happiness. Surely, in time, he would give in!

11. Sometimes she took a walk through the streets of St. Croix, which had suffered a drastic change, like a country maid degraded into a city tramp. Below Wolverine Motors, a dozen new factories had mushroomed, and beyond them stretched blocks of temporary houses, row upon row of boxlike shacks. These shabby places were sheltering the source of energy that kept the wheels of production spinning, the newcomers to town, the rootless thousands who had deserted farmland and village to flock to the industrial centers.

It seemed to Faith, as she watched the children playing in the muddy, unpaved streets, among trailers and squalid shacks, that they were as much displaced persons as the pitiful refugees of devastated Europe.

Main Street was changed, too.

There was a general mood of hectic prosperity and easy money, and the black market flourished like a green bay tree. Men and women of the assembly line demanded an outlet for their accumulated repressions and earnings, just as much as the lumberjacks of Eben Holmes's day.

Faith thought sorrowfully, Progress sits badly on the face of our town. And she wondered if the people could maintain the exacting pace of their material progress without becoming the dupes and victims of their own superior efficiency and ingenuity.

12. Since the Rentschler interests had brought Steve Pringle back to St. Croix as the new editor of *The Observer,* the paper had rapidly deteriorated, taking on the typical Rentschler pattern at the expense of its former individuality and its liberal policy. The reactionary overtones, however, were so adroitly hidden among the sensational stories of spies, love nests, glamour girls and murder that it appeared to have no policy at all.

A reporter from *The Observer* had sought an interview with Faith on her arrival, but she had refused to see him. So she was considerably surprised when, a month later, Steve Pringle himself came for a call.

He had visibly changed. The thick, wiry red hair had thinned to a few straggling locks plastered on the high bald dome. His former air of ribald good humor had given way to one of indulgent self-importance. Good food and plenty of bourbon had left thirty pounds of excess flesh, mostly around his jowls and abdomen. The distended blood vessels on his heavy cheeks and his hoarse breathless manner of speaking would have discouraged the interest of the most optimistic insurance man.

"Faith, sweetie!" He held out his arms with theatrical heartiness, and was not in the least abashed when she ignored them. "Say, you're still a mighty good-looking gal! St. Croix has more reasons than one to be proud of its favorite daughter!"

"Relax, Steve. And don't try to sell me a bill of goods," she said tartly. "If I know you, this call is not merely for old times' sake."

"You're right, Faith." He brushed the ash from his cigar, which had smudged his gray worsted suit. "I'm here on business. The Rentschler Syndicate is offering you a year's contract for a column. Personal observations on the post-war world. The sort of thing Dorothy Thompson does. But with more human interest. We're prepared to offer you . . ."

"Never mind, Steve. I'm not interested."

"You kidding?"

"I'm not kidding."

"Got something else up your sleeve?"

"Nothing you'd be interested in."

"What about the old school spirit, honey?" His sandy brows lifted. "After all, you owe plenty to the old paper."

"I'd hate to admit I once worked on that sheet," she said heatedly. "You've managed to violate everything Vrest Macklin stood for."

He whistled mockingly. "My, aren't we getting high hat?"

Her eyes shone wickedly. "Your scandal sheet is doing the town irreparable harm! Why, the way you're trying to sell Mayor Breedon and his gang to the people . . ."

He finished his highball. "Get off the soapbox, Faith," he said deliberately. "It ill becomes you. And sometimes, it's rather dangerous."

"It becomes me as much as pandering to Rentschler becomes you. You should be thoroughly ashamed of yourself, Steve Pringle!"

"Okay, okay." But he was unable to resist a parting shot. "Some day, honey, you may be needing us."

"As long as I remember Vrest Macklin," she retorted, "I have no fear of that!"

After dinner that evening she told Mark of Pringle's visit.

"You're quite right," he said. "Under Pringle, *The Observer* has become the mouthpiece for Mayor Breedon, Lewis Trout and the whole political machine. It's a damned outrage!"

"Mark, I'm sure that even in the old days, Lewis Trout was tied up with Breedon. Do you remember how the explosion in his plant was hushed up?"

He nodded. "But it's been even worse during the war years. The town's filled with migratory workers who've never made as much money as they're making today. The red-light district's wide open. And the profits are lining the pockets of Breedon and his gang."

He told her about the recently formed St. Croix Construction Company, owned by Lewis Trout and his henchmen. The company had been awarded contracts for all the new roads, sewer systems and water supplies.

"That outfit was even awarded the contract for the new wing of the hospital grandfather endowed." His gray eyes darkened with bitterness. "Actually, their bid was the highest. I put up a fight, but what good did it do? The other members of the board outvoted me. After all, they're cronies of Trout."

"What a pity Vrest's fight for clean politics came to nothing."

"Vrest is dead," Mark reminded her. "And Steve is hand-in-glove with the party in power. It's a Rentschler policy. The people complain taxes are too high, the town's finances are in a bad way—but they're too damned apathetic to make a move."

"There must be some way to wake them up!"

Mark shrugged. "It's hopeless."

She recalled his words, when late in the summer, they were discussing the forthcoming September primaries for the nomination of mayor. The incumbent party was so confident of re-election that it was putting up the most perfunctory campaign. Mayor Breedon was running again, of course. The party was back of him. The powerful paper, *The Observer,* was back of him. It was in the bag!

"Mark," she had repeated then, "surely there is some way to defeat Breedon!"

He snuffed out his cigarette with a gesture of frustration.

"Not a ghost of a chance. The machine's got a stranglehold on our town. It's my fault, I guess. It's the fault of every one of us. We're so proud of our heritage. We'll fight to death for a free democracy abroad, but we won't lift a finger to preserve it at home!"

He finished unhappily, "A fine state of affairs the boys are coming home to. . . ."

13. Even before the Nazis capitulated, Mark was making tentative plans for the return of the veterans. They would need homes and jobs. With the coming of peace, he wondered how St. Croix could possibly absorb the thousands of transient workers and the veterans, too. The problems of possible unemployment with all its attendant ills gave him many moments of anxiety.

Lewis Trout, on the other hand, wasn't worried at all. He displayed a shoddy optimism that infuriated Mark, when they sat in together on the Mayor's Committee for Reconversion and Town Planning.

"Mark, you're a pain in the neck!" Lewis Trout growled. "You and your damned gloomy outlook! Always putting a damper on progress. Let me tell you, this town has just started growing. You just watch our dust, boy!"

St. Croix had been watching Lewis Trout's dust for a good long while. He was the town's leading industrialist, taking precedence over Mark Holmes and other earnest, forthright businessmen by his rapaciousness and blatant self-aggrandizement. His celluloid plant was greatly expanded, now; he owned the new shipyard, too, and he was still chairman of the board of the Lumberman's Bank. He was a bosom pal of Big Bob Costello's, and was intricately identified with the political structure of the town.

"Every city needs a Lewis Trout," he boasted, "in order to put itself on the map!"

His wife, Madeline, had divorced him long ago; he was now a bachelor, going his merry way without benefit of clergy. No woman would trap him again; he was too smart for them.

Most of St. Croix' populace, blinded by his flagrant success, his talent for self-exploitation, forgave his indiscretions in love and in business. The few who recognized the viciousness of his character were helpless. Mark Holmes often said, "A vote for Breedon is a vote for Lewis Trout." The rumors, gossip, criticism, outrage did not disturb Lewis; he remained firmly entrenched in the front seat.

Chapter Nineteen

1. In August, Mark was asked to be on the committee to welcome home the first contingent of veterans returning from the European theater of war. A huge public reception was scheduled. Mayor Breedon was vexed at including Mark, well aware of Mark's dislike and distrust of him, but Lewis Trout insisted.

"Holmes gives the committee dignity," he added cynically. "After all, he's made arrangements to use a batch of veterans at Wolverine. The town trusts him. And the veterans' vote is a new note in the picture —one you damn well can't afford to ignore!"

The reception was to take place Saturday afternoon in Holmes Park, where a stand was being erected and an amplifier installed. The high-school band cleaned its red-and-white uniforms and polished its brasses. The Mayor's secretary sent *The Observer* the list of citizens on the honorary committee. Lewis Trout was, naturally, chairman and master of ceremonies; and the speakers included the Reverend Doctor Arnold, who would deliver the invocation, Major Andrew Scott, the brilliant young intelligence officer who was now back at his job at Wolverine Motors, two Bataan nurses on tour through the country, Faith Holmes, the beloved reporter of the G.I. and of course, His Honor, the Mayor of St. Croix.

Mark asked Major Scott to lunch with him and Faith at the Lake Shore Grille before the ceremonies. And Faith found herself liking the neat personable young man with his long, earnest face, shrewd blue eyes, and affable manner. From what Mark had told her, she knew the good manners hid a brilliant mind and an extraordinary talent for administration, which he used to great advantage as Mark's assistant at Wolverine.

"This speech has had me stymied," he confessed, as they drove to the park.

"What're you going to talk about?" Faith asked.

"Well, I thought I'd tell the folks of our experiences in Europe.

How much those people have suffered at the hands of the dictators. And how lucky we are here in America." He helped Faith out of the car. "What do you suppose the Mayor will have to say?"

"If I know the old boy," Mark answered, "he'll give us his customary biennial song and dance. What he's done for the town in the past. How much he'll be doing in the future. He'll enumerate all the industries that have come to St. Croix and take personal credit for bringing them here. Then he'll go on to crow about the town's big future. But he'll be mum about the vice on Grant Avenue, about high taxes and the corrupt police force."

"Isn't it about time something was done about the filthy local politics?" Scott demanded.

"It's a good old American custom, boss rule," Faith murmured. "The pattern keeps right on repeating itself. When I was young, I used to cry, 'Why isn't something done?' I actually bearded Lewis Trout in his office once. I was going to punish him singlehanded for his evil deeds. Well, look where he is now."

"Nevertheless, Miss Holmes, I'm surprised you haven't stepped out this time. You've got so darned much influence. Gosh, people will listen to you!"

"I've retired, Andrew Scott," she said with mock severity. "Henceforth, the only business I shall mind is my own!"

Mark grinned. "Don't let her kid you, Scotty! Faith's a born reformer. Of course, at the moment, she's been slapped around a bit, so she's licking her wounds, thank the Lord. But you can never be certain when she'll make her bow again."

Faith looked at him searchingly. She was suddenly uneasy. If there lingered in his mind any doubts, she meant to dispel them once and for all time.

"Never again," she promised resolutely, clinging to the vision of their small island, hers and Mark's, so far from the mainland. This time the tides would flow by, and never once endanger the foundation of their happiness.

2. The turnout for the reception in Holmes Park satisfied even Mayor Breedon. The families of the returned veterans and of the boys still in service, the kin of the young men who had laid down their lives at Pearl Harbor, Anzio, the Normandy beachheads, the workers from the war plants, and the town folk milled around the wooden platform, eating hot dogs and guzzling soda pop, as they waited for the ceremonies

286 HEAR THIS WOMAN!

to begin. This was indeed an auspicious day, a day when at last they dared look toward a future pregnant with the promise of peace.

Promptly at two o'clock, Lewis Trout stepped out of his black Cadillac with the air of a knight of old leaving his chariot. He threw a patronizing glance at the crowd as he walked flamboyantly to the platform, where he took a seat between Faith and Mayor Breedon.

When the invocation had been delivered, he strode over to the microphone and greeted the assembly with brash familiarity.

"Folks, it's sure good to see you here. It's good to be here—on this red-letter day in the life of our community. For today, we welcome back to our midst the first of our sons and husbands to return home. Fellow citizens, it is a great honor—and a great privilege—to extend our arms and open our hearts in affectionate welcome to our young heroes, who fought so nobly to preserve the ideals of democracy!"

He turned dramatically to the veterans, sitting bemused under the spell of his oratory. .

"Welcome home, fellas. It's sure good to have you back!"

The crowd cheered enthusiastically.

"But words aren't enough," he continued smoothly. "We've got to show our gratitude to our sons in a more tangible form! To the victors belong the fruits of victory—education, jobs, housing—the best of everything is none too good for our heroes!"

He began the job of buttering the veterans. And then Mayor Breedon took over where he left off.

A calculated move, Faith saw, putting the pompous old windbag first on the program, before the audience was worn out with boredom.

"We are humbled in your presence," the Mayor began in his most unctuous tones, "for we are fully aware of the glorious sacrifices you have made for our great country. We want to show you our deep sense of gratitude. As Lewis Trout told you, our town is yours, your problems ours!"

Sitting on the platform, Faith stirred impatiently. The glib meaningless phrases of a professional politician, angling for votes. She looked down at the blur of faces, lifted raptly. Wives, sweethearts, mothers of men who had fought and died in this war; older men and women who had witnessed death and destruction in previous wars. They listened avidly, longing for words of reassurance, wanting to believe they were on the threshold of a permanent peace.

How dare he delude them with empty and pompous ambiguities? While men like Breedon, Trout and Costello remained safely at home, operating the swindle machine for their private gain, the boys she had seen in Europe were offering up their hopes, their very futures to safeguard their country. Yes, Faith thought, these boys are old enough to die for their country, but not old enough to help govern it.

"While you were away, fighting our battle," Mayor Breedon warmed to his subject, "our town has grown. It has developed into a prosperous, progressive city. And as it continues to grow, so—I promise you—will the futures of our sons!"

He rumbled on, paving the way for more promises. "There will be jobs for all, good jobs, plenty of jobs—veterans preferred. Nothing is too good for these boys! The current administration will see that they get the best. Then, in November, the boys and their families will have their opportunity to show their confidence in *us!*"

He sat down, breathing heavily as he mopped his ruddy face. The applause reverberated through the park, and Lewis Trout clasped his hands above his head with the air of a boxer who had just kayoed his opponent.

Faith noticed the angry lines in Mark's face. And she thought, The old windbag is a menace now. . . .

Then Lewis Trout held up his hand for silence, and introduced her. "You all know Faith Holmes. She was born here, she went to school here, she married here. Now she belongs to the nation, but she has come back to us—the same Faith!"

Only she and Mark caught the malice in his words. And as she arose to face the crowd, smiling and at ease, she made up her mind to return the barb.

"I should like to welcome home the young citizens of St. Croix, the vanguard of many more to come, in the name of Vrest Macklin, the late, fearless editor of the paper that is still, unfortunately, known as *The Observer.*

"I am confident that Vrest Macklin would have disagreed strongly with His Honor the Mayor, whose welcome smacks too much of a pre-election campaign!

"The veteran doesn't want a bone thrown to him in gratitude. By fighting a war and winning it, he's earned the right to fight for democracy at home. That means a voice in the government he fought to preserve. And he won't be fooled by a gratuity! He demands first of all an honestly run civic government. Because he knows that education, jobs, homes and other benefits will then follow automatically in its wake. And"—she paused, wishing she could see the expression on His Honor's face—"in order to have an honest government, it is perfectly obvious to him that he cannot—*he must not*—support the party in power!"

When she returned to her seat, conscious of the violence in the Mayor's florid face and the chill, venomous look in Lewis Trout's eyes, there was a pause. The audience, rocked by her blunt words, hesitated, not quite sure. . . .

And then a storm of applause roared over the park, led by the veterans on the platform. They were acclaiming Faith Holmes, the beloved reporter. But even more, they were commending the brave forthright woman who dared denounce the forces of evil, the corrupt politicians, the false prophets within their very gates!

Mark's smile was proud and approving, and Major Andrew Scott saluted her respectfully.

When the ceremonies closed with the playing of "America," Faith was surrounded by men and women, congratulating her. Mrs. Ernestine Long, the stout energetic head of the Business and Professional Women's Club shook her hand enthusiastically.

"You've certainly given us something to think about," she said.

"Thinking isn't enough," a younger woman interrupted. "What can we do about it?"

"It's entirely up to you," Faith answered.

"Tell us how, Miss Holmes?"

With a tactful smile, Faith managed to avoid an answer. She wanted to get back to Mark and Major Scott, but Mrs. Long was insistent.

"Miss Holmes, will you give us a talk? Some constructive ideas, perhaps. I'm sure our clubwomen will listen eagerly to you."

"I don't know what I can add to what's already been said."

"You'll think of something. And I promise you we'll listen—just as this crowd listened. We may even go a step farther."

Faith hesitated. She turned to Mark who had made his way through the mob to her.

"Perhaps I should do it," she said uncertainly. "If I can be of any practical help . . ."

Mark said, "You've chalked up a few more enemies in your roster."

"It doesn't matter. Lewis Trout has been mad at me for years!" As they walked across the turf to the car, she was serious again. "I think I'd have kept my mouth shut—though it's not one of my virtues—if Breedon hadn't tried so hard to seduce the veterans! All the time he was spouting, I kept thinking, The war's over. We should have so much to look forward to. But instead of taking a stride forward, we're caught in the same old mud of stagnation. Men like Breedon are mouthing the same old platitudes—and their hearers are accepting it with the same old stupid docility!"

"I suppose the basic trouble is this," Mark answered, lighting a cigarette, "when we feel our way of life is threatened by a foreign enemy, the nation becomes a homogeneous unit. All unite for the common goal—self-defense! But the moment the danger is over, we're right back in our state of lethargy. That's why so much is accomplished during a state of war—and so pitifully little in times of peace!"

"That shall be the keynote of my talk," she decided.

"Okay. And while you're at it, you might tell the women that the salvation of the world lies in their hands! They've come of age. During the war, they had a chance to show their worth—and they did it, superbly! It would be a pity for them to abandon the beachheads they fought so hard to consolidate!"

Faith stopped dead in her tracks and regarded him apologetically.

"Here I go again! What the dickens is wrong with me? After all my good intentions—Mark, why didn't you stop me?"

He made no reply.

"Anyway, darling," she promised, "this will be my very last speech."

A slow smile lightened his stern face.

"Make it the next-to-the-last," he teased. "For you, I'm afraid there'll never be a last one."

3. The following Friday, she was present at the meeting of the St. Croix Business and Professional Women's Club, which took place in the new colonial building on Town Square. The outstanding women were all members—aging Dr. Alice Bannerman, who had pioneered in her field, and was today, because of Mark Holmes's encouragement and faith, head of the medical-welfare department of Wolverine Motors; Evelyn Ashmead, the lawyer; Leah Parker, the new owner of the Fashion Shop; Mrs. Alexis Jenkins, who ran the Lake View Tea Shoppe; Jenny Sullivan, head of the advertising department at the Bon Ton; Gabrielle Norton, society editor of *The Observer*; Kate Brown, who had built a hobby machine shop into a wartime industry.

Greeting old friends and new, Faith thought with a surge of pride, Here they are, alert, intelligent, understanding, surely the logical individuals to initiate civic reform. It was at this moment that she was con-

vinced that once the women of St. Croix pooled their resources and went
to work, they could clean house overnight.

After Mrs. Long introduced her, Faith stood up, smiling, with the
poise born of experience and self-assurance. She was wearing a beige
gabardine suit, and her softly waved hair was uncovered. She was
her old self, radiant and energetic.

"You're a select and privileged group," she assured them. "And
others of our sex should look to you for leadership. Whatever credit
has redounded to women is due to you, with your intelligence and
leadership in art, science, business. Similarly, whatever acts of omission
we're guilty of must fall on your shoulders!

"If as a sex, we're a flop, *you're* to blame!

"And we women *are* a flop."

She paused, allowing her audacious words to sink in.

"For a hundred years, we fought bitterly to gain the vote. When we
finally made it, the suffragettes were so happy. Equality at last! No
longer were women the greatest minority on earth. Now they were the
equals of men—they'd take their rightful place in the operation of their
government. . . .

"Well, we women have had the vote for twenty-five years. What've
we done with it?"

"We're hamstrung!" a voice shouted from the audience. "Men have
always considered us their inferiors. And their political machines have
kept us from holding office!"

Her listeners were dividing themselves into two camps, those who
recognized the truth of her accusations, and those who resented them.
There was a general commotion, and Mrs. Long pounded her gavel
repeatedly. "Ladies, if you have something to say, please address the
chair!"

A gray-haired woman stood up. "Isn't the Alliance for the Advancement of Women in Politics supposed to take care of such matters?"

"Yes. But up to now our tragedy has been that women have been
long on talk, but short on action."

There was a flurry of protest; a woman arose from her seat and
marched out of the auditorium, muttering, "I didn't come here to be
vilified."

"Very soon," Faith continued calmly, "Mayor Breedon will be running for re-election. We all know his record. It's enough to convict him
in our eyes. He is *not* the man to run St. Croix! Now, if we women are
in earnest—if we're serious about wanting to defeat him and the political

machine that's ruled St. Croix for thirty years—there's just one way to do it. That's to put up a candidate of our own—a man or woman honest, trustworthy, efficient and *free* of affiliations with any political machine."

She was improvising now as she went along.

"If the opposing party refuses to accept our candidate—well then, we'll have to put him up on a bi-partisan ticket. And attempt to draw the vote of every woman and a good many men in this community."

They were captured by her sincerity, by the sheer impetus of her logic and determination. She showed them the possibilities of their new role in an exciting picture. They would be the modern crusaders, sweeping evil and corruption from their midst, blazing new trails to good government.

"If every woman in St. Croix will make this election her very personal crusade, the fight for honest government in St. Croix will be won. I promise you this. And what's more, we'll become an example for the entire country. We'll show them what can be done when the women energetically put their minds to it. It's up to us now!"

Before the afternoon was over, the Business and Professional Women's Club decided to stage a political rally. Faith was chosen chairman, and it was her task to arrange for the speakers, among whom she immediately suggested Major Andrew Scott.

"Scott has intelligence and common sense and a talent for administration. He's just the man to give us practical suggestions on how to proceed."

But this time, Andrew Scott was less amenable. The reception for the veterans had cured him of all further oratory. And he was not in the least interested in politics. For he was certain that the Breedon machine was so strongly entrenched it would take more than the desultory efforts of a few women to blast it. A lot more.

"But Scotty, you *must* help us!" Faith pleaded. "Even if you do nothing more than get up on the platform and tell the women it's a tough job, but you know they can do it!"

He was stubborn in his refusal—until Mark persuaded him.

4. The sponsors of the rally asked for use of the high-school auditorium. The school board denied the request.

"I see Mayor Breedon's hand back of this move," Faith told Mark. "Is there any way in which you can help us?"

"I'm head of the Endowment Fund grandfather left," he answered. "Perhaps I can get the board to listen to reason."

Mark was always there when they needed him; Mark was generous with his time and money.

He succeeded again, as they hoped he would. And now he, Faith and Major Scott were driving to the auditorium through the hot, deserted streets. He parked the roadster at the corner of the athletic field and they walked up the path to the gray stone building, where they were immediately engulfed by a mob of women.

They had anticipated a crowd, but nothing like this! The auditorium was jammed solid and overflowing to the wings. Every women's club and society in St. Croix was represented, from the fashionable Book and Garden Club to the PTA, and there were hundreds of women without any affiliations.

"Considering this is neither a bingo party nor a bargain sale," Andrew Scott said, impressed, "it's really an extraordinary turnout!"

Faith said smugly, "You don't know the women when they're aroused. That's what I'm counting on to lick the pants off our dear Mayor!"

Here before her, she was thrilled to find the unknown quantity, the X-factor, the hidden potential. And once brought to life, once this inert mass was transformed into a dynamic force, why, there was no telling to what heights women could rise. . . .

"According to the records," she told her audience gravely, "there are potentially more women voters in St. Croix than men. That means we hold the power to break up *right now* the Breedon-Trout-Costello strangle hold on our town."

She described in detail the tyranny and corruption which the machine had imposed on them for so many years. She mentioned facts and figures on local graft and scandals.

"These crimes against us would never have been committed if we women had taken an active part in our politics!"

After she had goaded her listeners sufficiently, she spoke of the young veterans of St. Croix. To allow the Breedon party to remain in power was to deny these boys their birthright. And since they were ready to join the battle for good government . . .

"Major Andrew Scott," she finished, "will speak to you on behalf of these young men."

Before the rally was over that afternoon, the women of St. Croix decided Andrew Scott was their logical candidate. He was the only one who had a chance to defeat Mayor Breedon. If the opposing major party rebuffed them, Scott would run on a non-partisan ticket, sponsored by the St. Croix women, who hoped he would then draw the votes of all right-minded citizens of both parties.

"The primaries are only a fortnight away," Faith said breathlessly. "And there's so much to do!"

Instantly, the excited women rose to her challenge.

The hand that rocked the cradle and held the saucepan would sweep the politically greedy right out of their well-feathered nests. The best way to clean house was to wield the broom themselves.

"We'll win!" they vowed. "In unison there is strength. And for the first time, we are truly united!"

They meant to prove that once roused, women can be a force to be reckoned with.

Faith was too stimulated to sleep. Long after midnight, she sat at her desk, reviewing the rally and the wonderfully gratifying response of the women.

She no longer remembered she had come into the fight accidentally. Her blood stirred with excitement and her feverish mind pictured the almost unbelievable possibilities. The women living in the first half of the twentieth century, she thought, haven't the slightest inkling of their place in the destiny of the future. But some of us are awake at last.

5. She slept late and was still at breakfast when Mark arrived at noon.

"Have you seen *The Observer* this morning?" he asked, as she poured a cup of coffee for him. "Your old pal Pringle is certainly showing his claws."

She read the headlines:

FAITH HOLMES MAKES BID FOR POLITICS.

FORMS WOMAN'S PARTY TO CONTROL CIVIC GOVERNMENT.

In the center of the page was an old and unflattering picture of her, taken, she recalled, by Madeline Trout.

"Ouch!" She smiled. "They don't seem to like us."

Mark helped himself to a wedge of toast from the covered dish.

"The editorial pulls no punches, either," he said.

"St. Croix is bitterly ashamed this morning. For it finds itself in an unfortunate position as the birthplace of a new demagogue it would rather disown!"

"Of course," Mark added, as she threw down the paper, "I think they go a bit overboard comparing you to Huey Long, but that's not all.

They brand Andy Scott as the Jimmy Stewart of St. Croix. They call
the women of St. Croix the poor innocent dupes of an unscrupulous,
publicity-loving adventuress. That's you, darling."

He stared at her comically. "Just think," he sighed, "with what sort
of woman I've got myself involved!"

"That is going a bit too far," she murmured.

"Indiscretion seems to be the better part of cowardice. What do
you want me to do about your friend Stevie?"

"We'll answer him and Breedon at the polls!"

She was silent a moment, her eyes grave. "Mark, we aren't tilting
at windmills, are we? It's not impossible—we can make it?"

"Of course you will," he said heartily.

But as much as he admired her optimism and faith, which had such
an inspiring effect on the others, he was conscious of inner doubts. The
women had taken on such a gigantic task! How could they possibly, and
in so brief a time, vanquish a smooth-running, well-organized political
machine which had been in power so long?

Yet the succeeding days reduced his doubts. How ardent and inde-
fatigable the women were! The flame Faith had ignited burned zeal-
ously, lighting the way toward certain victory.

Even if they were to lose, he thought, a showing like this is the
greatest tribute to democracy St. Croix will ever witness.

The women, however, had no intention of losing.

First, they garnered more than the requisite number of signatures
on their petition, so there was nothing the Board of Elections could do
but allow the Non-Partisan Party to inscribe its name on the new ballot.

6. Faith took active charge of the campaign. Now her experiences
with Christine Ostbergh paid off, and she used to good advantage all of
Homer Sweet's precepts. She knew that much of the success of the
venture would hinge on proper exploitation and publicity. Since the
columns of *The Observer* were closed to her, she turned to the country
newspapers, but most of the editors were skeptical.

"This is just a flash in the pan," they said. "You women will never
make it. Breedon's mob has been entrenched too long."

They had no intention of being identified with some female, crackpot movement.

Undeterred, Faith sent out innumerable press releases throughout
the Midwestern states. She tackled the local radio station, demanding

as much time for Andrew Scott as the other candidates received. If it was a fight they wanted, the women would be in there pitching!

"Show the world how democracy works in America!" Faith exhorted. "And show America how democracy works in St. Croix. It's up to us, the women," she repeated, "to lead the way!"

During the last days of October all women's normal activities slowed down. Business at the Fashion Shop and the Bon Ton dropped; even the movies suffered; and at the last Chamber of Commerce session, Lewis Trout said glumly, "God help the world, if women ever decide to take over."

Never had the women worked so hard outside their homes. They organized themselves into small groups, each group covering a specific area, so that, eventually, the entire network of the town was covered. Thus, every voter was canvassed. They begged, pleaded, argued to make new converts to the cause of good civic government. No rebuff disheartened them, no insult daunted them. And from the headquarters on the second floor of the Lake Shore Hotel, Faith unflaggingly spurred them on to greater efforts, never letting down for a moment.

Whenever Mayor Breedon caught sight of a brace of women on their self-appointed rounds, flaunting their Non-Partisan cockade, his ruddy face grew purple and his blood pressure shot up high enough to ring the bell.

"Isn't there some way," he demanded wildly, "to stop these crazy women?"

"The only way," Trout retorted, "is to strangle Faith Holmes!"

Young Major Scott put all his energy and enthusiasm into the campaign. He pledged the voters an honest, efficient administration. He told them they were the stockholders of a vast enterprise, and the executives whom they elected were accountable to them not only at election time, but every day of the year.

"You're doing fine!" Faith encouraged him. "I think we've finally got Breedon worried."

7. It rained on the morning of Election Day, a bleak windy downpour that washed the streets of all signs of life, and whirled the dying leaves before it in angry little gusts.

No one could foretell how the rain would influence the election results. For the first time, Faith was showing signs of strain. She had thrown herself unreservedly into the fight, to the exclusion of her private life, and she could not face the possibility of defeat. It was not her ego that would suffer, but her sense of justice.

"We mustn't even think of defeat," she told her committee. "We've got to put it over today!"

The early hours saw the women at their assigned posts. Those who were ward captains checked on their subordinates, and saw to it that each one, in turn, checked on the voters for whom she was responsible.

The chill depressing downpour never slackened during the day, and the women requisitioned cars and chauffeurs to bring in voters from the isolated areas where the turnout was usually light. They checked off names in the polling places, challenged suspicious registrants, made sure each one knew how to use the machine, commandeered their own families, especially the young veterans, whose presence seemed to inspire the faltering ones to throw off the yoke of political bondage.

During the day, Faith, accompanied by Mark and Major Scott, toured the polling places, from the fashionable Heights, where Joyce Griswold was a watcher for the Non-Partisans, to sorry Ontario Place, where Tod Andrews was doing his bit.

"Dad," Faith hugged him proudly, "I wish we had a few more men like you!"

Twice, during the day, she returned to the Lake Shore to change into dry clothes, and went right out again. Mark had arranged for the Grille to send baskets of sandwiches and vacuums of coffee to the polling places, where the women were spelling each other for a rest. When the polls closed, Mark returned Faith to headquarters, where they sat around with Major Scott and the committee, drinking too much coffee, smoking too much, as they waited tensely for the first reports.

Mark put his hand firmly over Faith's. "Now, relax," he admonished.

She managed a flimsy smile. "I wish I could. The last half hour is the hardest," she sighed.

Just then, the first reports came over the radio.

The Heights gave Major Andrew Scott a sweeping plurality.

"It looks good to me," she said, brightening instantly.

Mark drained his fourth cup of coffee. "I'm anxious to hear how the West End votes. As Main Street goes, so goes the city."

At eight o'clock, a bewildered Mayor Breedon conceded the election.

When Faith awoke the following morning, punch-drunk but elated, it was to national acclaim. St. Croix was on the map—and not because of Wolverine Motors. The St. Croix Plan, whereby a group of inexperienced but determined women swept out a political machine, was the topic of the day, front-page news, a lead story for radio commentators.

Even *The Observer* announced reluctantly:
WOMEN THE VICTORS.

As head of the St. Croix Plan, Faith was news again. Among the mail she received were letters from people who had listened to her overseas broadcasts.

"You've done a swell job again," they wrote. And many added wistfully, "How can we clean house in our own town? Could you show us the way?"

The note which touched her the most came from Corrigan, who was covering a labor meeting in Cleveland. He had been out of the Department of Justice for several months and was doing free-lance writing.

"I've been wondering what kind of a rash you'd break out in next," he wrote. "It's okay, honey. You're doing fine!"

She showed it to Mark, and he said generously, "Why don't you ask Corrigan to spend Thanksgiving with us? I'd like very much to meet him."

"He'll like you, too," Faith promised happily.

They both met Corrigan at Union Station and drove him directly to Mark's apartment, where he would stay. Faith was enchanted with the way the two men took to each other. Mark responded to Corrigan's blunt, cynical candor, while Corrigan's dour nature warmed under Mark's generous, tactful hospitality. At dinner, Mark excused himself, saying he must get back to the office for some extra work. And Faith and Corrigan then caught up on the news.

8. Thursday morning, Faith arrived at the apartment early and helped Mark's maid prepare the turkey dinner. And the results were so savory that even Corrigan, who was usually bored with food, did ample justice to the festive meal.

Afterwards, they sat smoking and talking idly. As Faith rested her head against the back of the chintz chair, she found herself relaxed and content. The excitement was wearing off, and instead of the letdown that was usual in its wake, there was a renewed feeling of optimism. She sipped her coffee and listened to the men.

Corrigan was slumped on his spine in an easy chair, his long legs sprawled before him. He said that the events in St. Croix gave him the hypothetical basis for a number of political stories.

"Personally," he said, pushing a lock of lank black hair from his eyes, "I would never have believed women could rise to such heights. They're certainly unpredictable!"

"On the contrary, they run true to form," Faith corrected him. "The trouble is that the men have always underestimated them."

"If you'd have seen the way the women of St. Croix worked during this campaign, you'd have been impressed," Mark said. "I know *I* was."

Corrigan crawled out of his chair to fortify himself with a fresh brandy.

"I bet all the credit is Faith's," he said slyly.

"The credit," she retorted, "belongs to every woman in town."

They were silent a while, lost in thought. Dusk intruded now, and Mark drew the curtains and turned on the white lamps. Aware of his calm and casual movements, Faith thought, How self-possessed he is, how distinguished. And in his way, he is the fighter—while Corrigan is the passive cynic. . . .

"We've done such a good job cleaning house in St. Croix," she mused. "How wonderful it would be if we could repeat it nationally!"

"It's one thing to do a local job," Corrigan answered. "And quite another to meddle in Federal politics. That's no woman's job—at least, not yet!"

"Why not?" She sat up in the chintz-covered chair, her face flushed with sudden enthusiasm. "Look, Corrigan, since the St. Croix election, I've been flooded with requests from women in other towns, begging for help. Now, just suppose all these women could follow our example and clean up their local political mess—why couldn't they go on to a national housecleaning?"

He finished his brandy.

"Honey, you're letting your imagination run away with you—as usual. Your hot-headed fervor is one of your strongest—and weakest—characteristics. You do hate to come down to earth."

"But if all the women *united* . . ."

"*That's* your salient point, Faith. Getting women around the country to follow the lead of St. Croix. Waking them up to their responsibilities. Showing them they can't be good wives and mothers unless they're good citizens. If you can do this much, you will have done your country a great service!"

Then he added sadly, "But I suppose you're through with politics."

"I should be stepping out." She glanced apologetically at Mark. "But I must answer the many women who've been asking me for practical advice. Corrigan, I wonder if you'd be willing to help me map out a universal plan of action?"

"Help you? Shades of the Athenaeum!" He shook his head.

"But Faith needs you," Mark reminded him.

"I'm working. I couldn't . . ."

"Yes, you can," Faith said gently.

That evening, they sketched out their tentative plans. They were forming a Women's National Committee for Political Participation, with Faith as its head, and the St. Croix election as practical proof—and an inspiration to others.

Chapter Twenty

1. Making notes for her speeches, Faith thought, We all know the troubles facing the world, but we must never flinch, we must never become defeatists. It's so easy to say, "Yes, the world's in bad shape and there's nothing I, in my small way, can do to help. . . ."

She continued passionately, making notes on her pad. "We women must not retire to the kitchen again. We must stare discouragement in the face and yet fight on!"

When, finally, she finished writing the speech, the silver pencil dropped from her stiff fingers to the desk. Her shoulder muscles ached, and her head throbbed mercilessly. She gathered the sheaf of papers. They were important, most important, having to do with the pitiful state of the world. Nevertheless, she wondered, weary and confused, why she was preparing for a series of lectures, when she wanted only to be with Mark.

Harking back again to the night she, Mark and Corrigan had evolved the plan for the Women's National Committee, she recalled that she had intended being cool and objective about it. But her impulsive emotions had betrayed her again. For suddenly the Women's National Committee was a concrete organization, and she was booked for an extended tour.

Then, in the midst of her hectic packing, she stopped, brought short by the significance of her actions.

"I can't go!" she cried, her misgivings obvious in the distress of her face. "I mustn't go!"

But this time, Mark, sensitive to her dark fears, made an effort to soothe her.

"You're not leaving me, my dear," Mark said. "This isn't the way it was once before."

She listened to him, wanting pitifully to be reassured. Wanting and needing it, to ease the deep inner sense of frustration. Harvey Jessup had remained obstinate, simply repeating that under no circumstances would he ever agree to a divorce. Even the lawyers were pessimistic over her chances now.

Slowly she placed the notes in her briefcase. Be glad for the tour, she thought with a touch of bitter irony. For were it not for the tour, you'd be sitting here, waiting again. Waiting.

During her travels in the early spring of 1946, Faith gave her feminine audiences practical suggestions for making their voices heard politically. And before finishing, she went beyond local politics to world affairs.

"This is not the year 1946 A.D.," she told them.

"It is the Year 1 A.A.—The Atomic Age.

"On the first day of this year, a bomb fell on Hiroshima, marking the dawn of a new era.

"Shall we go on to a lasting peace—or final destruction? It's up to us. For what we do—or leave undone—today will determine a hundred years later whether a few survivors will curse us as selfish blunderers—or whether a grateful race of men will honor our memories as the saviors of civilization.

"In London, a few days ago, the nations of the world met with the hope of establishing a permanent peace. The wise men will sit around the peace table in futile talk. They're doomed to failure—because already the seeds of another war are germinating.

"Always, men made war and negotiated the peace. Women were never consulted when wars were launched nor allowed to participate at the peace table.

"Yet women are the natural proponents of peace. They are the creators—not the destroyers. The world over, women are bound together by a universal aim—to keep the family unit safe and secure!

"And that is the reason," she finished, "that there can be no permanent peace until woman has been granted a voice in world affairs!"

This she told them in schools, churches, colleges, auditoriums through large towns and small in Ohio, Indiana, Michigan, Wisconsin. This was the gist of her address to five thousand women in the auditorium in Washington. And everywhere, she inspired them with her own faith and fiery conviction. Never retreat, keep going forward, fighting, always a step ahead.

2. Sitting at the breakfast table in his apartment in the East Seventies, Homer Sweet scanned the morning papers. His coffee grew cold.

Damn that woman! Every paper in the country would be quoting her!

He reread excerpts from her speeches, attacking, debunking, calling women to arms. What a firebrand she was! If women in their emotional folly were to obey—Good Lord, what would happen to the country? He considered all women notoriously unstable and hysterical, they might well consider themselves the Anointed.

He dreaded Eric Ostbergh's reaction to her speeches. And just as Ostbergh was making ready to emerge from the anonymity of the war years. And Christine, now a prominent member of the Women's National Democratic Club wouldn't like it a bit!

It might be an idea for Christine to reply to her tirade, he reflected. He made notes on his memo pad. Consult Harvey Jessup. He might have an angle.

At any rate, she must be silenced.

3. Corrigan's cronies thought he was nuts. Why should a hard-boiled egg tie himself up with a bunch of hysterical females? What had got into the old boy?

Corrigan retorted icily that nothing had got into him. Corrigan said, "Did you ever see a drowning man clutch at a straw? Well, that's me."

After all the muddling, selfishness, hypocrisy, what's-in-it-for-me he had witnessed, he was willing to try anything possessing a vestige of sincerity. For years, he had been bellyaching about how stupidly public affairs were run. With women taking a hand in the government, conditions couldn't get any worse. Give 'em a break. It may be a start in the right direction. . . .

While Faith was on tour, he remained in St. Croix, where the plans for the Women's National Committee for Political Participation were progressing. Mark donated space for headquarters in the new Holmes Building off Town Square, and supplied the initial funds. And Mrs. Latham mailed Faith a generous check.

"My dear, I am so happy you didn't retire. For I was confident you would one day make a vital contribution to the cause of women," she wrote. "I'm so proud of you! Please do feel free to call on me for extra funds. Awakening American women to their political obligations is the worthiest cause I know."

Wherever Faith lectured, the women organized into a group for action. By mid-summer, there were several hundred branches of the new organization. Always, Faith made it clear that the Committee advo-

cated the candidacy only of people of high character, integrity and capa-
bility.

"It doesn't matter on what ticket a candidate runs," she repeated.
"We women are above party lines. We ask only that the candidate's
qualifications meet with our exacting standards. When they do, we'll
back him to the limit!"

She met bitter opposition as well as encouragement. A great many
of the Old Guard in national politics denounced her. Boss rule was the
basic structure of American politics, and was not to be tampered with.
Even the women's branches of both major political parties refused to
take her seriously, but considered her an upstart who would, together
with her group, die a speedy death. Mrs. Reynolds, president of the
Alliance for the Advancement of Women in Politics, accused Faith of
using this new society as a catapult for personal exploitation. But the
Over 21 Ladies backed her unreservedly, as did the Women's Voters
Guild.

4. Faith was on a full-time schedule now.

Although St. Croix was her home port, she was seldom there. For
periods she didn't even see Mark for a week or two at a time. No matter
how patient he seemed to be, the very fact that there were such interims
caused her grave concern.

"Darling," she wrote him, "I hate being away from you. I miss you
so terribly. But as much as I find myself rebelling, as much as I long
to be with you, I cannot quit yet. For this isn't merely another job. I
can't help thinking of it as a kind of crusade."

She prayed Mark would understand. She counted on it. For surely
he realized this was no manifestation of a woman's vanity, but a genuine
desire to do good. After all, she was not Christine Ostbergh, who
measured success only by the clippings she received. Faith had absolutely
no interest in self-glorification. All the adulation and publicity her tour
inspired, all the interviews that compared her with Eleanor Roosevelt
and Clare Boothe Luce, and prophesied she would become a bright star
on the political horizon—all these tributes she would have gladly surren-
dered were there anyone to take her place.

"You've started something that's more important right now than
your private life," Corrigan reminded her relentlessly, whenever he felt
she was weakening. "And until you've finished it, you have no right to
a private life!"

She stared at him, brought up suddenly, terror in her eyes. Was she getting out of hand again? Had this new project crept up so insidiously that it had trapped her before she could escape? Yet in the face of what was expected of her, she dared show no weakness, no indication of dropping out.

Only Mark's steady, reassuring letters kept her going.

Mark was concerned about her. The hot weather had set in, and she returned from trips wan, listless, exhausted.

"Can you take off a couple of weeks?" he suggested. "We'll run up to the northern camp."

Instantly she came alive. "Darling, I'd love it!"

She turned to Corrigan, who was present as he usually was these days. "Will you rearrange my schedule?"

"Absolutely not!"

Her brows lifted. "Aren't you being too much of a taskmaster?"

"Maybe. But next weekend, you're going to New York. Friday you have an appointment with Mrs. Russel Burton, the publisher of the *Evening Standard*." His moody dark eyes lit up with rare excitement. "If you can persuade her to sponsor the Women's National Committee, I'll wager the next election produces the finest bunch of officials this country's ever had!"

Faith shrugged wearily. "I'll do my best."

And to Mark she said silently, "You see the way it is, my darling."

5. At eleven o'clock Friday morning, she was shown into the office where Mrs. Burton awaited her.

The room was not large, but graciously proportioned; the walls a French gray; the Regency pieces and the Aubusson rug worthy of a museum. There was a Renoir nude over the mantel and a porcelain bowl of yellow tulips on the cocktail table.

Mrs. Burton, sitting behind her small handsome desk, was slim, elegant, distinguished. Her black suit was unadorned, but her tiny hat, sprayed with violets, rosebuds and misty pink veiling, sat like a crown on her silvery head. Her round, boneless, porcelain-white face resembled a Laurencin painting, pale, neutral, and dominated by intelligent dark eyes. Her manner was warm, quite at odds with her cool exterior, and Faith found herself instantly responding to the quiet ironic charm.

"A good many people who throw themselves into the fight for good government are unworldly idealists," Mrs. Burton said crisply. "But you, Mrs. Holmes, make sense. You are practical. You can do a great deal for American women, and indirectly for our country."

Over a lunch of melon, chicken salad and iced tea, served unobtrusively in the office, she questioned Faith minutely about the aims of the Women's National Committee for Political Participation.

"Our women," Faith said, "are the most intelligent and efficient in the world. Yet they're still pitifully backward about politics—as if it were something out of their sphere. Of course, the League of Women Voters and other such organizations are doing a grand job. But they aren't reaching enough women. That's where our Committee comes in."

They talked late into the afternoon. When Faith stood up to leave, Mrs. Burton held out her fragile, jeweled hand.

"Mrs. Holmes, you've convinced me. The *Evening Standard,* its syndicate and radio stations will throw their entire weight back of your Committee. It is my contribution to the cause of world-wide democracy!"

Faith was elated. What luck! This was precisely what they needed —something to lend prestige to their movement. How pleased Corrigan and Mark would be!

Before going home, she determined to have a showdown with Hank. This time, she would not allow him to demoralize her; this time she would not leave until he agreed to reason. She knew Hank's character well; he had his price. Whatever he wants, she thought, I'll pay willingly. . . .

6. Mark parked his roadster and strode over to the administration building of the St. Croix airport. The spring sun was a spotlight which brought into sharp relief the new blades of grass pushing up through the rich, moist earth, the pinkish pods of the maples, the glossy green of the rhododendron bushes. A tranquil Sunday hush swept over the countryside. In the valley, the bells of St. Croix tolled sonorously, blending with the chatter of the birds.

He walked around the building restlessly, his hands thrust in the pockets of his worn gray tweed jacket, a deep line between his dark brows. He was too early; there was still a fifteen-minute wait.

When at last he spied the plane in the blue sky, and heard the first sound of its engines, his face brightened. Faith, he thought, how can I ever tell you what you mean to me?

And there she was, walking down the ramp, tall and slender in her blue woolen reefer, a small blue beret with a jeweled clip tilted over her forehead, a fur scarf slipping from her shoulders.

He hurried forward to greet her, and then he caught sight of her set and bloodless face.

"No luck," she said woodenly. "This time Hank wouldn't even see me."

He took her arm. "You went to Hank?"

"Yes. I couldn't be in New York and not even try."

"What happened?"

She closed her eyes. In the brilliant sunshine, he noted the fine veins on her temples, the deep lines around her eyes.

"I telephoned Hank Friday afternoon. He wasn't expected until morning, so I tried him again Saturday. I tried a half-dozen times. Finally, I realized his secretary was giving me the brush-off. Hank had nothing to say to me." Her dark luminous eyes were haunted. "She referred me to his lawyers."

"Faith, you must take it easy."

"How can I?" Her voice broke. "What are we going to do with the rest of our lives? Stall, mark time . . ."

He must get her away from this open field, from the interested spectators in parked cars.

"Let's get out of here. We'll talk in the apartment."

"There's nothing to talk about," hopelessly. And as he helped her into the car, she whispered, "Oh, darling, what shall we do?"

"We'll figure out something. Just hold on to your courage."

She shouldn't have gone to see Hank, he thought. She shouldn't have done it.

"I've been trying, Mark. All the way home, I kept repeating, 'What a selfish beast you are, Faith Holmes, concerned only with your own problems.' But it didn't help, darling. I wasn't ashamed. All I want is to be with you. I don't care what people will say! Gossip wouldn't hurt me."

"We'll find a way," he answered grimly.

The gloom accompanied them to his apartment. Fortunately, Corrigan was in Great Falls for the day, so there was no need to discuss the Women's National Committee. Under the maid's reproving eye, they managed to eat a bit of lunch. Then Faith moved away from the table, and sat down on the sofa. Mark switched on the radio. The moving strains of the Prize Song from *Die Meistersinger* fell poignantly on the quiet air. She recalled the Sunday afternoons of their childhood—the two youngsters sitting stiffly on the gilt-legged chairs, beside Eben Holmes, listening to his beloved Bach.

We were safe then, she thought. But since we've lost the way . . .

After a while, Mark came to her.

"Maybe it is smarter to live for the moment," he said in a torment, with the desperation of a man who's tried all else and found it wanting. "Let life take its course. . . ."

She wanted so much to console him. But for both their sakes, she dared not raise false hopes again. She closed her eyes in anguish. And suddenly she put her hands to her face, and she wept without restraint.

7. Never before had she been in such a quandary. She had returned to St. Croix to be near Mark. Yet despite her determination to renounce the world forever, she became fortuitously the head of one of the most extraordinary movements in the history of the country, a movement which might well influence the course of future politics.

She should be pleased. For this was the *fait accompli* of her youthful dreams when she had cried to Vrest, "Why can't we do something?"

It was so ironic that now, when she wanted only to live peacefully with the man she loved, she should be offered the opportunity for which, years ago, she'd have sacrificed all earthly happiness.

Sometimes in a moment of introspection, she saw herself at the beginning of the race, hesitant and unwilling, taking the first steps apprehensively. But soon some inner force impelled her onward. And then, there was no stopping, no turning back.

She knew there was no compromise, and never could be.

8. Faith was in Mrs. Hussar's bedroom, bidding the old lady goodbye. Tod sat on the porch swing, in the cool shade, rocking mechanically. A fly buzzed persistently at the screen door, and a bee attacked the peony bushes.

It was on a day like this that he and Lotte had come to St. Croix, forty years ago.

Forty years.

He got up slowly, and in his slow shuffling gait walked down the stairs. He was thinking of old Schatz, the tortoise-shell cat Faith had adored. There was no longer a cat at Mrs. Hussar's. There was little else left; gone were the gaiety and hearty laughter, the clack of poker chips and the sound of beer mugs.

Life sure fooled you. Take your time, fella, the best is yet to be. The dream? Heck, you'll make it come true, only what's your hurry? Art is long and so is life. The little printing shop's right around the bend. . . .

Tod Andrews stared at his gnarled hands. I'm old, he thought with mild surprise, these liver-spotted, veined hands are mine. When did it happen? Where did time go?

The sun was pleasant on his bare head. He looked across the lilac bushes. A new gas station was coming up next door; an all-night-service place. The noise would bother Mrs. Hussar. She didn't sleep much without an opiate.

He heard the sound of steps on the porch. Faith was coming toward him. The pink linen frock she wore accentuated the womanliness of her body. She's always meant well, he thought tenderly. Even when she's made mistakes.

"Mrs. Hussar seems more cheerful today," she said.

"She always perks up when you come."

They were silent. Then she said, "Well, dad, I'd better be going."

"What time do you leave?"

"Four-thirty."

"Oh."

He took her hands in his, and regarded her with eyes over which wisdom and age had drawn a film of humility.

"Dad, Mark will be seeing you every day."

Mark! He shook his head, as if to clear it. It was of Mark that he had wanted to speak. She and Mark were growing older. They, too, had missed the bus. Time was racing past and where were they heading? Was this to be the perpetual pattern of their life—uncertainty and indecision? Would they ever pin down happiness?

She kissed him and opened the gate. Then he noticed the glint of the little gold locket on her neck.

Standing bareheaded in the sun, he was conscious of a strange chill. For it came to him suddenly that Faith was her mother! He recognized the febrile eyes, the intensity, the fanatic brooding intensity! Poor Faith!

He turned slowly and went into the house. Who was he to judge the path she was to follow? The decision had been made for her. And he thought, "What shall it profit a man if he shall gain the whole world and lose his soul?" Only for Faith, he substituted "happiness."

9. When Faith left for New York, where the Women's National Committee for Political Participation would work under the sponsorship of Mrs. Burton's *Evening Standard*, Corrigan and three of the staff accompanied her.

In the following months, whenever Mark managed a weekend in

New York, he was worried and upset over the problems of reconversion at Wolverine. Between his problems and Faith's increasing responsibilities they saw their hopes of an ultimate life together growing more and more dim.

This is it, Faith told herself starkly, I've left Mark again.

And Mark, worried in St. Croix, remained silent.

For Faith, there were fresh complications. As the Committee grew in scope and power, it made fresh enemies among the hidebound politicians who feared women's sudden awakening. She hit back just as boldly at the men of evil intent, among them Eric Ostbergh, who were seeking to use peace as they had used war, to further their own ambitions.

"We need fresh blood in politics," she said. "Just as we develop the flower of our youth at West Point for war, so we should establish training centers to develop potential leaders in the government—for peace!"

As her influence increased, reporters flocked to Faith, wanting to probe her past, to delve into her private life. Recently a young chap named Charlie Turner had turned up for information.

Faith refused to divulge her private life.

"It's the Women's National Committee that matters," she insisted. "If you want to write anything, write about the Committee."

Because she was so reticent, the reports about her were often based on conjecture and speculation.

"It's a very human failing to jump at conclusions," Corrigan said wryly. "And to want to accept the obvious. Besides, gossip lends itself so much more dramatically to a story than the simple unvarnished truth."

10. Mark was in town the day Faith received a summons from Homer Sweet. They were having roast-beef sandwiches and coffee at her desk in the Madison Avenue offices of the Committee, when Corrigan joined them.

"What do you suppose Homer wants of you?" he asked glumly.

Faith shrugged. "I wouldn't be surprised if my little speech on Eric Ostbergh last week hasn't something to do with it."

Corrigan helped himself to the extra container of lukewarm coffee.

"Ostbergh wants the public to forget he was on the wrong side during the war. And you keep reminding them."

"He's still on the wrong side." She was suddenly earnest. "And still a very dangerous man."

"Faith," he said, "there were a couple of guys around the other day, making pests of themselves—trying to check on your early days."

Mark spoke up. "What did they want to know?"

Corrigan lit a cigarette in the corner of his mouth. "They were asking a number of things. If Faith knew some guy named Trout, I think the name was. We finally got rid of them with the same spiel we give the press—Mrs. Holmes does not want any personal publicity!"

Mark stood up. "Think it's anything to watch out for?" he asked nervously. Everything concerning Faith worried him, the crackpot letters in the mail, the threatening phone calls, the prying reporters.

"Well," Corrigan answered slowly, "I really don't like it. Homer isn't asking Faith over to pin an orchid on her. He and Ostbergh have it in for her. And he's not one to let sleeping dogs lie."

Mark turned to Faith. "Must you go? If he wants to see you, let him come here!"

"Then he'd think I'm afraid of him," Faith said. "He'd like that."

"I'm coming with you!" Corrigan said.

"Thanks. But I'd really rather see him alone." She adjusted her small feathered hat and picked up her white gloves.

"Will you walk up with me, darling?" she said to Mark.

The October sunlight gave Fifth Avenue a luminescent quality. "What a lovely day!" she said, pushing the thought of Homer Sweet to the back of her mind. She linked her arm with Mark's. He had flown in from St. Croix this morning on his way to Washington. They planned to dine together and go to the theater tonight. She hadn't felt so fine in a long time!

At Forty-ninth Street, she stopped. "This is where I leave you, darling."

"Look, Faith," he said. "I feel the same as Corrigan does. Those prying men the other day—and now Homer asking to see you—I don't like it. I don't feel easy about it."

"It's nothing, Mark."

"Then let me come up with you. If he tries any funny business . . ."

"Mark, darling, your imagination is running away with you. I can take care of myself. Really I can."

"Shall I wait for you here?"

"Well, I don't know how long I'll be tied up."

He glanced down at his watch. "Suppose you meet me at the Plaza. About four?"

"Good."

She stepped into the elevator, and on the thirtieth floor, she walked swiftly along the air-conditioned corridor. Her heart pulsated against her ribs. She kept reminding herself of Mark's admonition to take it easy. Finally, she stopped before an opaque glass door marked: *Homer Sweet. Public Relations Counsel.* She opened the door and walked into the reception room, which was just as it had been always, a reflection of his carefully cultivated taste for the fine things in life. The same Chippendale pieces, the same hunting prints; even, she noted humorously, practically the same blond, extremely decorative receptionist.

She announced herself.

"Oh, yes, Mrs. Holmes," the girl said with flattering deference. "Mr. Sweet is expecting you."

Looking at the gleaming pageboy bob, the sticky mascara, the sweet crimson smile, Faith wanted to ask, What do you think of the Women's National Committe for Political Participation? It should concern you as much as Lana Turner, Senator Claghorn, Make-Believe-Ballroom, and your date for tonight. . . .

But the blonde was already absorbed in the tabloid hidden discreetly on her lap.

This time she did not have to wait long. From the door invisible behind a rare old screen, Miss Kelly emerged, seven years older, a little thinner, showing the ravages of diet and dye.

Miss Kelly, what do you think of the Women's National Committee for Political Participation?

"Why, hello, Mrs. Holmes!"

Faith smiled. "It's nice to see you again, Miss Kelly."

"Thank you." Poor Miss Kelly, torn between loyalty to her boss, and admiration for her old co-worker!

"Mr. Sweet will see you now," she said uncomfortably.

Faith followed her through the corridor and past the General Operations Room to the threshold of the Sanctum. How many times she had followed this path! She could retrace it blindfolded.

Miss Kelly opened the door.

Faith stepped in gingerly. "Good afternoon, Homer."

The man in calculated shadow behind the vast Chippendale desk moved slightly. A reflex action, as if he were taken back by her appearance. Seven years.

"Come in, Faith," he said softly. "We've been waiting for you."

He was not alone. The hostile stares of three other people were focused on her. Eric Ostbergh and Christine, his wife, and Harvey Jessup. Time had not been gentle with them, either. She was conscious of a prickling sensation in the region of her spine. The air of self-assurance about Homer warned her this was no impromptu session. Obviously it had been planned, and just as obviously, the others meant to use him as their mouthpiece.

He motioned her to a chair placed in the center of the room, conspicuous in the bright sunlight. How ridiculous of him, she thought, as if I were the defendant.

"I'll stand, if you don't mind," she said quietly. The air was charged with bitter, unforgiving hatreds, and the chill impassive faces reminded her sharply of a group of inquisitors, standing in terrible judgment.

Homer cleared his throat.

"Faith Holmes," he began pontifically, "you are the head of an organization that is deliberately misleading thousands of gullible women. You've made ugly accusations you cannot substantiate. You've sullied the reputations of innocent people who have done you no harm. You turned traitor to your old friends—"

He saw that Eric Ostbergh was restless and decided it would be wise to eliminate all further embellishments.

"When you attacked politics and politicians," he continued, "we were silent. But when you flung your scurrilous dirt at us—and the institutions we represent—as you did in your recent radio address—it is time to call a halt! We haven't forgotten that seven years ago you brutally betrayed the confidence we placed in you. Now, you are playing Judas again. . . ."

Faith was standing behind the chair, as if it were a shield. She turned her head to look at Eric Ostbergh, impatient and arrogant at the window; a monolith of a man, his heart as stony as his exterior. And Christine, aloof yet wary, the disdainful smile playing on her thin lips. She blamed Faith for her defeat at her last election, and she was right. And Hank Jessup, who was convinced that his misfortunes began when he met her. Hank could be an implacable enemy, too. They are afraid of me as they're afraid of all honest people—and that's what makes them dangerous.

It's just as well Mark and Corrigan have no idea what I'm up against! she thought.

"Homer, don't waste the double talk on me," she said coolly. "It falls flat. Nobody in this room—neither Ostbergh nor Christine nor Hank—has the right to accuse me of anything! But since you're putting on quite a show, you may as well continue. What do you want?"

Homer Sweet cast a triumphant signal to Ostbergh. He had been right. Despite her bold talk, she was frightened. The entire matter would now be settled quickly and expeditiously.

"Our demands are quite simple. Give up this hare-brained idea of yours. After all, you know as well as we do that women don't want a political consciousness! They're far better off where they belong—in the kitchen!" He stood up on the balls of his feet.

"After you have resigned from your organization, you will present the press with a retraction of your vitriolic attack on Eric Ostbergh. You will admit you erred—that your information was biased and false. Better still, confess you chose him as a target because the publicity would contribute to your egomaniac pursuit of glory."

Her expression remained level and undismayed.

"Suppose I refuse?"

A smug expression puckered his pale thick lips.

"We didn't summon you here to bargain with you. We're dictating. You see, we can force your hand. We have decided that you are retiring from public life. For good!"

For the first time, a spark of anger flared in her dark eyes. "Homer, you are being presumptuous. And you know perfectly well you have nothing on me."

"Indeed?" With a triumphant gesture, he opened the manila folder. "How do you suppose your loyal followers will react when they learn about the sex life of their beloved leader? How she inveigled a rich young man into marrying her—and dropped him when he went broke. How she sent her husband's best friend to his death. How she robbed another woman of her husband—and how she climbed on the backs of other men —even old men like Vrest Macklin—to attain success. Would you like to hear more, Faith? We have the complete dossier."

She watched him without speaking.

"The whole messy story is here—in detail, all facts substantiated! We could very well have broadcast this deadly information without warning you. That's the underhanded way in which you'd have done it. But we're being fair. We're giving you the opportunity to make amends by retiring gracefully. The choice is yours. If you refuse . . ." he paused significantly, "then we shall be compelled to reveal to the American press the story of your past—including, of course, your present relationship with your former husband. That in itself will ruin you!"

The others were watching her intently.

"Homer," she said softly, "you can do your damnedest—it still won't intimidate me!"

"I have no intention of intimidating you. I'm merely presenting you with the facts." He hid his chagrin and continued, "Your trouble has always been that you're obsessed with a wild imagination. No doubt, you are now picturing yourself as a modern Joan! I wouldn't even be surprised if you think you hear voices!"

"If I do," she retaliated, "they're the voices of the American people, who've been the fall guys for men like you and Ostbergh. . . ."

Harvey Jessup struggled to his feet, overturning the highball glass.

"For God's sake, don't let her sidetrack you!" he shouted. "This time she isn't going to talk herself out of her predicament. Because now, I'm holding the trump card!"

There was an electrifying stir. For the first time, Eric Ostbergh addressed him directly.

"What are you babbling about?"

Hank was in command of the situation, ready for his moment of precious revenge.

"For a year, she has been begging me for a divorce. Because she wants to go back to Holmes—he's rich and successful now. Well, I held out on her. I let her stew. But if she'll renounce her political aspirations —if she'll retire the way we want her to—I'll agree to an uncontested divorce!"

11. Faith regarded him quietly. Her anger was gone, she was conscious now only of a deep and ironic sorrow.

"I came back from Europe wanting only to be married again to Mark. I returned to St. Croix hoping I'd never see another newspaper or radio station again! Only Mark mattered to me. But when we found we could not re-marry, and this political situation arose . . ."

She was talking to herself, rather than to them. But her words were an impetus to Christine Ostbergh, who cried out, her voice harsh with savage fury, "What a fool you've been, Hank Jessup. What an utter fool! Why didn't you give her the divorce when she asked for it? Why didn't you let her marry this Mark Holmes, and retire to that awful little Michigan town and anonymity? The world would never have heard of her then. And she'd have left us alone, too: It's your stupidity that has made her the dangerous political figure she is!"

She stood up, her pale oval face blazing with contempt.

"For heaven's sake, give her the divorce—*without* reservations. And I only hope for all our sakes, it isn't too late!"

12. She was on the Avenue again, walking north. She couldn't remember how she got there. Her head was whirling, and she felt she

was not the same woman who had entered the Rockefeller Center building an hour ago. In Homer's office, something had happened to her, the ultimate crystallization of her spirit.

An hour ago, walking up here with Mark, her hand clasped in his, she had been afraid to dream—of long dark nights and the logs burning brightly in a stone fireplace; of white lamps like beacons at the picture windows overlooking the fragrant sleeping gardens; of the lake under the glistening sheen of the hot summer sun. The snug harbor, the peaceful haven; Faith and Mark together at last, protected by a ring of fire that shut out all intruders. . . .

No longer was it the impossible dream, to be wept over and shut away in mothballs. She was going to make the dream reality.

She was going home again, as Mark's wife.

Then, insidiously, the shadow of duty cast its gloom over her spirits, reminding her that she could not make such a drastic decision because she did not belong to herself. Resentfully, she pushed it from her. Hadn't she waited long enough? Hadn't she paid the price in full? Let another take up the torch.

Her eyes were shining, her head erect, her feet winged, as she hurried on.

13. Mark was waiting for her at the Plaza. In a secluded corner of the bar she gave him the good news.

"Isn't it wonderful, darling? He is setting me free! At last, we'll be together again—on our little island."

He listened quietly, his fine head bent; he did not give way to his emotions easily. Finally, he said, "Faith, there's no going back to the past. I'm afraid the island is closed to mature people. We've grown beyond it. From now on, we can be together in the midst of the whole world."

She smiled tremulously. She was young and eager and life was ahead of her.

"Oh, Mark, if anyone intrudes now, I'll say, 'Please don't bother me. I'm busy and content being Mark's wife!' "

He shook his head.

"No, Faith. You have your job to do—and I have mine. But they won't conflict because now, at last, we understand each other."

She was quiet a while; then she spoke up with new enthusiasm. "You know, Mark, I have a fresh idea for a radio talk." She grinned, remembering another day. "And this one will be my swan song, my very last."

His features relaxed in a tender smile. They were safe at last, he and his Faith, because they had found each other.

"Make it the next to the last," he suggested lightly, "because for you, darling, there'll never be a final one."

She took his hand. "Do you remember, Mark, what Grandfather Holmes always said? 'The longest journey begins with the first step.'"

"Yes," he said. "And I'll be there beside you."